ARCHON'S QUEEN

THE AWAKENED BOOK 2

MATTHEW S. COX

DIVISION ZERO PRESS

Archon's Queen
The Awakened Book 2
© 2014 Matthew S. Cox
Second Edition © 2018

Cover art by Jackson Tjota

Cover Formatting by Alexandria Thompson

ISBN (ebook): 978-1-949174-26-7

ISBN (print): 978-1-949174-27-4

The Awakened Series

Prophet of the Badlands

Archon's Queen

Grey Ronin

Daughter of Ash

Zero Rogue

Angel Descended

CONTENTS

AUTHOR'S NOTE

Archon's Queen takes place five years prior to *Prophet of the Badlands*.

SENT TO COVENTRY

D espair billowed across the sky in the guise of clouds. Formless, the shroud of charcoal mist devoured life and hope, leaving the city below to wallow in the tragedy of its own existence.

Rain, four days this week, saturated the ground with poison rivulets of muck. The rounded girth of an aging monolith of plastisteel and broken glass as black as the mud surrounding it glimmered wherever moonlight caught it. Old wires drifted from its side, reaching into the sky like the probing tentacles of some great beast searching for prey that would never come.

Coventry Tower clawed at the heavens, the raised finger of an enormous old crone. Its shadow spread ominous upon the field of debris over which it ruled. The old tower block apartment had been the only structure in the district to survive the airstrikes; fate itself had ordained it the home of the unwanted.

The barren land around it contained so little, even advert bots didn't bother with the place.

Annabelle squinted up into the rain. Angry faces glared down at her, evil shapes drawn upon her mind by the drugs in her blood. Clouds had become a roiling fog circling the upper parts of the building, alive in the images of demons and imps. Their eyes flickered from the glow of hidden moonlight. The shadow creatures tore open their flesh, wringing it out to bring more rain out of spite. Whorls of grey churned about in a devils' dance, the images shifting to ever more terrifying forms. Thundering voices called her by name.

She glanced down at her old boots while navigating the puddles dotting the blackened muck. The hiss of the downpour overpowered her squishing steps, allowing her to approach a group of four men, three crowded around one, without notice.

The three clad in black all wore a red smear on their sleeves approximating a capital 'E,' the mark of the East End Boys. The tallest loomed over the fourth man, a wiry figure who tried without success to avoid the rain with a poncho of dull beige plastic. The small man whined and pleaded, his effort to wheedle a bargain out of the Boys failing.

Annabelle shivered at a blast of wind reaching under her ragged half-shirt. The decrepit cloth flapped like a flag for the Manchester United Frictionless club. Her glossy indigo skirt of faux leather did little to stop the chill. Painfully aware she hadn't owned a pair of smalls in at least a year, she stared at the men, tugging with trembling fingers at the hem in an attempt to pull the skirt down a little more over her rain-soaked thighs. She had helped herself to Spawny's jacket, doubting Penny's boyfriend would need it any time soon since he'd gotten loaded and passed out, probably for the night. Water beaded and rolled off the treated synthetic denim; it held his fragrance as well as Penny's perfume. Either offered an improvement over the stink of the dusty chemical rot lurking in The Ruin.

She peered up at the sky while the men argued in dire whispers. The demons and creatures had faded once more to steely clouds wafting in the wind. She rubbed her face with one hand. A tremor started in her arm. The zoomer had worn off. Anna tuned out the conversation in front of her and pulled her jacket sleeve down to expose her left wrist and a tan patch of rubberized plastic. She picked a fingernail at the corner and tugged. In a moment, the spent derm came free, leaving a one-inch square red mark with rounded corners.

Anna winced as she rubbed cold rainwater over the chemical burn at the center with her thumb. She had been hitting the same spot too much, and the drug had eaten her skin. Drawing her arm against her chest, she shivered, trying not to think about how close to sober she'd let herself become. The demons of moments ago had been a flashback, not a high—a warning that withdrawal stalked her. She also tried to ignore the freezing rain that soaked her short white hair, or her miserable wreck of a life.

The gurgle of a breath startled her into looking up. Knux, the tallest of the Boys, lifted the little man into the air with a metal fist around his throat. He'd been the first of the East End Boys to have a whole arm replaced. Few dared ask where he got the money for it. She fixated on streams of water flowing around the dark plastisteel limb; for an instant, a feeling inside it called to her. Threads of electricity teased at her senses, appearing as tiny threads of amber light.

A perpetual beard shadow twisted as Knux frowned. "Oi Mate, what do you think this is, a charity?"

The man clawed at his throat, his attempt to speak emerging as wheezes and gasps. He kicked his legs back forth, emitting pleading moans. Annabelle looked down, thankful someone else got the business. The chirp of a firing circuit added fear to the cold, and she could no longer resist shivering. Knux stuffed his pistol into the face of his would-be customer. Rain beaded on the plastisteel frame, running over the glowing LEDs and onto his still-flesh left hand.

"You're into it for almost a grand now, bucko. The tap's cut off 'til ya make a payment."

Knux smashed the pistol sidelong across the man's face, simultaneously releasing his metal-fisted grip. The impact sent the man sprawling into the black mud on his hands and knees with a wet *splat*. Straw-brown hair hung from the hood of his poncho. Blotches of red appeared in the puddle below his face. Blood dripped from his nose.

"I'll get it, really I swear." The doser sat back and rubbed his neck, coughing. "I just need—"

The East Ender to Knux's right kicked the man in the face, flipping him over backward into a puddle large enough to count as a tiny lake. "Cut off means cut off. Bugger off 'til ya got at least half the dosh."

Poncho wailed in protest as the two Boys hauled him to his feet and sent him off with a boot in the ass, howling with laughter at his frantic sprint. She knew they'd kill him to make an example of someone who owed too much. In this case, Old Bill would likely do it when the man did something foolish to get money.

Knux spun on Annabelle, startled by her quiet presence. She cowered, staring at the ground where water pooled around her boots up to the shin. The glassy puddle made looking down feel like staring into the sky. Shifting leaden clouds rolled across the surface, swirling into each other and expanding. The sight gave her vertigo, as though she could fall into the endless sky.

He grinned, baring metal fangs where his canine teeth used to be. "Oi, luv. Mus' be in need if yer out in this parky mess."

She rubbed her hands up and down her arms, trying to find some warmth. "Me last zoomer's all clapped out. I'm in a bad way."

The other two returned from taking out the trash and the trio formed a half-ring around her as they had with the other man. Fear of what they could do with her added to the angst of her sobriety. In another life, they would have been cowering from her. The thought of it sent a tingle crawling up her spine. The Boys loomed, indelicate in their obvious gandering. The man on her right brushed a hand over her cheek, wiping the remains of mascara away. A thunderclap rolled across her mind, the image of a well-dressed man she used to work for smiled. *What was his name...?*

"Only got one left, but I'll give it to ya on the cheap. Hundred creds."

"Giro was light this fort." Annabelle sighed. "I got sixty five."

A hand on her ass, a voice in her ear from the left mimicked that of an old woman. "Your last sixty five on a zoomie, ya poor dearie, what'll ya eat?"

Quaking, she kept her gaze on ripples spreading outward from the walls of her boots. "I can beg for food… I can't beg for zoom."

She fumbled in a battered handbag, rifling trash and empty wrappers until she found a three-inch plastic fob: a credstick. The man on the right tugged her shirt up to expose her breasts. Anna stood stock still, afraid to protest or move. Cold air washed over her, speckled with freezing dots of rain. The part of her capable of blushing had broken years ago.

"Well then, this li'l scrubber's got quite the pair." Knux helped himself to a feel. "Noice li'l peaches."

The man to her left shook his head. "Gotta be fake. Too round."

Knux smirked, squeezing one of her breasts with his human hand. "Now where'd a slag like this git the creds fer 'at? They feels natch-rul."

"Yeah, Spid. This one blows her whole allowance on candy, ain't gonna afford any work. 'Sides, them things is way small for jobbers."

"Tim's got a point there, mate." Knux's throaty chuckle turned into a phlegmatic projectile that vanished into a nearby puddle with a *ploink*.

She stared at the ground. Numb, she ignored the grimy fingers smudging her pale skin. "They're real. Sixty-five and a show then? Will that do?"

"I'm thinkin' ya keep your creds and do us a favor instead, lass." The guy on the right winked.

Annabelle covered her mouth; the trembling lack of drugs in her blood added to the nausea of what they suggested. She hadn't reached a point of desperation that she'd shag three men in the middle of The Ruin where anyone would see. Oncoming withdrawal couldn't hide the presence of the thing in the back of her mind. With the drugs gone, it swam to the surface. The Boys continued pawing at her exposure. She looked to the right and bit her lip. At a sense of prickling warmth, she shoved her hand behind her back so they couldn't see the tiny spark crawling over her fingers.

"I'll get the rest of the creds in a couple o' days. If it pleases you lot, I don't fancy a feck in the mud."

Tim pulled her by the hips against his body. Hot breath flushed around her neck and filled her nose with the fragrance of synthbeer. He licked at her ear. Anna's heart raced, her throat tightened, and she found herself pushing at him to get away. The presence stirred in her mind, riding the wave of fear. Knux's metal arm flew into a spasmodic fit of twitching while Spid grabbed his head and screamed. A faint wisp of silicon smoke drifted on his breath and rose from the M3 plug behind his ear. Small bits of cybernetics in the Boys flickered in and out of her awareness like ghostly fireflies.

"Oi, what the hell." Tim let her go, rushing to his friend's side.

Annabelle scurried off a few paces, almost falling from her effort not to walk right out of her boots in the thick mud. Gulping, she pulled her shirt down and tried to calm herself. "Must be bum 'ware, shortin' out inna rain."

Knux swiped the credstick from her and offered a thin sheet of white plastic with two flesh-toned derms. "Take 'em, ya look a mess."

With that, he retreated to tend to his misbehaving arm and screaming friend. Anna trudged away, moving with urgency while trying to keep to areas where old paving peeked out from the mud on her way back to the tower. She peeled one of the derm patches from its backing and pressed it into the tender skin of her right forearm, two inches south of her wrist. Within seconds, the uncomfortable sharpness of sobriety faded away to the reassuring calm of a zoom high. The thing in the back of her mind roared, vanishing like a demon dragged down to the abyss.

She squatted, unable to walk due to the woozy onrush of the chem invading her veins. Once more, twisted faces in the clouds laughed at her. Raindrops screamed as they fell past, the sound of millions of tiny creatures falling to their deaths. Blue sparks arced from her bare legs, snapping at the water for an instant before vanishing. She tasted ozone in the air and curled tighter into herself. The howl of the wind mutated into a demonic roar and the rain came upon her like a hail of ice needles.

Anna sprang to her feet and ran, slipping and falling several times in her haste to avoid the sharp things dropping from the sky. A floppy-eared goblin darted out from behind an overturned car. Yellow eyes filled with greed gleamed out of the darkness. A tiny pair of tattered camouflage shorts covered its middle, the rest of its leathery skin bare. She drew up short, taking a step back, ready to scream. Its clawed hand raked at the air as it took a step closer.

Mottled green and brown gave way to grime-covered skin. The form changed, standing straighter. The claw became a hand upturned, begging. Glimmering greed melted away to curiosity. A young boy of about eight stared up at her. He realized she had no money or food, gave her a sad face, and ran off to the tower. She watched him until he disappeared among concrete slabs, and turned her gaze up to Coventry Tower.

The building felt inviting despite the lime green fire raging inside most of its windows. Seconds later, the rain ignited, falling on it like gasoline, turning the ebon spire into a torch illuminating the devastation around it.

She buried her face in her hands, struggling to rein in the hallucinations, the unpleasant side effect of her necessary evil. Years ago, the visions had been wild and terrifying. Now, for the most part, she recognized them for illusions… usually. A year ago, the visions lasted much longer. She developed a tolerance and could will away the sights after a short time.

Annabelle grabbed two fistfuls of her short hair, chanting, "It's all in my head," over and over. Wild, nightmarish changes in The Ruin lessened. She crouched there in the rain for a time with her eyes clamped shut. The Zoom gripped her brain, caging the writhing beast within. When she looked, the world had returned to bleak rainy normality with only a hint of faces above. As long as she concentrated, she would stay in control. The reassuring chemical fog formed a gate the tiny demon in her head couldn't breach. She wobbled to her feet and slogged over the mud toward the monolith of gloom.

Coventry Tower jutted up from the center of The Ruin, an area once known as Tower Hamlets before the war bombed it to oblivion and back. From Bishopsgate in the west to Hackney Road in the north, the crushed and flattened remnants of buildings came to an approximate end by

Grove and Burdett streets. Beyond that, abandonment left intact structures empty east to Gillender Street, but no Proper wanted to live in them, being too close to the refuse that collected here.

The Ruin had existed as a tangled mess of collapsed buildings, old cars, and crashed military craft for far longer than her short life. This place adopted those whom society no longer wanted, a refuge for people with nowhere else to go.

Annabelle called it home.

OL' JACK

Eyes closed, Annabelle rubbed her thumb over her smooth skin and the tiny square of rubberized plastic. A fresh zoomie felt like an old friend holding her hand. The cold wind stopped bothering her, and a thousand whispering voices in the dark came and went. Light hit her in the face like a solid object. She cringed, eyes open.

A quarter mile away stood Old Bill's blockade around The Ruin. Someone on an armored truck had spotted her. By the time she raised an arm to shield her eyes, the searchlight had moved on. She had no weapons and nothing of value. To the police, she had little use, merely another throwaway. The operator panned the spotlight over the debris field. Shiny black corners of the police van gleamed, a polished onyx brick. She stared at it, that they ignored her stirred both relief and anger.

She cringed away from imps and scuttling fiends dancing around the shattered brick and glass rubble. A grey creature two feet tall with an oblong head and floppy ears ran up and clung to her leg. She looked down at its black banded tail coiling around her boot. A mouth full of needle teeth opened in a creepy smile. She pressed a hand to the side of her head. With a grunt of concentration, the creature turned into a loose piece of windblown debris fluttering against her. She kicked it aside.

Anna ignored the various sights and sounds she knew to be false, and stumbled toward the only building here. The voices continued, their source circling about and changing at random. At least the raindrops had stopped screaming. Up ahead, a patch of paving offered refuge from the mud. She wobbled up onto it, standing between two slabs of wall that used to be the façades of shops, and ventured a glance at the shattered window frame where a thin figure drawn of shadow stared back at her.

A slow blink chased it away. With zoom fresh in her blood, she found it difficult to stay on her feet. Knux had given her a potent batch this time, not to mention it was almost two in the morning. The voices got louder. She wobbled toward Coventry tower, ignoring creatures that prodded and picked at her.

Hands seized her and wrenched her about. Another demon stared down at her, so tall she felt like a little child. Glowing eyes of fire widened in amusement. Two others, with flaming hell-spawn wings, held her by the arms. The massive one leaned back and laughed a scorching breath into the sky. He spoke in a tongue she couldn't understand and reached a clawed hand at her. Annabelle struggled to get away, but the demons held her in place. Oddly enough, the demon appeared to want money. She had none; they'd take the zoom.

"Oi, that's plenty enough you lot. Sod off!"

An amorphous humanoid shape of smoke coalesced at the source of the deep baritone. She knew the voice. The mass of shadow split down the center, revealing a man. The smoke rolled behind him as he walked, murkiness sent to oblivion by her recognition of Ol' Jack.

He had installed himself as the doorman of Coventry Tower, a protector of sorts, a role he'd fulfilled soon after she arrived. Despite his height and muscular build, he moved with the grace of a prowling tiger. Hands poised, his body language gave a warning absent from his calm face. She grinned at rain trailing over his dark skin, the droplets crying out in glee. She forgot the demons holding her, oblivious to everything aside from the singing raindrops on his leather coat.

The voice came from the creature in front of her. "Back off, chap. This li'l pikey's ours."

Her limp body hung by her arms; she stared up at the burning demon. In an instant, it vanished, morphing into a thug, some random piece of street drek prowling The Ruin. His scarlet hair soaked to his cheek in the rain, adhered to the jet-black of a wild beard.

When Ol' Jack pounced, he released her. She fell, bouncing once before rolling to her side. Landing ass to pavement should have hurt, but the zoomer turned the hard ground into padding, and she gawped at the air. Above her, a beating commenced. Meaty *thuds* interspersed with growls and 'oofs.' The scarlet-haired man hit the ground in front of her, face down for an instant before something dragged him out of her field of view. She curled fetal, grinning at the splash crowns the rain made in murky grey puddles inches in front of her face.

A soft electronic chirp came from above. Anna rolled on her back and looked up, searching for the birds.

Ol' Jack brushed the side of his nose with his thumb. "Bad move, mate."

Four hits came at the pace of a machinegun, then the unmistakable *crack* of a broken arm and a howl. Something fell onto her back and slid to the ground. After peeking, she rolled away, petrified by the mud-splattered pistol next to her. Her hope of seeing a bird died. The chirp had come from the firing circuit. The weapon seemed to stare back; she felt its heartbeat. It reminded her of the thing in the shadows of her mind. A well-dressed man who seemed somehow familiar faded in before her, not a speck of mud on his suit. He shook his head at what she had become.

Terrified of the *feeling* and of what Old Bill might do if they thought she owned a firearm, Anna kicked the gun away into the muck, shrieking, and crawled toward the building.

Behind her, an uncoordinated barrage of wet footsteps splattered off into the night. A hand clasped her about the arm. She screamed and fought until the presence of Ol' Jack's cologne flooded over her. Her panic ebbed and she looked up, raking her nails down his sleeve in a feeble attempt to cling. Skin wrinkled about his eyes. A faint green light blinked in a slow cadence between his left ear and his neck. Beads of rainwater on his shoulder caught the light, glinting in the dark with each pulse. A weave of amber threads appeared out of nowhere, glowing superimposed over his arms for an instant before they faded. She stared at the lines of his face, thinking he had to be about fifty or so. Too old for love, but he protected her. Smiling, she cuddled against him.

"Bloody hell, Pix... What are you doin' out here alone at this hour?"

She tried to speak, but only managed to spit bubbles into the air. His age made her feel like a kid. What he had done for her made him feel like her father.

With a childish giggle, she cooed. "Daddy."

He shook his head and pulled her to her feet. "You're feckin' legless aren't ya. That shit's gonna kill you."

She tried to walk, clinging to him, but wound up doing little more than twitching. He picked her up and carried her like a bride through the open archway into the tower. At the cessation of the pelting rain, she gasped and looked up at the ceiling as if the world had fallen apart.

"I dunno what gets inta ya, girl. Why do ya do this ta yourself?"

She rested her head on his shoulder while he carried her past blurry images of red letters painted on walls, the shadow of a stairwell, and a chain of dangling lights. The corridor became forest. She flew, arms out to the sides, the glow of blue pixie wings above her.

Ol' Jack sighed. "Let's get ya ta bed then."

3

TAXES

Dull grey-painted concrete spread out above, lined with the splintering cracks of abandonment. Annabelle raised a hand to her forehead, trying to rub away the dizziness of sobriety and the heaviness of oversleep. Eventually, the cause of her consciousness became apparent as a rhythmic tapping on the wall. A couple in the next apartment went at it full tilt.

She sat up to find her boots next to the bed and Spawny's jacket missing. Her bag rested upon the nightstand in a weak patch of light that made it past the grimed windows. White patterns decorated peach-colored walls. To her half-closed eyes, it looked as though someone had tried to paint flowering ivy wherever plaster flaked to the ground. Naked wires carried stolen electricity to a single fist-sized LED in the center of the ceiling.

Blood and dirt spattered her in equal parts, she had no idea where the blood came from. She did remember going out for a fix last night. *Ol' Jack pulled them off me again, I bet.* A few minutes later, she summoned the urge to move and staggered into the autoshower, still in her Manchester T-shirt and skirt. Once inside, she punched the console. Somewhere along the second run, she slipped out of her clothes and swayed with her best attempt at standing upright. During the third cycle, she peeled the spent derm off her arm and cast it into the swirling torrent around the drain. Arms over her head, she stretched, then ran her hands down over her face, chest, and stomach. She frowned at her prominent ribs.

The East Ender was right. I should eat more.

She stared at her body, the swath of milky skin broken only by a three-inch tall tattoo of a pixie on the front of her left hip. The tiny woman had short, white hair like hers with cobalt blue wings trailing tiny stars around her side. Anna traced a finger over it, grinning at the thought of Tommy, a long-ago boyfriend who had started calling her Pixie due to her slight build and short hair. He wanted it drawn tapping the top of her sex with a star-capped wand, but that had been too bawdy for her back then, so the pixie held the wand upright. Annabelle's wistful smile melted at the thought of his death—and how she had changed so much since then.

The autoshower kicked into its dry cycle, embracing her with a whirlwind of hot air. Coils of wire beneath her feet pulsed in the back of her mind; the current driving the inner workings of the fan motors pulsed in her senses. Every wire, every motor, every detail of the circuitry traced itself clear in her thoughts on racing threads of amber light superimposed over reality. She cringed in shame at the unnatural sight. Her father shouted out of the past, angry with her for breaking things. She flinched without thinking, away from an expected fist.

It's not my fault! It just does what it wants! Screamed her tween-aged voice in her memory.

Anna leaned her face against the tube, sobbing as her brain filled with memories of the house where her childhood began and ended. As much pain as she'd experienced there, she'd go back in an instant if she had the chance. It had been ten years since she'd last been inside the place, but she remembered every mark upon the walls as well as the smell of her old bedroom. As far as she knew, the place still stood vacant. It made little sense that a property in London would stand empty so long, but perhaps people didn't like that a man had died in it.

No matter how much she tried to control the thing in her head, it had destroyed her home. Her father's pleading with her to stop had become demanding, then drinking—which led soon to beating. His violence only made the little demon angrier, and the situation worse. The monster fed from her emotions.

Spawny tapped on the plastic.

Huddled on the floor inside the autoshower, arms crossed over her face, she couldn't recall how she wound up sitting, or how long she had been in there after the hot air cycle ended. She lowered her guard, frowning at the wiry and quite naked man hovering on the other side of clear plastic. Long black hair hung to his waist, his emaciated frame gave him the look of a famous holovid star well on his way to burning out before thirty. When her mind caught up to her eyes, she held a hand over them.

Spawny stood on tiptoe and shifted side-to-side. "Done yet? Our autoshower is shafted."

"Dammit man, I don't need to see your todger waving in my face."

A little nudge poked at the back of her mind. She wanted to be embarrassed but couldn't find the energy. Spawny had been on her for weeks about having a threesome with Penny, but some lines she still refused to cross. He always flashed the same smirking grin whenever he brought it up, lending enough doubt to his seriousness that neither she nor Penny had become too upset with him. The tornado of hot air had somewhat dried her shirt and skirt, so she put them on before opening the tube.

He leaned into her as she stepped out into the cold air; his chin hovered a touch above her eye level. Penny's scent surrounded him.

"Offer still stands, luv. Girl's got needs, right?"

She pushed past him into the bedroom. "No thanks."

"What?" He turned to face her, arms by his sides. "Penny's fine with it."

"No, she's not. Even if by some twisted parallel universe bend she was, *I'm* not."

Spawny inhaled as he entered the tube. "What so you'll wave 'em 'round a room full o' gits, but won't have a romp with your besties?"

Annabelle ignored him, retrieving her boots and purse from the bedroom before going across the hall to Penny's apartment. The air hung stagnant and thick, filled with the aromas of sausage, eggs, and sex. She entered, kicking small pieces of trash out of her way.

"Oi, Penny? You 'ere?"

"In the kitch." Her friend's voice came around the corner of the pale green wall.

A muted Frictionless match on the holo-bar flickered light on the walls of the living room to her left, but only a junior-league match, so she ignored it. Anna strode through the crumbling plaster doorway separating the kitchenette from the remainder of the place. The smell of cooking overpowered the fragrance of the other room. To her relief, she found her friend dressed, as much as a knee-length pink shirt with large holes could be called such.

Penny Dhara arrived in London a month or two after Anna ran away from home. A mail-order bride from Bangalore at the age of sixteen, she had been eager for a new life married to an executive. As it turned out, the executive never existed. The Syndicate purchased her for use in a brothel, but in a stunning miracle of competence, Old Bill had intercepted her at the shuttle port. Unable to afford to return home, and the police not willing to pay for a trip, she wound up stranded in London.

Anna had run into her by chance almost ten years ago. They'd become inseparable since. Penny grinned over her shoulder, her knee length hair swirling around. Anna took a seat and pulled her boots on over bare feet.

"Jesus, luv." Penny set the cooking aside and fussed over Anna's hair. "You're a right mess. You've gotta change somethin'. I hate seein' you like this."

"I'm fine." Anna leaned her elbow on the table hard. "Spawny's at it again."

"Oh, pay him no mind. He doesn't learn." Penny picked at her a moment more before returning to the stove. "You've lost control, Pix. The shit's no good for you, certainly not better than workin' for Mista' Carroll."

The lights flickered in response to a crash of sorrow, guilt, and shame. Anna bent forward, sniffling.

"Oh, I'm sorry, Pix... I didn't mean to make you think of Tommy."

Anna looked up, red around her eyes, and wiped her nose. "I... I couldn't save him. Bloody filth shot him because of me. He was always reckless, showing off." She covered her face as the tears came on strong. "Tommy was more afraid of Arsenal winning than us gettin' killed."

"Every time I ask how it was your fault, you change the subject." Penny's spatula scraped a pan. "Whatever you did for that bloke, you cannae keep it all ta yourself, ya know. I get that you're tryin' ta protect me, but you can't handle it alone."

"Is your autoshower buggered or did Spawny just want to peeping tom me?"

"See, that's exactly what I'm talking about. The water's a bit tepid, but it runs." Penny put two sausages on a plate with some eggs and set it on the table. "Probably wanted to gape."

"Figured." Anna tucked closer to her breakfast. "Thanks."

Penny fixed herself a plate and sat. Before she touched her food, she put a hand on Anna's wrist. "I've been looking after you for ten years, yet in some ways it feels like I barely know you. You don't need to shut me out of the important bits. You need to change some things, Pix. Ol' Jack said you were a mess last night, called him Daddy."

Her cheeks blazed with fierce blush. She poked at her food, unable to look up. "Yeah. I's just takin' the Mick. Everyone keeps callin' me a kid, so…"

"You can tell me, Pix. I don't care what you're hidin' from. I can't help unless you let me. You used to kill people for that sod Carroll, didn't you? You know the Syndicate never forgets. Is that what you're trying to protect me from?"

"No." Annabelle shuddered. "I dinnae kill fer 'em. Just… you know, did spy type stuff. Sometimes, we had violence. But I never punched a bloke's ticket." She pushed food around her plate. *On purpose.*

She stared into her breakfast, her mind full of flickering blue light, men screaming, and the scent of burned meat. The little monster in her head had turned her own father against her. She couldn't bear it if Penny reacted the same way. She had to keep the tiny demon down. She had to drown it in zoom.

"It's got somethin' to do with the way electronics tend to bugger themselves 'round you, innit?"

Anna cringed, biting her lower lip. "You noticed."

"How could I not?"

"Please don't make me say it." Anna sniffled.

Aside from the scraping of forks, silence held the kitchen for a few minutes before Spawny returned, still naked, and collected his breakfast on a plate. Anna leaned her head in her left hand, turning away from him.

"Good morning, ladies." Spawny slid his hand over Anna's head as he passed.

"Put some bloody clothes on. We 'ave a guest." Penny threw a napkin at him.

"Nonsense, luv. She can't 'elp but bask in the glory."

"You've an odd notion of glory," muttered Anna, too low for either of them to hear.

"Stuff it." Penny scowled. "You know she's sensitive about it."

"Oh yeah, real sensitive. Sensitive enough to dance starkers at BC."

Anna shrank in on herself.

"Lay off it, Milo," said Penny.

He cringed at his real name.

"The dole ain't enough to get on, and it's the only work she's got. Did it ever occur to you maybe she *hates* it there?" Penny slapped the table.

"Roight. Uhh"—Spawny scratched his head and swiped pajama pants off the back of a nearby chair—"Soz, luv."

"I should be off, then." Anna started to stand, but hesitated with a thought stuck halfway out of the womb. Words containing the truth left her brain, but before they reached her mouth, they changed to, "thanks for the brekky."

She forced a pleasant smile at Penny, left her plate in the sink, and walked out.

4

OLD BILL

London these days offered two types of weather: raining, and about to be raining.

Today had the latter, with a side order of strong wind. Anna's thin red jacket didn't do as well against it as Spawny's imitation denim. The Ruin, lit by the day, stretched out into a sea of black mud and puddles, bridged here and there by fragments of surviving road.

A trio of little girls wearing dirt and simple dresses giggled and climbed over an old tank hulk that mired in the ground long before their parents were born. A boy their age dangled from the bent barrel of its laser cannon. Jagged gouges scored the ground on the left, where the ancient e-cells had died a catastrophic death long ago. Anna watched the kids while balance-beam walking a fallen signpost across a huge puddle.

Poor kids... Anna shook her head, jealous of their innocence and pained by what the future held for them. *He's probably gonna wind up with the Boys, if he lives long enough.* The unrestrained joy on the girls' faces made her feel even lower at what she had become. *Why do Covs have children? It's cruel.*

"Oi, kids. Get 'way from that. Might be somethin' left behind in it could hurt ya."

The barefoot children darted off into the muck while Anna trudged as best she could along the paved bits toward the police line. Anywhere a route out of The Ruin was passable, the Old Bill had it blocked off.

It had been that way for three years now, ever since the Trafalgar Unrest. The people responsible for the attack had fled into The Ruin to elude the law. For all anyone knew, they still hid out here somewhere, assuming one of the gangs hadn't killed them. Old Bill wanted no part of going into the place. Everyone from patrolmen to politicians expected it would set off a massive gang war and give the Labor party endless ammunition to weaken the Crown. Despite pressure to bring the terrorists to justice, the authorities decided to wall it off. Rather than take the criminals to jail, they made their home into a prison. Maybe everyone would forget about it at some point and the police would go home, but no one held their breath.

At six cops to one Cov, they acted the lords of London; the other way around, they ran like chickens in black. Perimeter watch offered boring, inglorious work to a constable, so it had become a dumping ground for less-than-stellar officers. The longer a constable spent here, the less likely they would be redeemed back to being 'real' policemen. Most of the ones with no hope of being reassigned took out their vexation upon the Covs.

Anna hesitated behind a slab of concrete wall, staring at the checkpoint. Usually Spawny and a couple of his friends would walk her to town to lessen the chances The Filth would mess with her. She chewed on her lip, chiding herself for storming off alone, and brushed her cold fingers at the bridge of her nose in an effort to push her drug-addled mind closer to something resembling lucidity.

Forcing people not to see her used to be an easy task. She focused on the police, trying to get a sense of their minds. Her atrophied telepathic sense sputtered, producing only a feeling as though she eavesdropped on a conversation on the far side of a thick wall. *How did it go?* She recalled it had something to do with tweaking a person's mind to disregard her. She concentrated on the constables, trying to delete herself from their awareness.

At a snail's pace, she crept. *Do not see me.* A pair of police vans sat nose to nose at the street she chose to leave by, four men in black armor with yellow armbands stood guard at the wall of a small portable building.

It's working...

"Oi, Wot's your name?"

Shite.

A ponderous fellow, whose belt barely contained his gut, waved her to a halt.

Her words came as a pitiful squeak, a hair above a whisper. "Annabelle, constable."

"Annabelle wot then?"

"Morgan, constable," she said, gaze fixed upon the wet road.

The shadow of an armored man fell on her. A mixture of sweet pastry, sweat, and coffee exuded from every pore. She knew what meat felt like, sitting on a shelf being stared at by a hungry customer. She knew it every night working at the Bristol City Club, only here, she wouldn't be paid for it.

"Need some extra precautions with this one." He nodded to his comrades with a wink, waving her at the door of the little building. "Come on then, in ya go."

Keeping her head bowed, she offered no protest as he led her by a one-handed grip on her arm to the temporary pod building at the boundary line. Decorated in plain steel grey, the inside looked as bleak the land outside. One desk, two chairs, a plain chrome table, and a weapons vault complimented the communications suite at the far end. Beyond a tiny doorway, the presence of holding cells brought a shiver.

"There's a bit of a gate tax, luv."

Her mousy response sounded like someone else had taken control. "Yes constable, whatever your pleasure."

"'Ands up then."

She complied, passive as he handcuffed her over a bar on the ceiling, a posture that forced her up on tiptoe due to her short stature. Anna bit her lower lip, grunting from the discomfort of her weight dangling by her wrists. The large man walked around behind her, pulling off his gloves.

"Where ya off to on this fine mornin'?"

"Work, constable."

"Work?" Condescending surprise laced his chuckle. The gloves clattered to the metal desk. "What sort of work would that be?"

He patted her down, ostensibly searching for weapons.

"Dancing, constable, at the Bristol City Club."

A bellicose laugh thundered over her from behind. "Titty City eh? Well then, I imagine you know the drill."

"Yes, constable." Overhead lights weakened and flashed in response to a wave of fear gripping her. "I don't want no trouble."

Last night's zoomer had almost passed out of her system. Only the knowledge of the spare in her jacket pocket staved off outright panic. She shifted as best she could to avoid him while chained to the ceiling. He pawed her all over. A brush of cold air on her nethers when he pulled her skirt up made her gasp. Brown's amusement at her lack of panties gave her a few seconds' reprieve. One of the other dancers stole her last pair months ago. She hadn't bothered sparing the money to replace them—every last credit going to zoom or food.

Cold steel around her wrists reminded her of Tommy. He'd been into that sort of thing. Somewhere in the fog of the past several years, she had gone from fearing helplessness to using it as armor. The more pathetic she acted, the better people with any power treated her. Silent tears ran down her face. Anna blushed, mortified at how the handcuffs excited her despite wanting no part of the slovenly constable's attention. Her body found itself at odds with her mind. She tugged at the chain, a genuine effort to escape, which had the paradoxical effect of turning her on more. Warmth flushed her cheeks, her heartbeat quickened—she couldn't move. No matter how much she wished it, the man touching her all over wasn't Tommy.

She felt like a deer hung for cleaning.

Any sense of titillation she started to feel at her predicament gave way to repulsion and anger. A shower of sparks burst from a component at the corner of the room. The constable shifted toward the *bang*. She let all her weight hang on her wrists, trying to slip free.

"Constable, beggin' your pardon, you shouldn't. I ain't clean."

His armored potbelly brushed against her. He leaned in to kiss the back of her neck, leaving a sticky fruit-scented imprint of his gluttony. "Neither am I, luv. Just a trip to the clinic, wot?" He laughed.

Anna looked up past the cuffs at her reddening hands, wishing her payment of tax to be over as fast as possible. He fussed with his belt. She closed her eyes. Terror pierced the haze in her mind; images of men writhing in pain on the ground came back to her. The urge to do the same to the one behind her grew, but popped like a bubble. *Wouldn't help. His mates would kill me before I got loose.*

Rough hands grasped her hips. The truth of her situation banished calculated thought. She had no chemicals in her system to detach from reality. She whimpered, begged, and squirmed. Her protest only amused him. She stopped moving and tensed, waiting for the invasion. Shaking, she forced herself not to beg him off. If he sensed she didn't want it, he'd be worse about it.

Crackles erupted from something on his uniform blowing up in a shower of small electric arcs. He yelped and swatted at himself. *Go away.*

His warmth drew close. Without conscious thought, she lifted herself up off the ground to buy an extra fraction of a second before it made contact.

"Constable Brown! What's this then?" shouted another man, his voice ringing off the metal walls.

Anna jumped at the sound, and strained to look left at an older cop standing in the doorway. Short silver hair gleamed, backlit from the outdoors, a military cut. He shot a dour frown at the pudgy constable racing to put himself back into his pants. She shivered as if she'd been caught doing something wrong.

Despite her fear, she felt relief.

"Sergeant." Constable Brown coughed. "Just doin' a routine search of this scrubber for contraband."

"With your John Thomas?" The senior officer's voice echoed back from the holding cells. "I already told you twice, Brown, if I catch you at this again, I'll have you shuttled off to the Orkneys. Get your slovenly arse out of here this instant. This is the last straw for you, Brown. Out of my sight this instant!"

The heavyset man scurried off like a hound with its tail betwixt its legs. Annabelle looked away, struggling to keep her composure. The Sergeant's frown poked at a long-dead sense of dignity. He walked close. She cowered, expecting only chased Brown away so he could have a turn with her first.

"You all right, luv?"

"Yes, guv'na. No complainin' from me." She pouted at the floor. *Better a lying whore than a dead one.*

"Don't lie to me, girl." He shook his head and scowled. "Bugger all. These twats take advantage of you Covs so much you just roll over for it. Well, s'pose I'd rather you play possum than shoot at us."

The snap of a rubber glove made her jump.

"Calm yourself, lass. Since you're already in the posture, I might as well check for illegals, unless you'd like to request a lady constable?"

"Beggin' your pleasure, Sergeant. I ain't hidin' nothin.' I got a zoomer in me coat, but that's all."

She suffered a silent stare for a full minute before he spoke. "You're not lyin' ta me again, are ya?"

Her voice sank back to a pathetic squeak. "No, sergeant."

He took the plastic sheet from her jacket. A strip of light gleamed across it as he turned it over. Annabelle squirmed, trying to get her hand on it. He glanced between her desperate eyes and the small pliant patch.

"This 'ere is why you're stuck in the dustbin." He flapped it at her. "Never understood what drives you young people to this crap. Most of you are on the tit, and you spend it on this. Are you on the tit, Miss Morgan?"

"Yes, Sergeant."

"Well then, this bit of illegality belongs to the taxpayers."

The sergeant made a sharp heel turn and walked around the desk, slapping the sheet down at the corner. Anna jumped at the hollow metallic *slam*. Her lifeline was too far away to grasp with her toes, even if she didn't have boots in the way. Without the zoom, her mind would run away.

Things she couldn't control would happen, and *they* would find her again.

The sergeant fell into a chair and waved a hand over the terminal. A rectangular panel of black appeared in midair. The part facing her was opaque, while reflected amber light crawled over his face from images and text.

"Please, guv'na, that's me last one and I don't have the money for treatment to be off it."

He didn't look up, continuing work at the terminal. A Cov speaking to the police out of turn was a risk; one wrong word could bring disastrous consequences. He'd left her skirt flapped up exposing her nethers, and she wasted those words begging for drugs rather than her dignity. She bit her lip and lifted a leg in an attempt to cover herself.

At least he's not staring at me. Her head sank. *Prob'ly thinks I'm dirty.*

Anna stretched, trying to will her arms longer to allow more of her weight onto toes that barely reached the floor. Sometimes, she rather hated being so short. Shifting, she hoped a plaintive mewl of discomfort would send him a hint she had enough of being chained to the roof, but he didn't react.

Minutes passed in silence. Again, she glanced up at the shiny chrome around her wrists, turning and pulling in a futile effort to get her now-crimson hands out. The sound of the latex glove peeling from his fingers scared her motionless until she realized he took them off.

He asked her name again; she recited it. The panels of light on his face shifted, brightening. She imagined a picture of her in front of him now.

"Says 'ere you're twenty-three?" asked the Sergeant with a note of disbelief.

"Yes, Sergeant."

"Bugger. Thought ya sixteen. Looks like your father died eleven years ago…" His voice trailed off as he read, an eyebrow lifted. "Faulty food reassembler?"

The drugs couldn't suppress the shiver that time. The sergeant's terminal erupted in a flurry of blue sparks. He swatted at it twice. Anna turned away, muttering at the wall. "Yes gov'na. He got a right nasty zap from the thing."

His chair squeaked from his weight leaving it. The sergeant swiped the derm from the corner of the desk and carried it toward the disintegrator.

She struggled, all her weight dangling on the binders, pedaling her legs at the air. "Gov'na, beggin' your pardon, please don't. I've been on it too long, comedown could kill me."

"Zoom withdrawal can't kill, though you'll be wishin' it did. You're better off without it, lass."

In response to a wave of his hand, a panel slid open in the wall. Beyond it, the steel interior of a chute glowed yellow from light deep within. In slow motion, the plasfilm flew from his fingers, drifting like a snowflake toward its conversion to a lump of inert beige matter. Her mind's voice screamed inside as if he had taken a beloved pet away from her and murdered it before her eyes. The thing in the back of her head rose up, but she clamped her eyes shut and focused on staying calm. A police checkpoint was the *last* place a display of her talent needed to happen.

He walked up behind her before she realized she'd burst into tears. Hanging limp, she swayed about as he fixed her skirt back into place. Beeping above her head signaled her imminent release from the restraints, but even with warning, she fell when they no longer supported her. The sergeant caught her and carried her over to a chair by the wall, folding her arms in her lap and shining a small light in one eye and then the other.

"Shall I call for an ambulance?"

Annabelle glanced at the red marks on her wrists, thankful her 'gate tax' had taken the mild form of being pawed at, sore arms, and lost time. *That's what you get for storming off alone.* The nicety of this policeman seemed unusual, exacerbating her sense of being cheap and dirty. For a brief instant, she considered the shamble of her life as much her fault as society's. Most constables thought of people in her social strata as meat puppets for their personal amusement. The men became occasional victims of police combat training and the girls… well, the girls did whatever the constables wanted. Anna had no idea how to react to a cop who treated her like a person.

It hadn't much happened since she'd been thirteen.

She ventured a dazed smile and shook her head. "I'm all right."

"Are ya then? You look 'orrible."

"I just got out of bed, and…" She shivered. "The zoom's wearin' off."

He smirked in disapproval. "Cannae hide forever, girl. Sooner or later, you'll need to confront your demons. I'll git started on the incident report then."

"Incident?" She looked up, wide-eyed.

"That berk, Brown."

She swallowed hard. "It's no bother, sergeant. I don't want trouble. His mates'll give it to us twice as bad."

"Aye, suppose'n they would at that. I'll deal with 'im then. G'won, yer free ta take your leave."

He walked her to the door. Anna hesitated, glancing down at the portable metal steps between her and the rain-soaked street.

"Sergeant?"

"Go on."

Anna shivered, grasping the doorframe for support. "Thank you."

He nodded, a motion she caught from the corner of her eye. Wind whistled high overhead. Head bowed, she gathered her jacket tight and hurried away. The sergeant leaned against the opening with folded arms, watching her leave the puddle-laden mud of The Ruin behind for the intactness of London. Half a block away, she glanced over her shoulder to smile at him, but he had gone back inside. The dull shadow of Coventry tower resembled a smudge in the sky.

Annabelle walked down the street, surrounded by a bustling crowd that scarcely noticed her. More people had come out and about today, drawn by the rare lack of rain. A world apart from the tower, London brimmed with jostling bodies, flashing lights, whizzing advert bots dancing in the sky, and random aromas of food.

A young man collided with her. His hand swiped at her pocket, but came away empty. She offered a disbelieving glare at the disdainful look he gave her, as if she'd offended him by having nothing to steal.

The faint urge to zap him in the rear end formed in her head, but only caused the NetMini of a passing woman to burst into flames. Screaming, the Proper hurled it to the ground and jumped back.

Eventually, she left the nicer areas behind, and the pedestrians thinned accordingly. Block by block, she headed toward where people closer to her level congregated. She sped up to a jog past the tramps and street gangers who shifted out of their lazy rest to get a better look at her. Anna didn't look back until the glow of a giant pair of holographic breasts above a black-painted door came into view. It appeared so old she often wondered if it was real wood. Each time she knocked on it, the same thought waltzed around in her mind like the first time she had laid eyes on it. With the zoom so weak in her system, the texture of bubbled plastic appeared obvious in one of the gouges—Epoxil.

The door was as fake as most of the tits behind it.

Anna reached up a shaking hand and knocked again. An eight-by-two holo panel spread out in front of the door bearing the face of the club manager. His bushy black brows scrunched together, beady grey eyes glared at her.

"You're late."

"Sorry, Mr. Blake. Old Bill kept me for a minute at the border."

5

ACHERON

F lashing lights thrummed in time with oppressive music vibrating Anna's body. With each twist of her figure, her capsule-shaped cage jostled upon the three chains holding it off the ground. The six-foot enclosure of chrome-coated plastisteel didn't weigh much more than she did, bucking and swaying as she performed her routine. Faces massed into an ocean of lustful eyes at the level of her feet. Men stared at her with alcohol on their breath and sex on their thoughts.

She danced in nothing but a dark metal choker connected to a thin metal band encircling her chest below her breasts. Made to resemble leafy vines, the harness held a device the size of an egg tight against her back, from which long filament wings sprouted five feet to either side. Her alabaster skin glowed blue from the holographic appendages that fluttered, waved, or extended in concert with her every motion or change in posture. A headband of false flowers projected shimmering antennae of light up from her hair, a dangling pair of glowing orbs at their tips. Electronics in the headband picked up on her thoughts and controlled the wings' animation.

Annabelle clasped the bars above her head, fingers circling about the gentle curve of the metal where it came together. She swung herself about in time with the music pounding into her head, so loud, she imagined her brain compressing with each beat. Her feet sought purchase on curved bars with the precision of practice. Staying upright took more concentration than usual today. Anxious sweat came from knowing one misstep would result in a painful fall, her leg slipping between bars. The lack of chems in her system made everything tedious, every motion slower, each piece of her act necessitated deliberate thought about what she did. To the room around her, she flashed a smile as insubstantial as her wings.

She couldn't remember the last time she danced while sober enough to feel shame at being naked in a room full of strangers. Aside from suppressing her out of control brain, the chems mitigated her embarrassment. Without the gauzy layer of zoom covering her eyes, her stomach churned. Not yet two full hours into her shift, at least six men had commented on her red face. She couldn't allow her emotions to slip away from neutral. Her concentration spread between containing the *thing* and not wiping out. The combination of bare feet, sweat, and plastisteel made for tenuous balance at best.

Whenever she had to decide between the little monster or breaking her ankle, she chose not to fall. Few noticed the random spark overhead or a nearby NetMini dying a fiery death. Anna forced herself to move with the beat as she'd always done. Each time her skin brushed metal, the thought of being hunted down and killed seemed less unwelcome—at least she'd have clothing on for that.

Ten years ago, she would have been mortified to wear a skirt shorter than her fingertips. Ten years ago, she thought only 'bad people' did drugs or drank alcohol.

Maybe I should have let Dad kill me.

Under the haze of zoom, the Pixie persona often became real. Sometimes, the room full of perverts would melt away to a sylvan forest. Instead of being a whore in a cage, she turned into a real fey flying among the trees. She could forget her life. Today, she had no such shield, no such escape from reality. The leering eyes and wild howls hit her without the armor of drugs. The way these men looked at her made her glad for the first time that Blake locked the cages.

He had ignored her plea for a half hour delay. A guy she could score from lived only a few blocks away from the club. A trip there and back would take less than fifteen minutes. The worse her headache got, the more she didn't care if she had to streak in public to get her fix. The two minutes it would take to throw something on would take too long. He had given her a hard time about being late already and seemed in no mood to hear her request for even more time. When she'd asked him, he'd all but dragged her into the changing room and ripped her clothes off.

Anna grabbed the cage in front of her face, letting her head rest against her hands. *Being on Mr. Carroll's payroll wasn't that bad.* The idea of what *that* Anna would've done to Blake for even attempting to grab her made her already queasy stomach churn more.

I don't even know that woman anymore.

Working for Blake was one small step above being a slave, not that the police cared one whit about what people did to Cov girls. If she had the gall to go to complain to them, Blake would say she had made the lot of it up to cover her stealing, and they would put *her* in jail.

At least she made a little cred working here, what need did a Cov have of dignity?

The music shifted: lighter, faster, with a thrumming beat. She altered her routine, moving her body in waves against the cold enclosure as the virtual pixie wings buzzed. Reacting to her changing the dance, the somber blue holograms burst into a frenetic lime green that cycled to yellow and orange. She stared at them, wishing them real, wishing she could fly out of this cage and disappear into the forest she so often dreamed about. Her head pounded and spun. She caught herself testing the door. If it hadn't been locked, she'd have run, no matter what Blake would do to her. She couldn't stand it in here anymore. She'd do anything to get away from the noise, the stink, and the unrelenting eyes of perverts. Men close enough to see her struggling at the door assumed it part of her 'caged Pixie' act.

Trapped.

Her brain tensed, rage and panic gathered for an eruption, but dissipated at a *beep* from below. A hand stuffed an orange plastic ticket in a box hanging under her enclosure, a tip, physical tokens exchanged for credits at a booth near the door. On autopilot, she squatted low near the man who dropped the trinket, allowing him a closer look at her naked body. His gaze feasted upon her flesh. A moment later, he reached up and touched her breasts where they protruded past the bars. She acted as though she enjoyed the attention, smiling on the outside while her brain screamed at her to run off and find a dark place to hide. A loud *bang* erupted somewhere overhead; a holo-projector paid the price for her spike of shame. Everyone thought the noise part of the music.

Anna couldn't look at him, forcing herself not to flinch away from the pawing and groping. She stared off to the side until a rake of pain flared along her breast. She bit her lip to stifle a gasp of pain and cradled the fingernail scratches. One of the enormous bouncers had seized the man, who clamped down on her breast the giant man dragged him away from the cage. The bouncer hauled the man around by the collar and lifted him up on tiptoe.

"No touchin'. You wanna take her in back for half an hour, it'll be six hundred. In advance."

As people who exploited Covs went, Blake was on the more generous side. She'd get to keep at least sixty credits of it.

Pixie stared at the latch. Hearing this man sell her body regardless of her say in the matter filled her with shame, though far more than a simple locked door trapped her here. A fantasy played out in her mind: the man paying for her, the door opening, the bouncer reaching for her. She'd catch him by surprise, knee to groin. Once she let her panic out, let the *thing* go crazy, the chaos would give her the chance to escape. In her mind, she sprinted among a shower of falling sparks and confused perverts. She would run. As soon as the door opened, she would flee this place. It no longer mattered how little she wore, the cage had become intolerable. She had to escape this place and never return.

Anna gripped the bars of the door with both hands, flashing an eager smile the prospective John would misinterpret.

The customer pulled at his collar, staring at her sideways. "W... What'd I get for that?"

"Whatever ya fancy, 'cept don't cause permanent damage. You do anything to 'er a stimpak won't fix, I'll tear your boys off and feed 'em to ya."

She stood on tiptoe, licking the bar by her face and winking. The man peeled his gaze from her to babble at the bouncer. In the end, fear won over and he walked away. Her cage would remain locked. Anna wanted to turn her back to the room to hide the sudden tears that rolled free, but anywhere she faced held more depravity. Half the multicolored, strobing lights on the ceiling, as well as her holo-rig, sputtered and went dark. A keening feedback wail screamed from the sound system.

Bristol City became as quiet as a graveyard.

She swallowed her shame. Her emotion had let the thing out of its cage, and she had to cram it back in.

Calm down, Pixie. Calm down.

A few murmurs of "Bloody Hell" or "What the feck?" came from the customers who all looked around at the buzzing lights and speakers in the ceiling.

Seconds after she reined in the monster, all the electronics came back; the confused quiet gave way to the usual din.

Her body didn't want to continue. She held on to the bars, swaying and gyrating only enough to convey an attempt at continuing to dance. The flashing holographic colors and overbearing music swirled together in her mind, making her sick. She swallowed a hint of her breakfast again, gasping for air as she broke out in a cold sweat. The flavor reminded her of Penny. She wanted Penny to save her from Blake like she had saved her from the street. Anna shook the hanging cage, desperate to escape, wanting to go home. Greedy faces blurred at her feet, spinning and whirling into a sickening spiral of degradation. In a moment of panic, she strained at the door, trying to open it. The crowd cheered and clapped at her yearning look at the club's exit.

Stop looking at me.

She sank to the bottom of the cage and clutched one leg to her chest. The other dangled past the bars. The initial shock of cold metal upon her ass melted into comfort a few seconds later. Sitting felt wonderful. Her limbs shook, no matter how much she tried to will herself to stop. She leaned her forehead into a space between two bars, too narrow for her skull to fit. The chill offered momentary relief from the headache the sound system jackhammered into her brain.

The holographic wings curled forward. Blue again, they draped around her like a pixie asleep on a branch. She shivered, having gone from overheated to freezing. Beads of sweat raced each other down her extended leg like errant spiders. The trembling intensified. She let go of her breasts and rubbed both arms, trying to warm up. Staring eyes bathed her in a chill as though she sprawled out in the snow with nothing on.

Anna wanted a warm blanket, a bed, something softer than the rigid cage. A convulsion brought a trace of vomit into the back of her throat. She gagged and clamped a hand over her mouth, though a gossamer thread of bile slipped between her fingers and fell to the floor. Time lost meaning as she flitted in and out of consciousness, the numbing cold the only constant.

A man's voice wobbled within her clouded mind, asking if she was okay. A bottle of water came past the bars. She hugged it like a doll, sipping at it, still floating outside of time. In seconds, her stomach rejected the offering, winding into a knot and sending the liquid back up out her nose in a sputtering cough.

A loud *crack* of metal on metal jarred her out of her fog. She struggled to lift her head. The floor in front of her had emptied, except for Blake. He hovered outside, his cheeks red, roaring a series of incomprehensible things while spraying her with spittle. Even sprawled at the bottom of the hanging cage, she looked down at him. He banged on the bars with a truncheon again and again, whatever words he bellowed failed to pierce the haze in her mind.

She reached up to grip the bars and pulled herself standing. Being eye-level with her shins seemed to enrage him even more. Inch-thick plastisteel rods made for uncomfortable footing, worsened by the cage wobbling and swaying. Anna tugged at the door. Blake said he locked it for their protection.

Bullshit, he just likes hearing us beg to be let out. It's fecking kidnapping is what it is, but we're Covs.

The incoherent fog between her ears parted, allowing real-time sound to rush in. The music seemed much weaker than his voice.

"Oi, stupid bitch. This ain't naptime! Get your ass moving. You forget you're for sale? None of these gits wants to dip their wick in a zombie."

Anna grasped the bars, rattling the hatch. "Please Blake, I need to use the loo. I feel like shit. Lemme outta here?"

"You've only been at it for two hours. Your break's not for another. Get to it or you can spend all night in there."

"Come on, Blake. I'm not kidding, I feel lousy..."

Anger faded to laughter. "Oh, is that so? How many sick days do you have left? Oh, that's right... none." His joviality ended in an instant, voice dropping to a threatening growl. "I own you, bitch. Never forget that."

"It doesn't matter how much of a shit you are to me." Anna clutched the cage to stay upright, casting a hateful stare at him. "Answer's still no. You ain't gettin' in my knickers by being a bigger twat."

"You don't wear knickers, *whore*." He bashed the truncheon into the bar an inch above her fingers.

Anna jumped back, but her foot slipped and she landed on her ass, one leg wedged between the curved bars at the bottom of the cage. Pain from her tailbone crashing into metal rode up her spine and detonated a budding migraine into a cascade of vomit that splattered onto the floor. Blake jumped to the side, avoiding all but a few specks on his boot. She let gravity take her, and curled into a heap on her side, staring at the wavering blue antenna bobbing in front of her eyes. Everything hurt. The music thrummed into her skull, sending wave after wave of bile past clenched teeth. His voice repeated 'whore' in her head. Shame crashed into fury.

The sound system burned out with a deafening feedback scream.

She shivered, glaring at Blake who turned to deal with complaining customers. Blue sparks danced on her arms, lapping at the cage. Anna raised a hand, mesmerized by the electricity crackling over her fingers. The warm threads comforted her like an old friend holding her hand. She had only to want Blake dead. She reached out of the cage, straightening her arm, pointing at him.

She stared over her hand like aiming a gun, smiling at the thought of killing him. Blake blurred as her eyes focused back to the still-locked door. She couldn't get away. They'd catch her for sure. Her lip curled into a sneer. *Fuck it.*

Power built up around her as she gathered current from her surroundings. She concentrated on Blake's head, wanting the electricity to be drawn there. Before the arc leapt from her fingertips, a head-sized bot floated up outside of the cage, blocking her view of Blake. It projected a holographic advert for antacid.

A hair-thin spark leapt from her fingertip to the bot, which didn't react at all to it.

Anna let her arm fall limp. Her left eye felt as though a knife had pierced it; the migraine worsened. A few men wandered over to see what Blake would do. He handed them a few complimentary 'tip tokens' and ushered them toward other dancers less visibly sick before running over to scream at the sound guy for the music being off. The sales bot lost interest and glided away once her body succumbed to involuntary shudders. Searing threads of pain flickered down every nerve.

Fire filled her veins as if every blood cell scratched at her for denying them zoom. Heat and cold came in waves. Anna crossed her arms over her head in a futile effort to block out the light and sound.

Someone kill me...

6

MANKY

Silence crashed into Anna's consciousness with the strength of a loud noise. Darkness surrounded her, broken only by the glint of her glowing deep blue wings on the mirror-finished bars. Reality spun in circles around her head and numbness had replaced the feeling of biting cold. She leaned forward, reaching to grasp a horizontal brace connecting the bars. The holographic antennae perked up as she raised her head.

The Bristol City Club was dark, the place left to its own devices in the wee morning hours of the next day. Annabelle stared at the obstinate door. Blake made good on his threat and left her locked in, trapped long after everyone had left. Despite the futility of it, she struggled to break the cage open with brute force after pulling herself to her feet. Sensing her motion, the faerie wings batted as if she used them to help fight against the enclosure. Her attempt at a scream, a pathetic raspy squeak, made her aware of extreme thirst.

"Blake, you twat!" she croaked. "Let me the feck out of here right this instant!"

When her voice echoed back unanswered, she seethed in anger for several minutes. Snap flashes of blue lightning danced across the rafters above her. Again, Anna attacked the door, tears rolling unbidden down her face.

The bobbing motion sent her back to her knees in dry heaves. The flavor of hours-old vomit returned. She sagged, arms and legs draped past the bars, and stared into a bucket Blake had hung from the underside of the cage for her to use as a bog, scowling at the thought he cared more about his floor than his workers. She considered spiting him, but somehow found the presence of mind amid her shuddering misery to fear the beating it would earn her if she pissed or puked on the floor.

She reached for the water bottle she had dropped hours before. Blake left it there, no doubt knowing she would never be able to reach it. At her height, she could stand under the cage without it touching her head. She tried sticking her arms or legs out of the cage in every conceivable contortion, but never came closer than a toe ten inches from the bottle.

Numbness retreated, fading to oppressive heat. Sweat coated her, this time with woozy lightheadedness and flashing patches of burning sweeping in waves. The zoom had gone completely out of her system. All traces of it sat beneath her in the pail. It had been more than a year since she had let sobriety advance this far. Mercifully, she felt so awful that the presence lurking in the back of her mind was the farthest thing from it. At the moment, she would have happily glommed any chem she could find: a Zoomer, Narcoderm, Freelove, Flowerbasket, Smileys, Yellow Crumblies, Nightcandy, a Racer Dot, anything... except maybe Lace. She wanted to suppress the little monster, not kill herself.

After a brief repeat of her ineffectual battle with the door, she held her hands over the lock. Ages ago, she could have caused an arc strong enough to melt it. Her fried mind failed to summon even a static spark. Even her emotion racing from anger to shame to terror produced no effect in the surrounding electronics. The throes of withdrawal kept her power well and truly unreachable. She had become helpless, for real.

Is this what it's like to be normal?

She draped herself against the cage, letting her legs hang free, too defeated to move. In defiance of the lethargy that immobilized her body, her mind searched. Knowing she couldn't go off in search of the substance she so desperately craved made her want to scream and kick and shout. Her muscles spent, her angst took the form of a piteous whimper from her nose. Glimmering threads of blue light, the silver bars of other cages out in the dark room reflecting the faerie wings, mesmerized her. A tendril of drool descended from the corner of her lip, landing unnoticed upon her breast. She gaped at the shifting glow as if it offered insight to the deepest mysteries of the known universe.

An hour passed before the shivering came again. Involuntary spasms of protesting muscles rattled the chains from which her prison hung. Her brain cried out for zoom, the static reality of her surroundings displeased it. She stared at the keyhole and daydreamed about a vid she watched as a child where an evil magician kept a faerie locked in a jar to use as a lantern. Anna felt like that tiny woman, her immediate surroundings aglow in the hologram blue of slow-fluttering wings.

She traced a finger over her pixie tattoo and wondered how much it resembled what she must look like, though she didn't grin. Fighting the cage proved pointless, and feeling shame wouldn't help either. Anna curled into a shivering ball, forehead against her knees, and cried.

This is what I deserve.

Brilliant sparking explosions shocked her eyes open. She recoiled from a shower of embers sputtering out of media projectors in the roof. Shame and guilt had awoken the beast. She glanced at the wings, and let slip a detached giggle that they had survived. Then again, they didn't have much power in them. Anna tried again to melt the lock, but the limp tendril of current that leapt from her hand to the door only grounded into the ceiling. *Am I that rusty?* In order to melt plastisteel, she would need more energy than she could generate from thin air. She would have to redirect it from a mains supply. Alas, she couldn't feel anything nearby with enough power in it.

The wee hours passed in alternating moments of lucidity and delirium. The bottom of the capsule-shaped cage offered little comfort. No matter how she sat or curled, the bars pressed pain into some tender exposed bit of flesh. Only by virtue of withdrawal did she lose blocks of time. Anna hadn't eaten since breakfast the previous day, though her condition kept hunger at bay. Sometimes falling into a dream, she imagined herself a real faerie in a real jar, pounding at the glass and begging someone to let her out. She cradled sore hands to her chest as the line between real and dreamed pain blurred.

She tried to cover her body. Even the empty room made her feel exposed. Her prison hung near the center of the club, leaving her no direction to turn where someone couldn't find a view. *Is Blake going to leave me in here all day tomorrow? Make me dance without letting me out?* Anna sniffled, and screamed for help until her throat hurt. She slumped down and curled up. The only answer to her cries, the echo of her own voice.

This is kidnapping. Old Bill won't care.

Sleep teased at the edge of her mind and the sense of cold metal on her back changed to something warm and smooth. She opened her eyes, finding herself sprawled at the bottom of an immense bottle.

Hand-blown glass distorted the face of the mad wizard leering at her, chin to brow as tall as her height. *What the? Oh... I'm dreaming.* Anna backed away from the gargantuan man as the narrow, drawn face puffed up and widened. He shrank, his eyebrows thickened, and the ancient mage morphed into the face of Blake. Yellowed glass split like melting plastic, forming a shiny cage.

A sphere of an overweight man hovered near the cage, raking his truncheon back and forth across the bars until she sat up. The deafening cacophony made her grab both sides of her head. Her entire body ached as if she had been hit by a maglev train, then run over by another one going the opposite way.

Solid floor hit her in the face. She lay stunned, unable to remember the cage opening or climbing out of it. Fingers clutching a handful of her hair pulled her up on her knees. Blake stuffed the bucket into her hands. Her stomach rebelled at the stink of piss and puke, and she heaved more bile into it. The truncheon struck across her buttocks in a series of light slaps, urging her to stand and then to the bathroom. His hand on the back of her neck guided her to the nearest toilet, where she dumped the pail out. Blake shouted the whole time he made her wash it, though his words drifted around her brain in the form of random explosions of sound somewhere far away.

Compared to the bathroom, the cage had been warm.

The annoying rap of the baton upon her backside chased her on unsteady legs from the bathroom into a corridor where her face met the wall several times. Each time she stumbled, he helped her up with a harsh yank on her arm. Time stopped and started; her vision consisted of blurry still images flashing in sequence: hallway tilted left, floor, wall, hallway tilted right, ceiling, a bright LED bulb hanging on an exposed wire, and doors. From blur to magnificent detail, every grain of sand and every mite upon the surface of each picture stood out in her mind before it returned to blur. The cycle repeated until she found herself sprawled on tattered green carpet.

Blake gripped her shoulder. Breath thick with the smell of sausage, mushrooms, and gravy choked her gagging. "You lot think ye kin freeload here, eh?"

It should have hurt, but nothing made it past the full-body agony of absent zoom. He opened a door with her face and shoved her in. The blurring colors in front of her hinted at the shapes of a messy bedroom. His erection stabbed her in the back despite his pants when he stepped in behind her. Before she could turn, he shoved her forward into a flailing stumble. Everything spun and dragged down into slow motion. The fall seemed to take longer than it should have.

SHE LANDED ON HER CHEST IN A MOUND OF COLD, WET TRASH.

Anna lifted her head out of the plastic and stared into the rainy grey of an alley, wondering how a bed turned into a pile of rubbish bags. Her surroundings glowed azure from the false wings that still managed to work despite the rain. For several seconds, an empty can adhered to her cheek before it peeled away and fell back into the pile. Water pooled in the small of her back. Her soreness had receded to a point, shrinking out of her limbs and hiding in her head. Someone had wedged a cannonball between the lobes of her brain, and it crushed outward at the back of her skull.

With a soft whimper, she braced a hand to her head, surprised to find the band of imitation flowers still there. Nudging it caused the antenna to wobble in front of her. The nauseating motion of the azure orbs set her dry heaving.

When it passed, she tried to climb off the lopsided mound of garbage, but wound up slipping and rolling into a seated position on gritty pavement. Anna gazed with half-closed eyes at the cluster of trash bags, the wet pavement beneath her, then up at eighteen stories of fire escapes from which more water dripped. Grabbing the wall helped her remember how to stand. She spent a minute leaning on it and trying to understand how she had gone from the cage to an alley and why the sky held daylight.

Several advert bots swarmed her, displaying advertisements for clothing. When they failed to detect the presence of a NetMini signal or ImDent chip, they lost interest and rushed off, careening over each other around the corner.

Most of the population carried NetMinis, small hand-held devices that combined the function of a VidPhone and computer terminal. Linked to someone's Personal Identity Data, or PID, a wave of the device by a merchant's terminal let civilized people pay for goods and services. Alas, NetMinis weren't on good terms with Anna. Every time she'd gotten one, it had burned out in a week.

Hand over hand along the wall, she made it into the street and went two blocks over before the steady stream of gasps and insults reminded her that the pixie costume electronics were all she had on. She remembered the long-absent feeling of shame coming over her in the cage, but since she had somehow escaped, only one thought echoed inside her mind: zoom.

Nakedness didn't even register.

She bowed her head with a sullen frown, letting the words hit her and accepting them, cringing away from each voice. Whore was a popular one, tramp, slut, filth, street trash, and of course pikey. She lacked the coordination to reach up behind her back and turn the wings off, so she plodded along with them curled over her like a smashed dragonfly. One or two passersby clapped or whistled in appreciation for the unexpected show. They made her feel worse than the sanctimonious ones.

This part of the city saw few cops unless a riot or a raid wound up on the menu, but fortunately, neither one had been scheduled that day. The falling rain washed some of the filth of her miserable night into the gutter. The crowd parted for her, giving her some open space to walk in. Despite being one bad week away from winding up in Coventry themselves, the dregs of this part of town acted as if above her. Most had low-wage jobs with little prestige and lived ten bodies to an apartment, but even they looked down their noses at people from The Ruin.

Some took vids of her, others stared, one or two pawed at her, but drew their hands back with howls from unexpected shocks. Fortunately, the zaps her strung-out mind produced didn't amount to much more than coincidental static—enough to dissuade, but not injure.

She ignored it all, walking until a traffic signal stopped her at the corner. The crowd shifted away, half expecting her to do something crazy, steal, or perhaps they wanted to avoid a nutter streaking about with animated wings made of light. Her semiconscious gaze fixated on the crossing signal. Her half-dead body suspended the punishment of pain because she promised it what it wanted. The Propers following and harassing her meant nothing.

Plonk's flat waited for her a few more blocks straight ahead. Returning to the club in search of clothes hadn't even occurred to her. What he had was more important.

"Are you all right, miss?" asked a bookish man a few years her senior. He leaned close, gathering a sand brown coat about himself as if seeing her made him colder.

She turned her head, squinting at him past the rain in her eyes. It took some time for the message to go from brain to lips, but she muttered in a hung-over drone.

"Party… lost a dare."

The crowd muttered; she hoped they believed her about being wagered to do this. Anna folded her arms in a sad attempt at modesty, staring down at the water tracing icy lines over her naked body while wanting to believe she might not be all the things they called her.

Such hope was as empty as her life.

7

BLISS

Number Three, Dalrymple Road wound up being a bit more of a walk than she remembered.

Last time, she had the lingering haze of a prior dose in her system as well as clothes. Naked in two ways, the trip felt much longer. Derisive looks and hurtful words continued, though she cared only about finding one special door. For blocks, she had walked past disapproving stares and unintentional baths provided by passing cars striking puddles.

Her skin alternated from total numbness to such tender sensitivity the texture of the sidewalk felt as though she trod over an army of pins. The weather and a small crowd followed her to her destination, but only the rain continued past the yard gate.

Ian Mitchell, better known as Plonk by those with whom he conducted business, sat upon the stoop under the protection of an old awning. The Buildup, as it had been called sixty years prior, converted most of the residences in London to multi-level apartments to accommodate the growing population. The ground level looked much like it had ages ago. Above it, the pea-green metal structure reached into the hazy grey of a rainy afternoon.

Anna walked the steps, cold and dry compared to the pedestrian path.

"Well now, aren't you a sight." Plonk laughed. "You taken up the Bard then?"

"I think I got fired." She muttered, blinking, her eyes unable to focus on anything for much more than an instant.

"Well there you go. Why ya runnin' about starkers?" Plonk gestured at her. "You have a… wardrobe malfunction?"

She pointed in a random direction, which might have even been at the club. "Woke up in an alley. Had a bad comedown. I'ma die if I don't get a zoomer. Can you help me out?"

A smidge of emotion peeked out from under the dull deadpan of her voice, riding the last few words. She stumbled up to him and collapsed on her knees a few feet from where he sat. Plonk cringed at the sound of her bones hitting the porch, though she didn't feel it.

"Where you keepin' your cred stick? Or do I not want to know?"

"I'm out." She sighed. "Please, Plonk… I get my giro in a day or two, you know I'm good for it, I swear."

Sensing her anticipatory mood, the wings fluttered to life and spread apart.

"Well now, Pixie, ya don't get owt for nowt. I don't do the credit bit. Collection's a messy bit of business, and your little legs are too pretty to break."

She wobbled back, sitting on her heels with a desperate stare. "Zoom for a shag then?"

Plonk massaged his lips into a Cheshire grin with one finger. "Well, I'm too much a gentleman to ask. However, since you've offered, I think we can come to an arrangement."

He took her by the hand, helped her up, and led her inside. In the elevator, she sank to her knees again and went for his pants.

"Oi, luv. Not in the lift. I got a place, be proper about it and all. I'll even fix ya somethin' ta eat after."

She clung to him, trembling from the need. He had been around enough to know how bad the want could get. Were he the sort to be inclined to do such a thing, he could have rented her out to his mates for half the day.

As close to The Ruin as it was, this building played host to the sort of people who didn't pay attention to things normal people would pay attention to. They didn't much react to a naked woman with glowing filament wings faltering past their doors with half-closed eyes, or that Plonk had half the gangs in the East End coming to him for chems. Much healthier not to notice such things.

Grey carpeting spanned the floor of Plonk's flat. To the right of the door, a dingy kitchenette seemed aged by the unearthly buttery glow of a single lamp. Past it, the room expanded into a parlor where a large holo-vid player faced a leather couch. A highly-stylized representation of a nude woman on all fours with an oval of glass balanced on her back served as a coffee table. Anna squinted at the warped figure, far removed from realism, wondering who would consider it art. *Looks more like a tangle of icicles.*

Peeling lime wallpaper on her left ended as the jutting wall cornered at a short hallway. Between the living room and the master bedroom, it provided access to a single bath. Following his gesture, she approached the bed while he rummaged a number of locked cabinets at the other end of the room by a shuttered window.

"Blinds, eight," said Plonk.

The blinds whirred and narrowed, dimming the room to the point her glowing wings gave off more light than the day outside.

"Aha. There we are. You said you fancied a zoomer, right?"

"Aye right."

She looked up wearing the expression of an eager orphan begging for food, holding her hands together at her heart. He tossed it like a Frisbee onto the bed, landing the small patch in front of the pillow. Like a dog after a treat, she pounced, clambering up to it and picking at the adhesive. Her coordination dulled from withdrawal, it took some doing for her to work the thing free of the backing.

Plonk joined her on the bed, kissing her on the shoulder and caressing her body in an attempt to be at least somewhat romantic. She paid little attention to him or his roaming touch. The small square in her hand offered an escape from where she lived, who she had become—and the filth in which she wallowed.

She closed her eyes and pressed the derm into the tender skin of her wrist.

A whiteout flash of elation came and went, fading to a face full of pillow, her back end in the air. Whatever went on behind her didn't matter at all. What Plonk did to her was worth what she held in her hand. His whispers and grunts dissipated into a sublime sense of floating.

The cold sensation of zoom seeped into her arm. All the misery melted away in the onrush of contentment. She smiled, basking in the rapid absence of pain from being separated from it for an agonizing day. Anna became vaguely aware of Plonk inside her as reality, and the pillow, faded into a patina of too-bright greenery.

She sailed upon pixie wings into a forest of hallucination.

Giggling, she looped over branches and glided among the leaves. Birds flew up alongside her, chirping merrily. The storybook woods blurred by in patches of emerald and brown, shafts of sunlight offered warm rays among which she flitted before diving to frolic in the grass. Anna settled upon a leaf, drank it free of dew, and reclined.

After a moment of blissful rest, a poke in the rear end woke her. She glanced over her hip at a furry little animal with huge cartoon eyes. The diminutive woodland creature, looking a bit like a shaggy beaver with Plonk's teeth, clung to her rump and fussed with a yellow lamp helmet, flicking at the lens twice.

"Oi. Li'l help here luv. Can't do this all on me own and the wick's running out."

She smiled, cooing, and stretched back into the leaf—asleep.

8

DIRTY

Adrift in a listless breeze that matched her mood, Anna sat with her legs dangling through the balcony railing, and stuck her head out to gaze down past her toes at The Ruin, thirteen stories below. Her hair brushed at her cheeks in response to a gentle breeze. London cowered beneath an overcast sky, leaving her unable to tell if she woke up before noon or at almost dusk.

"You okay? Ye were all sixes and sevens last night," asked Penny, somewhere behind her.

Anna pulled her head out from between the bars and glanced over her shoulder, her face a mask of accepted disgrace. "Had ta cop off with Plonk again when I came to. Said the first wasn't 'nuff since I was as good as brown bread. He wouldn't let me leave 'til I *paid* him back."

Penny stooped, grabbed Anna's arm close, then turned her wrist up, smirking at the derm. "You ought to quit these, girl. They're not an Elastoplast for the heart."

"I can't." Tugging her arm back, she hid handcuff marks in the folds of an over-large nightshirt.

The breeze picked up, making her shiver. Penny tugged at her until she got up and went inside, then closed the sliding door to shut out the gale. Anna flopped on the bed and tried to rub some warmth into her arms.

"Budge up then..." Penny sat as Anna scooted to the side. "I'm just worried about you. You've never been the chipper sort, but you're a bit stroppy as of late."

Anna pulled the bedclothes over her bare legs, basking in the warmth. The little creatures giggling at her from under the bureau whispered about her. They gave voice to Anna's shame at Penny seeing the red lines around her wrists. Knowing the whispers to be a product of the drugs, she tuned them out.

"Your hair's nice," mumbled Anna.

"I've 'ad my hair like this since we've met. It's not changed." Penny sat on the edge of the bed, nudging Anna's eyes open wider with a thumb. "Oi, you're wrecked, aren't ya?"

Anna grinned, stroking her fingers at her friend's long, ebon locks. "I love this black."

"You know they 'ave dye. You could change it." Penny crossed her arms, feigning jealousy. "I don't see why you would though, yours is so exotic and pretty. Can't say I've ever seen anyone who's a *natural* blonde this white. You should let it grow out again. You're not runnin' with that Carroll gent anymore."

"Right." Anna let her hands fall in her lap. "Long hair got in the way." Tears welled up in her eyes as her face warped in preparation of hard sobbing. "I miss it long. I cut it off, didn't I?"

Penny threw an arm around her and patted her back. She rubbed Anna's shoulder for a while until the sadness weakened.

"Hey, it'll be okay." Penny squeezed. "Did something else happen wif Plonk? I haven't seen you like this since I found you in a rubbish bin all them years ago."

"Been thinkin' about my dad." Anna burst out laughing, wiping her cheeks dry. "I must've been a sight, aye. Guess I loved the bastard after all. Maybe I shouldn't 'ave killed him."

"Killed him?" Penny gasped. "Your Da? You said it was an acci—oh... The food 'sem, did you make it blow up?"

Anna regarded Penny for a full minute until her brain caught up to what had come out of her mouth. She'd been thirteen when they met; ten years was an age in Coventry time, most didn't survive that long. She wanted to confess about the thing in her head, but that sort of truth could ruin even the quasi-sisterhood that kept them alive.

"I-I." She shivered, staring at Penny. "He used to beat the hell out of me. I dunno why 'lectronics fritz around me. I got bad luck or something."

Penny, to Anna's surprise, didn't recoil away. "Oh, Pix... You've been blaming yourself for an accident all these years?"

Lying to her only true friend hurt as much as murdering her father, even if it had been self-defense. Penny consoled her through another bout of tears.

"No, Pen, I really did it. I wanted the machine to kill him."

"You were thirteen, and you witnessed it. I can't imagine the kind of nightmares you must've had. I don't believe for an instant it was your fault." Penny ruffled her hair the way she used to, ten years ago. "You really ought to get off that shit."

"It's better if I keep on with it. I can't afford the hospital and there's nothing at the chemist's for this."

Penny offered a comforting glance, begging her without a word to open up. A scrape of ice jabbed her in the chest from guilt. More so when Penny jumped at the faltering lights. If anyone in the world deserved her trust, Penny did. She wanted, no *needed,* to tell her the one thing she had kept to herself. Anna looked up, crying again when they made eye contact. It would be safer for Penny not to know about her. If *they* ever came for her again, not knowing would keep Penny alive.

Anna remained silent. After a pat on the back, her friend got up to leave.

"Stay in bed, hon, you still look like death warmed over."

"Pen."

Halfway to the door, her friend turned back with a concerned expression. "Yes?"

Anna grimaced, staring.

"You're either going to shit the bed with that face or you're dumping me."

She buried her face in her hands, laughing and crying at the same time. "I don't want you to hate me, but I can't take it anymore."

Penny rushed over. "It's that Carroll bloke, you've killed for 'im 'aven't you?"

"A couple times... by accident. Not like assassinations or anything, just bastards trying to shoot me."

"Well..." Penny sat on the edge of the bed again. "Spawny's popped a few East Enders, not tha' big a do."

Anna clamped her arms around Penny as if she were a five-year-old waking from a nightmare, whispering, "Pen... I'm psionic. I can't do it anymore; I can't keep lying to you."

The expected stiffening happened. Anna braced for rejection.

"I know, luv."

"What." Anna's head snapped up. "You know?"

"Oh, get off it, girl. You talk in your sleep. All the stuff what breaks around you? I've seen the sparks."

Anna sniveled. *She knows and didn't leave?* She whimpered, "I'm so sorry I never told you, I thought you'd hate me. My dad was a piss-artist, and in rare form that night. I practically got drunk from breathin' the same air. I buggered the holo during a Frictionless match. He broke my arm and had me in the kitch against the cabinets. I…"

"Shh." Penny kissed her on the forehead. "It's okay, I believe you."

Penny sat with her, rubbing her back until the high faded and she became drowsy again.

♌ ⚚ 🜔 🜂 ♎

ANNA POPPED AWAKE AT THE SOUND OF HER DOOR OPENING, UNSURE OF how much time had passed. Penny entered with a mug of chai tea, followed by a younger girl with long, straight blue hair who appeared to be around twelve or thirteen. The girl's childlike face stood out in a sharp contrast to the imitation leather jacket, T-shirt with the image of zombies in tutus, spiked chains, and knee-high boots. Her eyes glimmered with a combination of inexperience and a put-on sense of toughness.

From the look of her, Anna figured she had been out of a proper home less than a week. The overall effect of her black-and-white striped sleeves gave the feel of a suburban kid trying to act like a street tough. She didn't look emaciated and smelled of fruity shampoo.

Pixie took the tea, cradling the warm cup to her chest for a moment and basking in the steam before sipping it.

"Who's that?"

Penny shook her head. "Little miss tough hasn't said much. Spawny's taken to callin' her Twee."

Anna chuckled. The girl bristled at the term.

After a sip, Anna winked at her. "If you don't like it, speak up."

The girl's blue hair expanded upward, blowing in a breeze that didn't exist. The concentric black and white rings on her shirtsleeves started moving like barber poles while the undead on her shirt went into a mosh dance.

Rubbing the bridge of her nose, Anna groaned before staring at the

derm an inch from her eyes upon her wrist. "Cripes, this one's strong…
What's it been? Six hours and I'm still seeing shit."

"Faye." The girl fidgeted.

Lost to uncontrolled giggles, Anna laughed to the point where Penny
had to stabilize her tea. The blue-haired girl frowned and blushed.

"Why is that funny?" Penny smiled at the new arrival, trying to make
her feel better.

"I'm Pixie… She's fey."

"Don't mind her, luv." Penny gestured at Anna with both hands. "This
is why you shouldn't do drugs."

The young girl's voice carried a surly undertone, some of the venom
leeched by unfamiliar surroundings. "This place is a grotty shithole.
Umm, can I use your shower? I haven't had one in like three days. Is there
even one here?"

Anna stopped giggling as if a switch had been thrown, sitting up with
a straight face and taking her tea back. "I suppose. You should run a clean
cycle first so you don't get any Plonk on you." She downed the tea in a
series of long gulps.

Faye whirled with a raised brow. "The eff is Plonk?"

"You don't want to know," said Penny and Anna at the same time.

"Why is she here?" Anna held the empty cup tight in an effort to
extract any remaining warmth.

Penny's gaze followed raindrops down the patio door. "She needs
somewhere to stay."

"I know that." Anna made a playful batting gesture. "I mean she's so
little… Why does she need to be *here*?"

"I ain't *little*. I'm thirteen." Faye shot a sour look at the wall.

She doesn't have a monster in her head, she can go to the police.

Penny sighed. "Some nonsense with her parents… Isn't it always?"

I was the same age when I made myself homeless. The thought of her old
bedroom, and how badly she wanted to be back there right now, opened
the dam. Tears flowed free down her cheeks.

Anna leapt on Penny, draping herself over from behind and hugging
the wind from her lungs. "You kept me alive." She sobbed. "I never said
thank you. I've showered three times today, but I can't wash the feckin'
dirt off."

Faye backpedaled, pointing over her shoulder with a thumb. "I'll just,
umm, give you two some privacy. Yeah…" She darted into the bathroom
and closed the door.

Returning the hug, Penny comforted her friend's drug-fueled burst of emotion. "I know. Some stains soap can't get rid of. I'll always be here for you."

"I shouldn't be this up. I must've taken another patch when I left."

"Go on then, hon. Get some sleep." Penny put a hand on Anna's forehead. "You still look a mess and you're a tad overheated. I'll take ya into town tomorrow."

"I'm out of control," whispered Anna.

"Smidge, aye." Penny smiled. "But ya cannae just up and drop that shite. We'll get ya through it."

Anna relinquished the tepid cup, smiling at Penny as she slid into the warm bed. The repetitious thrum of the autoshower, knocked her out before the lights went off.

⚶ ⚚ ⛉ ⚱ ♈

Soft sobs from nearby cracked Anna's eyelids open.

Curled on her side, she gazed out the window and took in the faint glimmer of morning lighting the horizon. It had been many years since she had been awake this early, something about it seemed unnatural even if she had gone to sleep at four in the afternoon.

The quiet weeping continued behind her.

Anna rolled onto her back and found Faye curled up on the bed in her undergarments. In response to her moving, the crying quieted.

A small whisper broke the silence. "Sorry if I woke you."

"If you're gonna pinch my bed, at least use the covers. You'll freeze."

The girl shifted under the blankets and smiled at her. Runny eyeliner ran in dark streaks over an innocent face. "Thanks. Penny said it would be okay. T'other flats on this level are a mess, and Spawny didn't want a kid watchin' 'em shag." She frowned. "Not that I'd wanna see him anyway, the man's a hairy mess."

"I'm surprised the bastard didn't suggest you join them."

Faye shot her a dire look. "He's not one of *those* is he?"

The girl had reacted with such immediate fear, Anna couldn't help but peek into the child's surface thoughts—someone had tried to molest her. The man's pasty face leered at both of them, a suburban kitchen in the background. Faye's memory of him grabbing her from behind made Anna jump. She sat up and pressed her hands to her face. Ugh. Zoom's gone. I'd *almost forgotten I could listen to thoughts.*

"No, Faye, he's a horny idiot that's been after me for months. I can't even tell if he's serious. If he knows yer only thirteen, he won't bother ya."

Anna took a deep breath, letting her body adjust to the reality of being awake at seven in the morning. When she touched the shivering girl's shoulder, Faye cringed away, then offered an ashamed look.

"Sorry…" Anna knew the reaction. "Who was it then? Your father?"

"Nothing really happened." Faye sat in silence for few minutes before she broke into crying again.

"Figure it must be your dad if you're out here at your age. Mine died when I was twelve."

The girl quieted. "Mine's not dead. He doesn't believe me. Sorry 'bout yours."

"Don't be." Anna patted her shoulder. "He deserved what he got."

The girl rolled on her back, glancing up at her past a curtain of sky blue hair. "Did he…?"

"No. He wasn't like *that*. Dad beat the hell out of me… almost killed me."

Faye sniffled and wiped her cheeks. "Mr. Bell, next door. 'E paid me to watch his terriers sometimes whenever he went off on some errand or other. Used ta do it for 'im for years, ever since I was like ten. The last time when he came back… He had me against the wall and…" She choked up.

It had been some years since she made deliberate use of telepathy. In her present state, it required concentration to even peek into a person's surface thoughts, a task that used to be trivial. Great emotion all but projected Faye's shame into her head.

Anna forced mental images of an unwanted tongue kiss and a roaming hand out of her mind and broke mental contact. At least he'd only pawed at her through clothing. Anna tried to contain her anger while offering a sympathetic frown and consoling words. She closed her eyes and thanked the zoom for dulling the spike of rage.

"My pa didn't believe me. They think Mr. Bell is such a nice man. They think I'm lying to stir up trouble 'cause I dyed my hair blue and listen to The Dead Ballerinas."

"Did you go to the police? Ya should go now when you can. If'n ya spend enough time 'ere in Cov, they'll stop listening. We're not people anymore."

Faye's body tensed. "Yeah, they didn't believe me either because I got away from him before he did anything a med-scan would find. Bell's a dean or deacon or something in the C of E." She took on a sarcastic tone. "He would never do such a thing."

Anna rolled her eyes. "Donnae know how anyone still believes in that rubbish."

"I know, right." Faye sighed.

Anna figured the girl had run away from home to avoid the neighbor or as an aftershock to a nasty spat with the parents. In a day or two once the reality of this place set in, she'd try to talk her into going back. For now, she would let the kid cool off.

"Sorry for laughing at you yesterday. It struck me funny how our names related. You kin stay here with me 'til you figure out what you wanna do."

The girl's voice weakened from approaching sleep. "Thanks."

"If you wanna talk…"

When no response came, Anna eased out of bed and headed to the bathroom. After a shower, she leaned on the doorframe, staring at herself ten years ago—though she had been shorter at that age. A pang of jealousy reared up at the girl still having live parents, obtuse or not, and a home she *chose* to leave. Anna would take a nonce next door, no monster in her head, and *two* living parents ten times over instead of her present reality. She'd never asked to be a freak.

She glanced down at her hands… hands that had killed her father. The bathroom lights behind her flickered and died. A tiny azure spark lapped up her fingers in time with the memory of a brighter bolt going over her head and her father screaming.

No point lying to herself.

She had very much made a choice as well.

9

THE DOLE

Anna stared straight ahead at a stripe of reflective paint on pale grey cinder blocks while clutching a worn, metal railing so tight her knuckles whitened.

The constable patted and squeezed her here and there. For once, the cop behaved somewhat professional and only touched as long as he had to in order to check for contraband the sensors couldn't read at a distance.

"Clear," said the man, his voice inches behind her.

The unexpected voice made her jump. The expected slap on the ass didn't come, only a painful grip around her left bicep guiding her to a waiting area while he rummaged her purse. Today, she planned to be smart about it: she'd get zoom in London after leaving The Ruin.

Another constable dropped Penny's larger handbag on the desk next to hers. The closest thing she had to a sister pressed up against her from behind, clinging and eyeing the constable who had searched her. He walked past them, winking at Penny while muttering something in Hindi. Penny's face brushed the back of Anna's neck when she turned away. Anna twisted around to meet her eyes, opening herself to the din of the woman's thoughts. The man had groped her while telling her all about what he wanted to do to her, if only they'd been alone.

Anna scowled at his sanctimonious grin. She knew the type—all talk. Holding Penny's hands against her gut, she offered a reassuring pat and projected hatred at the sorry excuse for a public servant. His police armor brimmed with electronic devices: sensors, communication and targeting systems, bio monitor—a full military suite. Energy paths appeared superimposed on it, lines traced in glowing amber visible only to Anna. She tugged at the electricity, drawing it out in an uncontrolled release. A flower of lightning bloomed around him, crackling for less than a full second with a *crack* like a rifle shot. He screamed and hit the ground, twitching. Three small fires started on his suit.

Two other officers rushed to his side, shouting in a panic as he convulsed. The remaining four pulled guns and spun around, searching for a sniper. After a moment, the lech sat up, shaking. Anna backed into the wall with her hands up, acting surprised and frightened. She wanted to turn and give Penny a proper comforting, but not in front of Old Bill.

The police made them wait while a MedVan flew in to extract the wounded man. Once the scene calmed and a search discovered no contraband in either bag, a constable waved them past the checkpoint.

Two blocks into London, they paused on the corner.

Anna took the opportunity to hug Penny. "Are you okay? It's not right what they do to us."

She shook her head. "There's no need for pat-downs like that. How do you keep going back to that club? It's…"

"Dirty." Anna squeezed her. "What can we do? They're the Met. They could kill us and no one would care. We're not even people to them."

Penny's large brown eyes filled with tears and futility, unable to argue the point. No one who lived in the dustbin, as the Propers called it, got any respect. "Have you thought about the Moon?"

Anna blinked. "The Moon? Are you daft? We couldn't afford the shuttle ticket, and I'm not about to lick that much todger. I don't even want to go back to BC."

"You shouldn't, after what that bastard did to you… locked up all night." Penny scowled. "Maybe we *should* go to the Moon."

"I hear they don't trust dolls up there, so there's jobs for people wit' no schooling."

"They don't trust dolls here, either. The king's a bit touched, thinks one'll kill him."

Penny looked to the sky. "We'll find work. I saw an advert yesterday 'bout this place lookin' for executive assistants. We could do that… assist executives, right?"

"It's a bit more than makin' coffee and bein' a pretty face on a

VidPhone; ya gotta know *biz-ness.*" Anna leaned on the last word, making air quotes. "We'll wind up serving food or mopping floors."

"This is backward." Penny giggled away tears. "I'm usually the one trying to put you back together."

"You needed a break." Anna held her hand for a moment. "Terrible shame about that bastard's hardware malfunctioning like that... outta nowhere. Probably hurt quite a bit."

Penny blinked. When Anna flashed a sly grin, she covered her mouth and laughed.

A few minutes of walking later, Penny approached the door of a small ground-level flat while Anna waited on the sidewalk.

"Well we could wait tables then or something... cleaner." Penny offered a consoling look, fixed herself up, and pushed the buzzer. "Get away from this place."

"*This* place is fine. It's *that* place what's the problem." Anna nodded toward the ominous grey smear in the air behind them.

A brick-red door slid to the side with a hiss. Penny chatted with an Indian woman a few years older than them for a while in a rambling language Anna couldn't follow. When their conversation ended, a small boy of about three emerged from the house, bundled in a beige coat. He waved at Anna and leapt into Penny's arms, happy to see her. The woman also left the house, using a NetMini to summon an autocab.

As the trio continued down the street, Penny doted over the boy, who occasionally pointed up at the army of advert bots whizzing overhead. He'd plead for whatever treat or toy caught his eye, but Penny kept distracting him well enough to keep tantrums at bay. With a child in tow, the Propers stopped looking at the two women the way Anna had become accustomed to. They became two people among many thousands, largely ignored until they arrived in the lobby of the public assistance office and got on line.

Sighing, Penny bounced the kid on her hip to keep him from fussing. "I can't see why they don't automate this."

Anna kicked at the floor. "I don't have a 'mini, plus they gotta check us to make sure we're not wasting the dole on drugs or booze."

Penny's smirk made Anna burst out laughing, drawing a few stares.

"Oh don't give me such a sanctimonious look. I'm not the one pawning someone else's kid off as mine to fatten my giro. To think that woman pays you to babysit on top of it."

"One of these days, you're not going to get so 'lucky' and have a sensor blow out." Penny bit her lower lip. "What'll you do when they pick up the shit in your blood? How long does your psych cert last anyway? You ought to stop dodging the doctors."

Anna scuffed her boot side to side over the pale green and yellow tiles. "I dunno. Watching my father die when I was twelve affected me deeply. I don't think I'll be right in the head ever. Lucky for me, the sensors keep failing." The complete lack of emotion in her voice gave away her lie, but then a thought brought forth genuine sorrow. "I'd give almost anything to..." Her throat closed off with grief. If she could do her life over—without the damnable psionic mess—she'd give anything.

"What's that?"

She looked up, trying not to blush or cry. "Nothing... Yeah, you're right. I'm getting lucky. I should stop taking zoom. Not good for me."

"Anna...," said Penny in the tone of a scolding mother.

She stared into her friend's eyes. *There's something wrong with me. The zappy thing happens on its own. I can't control it. Whenever I get riled up, it just goes off willy-nilly.*

Penny jumped, gasping and blinking at her.

Soz. I don't wanna say this out loud. Yes, I'm a telepath. Anna hung her head as if confessing to a heinous crime. *I started taking zoom to hide my power... I just—it's such evil shit. I lost control. It's got me, and I can't fecking stop. I want to, but I can't.* Anna's face reddened with shame.

Penny prodded her in the arm with the child's shoe, squinting. "What about li'l Twee then. She's fond of you. You're the tough street bitch she thinks she is."

They both laughed.

"She sees you using, she'll pick it right up too." Penny shook her head. "You don't want that, do you?"

Anna stared guiltily at the floor. As they neared the window with the clerk, Penny stopped talking. When it came her turn, she scanned her NetMini and smiled, speaking only Hindi at the flustered young man behind the counter. The little boy in her arms grinned at him, as she had asked him to, and the two of them vanished into a doorway to the checking room.

A moment later, the next clerk waved Anna over. "Name?"

"Annabelle Emily Morgan."

"Swipe."

She flashed a cheesy smile. "Sorry, guv'na. Don't got a 'mini."

"Gander into that then."

He pointed at a small box mounted to the frame of the window. Dark brown rust peeked out from under flaking lime-colored paint above and below the mechanism to which she pressed her forehead. She hated the way the machine smelled, hated the way the breath of the previous fifty people pooled within the hollow confines of the shroud enclosing her face. Flickering bands of blue and green light went up, down, and crossways over her eyes. Once it beeped, she leaned away, blind for several seconds from the glare.

"Righto," said the man behind the window. "There you are. Bloody shame about your father, that."

"Thank you." She offered a pleasant smile.

"Been eight months since your last visit with the doc. You're due up for another psych eval."

"There's been a bother with the authorization; I'm waiting for NHS approval."

A lie, but a believable one. Half the room behind her moaned in a shared complaint about the agency's pace.

"Hope they get that sorted for you. No physical issues an' you're young yet. Gonna need a shrink to sign off on your assistance, or you'll have to get a real job."

"I understand."

The limp sense of indignation at yet another person belittling her barely registered. Better they thought of her as a freeloader or a harlot than they learned the truth. She shied away from the holographic posters on the walls asking 'concerned citizens' to alert authorities to potential psionic terrorists. Anna really hated the 'it could be your own daughter' one.

"Right then, through the door on your left." The man closed a shade over his window.

When the door beside the counter slid open, she followed the clerk into a cramped exam room. A sleepy nurse waited by a cushioned table. Anna shrugged out of her coat, dropped it on a chair by the wall, and climbed onto the examination bed. She lied her way past questions about drug use, enduring another light in her eyes and other discomforts of an abbreviated physical. Once again, Penny's skilled hand at makeup covered the red squares on her arm. Any medtech who bothered to put in more than minimum effort could've spotted the derm tracks with ease. In this place, they wanted to process people fast. During a few prior visits, the techs gave her sympathetic looks, silent offers of help. No one wanted to deal with the proverbial paperwork of filing a report about her using. Eventually, the wide-bodied nurse came at her with a portable medical scanner, touching it to the skin of her bicep.

Anna concentrated on it, trying to simply make it conk out, but fear of them scanning zoom in her blood kicked her power in the arse. The device blew up in a flickering electrical discharge that burned the nurse's hand as well as the spot where it touched Anna's arm. The nurse screamed and tossed the device, which burst into flame before it reached the floor. Silicon smoke hazed the air between the three of them. Anna bit her lip, begging fate that the public assistance man would tell the nurse not to bother with the chem test.

He took a step closer. "Crikey. Are you all right?"

"Yes," said Anna and the Nurse at the same time.

Anna smiled, rubbing her arm where a small red dot remained from the burn. *Please... Skip it.*

"S'pose you'll need to fetch another unit then?" He nudged the nurse toward a rear door with his eyes.

Terror.

All the LED lamps in the ceiling exploded like flashbangs at once; snapping blue sparks lit the subsequent darkness for seconds afterward.

The assistance man yelled, pulling Anna to the floor as if to shield her. "What the bloody hell was that?"

"All the others are in use in the other rooms. We've been losin' one a month lately. Damn cheap Paki machines." The nurse grumbled and smacked the dead scanner.

Backup lights turned the room red. The man gave Anna the once-over and shook his head.

"Bugger it then. You don't look strung out. Don't let me find out you're on somethin', luv."

Anna managed an innocent smile. "Wouldn't dream of it, guv'na."

A LIFETIME AGO

Advert bots massed around the public assistance office like flies searching for the perfect spot of turd to settle on.

Whenever someone walked out the door, they suffered a bombardment of ads for a block and a half, until the floating orbs gave up and returned to the throng. Anna and Penny ignored the barrage of holo-panels, walking astride for a few blocks to the small sidewalk café they always visited on the day they collected the dole.

They seated themselves and ordered the least expensive breakfast they could on the holographic menu projected from a terminal at the center of the table—fried eggs and chips. Anna leaned back in the chair and turned the credstick over in her fingers, staring at the glowing digits on its end with a frown.

"Eight twenty-five. What do they expect anyone to do with that?"

Penny spoke between the noises she made at the boy whilst trying to feed him some of her eggs. "They'd give you double if you popped one out. Still, for one person it's not a bad two week stipend."

After some quick mental arithmetic, Anna scowled. "Are you serious? The cheapest food I can get is about twelve credits a plate. Three times a day for two weeks, almost all of it… Five hundred or so—"

"Five-oh-four to be precise." Penny swabbed synthetic mayo on a thick chip and tossed it in her mouth.

Anna did as well. It almost didn't taste like both had been reassembled at a molecular level from the same bland paste. A half hour ago, both the mayo and the chips had likely been goop in the same canister of OmniSoy.

"Still." Anna stuffed the credstick into her pocket. "That leaves me C321 for rent, clothes, travel, and whatever else. The cheapest one-room apartment within a two-hour ride of London is damn near C2800 a month, and it's basically a bed next to a toilet."

"We don't pay rent, you don't travel, and you've worn the same outfit every day for six months. I'm astounded that skirt isn't walking on its own."

Guess I at least owe Plonk for getting my clothes back from Blake.

Anna scowled at the distant city. "They treat us like such trash, but they don't give us a chance. We don't pay rent 'cause we *can't*. Where else would we go?"

"There's always the Moon." Penny grinned.

"Bugger that." Anna leaned to the side, nibbling at her food.

"Buggerat!" yelled the little boy. "Pixie funny."

Anna rubbed her arms. Withdrawal started in the form of full-body aches, as though her skeleton had bruised everywhere.

"You could always get a proper job. You're always so miserable whenever you come back from the club. Why do you do it if you hate it? Carryin' food to tables can't be as demeaning as wagging your chesticles at a room full of drunken men."

"They're not *that* small." Anna whined, pulling her grey parachute jacket closed over her breasts. She calmed after a few seconds, and shrugged. "Blake don't care if I'm high, don't ask questions, and I don't have to think about it."

Penny held a piece of toast up for the boy to gnaw on. "Those tits won't last forever, hon. And didn't you say you don't want to go back?"

The child waved his arms, yelling "tits" at the top of his lungs, drawing horrified looks from pedestrians.

Anna pouted, folding her arms tighter over her chest. She hated the cage, hated Blake, hated everything about Bristol City... but she also didn't have much choice. If she tried to get a job somewhere legit, *they* would find her. The same people she'd turned to zoom to hide from. Not that any real job would hire someone who used that shit.

"What's really on you then?" Penny leaned forward. "Please, tell me."

"Look, even if I was able to hold it together without the chems... I'm hopelessly onto it. I'd need a doctor to get me off it now and..." She teased a plastic fork at her eggs. "I don't have the strength. I want off it, but… I'm too weak."

"You're not weak. I'll help you through it. What are you afraid of?" Penny squeezed her hand.

Anna looked up with a hurt pout. "It's more than the chems. I stopped workin' for Carroll after a close call. I don't want you to get involved, a nasty bit of business."

"Organized?" Penny's eyebrows climbed her forehead.

"Tits," shouted the boy again, clapping.

"You're a bit old for that, mite." Penny placated him with jellied toast, and ordered a glass of milk.

"No, I'm not talking about the Syndicate." Anna leaned close, whispering. "Government nasty." Her blood ran cold.

Penny's expression shifted from fear to concern. Minutes of silence passed as they finished eating.

"I'm…" Anna glanced to the left. *There's no way in green Hades I'm going to cage dance sober.* She shivered at the mere thought of being locked in that damn cage again. The mere sight of it would probably make her panic. *If I'ma gonna kick this shit, I need to find my old groove. I need practice.* She stared into space until the pedestrians smeared into an ever-shifting mass of color. "Gonna take a walk, get somethin' nice for Twee. Take the li'l bugger home. Don't want you gettin' caught up in it case the blag goes pear shaped."

"Blag?" Penny whisper-shouted and stood, gathering the boy. "Anna, please don't do anything stupid."

"I won't." Anna hugged her. "If I'm not back by midnight, don't call the cops."

Penny's eyes watered. Something cartoony on a passing advert bot drew the child's eye and he wriggled, pointing at it and yelling "*Cāhanā, cāhanā, cāhanā.*"

"Oh come off it, I'll be fine. The zoom's gone… I got me head back on." Anna shied away from her reflection in the café window. She looked way too thin.

Penny waved her NetMini. "Vid me if you need anything."

"Heh." Anna turned out her empty pockets. "If I can find a public. You know mine keep breaking."

ANNA FIGURED SHE HAD ABOUT FOUR HOURS BEFORE THE LACK OF ZOOM started to hurt.

She'd reached the less than pleasant stage-two of the post high. Now, the drug ceased affecting her concentration and she needed to work to rein in the critter in her head. She'd had enough practice at bone-ache stage one to tolerate it. Another hour or so, and the flu-like mess would start.

Hands tucked in her pockets, she went in the direction of High Street, not paying much attention to the route. At the sight of a familiar warp in the footpath, she glanced up and came face to face with her old home. The edifice of plastisteel and false wood slats floated there as though she had walked into a waking dream.

Number Six Woodseer Street looked no different than it had when she last saw it, a modern construction with six mushed-together flats crammed into a giant house. She recalled her father once bragging to his friends about getting into a place built after 2350, a task somewhat difficult to do that close to the heart of London. She had lost track of the current date. Anna hadn't cared about keeping track of a calendar since she had a bed full of dolls and a warm place to go home to at night. That had been 2403, roughly eleven years ago.

For a moment, she almost missed the beatings.

Dates and times didn't matter to a twelve-year-old who no longer went to class. If not for Penny's assistance, she wouldn't have bothered finishing primary school. Pen had pretended to be her foster parents' older daughter whenever the teachers wanted to talk to a parent.

Anna leaned upon the well-kept railing surrounding the laughably small front yard and stared at the dark square of plexi that used to be her bedroom window. Despite having no legal claim to the place, she struggled to push aside the feeling it was still somehow her home. Her gaze drifted down to a wisp of pink metal among the ill-tended lawn, an old bicycle, white tire squeaking around in a pathetic breeze. There had been a few good years, until the thing got out of control.

"Checkin' the place out, lass?"

Anna yelped, holding onto the rail to keep from falling. An elder had snuck up on her, quite unintentionally. He clasped a hand over his chest, startled by her jumping. His wispy silver hair wavered in the breeze, threads of cotton held to his scalp by the weight of a tweed cap.

"Sorry, dear." He offered a grandfatherly smile, fidgeting at his a powder blue sweater. "Not many come to check the vacant one out."

She tilted her head, a hand on her chest. "Vacant?"

The man shook his head, casting a disdainful scowl at the lawn. "Man what used ta live there wasn't right in the head. Used ta beat his little'un somethin' fierce. Poor thing, nae wonder 'is wife left 'im. Old Bill'd come here two or three times a week, but they did sweet Fanny Adams about it. Someone should'a done somethin' for that girl."

Anna looked up at the black window. She remembered being on the other side of it, shaking from the pain that had been strapped across her backside, staring down at the neighbors, people who had heard the screaming, wondering why no one helped her.

"Aye Mr. Harrison... Someone did."

He blinked at her, squinted, and then took a step back. "Gor Blimey, is it you? O' course, it has ta be. How many ladies yer age got 'air that shade o' white."

She leaned on her elbows, nodding with a regretful smile. "Aye, 'tis me. I hadn't realized where I'd wandered to 'til I saw the place."

He ambled closer, patting her on the back. "You doin' okay lass? We all been wonderin' what happened since..." He fidgeted. "Well, you know."

Lying came too easy. "Social welfare put me with some fosters. I got a job on the West End now, acquisitions."

"Oh that's jolly for you. Good ta see ya bounce back from that dreadful mess. Edith hasn't touched the 'sem since. Thinks it'll blast 'er right outta 'er knickers." The old man winked.

Anna chuckled. Everyone thought the food machine malfunctioned.

She chatted for a bit with her former neighbor, spinning a milquetoast web of lies about her flat uptown, a fiancée, and a pleasant but boring office job. He didn't ask much about her father's death, commenting only enough to attribute it to a karmic act of the divine since the police had done such a cack-handed job of protecting her from his beatings. Once word got out that a man died in the place, it had been difficult to rent it out. The obstinate property manager held out for full value, figuring location would outweigh superstition soon enough. Some part of her wanted to buy it, but she had about as much chance of affording it as sprouting wings. According to the elder, someone came by once every few weeks to look at the place, but none ever stayed long and no one had ever bought the place.

Mr. Harrison looked left and right as if afraid of being overheard. "Last bloke what came ta check the place said he heard footsteps an' felt a hand grab his shoulder. Ya' believe that rubbish?"

Anna couldn't help but sense something *off* about the place, but ghosts? Bah. Those sorts of feelings came more from zoom and or the guilt she tried to convince herself she didn't have.

"Not really, Mr. H. Bunch of wank."

"Aye." He chuckled.

The thought of squatting occurred to her, followed by an involuntary tightening of her throat. She missed her old life. How had she gone from an innocent, normal kid to a worthless dancing harlot? Her head sagged forward under the weight of lies and shame.

Dad would've killed me. I had to do it. It was me or him.

Anna curled over the rail, trying to maintain the smiling contentment of her imagined life for her elderly neighbor. She worked so hard not to cry that the thing at the back of her mind slipped free of her grasp. The melancholy howl of a distant wind drowned amid a cacophony of blaring horns, wailing sirens, and flashing lights. Every anti-theft mechanism in every car a hundred yards in either direction along Woodseer Street went off all at once.

Poor Mr. Harrison nearly died of shock.

BLURRED CLARITY

Morris & Baker was the sort of shop where the working man could secure a bit of pretty for the one he loved, the kind of place that sold baubles considered nice but unremarkable in a way that lent them handily to pawning. Something too big and rare would be traced. Too cheap, and not worth the risk.

Anna considered it perfect.

She leaned against a vendomat a half block away, sipping artificial tea from a bioplastic cup that would be little more than a puddle of glop half an hour after it cooled. Her heartbeat had about returned to normal from the explosion of car alarms. The blast of nerves threatened to undermine her resolve, but she swallowed her worry and decided to proceed. She gazed through the name of the shop, spelled out in glittering gold hologram over the window, watching patrons with the intensity of a cat waiting for a tasty mouse.

The zoom no longer clouded her mind. She focused on her purpose, pushing worry of withdrawal out to arm's length. If she let her emotion run off, it would ruin any chance she had. She needed the little monster half out of its pen to do this at all. Eyes closed, she inhaled the steam from the Earl Grey—or at least the best attempt possible at Earl Grey via molecular assemblage. Her father had mentioned once in passing that her mother had been fond of it, but he loathed the stuff. As a child, whenever she asked for some, it made him angry.

As an adult, whenever she drank some, she spited him.

A sudden distraction of violet light drew her attention to the left where a loaf-shaped advert bot the size of a cat hovered at about eye level, projecting holograms of lingerie ads.

It knew.

Her cheeks flushed crimson. She tugged at her tiny skirt, trying to make it longer. "Damn nosy thing. Sod off."

Anna turned away, a rush of embarrassment made its holographic panels fill with static. Small orange sparks flew from the bot as it careened off along the street in a whirling spiral, all the while emitting a high-pitched digital version of an agonized scream. The chaos halted with a metallic *thud* a few seconds after it dipped out of sight around a corner four blocks distant.

She looked down, tapping the toe of her boot against the footpath, dawdling until a short blonde woman caught her eye. An air of credits wafted from her like perfume. The woman didn't seem so wealthy she would find this place undesirable, but appeared well off enough she would ask the store clerk to see something worth nicking.

Anna tossed her empty cup into a bin and followed the woman in the door. While her mark went for the counter, she meandered about the shelves for a moment before stopping at a column-mounted terminal. Various pieces, custom ordered of course, appeared at ten times scale in full holographic glory. Anna pawed at the light, flipping virtual pages and pretending to be interested in ordering something.

The blonde went straight to the attendant and struck up a conversation. Anna's anticipatory thrill came to a cold halt when she remembered her little 'invisibility' trick only worked on people, not electronics. She took advantage of her short skirt and exposed midriff while sashaying around to keep the other clerk's eyes on her body rather than notice her scoping for cameras. His attention locked on her chest, face reddening. She couldn't tell if her prominent nipples in the thin fabric excited him, or the Manchester United logo between them incensed him.

Either way, she smiled. Distraction complete.

She noted four security domes in the ceiling. One by one, she focused on them.

Delicate threads drawn in amber light illuminated deep inside the recorder spheres, wherever electricity traced a wirepath. She *felt* every shifting mass of electrons racing along their conduits and the strong surge of the tie to mains power. Anna stretched over the counter, forcing her breasts tight to the shirt, and tugged with her thoughts at the first camera.

Electricity heeded her call, flooding into the device, which sputtered a brief wisp of black smoke, staining the white paint around it. The subdued *pop* went unheard beneath the din of the eager blonde assaulting the shop worker with an endless prattle of questions about which bauble he thought worked best with what outfit. The poor man smiled and pretended to be interested, hoping for a sale.

The rumble of a truck passing by outside afforded her the chance to zap the second recorder. She waited to see if anyone noticed. Perhaps a man in the back room watching terminals would come running to see why his screens turned to static. Then again, a store this small might not have a man in back. The clerk near her leaned closer, staring with greedy eyes at the taut fabric. His surface thoughts focused on her breasts, not Frictionless.

"Can I be of any assistance, Miss?"

She acted as though she wanted a gift for a young niece, something cheap that wouldn't create too big an issue if she wound up having to buy it. He retrieved a set of five-petaled pink kunzite daisy earrings. Sixty credits for the pair.

She pretended to drop one out of clumsiness while holding it up to let the light play with it.

"Oh, heavens," she said, pouring on the ditz. "I'm sorry."

Turning away from the counter, she eyed the blonde across the room and bent down to pick the dropped earring up. At the *thud* of a knee meeting the counter behind her, she assumed the clerk had leaned up, probably hoping she bent a little farther. At that angle, only about one inch of skirt remained in the way of his discovering she didn't own underwear.

With the clerk behind her eminently distracted, she coerced more electricity into the two remaining cameras. The blonde gasped with alarm as black smoke poured from the one on the left.

Bollocks!

Anna stood with the earring in hand and flashed an apologetic smile at the dumbfounded clerk. The right corner of his mouth twitched twice before it curled into a smile. She set the pink daisy on the glass with a *click*, and glared sideways at the debutante about to ruin her entire plan.

When the smoke proved to be a brief wisp and not the start of a fire, the woman lost interest and returned to her chat. Anna exhaled in relief and set the earrings into their pink satin case.

"These will do nicely."

By now, a number of pieces sat out on the counter in front of the blonde, mostly necklaces and pendants. Anna walked sideways to the register, appraising them. The attendant seemed on edge having four items of inventory out in the open, and watched the woman intently, no doubt suspecting her of something.

Anna handed over the credstick, paying for the cheap earrings. When the man returned it along with a bag, she thanked him and walked toward the exit. As soon as he looked away from her, she took a breath and held it, trying to remember how to open her telepathy to the world. It had been a while since she'd allowed her head to clear from zoom this much, and after a few seconds of *wanting* to use her abilities, it mostly came back to her. Forcing people not to see her offered a far better option than having to kill, so she had used 'telepathic invisibility' constantly while in the employ of Mr. Carroll. The presence of three sentient minds hovered around her. Anna reached into their thoughts, masking the conscious realization she existed from their perception. To the people in the room, she vanished.

For added reinforcement, she pushed at the door to make it beep as though she had left. Their expecting her to be gone from the room cemented her telepathic invisibility. She crept to the far counter, but neither attendant reacted to her. With the clerk focused entirely on the blonde woman, Anna palmed a necklace of dangly gold bars with small rubies affixed to the ends into her shopping bag and backed away.

The clerk continued showing off a different piece, unaware one had walked away.

Anna backed to the door, continuing to project her nonexistence into their minds. The entire area pulsed with electrical power: the door beeper, the holographic sign, and the anti-theft field emitters that would certainly sense the purloined necklace in her bag. The room glowed around her from hundreds of glimmering amber threads wherever a wire carried electricity in the wall or the circuitry paths in the machines. A three dimensional construction drew itself into her reality. She merged her thoughts with the essence of it, pushing the electricity out of the security system and the door. For all intents and purposes, everything powered off.

She slipped out without a beep, chime, or siren. Neither clerk nor the woman noticed her leave. A block away, she glanced over her shoulder, smiled at the lack of alarm, and became part of the crowd.

Just as easy as it used to be.

ANNA HADN'T BEEN TO MASON'S, AN OLD HAUNT OF HERS, SINCE SHE WAS sixteen and fell in with Mr. Carroll. Dingy and decrepit as ever, it sat in a part of the East End where no Proper would want to be after dark.

A certain rustic charm dwelled in actual bronze bells rigged to the door and how she had to kick small objects out of her way to make it down the aisles. Air at the rear of the shop hung thick with the combined smell of beer, cigars, and Middle Eastern incense. She stopped at a counter with a bullet-resistant barrier made of polycarbonate resin and metal mesh. Several gouges and twisted strands of wire gave away where vibro blades and bullets tried and failed to rob the place.

Behind the protective barricade, a large man in every sense of the word leaned back in a chair that creaked beneath his mass. Easily seven feet tall, he still looked quite muscular beneath the paunch of a sincere love of ale. Unkempt black hair jutted at random below a fading blue bandana, and pins and knick-knacks from various motorbike events studded his imitation denim vest.

Anna sauntered up to the counter. "Oi, Mason, long time."

He leaned forward, letting the wooden chair legs strike the floor as his weight shifted. It took a moment for his eyeballs to appear out from under furrowing brows, and another for them to widen with recognition.

"Anna? 'Zat you?"

"Aye." She upended the bag, spilling both necklace and earring box onto the counter.

Mason reached through the tiny opening for the small white cube, but Anna snatched it before he could grab it. "Not that one, need to flog the gold. This is a chintzy bauble you wouldn't want." She opened it enough to show him the kunzite, and pocketed it after he nodded.

He drew the necklace from the tray and dangled it in front of his face, rubbing his coarse beard in thought. The old, familiar fear came back. Nothing could really stop him from keeping it and telling her to get lost. No matter how much she'd brought him, as soon as the loot wound up on the other side of bullet-resistant barriers, she dreaded he'd stiff her every time. Mason never questioned how she had come to possess anything she ever sold him. He knew why street youth visited him. He lowered the jewelry to the counter, letting his weight rest over the chain.

"You know, lass. You're gettin' a wee bit old for this now. If you get pinched, Old Bill won't let you off with a rap on the wrist and a free supper." He grinned, flecks of green leaf clung to his teeth. "Kind of miss the glory days. I've you to thank for much of my current state of comfort. Shame you got in with that uptown lot. You were the best little filch. I still don't know how you got away with half the crap you did."

She stared off, wondering how she'd blown through so much money so fast. Even accepting Mason's ripoff prices, she'd made enough to keep her and Penny well fed for a while.

"Look at you, gone out then? Oi." Mason snapped his fingers in front of her face.

She scratched at her arm. "I know. It's a one-off. I'm not lookin' ta go back to that life if I can 'elp it. Too risky. 'Specially now I'm of age."

"Buck up, lass. You'll get no trouble 'ere." He winked. "Figger I kin do bout eighteen hundred for it, if'n you'll 'ave it."

"That's fine then." Anna scowled in her mind. The store charged ten thousand. He'd probably sell it for eight. Still, what he offered felt like a fortune now.

Mason slid the credstick past the bullet-resistant barrier, eighteen hundred credits richer than it had been a moment before. When she grasped it, he gripped her fingers in the sunken channel, a silent offer of help. Anna thanked him, not moving until he let go.

"Thanks," whispered Anna. Despite his slovenly appearance, she trusted him. One of the few men who'd never looked at her *that* way. "I appreciate it."

Once outside, she glanced behind her at the sense of a small sphere of electrical power. A volleyball-sized orb hovered, peeking past the corner of the building at the end of the street. Anna thought it strange an advert bot tried to hide rather than bombard her with things to buy.

She thought it even more peculiar when it followed her at a distance, but paid it little mind.

Probably a perv hacker checking out her ass.

UNREGISTERED

S ubsequent a credits-only transaction at Plonk's, Anna stopped at the market.

She had popped for a case of Panda's instant OmniSoy meals, the more expensive brand, and a small white teddy bear. Carrying one parcel under each arm, she approached the police line around The Ruin.

Because she had zoom in her purse, she had half a mind to Invisibility her way past the cops to avoid the hassle. The irony that she pondered using her power to protect the very thing she used to make the power go away struck her. Of course, constables tended not be as dim-witted as the jewelers; they *would* notice their cameras burning out. One tiny lapse of concentration and she'd seem to appear out of thin air among them. That would invite unwanted attention. She debated internally about whether she should tolerate the derision she deserved, or risk the attempt to avoid it altogether. Before she could come to an accord, a voice ahead of her shouted.

"That's her."

Her heart stopped. She looked up at a half-dozen police, two female, with rifles aimed. The little white teddy bear trembled with her.

"'Old it right there, then." The man in the center took a step forward.

She blinked. "What's this about?" *What the hell are you doing? Don't give them attitude.*

"Special request, lass. Drop the stuff and up against the wall with ya."

Anna stared at the road, dreading what she knew would follow. Perhaps all six of them would take turns this time. The nice sergeant was nowhere in sight. After stepping to the nearest wall, she set the crate of meals down and placed the bear on top of it to keep it off the muddy ground. The hunger that had been forming in her gut twisted into a knot of queasiness as she assumed the position against the grey bricks.

They shuffled up to her, keeping a wary distance, which she thought rather odd. One of the two female officers approached, slinging her rifle and performing a cursory squeeze-down to check for weapons before peeking into her tiny purse.

The officer's visor flickered, bathing her face in green light. "Not seeing any weapons."

"Check again. These Cov vermin kin 'ave plastic knives on 'em," said a man.

Anna remained passive while the constable secured her hands behind her back. The cold metal about her wrists made her think of Tommy. Fear kept her thoughts from drifting into the realm of sex as the constable searched her pockets and reached under her shirt. Upon noticing she had no bra on, the woman jerked her hand back. Strictly professional. Anna endured it without protest, even giving the woman a grateful glance. The constables' nervousness bothered her.

Something's not right.

The woman spun her around and led her along by a hand on the elbow, taking her to the same room where Constable Brown had strung her up like a side of beef. Another slice of dignity sloughed off at the thought of it. She followed the constable's pointing finger and took a seat in a chair by the steel table. The officer left her to stare at her knees while one of the men set her purchases and purse on a table to the left by the wall. The female officer traded her weight from leg to leg, inching backward with each shift. With the other constables leaving, the woman broke into a run out the door, leaving Anna alone.

The feck are they scared of?

Paths of electricity in the lights above thrummed in her mind, as did wires running inches below the floor plate and near her wrists in the powered restraints. She closed her eyes and let her unnatural senses probe the binders. Amid the black, her mental vision flew down, skimming above a landscape of glowing amber contacts, circuits, and pathways that looked like a network of suburban streets with all the houses removed. Anna grinned to herself upon locating the contacts to the hasp motor. A small jolt of power there would open them.

For now, she tried to keep her emotions neutral. If she blew out the restraints, she would be stuck in them for hours while the police scrambled for a tool capable of cutting them, an experience she didn't want to relive. She played with opening them, but put them back on, afraid of the beating it would earn her when the police returned. Her body stiffened when she eyed the cameras in the corners of the room. Hopefully, no one had seen the cuffs open and close. Trembles took over; withdrawal or fear she couldn't tell. Popping the cuffs required precise manipulation of tiny voltages, not something she'd be able to do in a panic. If she wanted to run, she'd have to commit to it before the situation escalated. Of course, committing to fleeing would escalate the situation.

Murmuring voices hovered outside the door, too weak to make out. Anna wondered what the devil they wanted. She expected to be bent over a desk by now, not left alone in a room. In some odd way, the oddity of being treated civilly felt worse than being used. She wondered if she missed a security recorder at Morris & Baker, or if Mason had tried to 'help' her by getting her off the street.

No, this doesn't feel right. If it was about the necklace, they'd be working me over already.

Quiet as she could, she eased her weight onto her feet and crept up to the door to peer out a tiny square window low enough for her to reach on tiptoe. All six constables clustered in a group outside, chatting away as if they had some kind of monster locked in the office. The thick armored concealed their words, but their body language gave off palpable fear.

Minutes later, a gloss black hovercar with opaque windows settled onto the pavement about ten meters from the police, spraying them with rainwater. Both gull wing doors opened, disgorging two men.

On the near side, a wiry man in his early thirties extracted a pair of dark glasses from his breast pocket, which he flicked open with a smooth whip-like gesture before sliding them on. Of average height with thin brown hair, his form vanished amid the fluttering folds of a long black coat. Military boots and gloves left only the ashen skin of his face visible, wrinkled with lines beyond his years.

The other man was taller, a pillar of military training. His shaved head caught the baleful light filtering down from the grey sky, a neatly trimmed dark mustache and goatee encircled his mouth. He wore the same coat, open unlike the smaller man, revealing a black armored vest bedecked with various small items. As he reached his full stature, the thin man turned to glance at him over the car.

Anna's heart fluttered at the sight of a tiny scrap of metal.

A silver triangle the size of a pinky nail behind his left ear glinted in the sun. The mark of registration—an implanted detonator designed to kill a psionic with the push of a button. Some bureaucrat in a plush office could determine risk exceeded benefit, or perhaps decide not to like you, and make a vid call. A minute later, a disinterested low-level military person barely out of high school would flick a holographic switch and kill someone they would never meet and knew only as a thirteen-digit code.

Two lamps sputtered in the ceiling, shaken by a wave of fear. Somehow, she kept it in check. Exploded lights would be impossible to explain. Someone must have reported her as an unregistered psionic—but who? She struggled at the handcuffs, too out of sorts to feel the circuit path. Their transition from nuisance to captivity added to her panic and made concentration even harder.

"Fuck!" she gasped, trying to calm down, but couldn't.

Anna sprinted across the room and leapt butt-first onto the shelf, straining to reach into her purse. Her probing fingers found the hidden zipper and slipped past it to the sheet of zoom. She peeled one away and scurried to the chair two seconds before the door cracked open. Anna stuffed her icy fingers down the back of her skirt, pressing the derm onto her left ass cheek to milk the chem out of it faster. She had to hide from the telepath. She had to send her mind over the edge.

The thin man entered with a pleasant smile, followed by two police officers. The large, bald soldier remained outside, observing from a distance. None of the constables came anywhere near the doorway. She pushed at the derm to squeeze the chem out of the pad faster.

The thin man spoke in a much deeper voice than she had expected from the look of him. "Good afternoon miss…"

"M-Morgan," she stammered, already feeling the effect of the drug. The subtle presence of something else joined her thoughts. When she looked up, the room melted as though she had stumbled into a surrealist image. Walls warped, the table liquefied, and the ceiling lamps descended on stretching cables. Only the thin man retained a normal appearance.

"We have received a report that you might be off the books." He walked to the left, entering a slow circling prowl.

Anna wobbled in the chair, unable to focus on anything after slamming the zoom. "I've not been to school since I was little."

The white teddy bear giggled and waved at her. "Can we go home now?"

"Not yet," muttered Anna.

"Not yet?" The thin man's voice slithered over her right ear.

Twenty seconds later, she jumped. Something shifted in her mind like a goldfish moving under her scalp. The thin man emitted a grumble of displeasure and walked a few steps to the right.

"Sorry, guv'na. I'm not sure what you're gettin' on about. I'm just a piece of shite from Coventry. Thought Old Bill wanted to take 'is rights with me."

Random objects in the room changed, morphing into sexually suggestive things. The metal of her seat became steel hands forcing her thighs apart. Again, the thin man remained normal. The teddy bear squeaked as it dry-humped the box of instant meals, aiming for the mascot panda. She giggled uncontrollably as the creature inflated away from the label and became a three-dimensional cartoon panda, which proceeded to have sex with the bear.

A disingenuous smile spread across the thin man's. "There is no need for subterfuge. We are already aware of what you can do."

The zoom surged into her consciousness. Dangling lights sang to her, the muffled voices of her breasts screamed in agony as the devil in the Manchester United shield stabbed at them with its pitchfork. The steel floor splashed like water under her kicking boots.

"Very well then. We have other means at our disposal." The thin man's face peeled forward, floating at her, still speaking as it expanded to four feet wide.

Like a wrung-out dishtowel, his stretched face wound tight, spiraling into a twisted tentacle of flesh that lanced toward her while the body stood rigid as a concrete post. She leaned back in the chair as the twisting whorl of skin speared into her forehead.

Anna shrieked at the sensation of a warm spike piercing her skull, sliding between the lobes of her brain. She thrashed about, kicking the liquid steel floor at him. Her attack did little to stall him; his body agitated like a fidgeting man on sped-up video. The flesh drill surged between the lobes of her brain, swishing around, one half, then the other.

The teddy bear cowered, shielding its eyes from what must have been a gory sight. The panda screamed, diving for cover back into its label, once more a two dimensional picture. Anna shouted at the stuffed animal for help. Geysers of hot blood rolled down her face from the hole drilled in her forehead, soaking into her shirt. Lost to terror, she strained at the binders and fell out of the chair into churning liquid metal that used to be a floor. Ebon forms crowded around her, foiling her attempt to slide away from the tentacle still burrowed into her skull. She kicked and thrashed like a wild creature. Her right foot hit something soft. A demonic wail followed the *thud* of a body striking the floor.

Shimmering vaporous wraiths swarmed over her, solid black except for fluorescent yellow bands circling their arms near the shoulders. Sputtering, she tried to sit up out of the drowning liquid steel. The wraiths howled spectral cries into her soul. Lost in the world her runaway mind created, she clawed, kicked, and thrashed as best she could to escape.

Another wraith glided over her, tearing her legs off below the knees. She screamed again, hyperventilating as the shadowy figure handed the severed limbs to another. When she looked back down, her skin regenerated into clean bare feet, which smoky hands pinned together. The black ghost conjured a tiny white serpent that coiled about her ankles and cinched tight, devouring its own tail. Off to the side, one of the wraiths moaned, dragging itself along the ground in a strange ungainly posture, as if it lost the ability to float.

She tried to fight, but her arms wouldn't respond. Trying to figure out why she couldn't move her arms, she looked down at bloody stumps. The sight shocked her mute. Two wraiths flipped her onto her chest. The bastard floor picked that moment to go from liquid back to solid. Her cheek struck it with a hard *slap,* and the remainder of her head shattered like a porcelain vase, the fragments scattering forward before her eyes.

Anna shrieked in blind terror, staring at shiny crystalline fragments of her brain.

The apparitions attached themselves to her shoulders, morphing into wings of tattered blackness that carried her aloft. Blurs of color drifted everywhere in a nauseating spiral. No matter how hard she struggled, she couldn't move her arms or legs. Her body became a winged worm flying down a square passage. Glowing brick-shaped creatures clinging to the ceiling cackled at her. After an eternity of floating helpless, she came to rest on a soft pad.

Her shadow wings tore loose from her shoulders, dispersing into clouds of black fog that slid away along the walls.

Covered in sweat, shaking from fear both real and imagined, Anna curled into a ball and closed her eyes. Time sank away as the surface upon which she lay alternated from cloud to spider web to cotton candy. The white substance became sticky, wrapping around her and clinging. Anna struggled to escape, but she still didn't have arms or legs. Her wormlike body twisted back and forth but she couldn't free herself from the clingy slime that tangled around her face and dragged her down into the dark.

Anna awoke to find her mouth full of cheap paper-coated pillow.

The overwhelming rush of zoom had passed, leaving her soaked in sweat and shivering with trembles she couldn't control. Snot and drool foamed out of her mouth and nose. When her arms ignored her attempt to move, she wiped her face on the mattress. Her muscles felt like dense bundles of rubber creaking beneath her skin. Belabored shallow breaths filled her chest with pain on every inhalation. Images in her eyes ghosted. Every object became a trail of two or three copies superimposed. The room shifted back and forth from too bright to dim.

She rolled on her side and moaned at the sight of a tiny holding cell. Metal restraints squeezed her wrists, plastic riot-ties dug into her ankles. Anna struggled for a little while before giving up and falling limp with a huff. She glanced at her feet and grumbled, wondering what had become of her boots. Replacing underwear was outside of her budget. She couldn't possibly afford new boots unless she gave up eating for three weeks. The idea of being stuck barefoot in The Ruin made doing time feel like a welcome fate. She tried to concentrate on the metal binders, but the zoom blocked out her power. For a few minutes, she alternated between lying still and impotent wriggling. Eventually, she fell sideways into the pillow and gave up.

Out of breath, Anna stared into the hallway. The bars of her cell blurred as the four empty cells on the opposite side of the hall came into focus. Despite her skimpy attire, the mega-dose left her roasting. She rolled flat on her chest and waited for the pain to hit.

Why the feck did the bastards leave me tied up like this?

Anna lay on her stomach for what felt like hours. When she could no longer tolerate feeling so helpless, she again squirmed in an ineffectual attempt to escape. The zoom sat upon her brain like a lead block, preventing her from sensing the wiring in the restraints.

She didn't want to wear puke twice in the same week, so she attempted to sit up. Her muscle response came delayed, causing her to overcompensate and tumble off the bed to the cold metal floor. She did manage to hold her head up to keep from cracking it. Groaning, Anna shuffled around, up onto her knees, then moved with an erratic series of hops and slides to the toilet. She thrust her face into it not a second before the fragrance of chemical toilet triggered a vomiting fit.

The hiss of a distant door and tromping boots leaked into her perception between agonized bursts of foul liquid expunging itself from her insides.

"Hey, Virji, think she's still away with the mixer?"

At a break in the heaves, she glanced past the bars at a pair of constables. The taller one on the left squinted with anger, face reddening. Tall, bald, and carrying an excess of weight, his chin sagged over his chest as though his head were made of melting wax. Not as paunchy as Constable Brown, his body stored fat in odd places that left him looking like an experiment in proportion gone awry.

The other looked younger and athletic; an Indian man in his middle-thirties with salt and pepper hair cut short. His stare almost held a trace of pity for her.

"Unfortunately, lass, you managed to hoof Constable Hargreaves in the knackers while you were beaked up."

Anna tried to apologize, but only barf came out. Her face dripped with it, and no matter how she squirmed, she couldn't get a hand up high enough to wipe her cheek. Beige slime streamed from her nose. She huffed at it, spitting, but couldn't dislodge the wavering tendril. In her foggy reality, she might have begged him to clean her off, or perhaps the voice only existed in her mind.

Constable Virji disappeared from the corridor and reappeared behind her, the product of a time burp. She hadn't noticed the cell open or him walk in. He held her chin and wiped her clean with a microfiber towel. Submissive as a two year old in a high chair, she endured it, thanking him when he finished.

Hargreaves had his nightstick out, a look on his face as if he wanted to pay her back for making him look like a fool in front of his mates.

"You know, Harg, she was stonkered. Highly unlikely she *intended* to catch you with her boot. Bet whatever that CSB chap did had a part to play as well."

"Bad business, all of it." The big man grumbled, sliding his truncheon back in place on his belt with a loud clack. "Bloody psios. Should kill the lot of them... or ship them off to the UCF. They seem to like 'em there."

Anna curled her legs behind her on the ground, picking with an idle finger at the plastic fusing her ankles together, trying to make her skirt longer by sheer force of will. A spark between her thumb and forefinger could melt the riot ties off, but she couldn't explain that away. Assuming, of course, she could even form the requisite concentration to make the lightning obey.

"I'm sorry." She bowed her head. A mild convulsion preceded her swallowing the urge to continue retching. "Got some bad zoom. If'n it has your pleasure, constables, I'll do whatever to make it up. I'm just a useless Cov."

With those words, she felt as though she had signed her own death warrant. As soon as the police knew they had a Cov on their hands, open season. Anna flashed into a waking nightmare of the small bit of NewsNet space her naked body would get tomorrow when some river scav or boat pilot found her on the side of the Thames. She hoped they would at least pose her with a little modesty.

"Bother it all." Hargreaves frowned, his jowls wobbling as he shook his head. "Not touchin' that povvy growler with a borrowed truncheon."

Virji laughed. "The face you made when she booted you, I'd expect you'd *have* to borrow a truncheon."

Hargreaves shook his fist at his partner, growling.

Constable Virji held her by the armpits and lifted her up to sit on the bed. "You still feelin' a bit of the violent, lass?"

"No, constable." She stared into her lap, whimpering in the same voice she had used the night her father died. "I got me head on now, swear. I don't remember anyfin' at all, whatever the man did to me…"

"CSB wanted to check you out, they got it in their 'eads you might be unregistered. Guess they're getting bored these days, can't tell a psionic from a strung out pikey," Hargreaves said. "Lot of effort for a false alarm."

"Dodgy lot, that." Virji muttered.

The entire meeting with the thin man had all but escaped her memory, lost in a cloud of zoom-dreams. Flashes of a black coat danced at the edge of her mind, a glimpse of the man's face stretching and twisting into a flesh tendril made her tremble. The government men hopefully thought of her as nothing more than another drug-addled piece of street trash who went crazy while in holding.

She tried to sound younger than her twenty-three years. "Beggin' your pardon, constables. I think he made the chems worse. I never had a trip that bad before."

Virji removed the restraints and handed her the towel. "Still got some chunder on ya. You're free ta go. There's a loo down the hall if you need to clean up a bit."

Hargreaves trudged out of sight. Anna dabbed at her face, and smiled at Virji. She strained to peek at his thoughts, but read only a wall of zoom-fog.

"Sorry if I was any trouble."

13

CHIVALRY

Anna never imagined the black mud of The Ruin would be such a welcome sight.

She tried to keep to the fragmented scraps of paving as much as possible, avoiding the minefield of puddles. Some appeared small, but could swallow her whole. It defied belief that not one, but *two* different members of the Metropolitan Police Force in short order had been nice to her. They didn't even steal anything.

What's the world coming to when Old Bill treats a Cov like a person?

The sergeant had left her hanging with her naughty bits out even if he did spare her from Brown. Virji had been nicer, though he could have taken the binders off a lot faster than he did. Then again, the more she thought about it, the more restraining her made sense given her violent outburst. A naughty smile found a home on her lips as she pictured Constable Virji out of uniform.

Her butt stung where the zoom patch had been; she had overdone it bad by squeezing it so much. Without the tolerance she had built up over the years, a smash like that could have killed her. Limping along under a misting rain, she pieced together that the flesh tentacle had to be the zoom's reaction to a mind-probing telepath. Apparently, the drug had muddled things enough for him not to find her secret. If the chem could dull her brain to the point where she couldn't use her powers, it made sense it could mess it up so bad a telepath couldn't read her psionic ability. The reality of her predicament knocked her into a shaking squat. If the zoom hadn't worked, or if she had tried to fight her way out, she would be dead now, or worse—hauled off by the CSB.

No one ever reappeared after the Clandestine Service Bureau got their hands on them.

They'd almost gotten her once after a job for Mr. Carroll went pear shaped. She still couldn't quite figure out how she'd managed to elude them. Because of the CSB, she'd turned to zoom. The government would put a tiny bomb in her brain. She couldn't keep a NetMini for three days without cooking it by accident… she'd kill herself in hours. Anna had to do *anything* to hide. Even getting into an impossible fight with zoom.

I'll only take a little. I can manage the dose. It won't control me.

Laughing and crying, she forced herself up and wobbled to keep her balance without dropping the case of meals or the little white bear she tucked under her jacket to shield it from the rain. The stuffed animal made her think of Twee, something pure and innocent brought into this awful place. Anna gazed up the shiny ebon walls of Coventry Tower, ninety stories of human refuse gleaming in the darkening light of dusk. Here and there, shadows moved in the windows.

Anna sagged. Futility came on strong. The black building, the grey clouds, the never-ending rain—all of it crashed into her with the idea that perhaps, next time, she should fight. That way, they would kill her and take her away from all of this. She thought of her father.

I should have let Daddy kill me.

For minutes, she wallowed in crippling guilt until she caught a glimpse of the teddy's tiny pink bow peeking out from under her arm. Thoughts of Faye made her self-pity less overbearing. The kid needed help she wouldn't find anywhere else.

Anna glared defiance at the jet-black scar in the sky. The unwanted lived here. One couldn't be any more unwanted in the UK than a psionic.

"You awright, luv?" asked Ol' Jack.

Anna jumped. He'd come out of nowhere while she daydreamed, leaning on a fragment of concrete wall tilting out of the muck. Somehow, his sunglasses avoided the rain, but his leather coat ran with thousands of trickles. The white of a smile broke the darkness of his face when he held out a hand.

"Blimey, Jack. I'm shitless." She pressed a hand to her chest, breathing hard.

He laughed, taking the case of instant meals. "Sorry, Pix. Saw you out here alone, and what with it bein' dark and all."

She stepped closer, letting him put an arm over her shoulders. "Damn fine of you, Jack."

"Penny's been climbin' the walls."

"I'm sorry. Damn filth got me again."

"Shiftless bastards." He grumbled. "Did they at least use a nodder?"

She looked up at him, eyes wide in confusion. "That's just the thing, Jack. Twice now, they didn't touch me… Was almost like I's a Proper. Makes me worry."

"Bah." He squeezed her in a one-armed hug. "Nothin' wrong with ya, lass. S'pose yer gettin' lucky to find the ones wot 'ave morals I guess."

"Old Bill has morals?" Anna blinked. "Well maybe to the Propers and moggies."

He carried her over a huge puddle. "You'd scrub up right nice, Pix. Change your clothes and they couldn't tell you weren't a Proper yourself."

She blushed.

"Oi, darkmeat. Give us a go with the bint," called a man on the left.

Ol' Jack stopped and turned to face the voice—and six East End Boys in a half circle around them.

Anna clung to his arm, unsure if her fear of the gang punks came from truth or she merely pretended to put them off guard. For an instant, she thought back two years… a pack of private security blokes. One shaft of lightning and they'd all gone down. Erasing herself from the memory of the unconscious had been simple. But now… the zoom spot burned like a dagger wound in the ass.

Jack met their stares without a flinch, cracking his neck with a left-right tilt of his head.

"You lot'll naff off if you fancy continuing in your ability to breathe."

Anna looked up at Jack, shocked at his total calm. Faint green light reflected on the inside of his sunglasses. *He's augged!* The realization stunned her. She'd always been so high around him she never noticed how much electricity suffused his limbs before.

One of the gangers stepped in, raising a pipe. "You got some cods, mate."

A second man pulled a sword off his back. "You know the rules. Any piece out after dark is up for the takin'… now back off."

The others all produced improvised weapons. Cloud-filtered

moonlight glinted from pipes, knives, and spiked knuckles as the men closed in on Ol' Jack.

"Jack, you don't have to—"

"Hold this." Jack handed her the box of instant meals and pointed at the Boys. "Look 'ere you planks. I'll not warn you again."

The East End boys grinned at him, confident in their six to one ratio. When they showed no sign of relent, Ol' Jack blurred into a streak at the man with the sword.

In the span of two seconds, a right hand punch to the gut cracked ribs, a left hand jab to the side probably ruptured a kidney, and a spinning kick to the face coincided with Jack tearing the weapon loose from the ganger's hand.

Ol' Jack came to a halt, his coat fluttering to rest behind him. His augmented strength launched the East Ender fifteen meters away, where he landed with a muddy *splat*. The motion had been so fast the others still stared at the water pooling in the footprints he left next to Anna.

Another Boy lunged at him, swinging a pipe. Jack caught the end with his left hand, bending the metal. A stomp kick into the chest launched the punk out of the fray; he hit the mud and slid into a brick wall, which crumbled into a rain of wet splats.

Like a dervish, Jack whirled at the rest of the gangers. He ducked a pair of nunchucks and walloped the man on the back with the pipe, driving his face into the mushy ground. While stepping over that one, he threw the pipe into the groin of another punk running in with a vibro knife. The man dropped to his knees, emitting a pitiful moan.

The fifth ganger swung a chain, which wrapped about Jack's right forearm. The Boy tried to drag him off his feet, but Jack took only one step forward instead of lurching over onto his chest, then adjusted his stance and wrenched back on the chain, dragging the East Ender into a one-handed choke hold.

He hauled the gurgling man around in a spin, tossing him like a shot put over a twelve-foot high fragment of wall. The body landed out of sight with a painful *crunch* that could've been old furniture or bones breaking. The final Boy backpedaled when Jack turned on him, lowering his pipe and fleeing into The Ruin.

"You kids shouldn't run about wit' sharp things." Jack shook the composite broadsword at them. "I'll be keepin' this so you don't hurt yourselves." He pivoted the weapon over his hand in a series of fluid practice swings. "Now, where in the hell do gang trash get their hands on a military blade?"

Anna stood from where she had crouched behind a chunk of plasticrete. She'd dealt with many augs while in the employ of Mr. Carroll, but few came close to the speed and strength she'd witnessed. *Military spec. Maybe even Mi6.* "Bloody hell Jack, what the devil was that?"

"Composite blade. For starship boarding tubes. Army don't much care for guns in a plastic tunnel."

"No, dammit. I mean what the crap is this?" She extended a hand at the moaning bodies.

He took the case of instant meals again, offering her his elbow with a smile. "I've had an interesting life."

She accepted his elbow, this time noticing the firmness of plastisteel under his coat. The sense of electrical energy in him glowed in a dazzlingly beautiful whorl of amber threads. He had a lot of cyberware. Both prosthetic arms looked identical to natural limbs, complete with synthetic skin that matched his dark brown shade perfectly, but had a surprising amount of power and speed. That definitely meant high-end military gear. He also had one artificial eye, also indistinguishable from biological in appearance, and full-body speedware.

The fog in her head had faded enough to let her peer into Jack's thoughts, but only to a shallow level.

Flashes of red desert drifted across his mind as they navigated The Ruin. The sword reminded him of his time with the SAS doing black ops on Mars. Old army buddies leaned on frightening looking vehicles with tires taller than people, smiles and waves shifted in the fog of years. Under it all, he seemed oddly focused on Anna's welfare. The name Hannah formed and faded as he looked at her.

Anna worried he might still be with the government, helping those two men who showed up at the checkpoint. Alas, dulled by zoom and lack of practice, her ability couldn't reach beyond his surface thoughts. When he smiled at her again, she sensed only relief at having protected her. He couldn't possibly be working for *them,* he'd been here for years. If the CSB suspected her that long ago, she wouldn't still be free.

Or alive.

BOTTLES CLANKED AND ROLLED ASIDE AS ANNA'S BOOTS PLOWED THE TRASH up twelve stories of pale concrete stairs.

On the landings, she stepped over bodies of those too strung out to find their hovels. Here and there, holes gave away where an errant bullet or ten had gone by.

The thirteenth floor, labeled fourteen, offered junk of lower density to wade past as Penny spent much of her time cleaning while not babysitting. Tidying the place gave her a sense of purpose and made it feel more like a real home than a squat no one cared about.

Anna walked around the corner, heading for her room. Ten doors past her flat, the area broke apart into one wide-open space; half of the thirteenth floor had blown out and all the apartments had merged into a giant, commingled mess of hanging tarpaulins and jagged metal struts. Few Covs had the desperation necessary to make their home there. With the east wall missing, it amounted to sleeping outside, only with a roof. Here, behind the protection of a ninety-degree bend, their apartments felt like a home.

Anna raised her leg and kicked. Her boot left a scuffmark on the dull orange door of Penny's apartment before she walked into hers. Faye sat cross-legged on the bed, still in her skivvies, listening to some horrendous loud music piped into wireless earpieces from her NetMini. The girl looked up at Anna as if disappointed to see her back.

"It's not your apartment yet, kiddo." Anna smiled, hiding the discomfort of her aching body.

The music stopped and the girl tilted her head at the giant box under Anna's arm. "Wot's that?"

Anna flopped on the end of the bed. "Got you some things."

She set the case of instant meals down and handed her the bear. "Couldn't resist when I saw it."

Faye smirked at the offering, calling it 'uncool' with an eye roll.

"G'won then. You don't need to act hard all the time." She dropped the bear in the kid's lap. "Oh, and there's this too." She handed her the box with the earrings.

"What's all this for?" Faye glanced at them, throwing back a suspicious stare.

"Saw them and thought of you. Figured you could use a cheer-up."

A little crack appeared in the girl's shell. Her nascent smile ran away from a crash at the front of the apartment.

Penny burst in the door, running up to Anna with a bog-eyed stare. "Cripes, girl. Where the hell have you been? I thought you got nicked."

"I did, but it was just a border check."

Penny hugged her. "Which border did they check?"

Anna laughed. "I got lucky again."

"You look awful." Penny fussed over her. "What is that smell? Did you hurl?"

"Stonker of a comedown this time…"

"Dammit girl." Penny shoved at her. "You need to get off the shit."

Faye set the bear to the side and helped herself to one of the instant meals. Ten seconds after she yanked the pull strip, the room flooded with the scent of Chinese noodle soup. She picked at the corner tab and drew back the plastic sheet, loosing a cloud of steam into the air. Translucent noodles swam in a yellow broth, interspersed with hunks of vat-grown shrimp and hydroponic farm vegetables. The girl started on it straight away, so hungry she seemed oblivious to the heat.

"You nicked a case of ramen?" Penny rubbed the bridge of her nose. "Cripes, this is the good stuff. This one's like a hundred-and-a-half credits?"

"I bought the food… nicked a necklace." Anna drew a finger around her throat and flashed a drug-dulled grin.

Penny swatted at her. "Anna, you're being an idiot. You know if you get pinched for it now, you'll go away. I don't want to lose you." The batting became a hug.

It was just practice, said Anna telepathically to Penny. *I'm not gonna keep at it. Too dangerous. I'm not gonna overdo it again. Almost got bagged once, ain't riskin' that again. Eventually, being careless will get me killed.*

Penny squeezed her tight.

"You two munch rug or something?" Faye slurped at her noodles.

Anna snickered.

Penny blushed. "Twee! Certainly not."

"Well, she's got a man at least." Faye nodded at Penny.

Anna's laughter faded to a shameful stare at the ground. She didn't want to admit to working at a strip club or being rented out for six hundred credits an hour. "I haven't met the right—"

"Bullshit." Faye slurped again. "I saw the faerie hologram rig. You're a stripper aren't you? You on the game too?"

Anna looked at the nightstand, at the leafy metal harness that lay like a dead spider on the imitation wood.

"It's cute." Faye slurped noodles. "I tried it on. You don't have to sugarcoat shit for me. I'm not as innocent as I look. Izzat why they call you Pixie?"

No way this girl was anything more than a spoiled suburbanite. Anna figured it for posturing, Faye likely wanted to be seen as tough despite being homesick and scared to death.

Anna had nowhere to hide… and maybe the truth would send the kid home. "Yeah. There isn't much other place for girls to go out here. The name came first, 'cause I'm five nothin' with a sprog's face and little titties." She laid it on thick as she described the club, saying she could keep forty credits of the six hundred her *manager* charged a man to use her. "They basically own me, Twee. If someone pays Blake, I have to sleep with them. I don't get a say in it."

Faye fidgeted, no longer able to make eye contact with either woman.

Penny chirped up. "You could babysit… Walk dogs… And your boobs aren't *that* small."

"Oh yeah… Me, babysit?" Anna slapped herself on the thigh. "Parents would take one look at me and lock their doors."

"Or ask who's babysitting you while you babysit their kid." Faye squinted at her. "Don't call me Twee. You look like you're fourteen."

"P'raps they wouldn't if you got off the shit… I think you keep half the corner-chemists in London in Armani."

Anna sighed, glancing at Faye. "It's not an easy thing to let go of."

14

BRISTOLS

Anna smiled at the fond recollection of Faye cuddling the teddy bear in her sleep.

She had slipped out of bed and left the girl undisturbed before tiptoeing out of the apartment. At a touch past noon, several dozen people crowded around massive grills made of old cinder blocks and rebar near Coventry Tower.

The wind carried the quasi-edible scent of purloined meat blackened by repurposed elements from industrial water heaters. Spawny and his cohorts had tapped the municipal mains to bring electricity into the place via the abandoned sewers. They had to repeat the task every few months when the Power Authority located the splice and fixed it.

She swooped in and swiped something masquerading as a hamburger patty, smiling and waving at a couple guys mockingly protesting her for darting in front of them. *They sound like schoolboys.* She munched on it, navigating The Ruin on her way to the police checkpoint.

Anna prepared herself for the usual 'against-the-wall,' but she had no zoom on her, no contraband, and felt altogether too strung out and fatigued to put up a fight. Despite resigning herself to not protesting an expected early morning body cavity search, the constables merely watched her go by without even speaking. Something about their stares made her uneasy, as if they were afraid of her. Not wanting to garner more scrutiny, she averted her eyes and walked faster.

Four blocks into the city, she mingled into a disreputable crowd at the end of a back street and waited her turn to talk to Everybody's Friend.

A man of mixed African and Indian heritage, EF appeared to be somewhere around nineteen. His hands slid among those of the people, passing credits and chems while returning gestures of respect. Most of his head hid beneath a floppy cloth cap, his clothes oversized and too expensive for someone who spent so much time in an alley like this. What she needed lurked deep within the great hooded mass of maroon cloth covered in a repeating pattern of beige fleur de lis.

"The Pixie…" He smiled when she reached the front of the line. "Sex on legs… You lookin' for Faerie Dust?"

"Got any of the usual?"

"Naa, girl. All out of the zoom. Been a run on it lately. This upsec dude showed up couple hours ago, got a real thing for it."

Anna shivered, stuffing her hands in her jacket pockets. "Got anything close?"

"Closest I got is a couple o' smileys."

"Need somethin' that'll keep my head in a fog… keep me Zen. Nothin' too rough though."

"Delicate." He brushed his fingers over her cheek. "Couldn't sleep if I broke the wings off the Pixie."

With a wink, he produced a clear plastic pouch holding four small yellow spheres, each about the size of a pea, letting them rest between his index and middle finger. Opaque and waxy, black smudges gave the impression someone had attempted to turn them into smiley faces. He had managed to get them all to line up with their silly expressions pointing at her.

"Looks like balled up ear-wax."

"These don't give the kinda light show you're used to, but they'll keep your head out of the now just as well. Whatever you feel, you *feel*."

Anna glanced off down the street, her body already shaking from imminent withdrawal. "Fine, smileys it is then."

"Eighty."

Her credstick and the pills moved around in his ornate hand-play, somewhere between a palm rub and a shake. Within the finger ballet, he plugged it to a metal box in his pocket and the beep of a transaction preceded it flowing back to her. They exchanged a grin and she turned back to the street, one of the smileys dissolving under her tongue.

A hint of lemon lurked beneath a flavor like well-worn floor.

⚶ ✳ ▥ ◔ ⊜

BRISTOL CITY SAT DARK AND QUIET, A SCARCITY OF LIGHT LEAKING FROM the light rods in the ceiling.

Lawrence glanced at her from the bar, his preparatory work coming to a halt as he tracked her with his eyes across the room. The scuffing of her boots thundered over the stillness.

Beyond a door into the back hallway, the air vibrated with the chaotic din of a dozen girls chatting about this and that, a feminine sound that slipped out from under the distant frenetic shouts of Sanjay, the club's owner. He railed at the VidPhone again, yelling about an uptick in the price of synthetic beer.

Anna shoved the dressing area door to the side with a loud squeak, and walked into a garish pink space with benches, lockers, and a dozen other women in various states of dress. The club didn't open for another hour, so they sat around killing time chatting, fussing with costumes or makeup, or lost in cyberspace on portable sens-rigs.

Anna set her bag at the end of one of the benches, sat next to it, and pulled her boots off. Her feet seemed whiter against the hot pink tile floor. The cracked and chipping blue polish on her toes needed a new coat. As much as she dreaded letting the police have their way with her, in two hours' time, she would be prancing about for anyone that happened to be in the room. The smiley lacked the punch of zoom, but mellowed her feelings enough that she could endure the humiliation. Anna slipped her shirt off over her head, stuffed it in her bag, then removed her skirt. She had showered before leaving home, but the reek of Coventry had seeped into her clothes. Sitting there naked in a room with other mostly-nude women hit her over the head with the feeling of being a piece of meat at market. Feelings of abject worthlessness filled her eyes with tears, but before she could sob out loud, her emotion leapt into titillation. Anna squirmed, fighting the urge to touch herself. Seconds later, her mood crashed to blankness.

Damn. I hate smileys.

She stood like a zombie and climbed into one of the autoshowers, ignored by the other girls. Soon, a spritz of cheap jasmine whore replaced the reek of her life outside the club, some knock off perfume Sanjay, the owner, had added to the rinse cycle.

When the tube released her, she plodded back to the bench, dry and smelling like sin.

After a moment or two of staring into space, Anna took her hologram rig out and put the metal choker on before swinging the projector around between her shoulder blades. The egg-sized pod landed cold on her back. She fumbled for the second strap and snugged the thin metal band across her chest right beneath her breasts. No point in turning it on yet, that would wait for her to be on the floor. The only question would be if Blake would put her back in the cage or send her to the poles today. If he remained angry, he might make her wait tables or worse yet—lock her in one of the back rooms to wait for the sort of client that doesn't care what the girl looks like.

Anna gripped the bench, staring at her toes. The mere thought of Blake caused her to throw up a little in the back of her throat. *I don't want to be in that cage again. I'm going to tell him to get fucked if he tries.* A deep wave of mortification came on, and she crossed her hands in her lap to cover her crotch. *Where did that come from? Stand up to Blake? He'll beat me to death.* She bit her lip, daydreaming about her old life with Mr. Carroll and what she would have done to Blake if they'd met a year ago. Deep in the bowels of her mind, the image of a man twice his size begging her not to kill him surfaced.

Her head sagged like a stone atop her neck. The smiley's effect crept into her mind, magnifying her mood. Disgrace that had up until this point tiptoed past her consciousness flung off its clothes and pranced in front of her. She bawled, bending forward and hugging her legs.

Hands touched her back. She looked up; two other women had come to investigate the outburst. At their concern, she brimmed with gratitude and love, hugging them like long lost sisters.

The sluggish high did at least prevent her electrokinesis from running away with itself, though it lacked the potency of her usual fix. Zoom gave her hallucinations impossible to differentiate from reality. Smileys shoved her emotions along the path of least resistance, but with the knowledge the drug did it. Anna's mood went up and down like someone else had control of her, but she didn't care enough to do anything about it.

She chatted for a while, alternating between casual, clingy, crying, and paralyzed with humiliation for sitting around nude. The girls were friendly enough, save the two oldest who'd always been jealous for no other reason than her being half their age. Anna lost herself in a giggling fit when they teased her about her height. None bothered asking for her diet secret to staying so thin—all of them knew it: being too poor to eat.

To spite one of the forty-somethings, she bragged her boobs were natural despite being small by sex club standards.

"By any standards," said one of the older dancers... Iris?

Anna narrowed her eyes. "You've got so much plastic, Old Bill's gonna nick you mistakin' you for a doll."

The women gasped.

What's gotten inta me? I never let the cattiness get to me. Iris seemed about ready to launch into a tirade, but froze with her mouth open, looking over Anna's head at something behind her.

"Anna... Come here please," said Sanjay.

A pall of silence fell over the room. The club's owner stood at the door, smirking at the assembled women. If not for the power he held over them, his overlarge peach-colored suit and pink shirt would have made them laugh.

The newest girl, Brittany, gasped at a man entering the room. Anna stumbled to her feet, swaying over and hugging him with a big grin.

Sanjay remained statuesque, indifferent to the nudity of the woman draped around him. His cigar-sized Nicohaler migrated from one side of his mouth to the other, and the end flared blue. Red-tinted glasses rode up the bridge of his nose, driven by one fingertip. He frowned.

"Hi Sanjay," she purred. "You look hot today."

He grasped her by the shoulders and pushed her off him. "No point in your being an arse-lick, girl. You are stonkered again, aren't you? I can see the glaze over your eyes."

"Just had a smiley." She covered her mouth with both hands, unable to stop giggling.

"Blake tells me you spent all day Friday night hanging there like a turd in the pool."

The giggle fit ended with a confused grimace. "All day... night? What?"

He slapped her, not hard enough to knock her to the ground, but sufficient to turn giggling into cowering. "You spent more time blowing chunder than dancing. I am not making money from chunder."

"I'm sorry, Mister Sanjay. I was in a bad way... The filth took my zoomer and I started crashing. I would've been fine if Blake let me get more, but he threw me in the cage. Won't happen tonight. I promise."

One of the old jealous bitches muttered under her breath with a spot-on exaggeration of Sanjay's accent. It escaped his ear, but Anna burst into snickering again.

He wagged his finger at her. "You are damn right it is not happening again! You are all ballsed-up? You keep coming in here three sheets to the vind. I have no need of girls who cannot function. No one wants to be shagging a sack of warm meat that doesn't even know its own bloody name… and chundering. Go on. Get out of here."

The smiley jumped on Anna's emotion, riding it into an enormous crater. She sniveled like a six-year-old being grounded. "But, Sanjay… You can't give me the sack. The boys like me. What'll I eat?"

"Pixie, honey," said one of the older dancers. "You *don't* eat."

Why am I crying? I want *this. I want out.*

"The customers vant a girl that can dance, not a druggie slag who is not capable of even moving. And they do not like chunder." He put a hand on her shoulder. "Look… You clean yourself up and I think about putting you back out there. While you're still on the shit, you're no good to anyone."

He walked off leaving her slouched there, clad only in tears. Blake leaned in from the shadows by the door with a leering grin. Anna offered him a pathetic glance, but he seemed amused by the situation. The girls offered their condolences while the older ones smiled at having one less pretty twenty-something to steal men away from them.

She couldn't contain the whimpering sniffles the whole time she removed the holo-rig and got dressed. Cloth slid over her skin, feeling like armor and easing her nerves. Under the effect of the smiley, her confidence brimmed to dangerous levels—taking a shiv to Blake's gut seemed like a right brilliant idea. Alas, he'd walked out of the room. She stormed out, but by the time she reached the main room, she again felt like a total failure and hung her head on the way to the exit.

A patch of flickering green by the door caught her eye. The board always contained announcements: people trying to sell an old bike, concert promotions, coded messages for where to obtain drugs, and other random ads. From a battered emitter, plastered over with a Dead Ballerina sticker, an ad that had been there for weeks beckoned. She never looked up at the board before, never caring to see what went on outside of her miserable existence.

An offer of a hundred credits pulled her in closer. The holographic poster floated two inches from the wall, shimmering with falling dust and flickering every few seconds with the sputter of a faltering circuit. The advert looked for models willing to pose during an art class at the university. Two hours of sitting nude in a room full of people for a hundred credits. She wiped her cheeks dry while reading it, committing the address to memory. The money wasn't great, but it seemed less sleazy.

I guess those university types are smart. Where else would they find someone willing to do this?

DUST SPARKLED AMID SHAFTS OF SUNLIGHT SHINING IN BETWEEN ANGLED wooden slats over ancient glass. Anna wondered how old the building was. The blinds appeared to be real wood, not Epoxil. The scent of polish, paper, and age swam thick in her senses.

She perched like a nude Greek goddess on a pedestal at the center of the room. Crumpled white cloth bunched around her hips and her right thigh, extra folds draped over her perch in an attempt at comfort. Two dozen university students peered from behind easels, sketching with fervor upon giant pads of actual paper. Professor Gresham, a purist, insisted his charges learn the rudiments of art before they moved on to modern tools like holographic tablets, light pens, digital animation, or full on cognitive artistry by means of cybernetic implants. A living anachronism, he made her feel like she had gone centuries back in time. The experience couldn't be more different from Bristol City. True, a room full of people stared at her naked body, but with earnest and studious expressions—not leering.

Rather than gyrate around, she had to remain as still as possible—the direct opposite to her old job. Blake would give her crap for standing still even for ten seconds. Despite longing for a break, the reality of holding motionless proved easier contemplated than executed.

Heavy footfalls echoed over the fervent scratching of charcoal sticks while the instructor paced around. He passed close behind her; a wisp of cologne emerged from the ambiance for a fleeting moment. Every so often, he would pause to comment on someone's work, sometimes complimenting, but usually suggesting adjustments to the technique.

Before she started, he'd told her to relax as if the only thing that could see her was the one object she picked. Anna chose an old stuffed owl on the wall in the corner to stare at. She tuned out everything else in the world but for the dusty, timeworn bird.

Despite her responding to an advert in a seedy adult club, he spoke to her as though she had no experience exposing herself in public. She rather enjoyed being thought of as a Proper woman, and didn't disabuse him of the notion she was anything but. The sheet tickled the small of her back with each breath; she wanted to close her eyes. Sitting still for two hours exhausted her more than dancing in a cage.

The professor's footfalls mutated into thunderous booms like great blocks of stone falling to the floor, a heavy metronome reverberating in her mind. She shivered, trying to keep her emotion on an even keel. Free of the club's pounding music, she found the silence tortured her the most. Continuous scuffing of charcoals on paper couldn't drown out her rambling thoughts. Here she sat, still being paid to show her tits to the world. Different, yes, but a degree of indignity came with it nonetheless.

Is this all I am? A pair of bristols?

Penny kept at her to quit taking drugs. Anna didn't want Faye to start, and now even her 'employer' wanted her off the shit.

What nerve.

A pimp—what Sanjay essentially was no matter how he dressed it up —telling one of his ladies to *stop* taking drugs. She clutched the bench until her knuckles whitened, far angrier than she would have become without the smiley in her. Knowledge the drug did it let her keep the rage out of her face and maintain the placid stare of disinterest at the ancient taxidermy bird.

How fucked up am I that a bloody pimp tells me to lay off?

Tears banged against the back of her eyes, trying to get out, but she held them in. Crying only helped if someone gave a rat's ass. She would have a good sob on Penny's shoulder later. These people didn't need to see such a display.

Perhaps being sacked would help her. Every time she walked out the door of Bristol City, she left a little dirtier and a little less human. Penny may have been right. She should try to watch tots or walk dogs. Maybe she could shake off the rust and go back to pinching things. Working for Mr. Carroll had been risky, but at least she had dignity there. *No, too dangerous. That will draw the CSB.*

Either way, Anna decided the time had come to stop letting life give it to her in the bum.

The commotion of people shuffling about snapped her out of her musings.

Who am I kidding? I'm just a tramp sitting naked on a box.

Professor Gresham approached, offering a grandfather's smile and gesturing at the easels. "That's all for today, luv. There's some good work about. Can I interest you in coming back tomorrow, say another hundred for your time?"

She eased her weight off the wooden cube, stretching the stiffness out of her legs. Her clear lack of modesty brought a touch of crimson to his cheeks.

"That's fine, guv'na."

He turned away. She found his courtesy strange. It made tears rush to the brim of her eyelid to get a closer look at him.

"I'll leave ya to get your kit back on then, lass. I'll be in my office at the end of the hall when you're ready to collect your pay."

Motionless, she stared at the figure in the dull blue sweater and tan pants. He left without trying to sneak a look back at her, disappearing behind the dark chestnut door below the owl. When he had gone, she padded to the partition behind which she had stripped before class. *What was the point of this?* She frowned at the old folding barrier, gold-hued wood painted with white orchids. *They're goin' ta see me anyway.*

An old NinTek 900 sat on a desk nearby under a layer of dust, collecting more. Two feet tall, three feet long, and half a foot thick, it now served as a bookend. She gathered her clothes from where she tossed them, staring at the archaic terminal. Before holographic displays or M3 jacks that plugged the brain into the net, it had been the latest and greatest. It had to be a hundred years old.

Anna looked down and pulled her skirt into place, ashamed her only thought about such a curious relic was about how much it would fetch at pawn. The old prof had been civil with her. She would feel guilty swiping it. Not to mention its size, something like that wouldn't be an easy lift.

Once she dressed, she tugged at the hem of her skirt. So short and without panties on, it felt *more* embarrassing than wearing nothing. Penny offered to lend her some jeans, despite being almost four inches taller. Anna fidgeted with the material, wishing she had taken her up the loan. *Maybe this is why Old Bill keeps giving me the biz.* Wearing something so skimpy made her feel like a cheap slut. Then again, she didn't *have* anything else. What wardrobe she'd once owned had all vanished down the endless pit of her need for zoom—or been stolen by her 'neighbors'.

Anna steeled herself and walked past the easels. The students would be back the next day to continue working, so they left their work in situ. Curiosity gnawed at her, and she lifted the shrouds, peering at the smudges of charcoal.

The angelic figures posed upon the pages looked so far removed from any way she had thought about herself. Seeing how the students had restored innocence in her face that had long been absent choked her up. By the fifth sketch, tears escaped, lost in the purity of it. *Is this how people see me?* Did people see her that way when they didn't know she was from Coventry, or high... or a whore.

She crumbled her fingers into her mouth, trying to stifle the sound of sobbing.

Memories flickered in her mind as she walked among the standing frames: watching a sheet-covered gurney wheeled out of her old house the night her father died. A close call with a psychologist who saw her create lightning. Running away. Twelve-year-old Anna begging at restaurants, and then the ignored beggar learning how to steal. The counter of Mason's pawnshop appeared again and again, lower with each repetition. She had grown up dropping purloined goods on that pale blue surface. She and Penny had enjoyed some good times... two kids with no parents, no responsibilities, and several thousand credits.

A face appeared out of the dark, the picture of exaggerated handsomeness mounted atop an impeccable black suit. Stealing from the wrong place earned the notice of the Syndicate, and Mr. Carroll. They somehow realized her as more than a simple thief. She had made good money with him doing unsavory things for unsavory people, but those sort of things attracted the CSB. The zoom worked at first to hide her from the government. She'd thought she could take only enough to hide the monster in her head. She thought she control it.

She'd been wrong.

Anna swallowed; the sandy grit of the smiley scraped at the underside of her tongue. People used them to enhance pleasure and happiness, especially when having sex. The drug oiled the path her emotions tried to walk, and they slipped in it, falling headfirst into a spiral of sorrow and regret.

The warm brown-orange glow of this time-forgotten space cloaked in ethereal serenity. She basked in the fading sunlight among the henge of easels. Her doppelgängers looked off at an unseen bird. The sketched versions of her changed facing a few degrees from one easel to the next. When she reached the students who had a clear view of her from the front, she sniffled at the paper.

They hadn't focused on her sex. One man had spent the most effort on her eyes and the delicate nose between them. Another had gone over and over her hair, capturing every strand of her pixie cut. A third had defined the curves of her silhouette with near photographic precision, faint smudges of his fingers bringing her musculature out in three dimensions. Only one hinted at anatomical correctness, a simple curved line suggesting the physicality of her femininity. The flick of an artist's wrist to indicate a change of light, a passing charcoal acknowledged her womanhood without dwelling upon it.

The sketch with the most attention paid to the breasts had been done by a girl. She marveled at the roundness, wondering if the artist had given her too much credit. Two dozen black and white apparitions stared into the air, proud and innocent—two things Anna felt far removed from.

"Are you all right, miss?" asked Professor Gresham. "It's been almost an hour. I thought you'd snuck off."

She jumped at the voice.

Blushing at being caught with wet eyes, she looked at the floor. "I'm fine... these are beautiful."

His grey mustache curled with a smile. "They have potential, but still have much to learn."

Anna offered a sheepish nod, and walked with him to collect her credits.

I suppose I do as well.

15

CHIPPER FIX

Anna dug her fingernails into her palms and tried to keep her mood level, knowing the smiley had to have worn off by now. The rat of sobriety gnawed upon her brain stem. She gathered her thin coat about herself and moved among the crowd. People's usual reaction to someone of her obvious station never bothered her as much as it did right then, but she clung to technically no longer being a stripper for a tiny scrap of self-respect. The wind tugged at her microskirt, causing a few men to stare.

Even the advert bots seemed to ogle.

She had made a career out of flashing her assets in the faces of drunken men, but now she wanted to disappear. For the most part, the citizens obliged and disregarded her. She wanted to turn invisible to all of London, but at best she could blot herself from the heads of two or three people in close proximity. Every gust of the breeze made her feel naked. Head down, she shuffled among the crowd. Telepathic invisibility couldn't help, but far more mundane solutions would help.

Anna headed for a store.

A few minutes later, two panels of inch thick glass slid out of her way, granting entry to a small clothing shop. She flashed a grateful smile at the mechanical doors that spared her the need of having to uncurl her arms from around her chest. The smiley's brief effect had faded, leaving her once more staring the absence of zoom in its cold, dead eyes. She had to focus and keep her mind on an even keel or she would attract the wrong kind of attention from the wrong kind of people.

A dozen freestanding shelves jammed into the center of the place made walking through it a bit of a challenge. Clothing, still a popular item for physical stores, hadn't done quite as well with the to-your-door market. People much preferred to see and touch things they wanted to wear before spending on them.

Anna selected a pair of loose black pants, the kind with pockets down the legs, and checked the size by holding them against her hips. A passable fit; her boots would absorb the extra length in the legs. Two hundred and sixty credits, a hair less than a quarter of her remaining money, but she wanted it bad enough. There would always be more pieces of jewelry to steal, and she couldn't put a price on dignity.

The clerk's eyes hadn't left her ass since the moment she entered. If any zoom had been in her system, she would have changed right there in the open in hopes of a discount; sober, she retreated to the dressing room. Thin black material slid up and over her legs, cool, smooth, and best of all —form obscuring. The belly-baring shirt didn't bother her even an eighth of what the skirt had since a lean too far gave people a show.

She decided to keep the new pants on, and wadded the skirt before stuffing it into her purse. On her way back out, she selected a thin nylon belt and put it on right from the shelf. After ripping the tags off both, she approached the counter and set the stubs by the drooling young man. He made perfect eye-to-tit contact and smiled. His hand missed the tags twice before she pushed them under his pawing at empty glass.

"That'll be all then, miss?"

"Quite."

"Two sixty for the Ruperts, thirty five for the belt... after tax that'll be three forty-five."

"Oh..." She stuffed a hand in her purse. "I'm exempt."

"Wha?" He made eye contact at last.

"Tax. I'm on the dole." She rummaged for the laminated card. "Here."

Anna imagined his hard-on drooping as fast as his face. The lust in his eyes became contempt. He swiped the card at the terminal as if loathe to touch it. She pondered zapping him out and helping herself to the credit transfer machine, but he had scanned her card and the authorities would trace anything she did here back to her. She glowered, ashamed of the way he had looked at her at first, and furious at the dehumanizing sneer he gave her now. Society shunned her kind; it wasn't *her* fault she had this life. Now that she tried to pull it together, he *still* had the nerve to look at her like that. The little voice in the back of her head whispered 'do it... do it...'

Sanctimonious bastard.

The merchant terminal burst into smoke and sparks.

Shrieking, the man dove to the floor.

Dammit... She cringed, and pretended to scream at the fire.

PURSE TUCKED IN THE CROOK OF HER LEFT ELBOW, ANNA HELD HER HEAD high for the first time in many years. The swish-swish sound of the synthetic fabric kept up a continuous reminder she no longer attracted every eye in the crowd. No one around her saw her as a Cov; as far as they knew, she was a Proper just like them. It couldn't all come from wearing pants instead of a micromini. Anna smiled. The way she carried herself had changed.

The whirr of a hovercar weakened her good mood. The Crown permitted only the police and the military to use them in London. Off in the countryside, anyone with money could have them, but King William had become possessed of an irrational fear some drunk would have a smash up with some irreplaceable treasure. Never mind that onboard crash avoidance systems would render such an event an order of improbable as to be nonexistent—unless someone disabled the safetys.

She looked, against her better instinct, at the unmarked black vehicle gliding overhead. At the speed of a walk, it crawled over the crowd. Too slow for a routine patrol, they had to be looking for someone. Anna ducked her head and stared at the footpath, hoping the facial recognition system hadn't captured her yet.

A block later, she darted into a chippery to get off the street—and because the smell had enticed her. This close to the heart of the city, nothing would be cheap, but that didn't matter to her at the moment. She wanted to feed the illusion of being a real person.

Small, disc-shaped bots crept about the floor, cleaning and polishing. Anna took a spot at the end of the queue and glanced at the teenagers behind the counter. An older woman mopped up a spill too large for the wheeled bots.

Across the pond, where dolls hadn't been banned, they'd taken jobs away from people like this. Poor, undereducated workers had little opportunity over there. They would have to go to the moon or off to a colony world to find decent paying work. At least the King, being fancifully paranoid about dolls, kept doors open for unskilled laborers. Anna grinned, remembering the gossip. A fortuneteller hired by the Queen claimed a doll would assassinate him, so he all but banned them from the city.

Most citizens found it amusing to watch the BBC whenever an ambassador from the UCF arrived with a doll bodyguard; the lengths the royal handlers would go to in order to ask them to stay behind without making a political incident out of it often created awkward scenes— doubly so when the doll had a human brain.

"What'll ya 'ave?" asked a pale teen girl with jet hair and green eyes.

Anna startled, and whipped her head forward, staring at the girl. Clicking fingernails painted with the Union Jack drummed with impatience upon the glass counter. Anna gazed up at holographic images of food, a menu above the counter. She didn't reach for her dole card, deciding to pay the extra credits for the pride of not suffering the ignominy of being stared at like a peasant twice in one day.

"I'll 'ave the number three, and an iced Earl."

Ten minutes later, she studied the tray, sixty-two credits worth of battered cod and hydroponic chips, while walking to take a seat at the back of the room. She'd made it a whole four steps away from the register before she regretted paying that much for food. In her present state, that much money for *one* meal was an unthinkable amount—even if it didn't come from OmniSoy. An hour from now, it would be cold, but still fish and potatoes rather than a lump of beige slime.

What sat on her plate never swam in any ocean or sat at the bottom of any fishing boat, but on a genetic level, it was cod. Hunger waged a catfight with a dull ache, her body's protest at the denial of zoom for two whole days. If she got lucky, this fish would digest before she became sick enough to reject it. The thought of quitting, as Penny and everyone else seemed to want her to do, seemed rather plausible at that moment.

Of course, in four or five hours, she'd be a right mess. Some zoom-heads had been known to kill their own families for a score once desperation set in deep enough.

Anna sighed at the plate, feeling like a condemned convict eyeing her last meal.

Already paid for it, may as well enjoy it.

Midway through her banquet, she looked up at the sense of eyes on her. Half a chip fell from her frozen lip back to the plate. There, in the back end of Chipworth's, sat Mr. Carroll—smiling at her.

He looked older than she remembered him, silver highlighted the hair over his ears and his face had thickened with years. She figured him for almost fifty now, but still a pleasant looking man despite his increased weight. The black coat remained the same, joined by a cap and gloves folded on the table near his plate.

They traded intermittent eye contact while she finished the rest of her meal. Whenever she glanced up, she caught him observing her, a curious smile on his lips. As she got up to leave, he waved her over. One didn't ignore the Syndicate and expect to keep vital body parts attached. Or at least ignore private contractors who worked most often with the Syndicate. Anna put a hand on her gut to keep the butterflies down, and walked over.

He gestured as if tipping a hat. "Curious running into you here, luv."

"Innit." Anna looked down, flicking at the pockets of her new pants. "Long time."

"Fate and circumstance..."

"How are they then?"

"What?" He cocked an eyebrow.

"Your dogs."

Mr. Carroll chuckled, patting his leg as he remembered. "They're resting peacefully now."

Anna sank into the seat opposite him, captivated by the pattern in the table. "Soz."

"Pay it no mind, they had a good life. I meant it is fortuitous we have crossed paths. I could use your talents again if you're available."

Anna sat on her hands to hide the trembling. "Might be... This isn't for Mister Cooper is it?"

Carroll chuckled. "No, lass. That ol' turf accountant's got his own men now; he doesn't contract with blokes like me anymore." He lowered his voice. "That business with Thomas was most unfortunate, but it's good to see you're still alive. Word is, you'd fallen rather hard on your derriere."

Mr. Carroll was the sort of fellow who put people with needs in touch with people with skills. The last time she had worked for him, she made a touch over twenty grand for two days' effort. At the time, she considered it a little shy of fair, but now it felt like a king's ransom. He held her ticket out of Coventry, but to claim it, she'd have to keep it together. The risk of the CSB lurked like a shadow at the back of the room, breathing cold vapor down her spine. Between them and Blake's cage… the government sounded like the better option.

She leaned forward, leaving her hands under her knees, her voice a touch above a whisper. "I've 'ad a bit of a rough patch. I s'pose I couldn't handle it as much as I thought."

"Rough patch." Carroll rubbed his chin. "That's one way to put it. What about that unpleasantness at Bristol City? I could always arrange for a little accident."

Anna shrugged. "They're scum what ain't worth the effort or the owin' you a favor. I'm feelin' better now. I'm off the stuff."

"For how many hours? You look like Death's little sister." He took hold of her arm and rotated it to examine her wrist. "Why aren't you eating?"

"Money." She cringed. The sad stare from a man who knew her before her fall hit her harder than those who frowned at another dole-taker.

"Now… that I can fix." He smiled. "If you're in any shape to work."

"Sorry, Mr. Carroll." She lowered her voice, leaning across the table. "CSB's was sniffin' about. Just like before. S'why I ran off."

"I imagine they would be rather keen on someone with your talents. I still have friends, girl. If you're one of mine, they'll leave you be. The Syndicate and the Crown are not so different. Credits smooth over a lot of paranoia."

"What's the earner then?"

"A client of mine is in need of a guardian. The usual sort of chap I work with these days is not nimble enough for this one. The client wants to get to the top of some dreadfully tall place and tap a local."

"So all I need ta do is watch his back?" *I can do this.* "What's the pay?"

"Fourteen five."

Kinnell! The yell stayed in her mind. She hoped the shock didn't leak from her eyes. "That'll do."

He reached forward and propped her chin up. "Guess the times really are as rough as they look on you. You used to quibble the change."

"Bit of a transitional period, I'm in. I'm fine." She forced a smile, ignoring the twitching.

"Still no 'mini?"

She shook her head. "You know why."

"Right then. Make contact with our man at the corner of Neal and

Long Acre tomorrow at eleven pm. I'll meet you here with a stick when the thing's done."

"Who'm I lookin for?"

"Calls 'imself Mr. Orange." Mister Carroll smiled. "Trust me, lass. Ya can't miss him."

16

BLAGGING THE BULLET

Anna clung to the autoshower's handrail so she didn't fall over.

Her body screamed in protest at the lack of zoom. Nerve fibers burned like fuses up and down her limbs. Constant, subtle trembling destroyed most of any coordination. At an unexpected *bang* behind her, she jumped and nearly fell on the wet, slippery floor.

Spawny's face appeared in the foggy curve of the autoshower tube. A spike of abject humiliation ran from head to toe. Heat welled in her cheeks. She shied away from him, wanting to cover herself, but refused to release her grip on the handrail lest she collapse in a heap. Her heart throbbed in her ears and the rush of spraying water seemed to peel back, as if it came from a faraway place.

Anna hadn't noticed she closed the bathroom door until Spawny barged in. She had never thought twice about leaving it open before, but that morning, she wanted privacy with her shower. Sleep had been fitful, so she exiled herself to the tattered couch in what had once been a living room to spare Faye from her endless tossing.

She felt as trapped and helpless as when Constable Brown had chained her to the ceiling. *Stop looking at me.* A brilliant blue spark leapt from the metal console in front of her chest, licking at her breasts without harm, her power drawing current from the tube. She sensed it preparing to leap to Spawny and forced it down the drain. The autoshower went dark.

"Crimey, what the hell!" He jumped away.

"Spawny," said Anna in a demure tone, turning her back. "Please let me have some privacy. I'm not in the mood for your antics today."

The weight of his stare seemed to linger on her back for a moment. "Well, all right then. F'ya need anyfing, I'll be 'cross the hall." Light shifted on the wall as he filled the doorway. "You okay, Pix?"

"Just tickety-boo," she muttered.

Seconds later, the shower tube came back online; the wash cycle restarted in time with the reboot.

"Twee?" she yelled, her voice echoed in the confines of the tube.

"Oi?" The girl stepped into view.

"Be a dear and close the door please?"

She reached for it. "Why's 'e walk in on ya like that?"

Anna pressed her forehead into the tube side. "It's the way he is. Thinks it's funny."

"I'll hoof him in 'is bleedin' plums if he e'er does 'at ta me." Faye shook her head and closed the door. "Perv."

Thirty minutes later, Anna dragged herself out of the tube and dressed in her lovely new pants. She admired them, drinking in the feeling of impersonating a Proper. With one hand on the wall to guide herself, she ambled out of the bathroom and found Faye seated in the kitchenette munching on some of the cereal she'd brought home the night before. Anna shambled over to the counter, poured herself a bowl, and sat down next to her. They chewed in silence for a while.

"Nice trousers," said Faye. "They make yer legs stiff or what?"

"Tryin' ta get off the zoom. Kickin' me arse." Anna pushed the spoon around her bowl "Got tired of givin' everyone a show whenever I moved."

"They have these things called panties…" Faye grinned.

"Haven't had the readies to waste on them."

"They ain't that much." Faye blinked. "So nick a pack."

Anna swatted at her. "Not the way to think."

"I'd give ya some o' mine but they're 'ome. Didn't rightly pack a bag."

"What for, you're starkers more than dressed anyway," yelled Spawny from across the hall.

The lights flickered. Faye stared up.

"Oh, hell, it's only been two weeks!" shouted Spawny. "Bastards are getting quick."

Faye stirred her cereal. "You don't look so good."

Anna shrank into her seat. "I'm on the rattles."

"They had this cheesy presentation at school about drugs. Bunch of fat wankers in suits think they know what's good for us."

"Twee…" Anna reached over the table to hold her hand.

"Don't call me that. I'm not five."

"Sorry. At first, I thought I could control it. I had a… chronic sort of problem that I figured it would help. I was a completely different person then. Confident… I convinced myself I'd only take enough to dull the edge. I couldn't control myself. It got me. I used to live with Pen in a nice place in town, had a car even. Money, all the clothes I could want."

"You sound just like those fat bastards."

"I'm serious, Faye. Look at me. I'm a bloody mess. Two years ago, I was practically wealthy. Now I have to show my tits to eat. I let Blake and…" Snaps and pops emanated from the floor above them while every visible electric light fluttered. "I used to think nothing of dropping ten thousand credits on a handbag or a cute figurine… now I can't even afford a pack of fecking smalls."

"What the bloody crap?" yelled Spawny. "If Eric's pissin' in the breaker box again I'll feckin' stuff his bollocks down his throat."

Heavy footsteps tromped by outside in the hall.

The girl rolled her eyes. "And you don't want me ending up like you."

"Dammit, Faye," shouted Anna, startling the girl into dropping her spoon into the bowl. "You don't belong here. I've already thrown my life away, and I don't want to watch you do the same thing."

Faye retrieved her spoon from the milk, and flicked her gaze up. A puff of blue hair hung over her left eye. "Why'd you get started then if it's such a bad thing?"

"Work." Anna's mind leapt to the first plausible lie it found. "I had to sneak inta some place posing as a zoom-head. Wound up getting the fake patch mixed with a live one. Once was all it took and I was trapped. Couldn't stop."

Faye stared down at her cereal. "I can't face them. They think I'm a liar."

"I could talk—"

"No!" Faye covered her reddening face. "I hate them. I don't wanna ever see them again."

"I understand…" *Telepaths cheat.* "Right when you needed them most, they weren't there for you."

Faye shuddered, on the verge of either bursting into tears of screaming obcenities.

Anna drew a breath to speak, but hesitated when Spawny traipsed in, Penny in tow.

"Cripes, Anna," said Penny. "What the devil."

"She's on the rattles," muttered Faye, wiping her eyes.

"No shit." Spawny looked her over. "Fink ya lost more weight too. Didn't rightly think that possible."

"Really?" Penny's face lit up. "You're trying to quit?"

"Yeah," moaned Anna, running a hand over her face into her hair. "It's gonna suck."

"Zoomers go nuts after about three days. Guess we'll have to tie you to your bed for a while." Spawny winked. "Clothing optional."

Faye glared at him.

The lights faltered again.

He looked at the ceiling. "Damn Eric. I'm gonna slap the shite out of him."

"Thanks, but no. I don't really want to be helpless around you." Anna winked.

"What, I'm not enough for ya?" Penny smacked him with her purse.

"Just teasin'." He cringed, in playful defense. "Hey, Pix, we're goin skimmin'. Wanna come with?"

Anna cringed. She didn't want to get caught up in that, but it would be easier to make it past the checkpoint in a group, and going out to do something might keep her mind off zoom. Sitting around here staring at the wall would be sheer torture.

"Faye you gonna be okay for a bit?" asked Anna.

She scoffed. "I'm thirteen, not three. You can leave me home alone."

"She's got all the answers." Penny put a hand on Anna's shoulder. "Just like you did."

Faye stared at Penny's hair as it floated off her shoulders. "Kinnel?"

Anna, unable to look up at either of them, touched the toes of her left foot to the metal table leg to ground out. "Guess there's a lot of static in here."

THE MAGLEV ORBITAL CIRCLED LONDON PROPER, CROSSING THE THAMES twice on its route. Anna sat at the rearmost part of the rearmost car, the tram's motion jostling her about. Despite the lack of contact with the rail, she felt the disturbance in the energy fields as a rhythmic pulse in her stomach each time the car slipped over a seam in the track. The conversations flooding the confined space drilled into her head: a rotten boss, a lousy breakfast, some Frictionless fans upset at a referee. Anna almost got interested until one of them said something in support of Arsenal, pitying them for an injured player. Her inner voice yelled *Good for 'em, bloody twats!* but her physical voice lacked the energy to escape her lungs.

Sweat tickled its way down her chest in threads. A woman's distant laugh pummeled her skull like a hyperactive woodpecker. Anyone looking at her would think she had a fever: bleary unfocused eyes, red face, sweating, delirious, hands that couldn't stop trembling. With nothing to do, she didn't waste the energy trying to keep up outward appearances. She pulled her legs up, tucking the heels on the seat, and hid her face against her knees.

Kicking zoom was a rotten idea.

Her friends had been right. Another day or so from now, she'd go into the worst part: the crazies. Something deep inside her mind would take over, driving her body to do whatever it had to for more zoom. Penny had once likened it to a parasitic fungus or something that turned ants into zombies. Zoom heads had been known to kill close family members in that phase. Tying her to the bed *did* make sense. As much as it would absolutely suck, she deserved it.

Or, she could admit that quitting sucked more, and find more zoom.

Spawny draped himself over the bench between her and Penny, tinkering with a little electronic device in the pocket of his imitation denim coat. He held the fabric to conceal it from view and fiddled with knobs on the side to adjust its transmitter range and sensitivity. Penny had one as well, but didn't care so much about the tuning. He babbled under his breath as he worked, mangling some old nursery rhyme with a forced Cockney accent that made it incomprehensible, even to people used to him.

Heavy as stone, Anna's eyelids drooped. The thing in the back of her head spun like a tiny cartoon Tasmanian devil, whirling about in search of anything it could use to get out. Her momentary calm trapped it, but the effort made her headache worse. Great amounts of power in the car below unfurled into her view as shimmering amber pipes with scintillating bright pulses shooting down their length every few seconds. The ephemeral light crept along the route of electrical wirepaths in the sidewalls in much thinner threads, up into the ceiling.

Lines traced themselves out as smears of yellow-orange, holograms in the brain.

Her mind played with it, an old atrophied muscle struggling to shake off two years' worth of chemical paralysis, flexing and releasing. Redirecting existing power took far less effort than generating lightning bolts from ambient static. It also proved far more deadly. She pressed her back to the wall wearing an expression most would mistake for an orgasm. For a brief moment, the power brought a sense of confidence and safety she hadn't known in years.

Her head sagged to the left, and she wound up staring into Spawny's pocket at the handful of light flakes dancing in his hand. Energy inside his machine glowed intense around the power source: a rectangle three inches tall, one wide, and half an inch thick, an e-mag. That moniker rolled off the tongue easier than Meissner Cell, though some old-schoolers still called them that. Developed at first by the military for use in energy-based weapons, the ubiquitous super-batteries had infiltrated many aspects of civilian life as well. No reputable company produced skimmers—Spawny had hand-built these. Naked wires attached to the contacts of the e-mag sparked and seethed.

Anna stared at it, her memory flashing back to a dim hallway and a man in a dark coat. One of Mister Carroll's enemies—and the man had lots of them—had sent him to kill her. None of the poor fools ever really knew what they were getting into coming after her. She'd jammed an e-mag into his throat and forced it to discharge all of its power at once. The man's head had vaporized. Anna from two years ago took shit from no one, certainly not a drek like Blake. Still, she *hated* having to kill people. It always reminded her of how she'd felt the night she'd murdered her father.

"You all right?" asked Penny.

Glimmering amber threads faded away at a hand shaking her listless arm.

Anna squinted. The window-light framing Penny's face burned her eyes. "Yeah, fine. Just a… bad memory. I need a feckin' zoomie."

Penny reached over Spawny and grabbed her by the lapels, shaking her. "Look at me, Anna. You do *not* need a zoomer. I'm here for you." Tears streamed down her rich, brown cheeks. "It's as much my fault… I never should've let you start."

"We're boaf 'ere for ya, luv." Spawny ruffled her hair like he tried to cheer up his kid sister.

"Thanks. Kinnel, this sucks." Anna doubled over, arms braced to her gut. "I shouldn't have eaten."

"Bollocks, girl. You're a twig."

"We're gonna take a stroll. Yell if you need us," said Spawny.

Penny glanced between the two of them. "You sure that's wise?"

"She'll be fine, Pen." Spawny bounced to his feet. "We're just goin' up and back."

Anna's arms fell slack on the seat as her friends walked down the asile. Gentle rocking of the tram taking a curve caused her to slip back into her semi-awake daze, her attention drifted between small diaphanous blobs of power manifesting from people they passed, flying into Spawny's pocket or Penny's purse.

That's twisted. I've never seen EM before.

Her friends had turned on the skimmers.

Sometimes the glop of energy leapt out of the back of a hand where an ImDent chip lurked.

The skimmers simulated merchant readers, siphoning off credits in small amounts from every device they came in range of. The amount randomized from one ping to the next, the software wouldn't tap the same source twice in less than a month. Most people didn't notice. Even if they looked at a statement, the odds were good they would overlook it since the transactions stayed small and appeared to be something common like coffee, a snack, or a toll.

Her friends reached the end of the car, the tiny acknowledgement chirps of NetMini's lost amid the din of the cabin and layers of clothing. One of the reasons Spawny preferred to run skims on the tram—noise. A cyan retaining field at the end of the cabin dissipated, popping like a film of soapy water as Penny hit the button. They advanced to the next car.

Anna lay like a corpse for a few minutes until the feeling of being alone and vulnerable in a box full of mostly men gave her the wherewithal to stand up. No one had made a move, much to her surprise. Perhaps the pants worked.

She lurched in pursuit of Penny and Spawny, falling into the standee posts one after the next to forestall an intimate meeting with the floor. A few people asked her if she was all right, another new feeling. Anna offered pleasant smiles and claimed a bit of fever, which made them lean away and nod.

At the end of the car, she smacked the wall a few times in a disorganized attempt to find the button to sap the field. A nearby businessman watched her fumble for several minutes until he seemed more uncomfortable by her proximity than bothering himself with another's problem. He reached forward. She tensed, expecting his hand to go for her ass, but he pressed the button for her. After a thankful nod, which almost sent her spilling into his lap, she wobbled past the opening. Her friends had made it three cars down. Anna searched the aches and pains for the ability to move faster.

She'd have to do something about that before tonight. All the horror stories of zoom withdrawal hit her at once. *Maybe Spawny was right.* Anna froze in place for a moment, lost to a waking daydream of being tied to her bed by strips of cloth, screaming and thrashing as if being burned alive. Reality came back in a flurry of conversation, swaying bodies, and the *whuff-whuff-whuff* of passing gaps in the monorail.

Her arms moved like a rubber figurine with stiff wires for bones. The job she'd agreed to do for Carroll required more flexibility than a piece of jerked beef if she would be of any use to the client or stay alive. Anna grunted from the impact with a metal pole she failed to see. Her hands clasped it out of reflex; she clung to gather her balance as well as her thoughts. The maglev went into a gentle rightward curve. Anna slipped and spun around the standee post. If not for the number of people packed in there, she would've hit the floor.

More zoom would make her feel better without delay, but it would dull her abilities and set her back. Then again, dulling her abilities had been the whole point of starting it. The drug proved rather effective at keeping her electrokinesis from running away with her emotion, but it also made it a chore to call on when she wanted to. To work for Mister Carroll again, she would need to be able to find the little monster in her head. To return to his employ as a matter of routine, she would need to stay clean. Could it be true he had the influence to keep the CSB off her?

No... Zoom's right out. Maybe I'll take up yoga or tai chi.

Pulling herself to her feet, she thought about visiting a clinic and buying a pacifier. Those autoinjectors could ease the withdrawal, but they ran about a thousand credits. Little more than weakened narcotics, they dulled reaction time almost as bad as the zoom itself. The only difference was the lack of hallucinations and a shorter high. The NHS called them non-addictive, but she knew that to be a lorry full of codswallop. Anna stopped, staring out the window at the passing grey city, wondering why the illegal drug was a hundred credits a dose but the path to freedom cost a thousand. She lost track of how often Old Bill had let her skate with the supposed contraband.

Bloody government's probably in on it.

Five doors later, she caught up to her friends. They had stopped at the midpoint of the car, facing away from the forward end to duck the gaze of a pair of constables by the door. The Filth's body armor had hardware capable of detecting a skimmer if they got too close, but turning around at the sight of the police would arouse suspicion.

Spawny eyed the cops via their reflection in the window. "They're watchin' us. Hey… you two lock lips, give 'em somethin' to really stare at."

Anna closed her eyes, trying to force the idea of it out of her mind. "Do you want to see my lunch again that badly? She's like my sister."

Penny grabbed her, kissing her on the lips before whispering. "Do you want your sister in jail for ten years?"

It could have been the motion of the tram, or a fragile stomach already upset from her body's demand for zoom. The thought of crossing tongues with a woman somewhere between sister and surrogate mum was the last straw. The taste of her lunch burbled in the back of her throat. She tried to steel herself, focusing on the thought of Old Bill carting Penny off for skimming. Her mind retreated behind a curtain of logic—tolerate this or Penny goes to jail. Blake had rented her to both men and women. She closed her eyes and pictured one of those clients, pushing all thoughts of Penny out of her mind. Spawny behaved as if filming them, muttering like a director, holding the skimmer up like a camera.

You cheeky bastard.

In a few minutes, the Met went on down the tram.

Anna let her head fall onto Penny's shoulder. "I should have skipped the pickles."

Penny patted her on the back and said soothing things, and led her to the nearest vacant seat. The near miss scared the pair of them off any more skimming for a while. Holographic adverts appeared inside the maglev's windows, courtesy of the occasional bot brave enough to fly up alongside in an effort to gain the attention of a passenger. By the time they arrived at the next station, Anna had a firm grip on her food. They disembarked, eager to avoid the police, but Spawny couldn't help himself and walked a skim past the people waiting to board the train.

"Oi!" shouted a tall man.

Spawny ducked the hand reaching for his shoulder, evading the man's grip.

The giant wore a heavy black trenchcoat, the entire back of which bore a hollow silver cross filled with thorns and roses. He lunged at Spawny, missing a second grab.

Crossmen. Anna's throat constricted with dread.

Two more men in similar coats, one with silver metal eyeballs, the other a crimson-and-green hairdo that resembled a dead peacock, turned on him and growled. Spawny squealed and took off at a full sprint, the rubberized soles of his shoes squeaking on the metal of the maglev platform. Penny ran after him, down the switchback stairs to the street level. Anna stood there as if detached from reality, watching, unable to move.

Tower, Peacock, and Silver-eye stormed off after her friends.

Seconds later, a flash of adrenaline chased away the knots in her muscles. Vaguely aware that some people might want to hurt her friends, Anna stumbled after them moving like an off-the-street extra from a bad holo-vid about zombies. Penny caught up to Spawny and grabbed his hand, dragging him along faster than the three Crossmen who pursued without a word.

The chase spanned the length of two blocks before an ill-chosen left turn stranded them in a dead end alley among stinking hulks of restaurant trash compactors. Spawny skidded to a halt at the bricked over fence at the end, grabbing Penny by the hips and hauling her up.

Tower checked him into the barrier, smashing the air from his lungs and sending him sliding to the ground.

Penny's grip failed, and she fell into the waiting arms of the near-seven-foot man. He threw her like a slab of meat to Peacock, who stepped back, trying to contain her while she flailed and screamed.

"So friend, you fink you kin skim the Crossmen, eh?" The big guy drove a massive boot into Spawny's side, flipping him over onto his back. "I'm gonna beat seven shades of shite out of ya. Hope you got a box ta put yer hampsteads in when I'm done with ya."

Spawny howled, lurching to his feet and punching the huge man straight in the jowls. Beard shadow bunched up over his fist, hardly moving the skull behind it. The attack made the tall, shaven-headed Crossman grin wider.

"Not bad, mate. My turn." With that, Tower slugged the stunned Spawny in the face, bouncing his skull off the wall.

He fell with the grace of a limp noodle to the pavement.

"Stop, please don't kill him!" Penny kicked and thrashed, pleading. "You can take it all, just don't kill him."

"Damn right we're gonna take it all," said Peacock, "right after we're done with yer little toy-boy."

Silver-eye stood back a few paces, like a Frictionless goalie ready to catch either one of them if they managed to get past his mates.

Anna stopped a few meters behind him, trying to work out the best way to help. Three soft *pops* came out of the darkness to the left, followed by an inexplicable spout of water from a puddle as if someone had dropped a rock into it. She glanced in that direction, feeling oddly watched, though saw nothing.

Tower shook his head, blinked, and continued kicking Spawny in the gut. Penny took advantage of Peacock's momentary disorientation and tried to run. One hand pressed to his temple, he snagged her by a grip on her shirt collar, and dragged her over backward to the street.

Silver-eye spun toward the splash and spotted Anna. Red glowing lines moved sideways over his metal eyeballs. A small trickle of blood ran down the left side of his neck. He regarded her with pity for a few seconds, confusion for a little longer, then his expression warped with lust.

"Looks like we got a bonus, mates. This one's worth a squirt as well."

Anna, distracted by the distant rattle of a ladder, didn't react as the man rushed over and grabbed her about the chest. It felt unreal, like a dream. The withdrawal had gone from hypersensitivity to numbness. She couldn't move her arms or walk away, but the exact reason of why dangled over her conscious mind like a treat held out of the reach of a dog.

She stared at the hands clasped together over her stomach without recognition of what they were or that they had anything to do with her immobility.

"Yearrrgh." Spawny howled, leaping up with a series of rapid punches to the big man's groin.

Tower doubled over, wheezing. Taking the opening, Spawny kicked him in the face and bloodied his nose. Like a rabid Chihuahua, the wiry man leapt and dove at Peacock. The man turned away and bent forward over Penny, giving Spawny his back and all but ignored the barrage. When he'd had enough, he flung Penny face-first into the metal wall of a Greek café. She slumped to the ground in the corner while the Crossman grabbed Spawny by the jacket and held him up over his head.

"Bloody flea," growled Peacock, before slamming Spawny down flat on the wet pavement, and kicked him in the ribs.

Barely able to breathe, Spawny rolled onto his side and caught the sole of a boot in the stomach.

Pain seeped into the fog enshrouding Anna's brain. She became aware of a rough hand squeezing her right breast. With solid pants on, her nether bits seemed too difficult a target for a quick feel. The one holding her had slipped his mitt up under her shirt and worked her boob like a lump of dough.

She scrunched her face a little as if that act presented such a minor a breach of etiquette it left her unsure if it really warranted a reaction. The detachment removed her from the now, as if she watched it happen to someone else. Anna peered down at the undulating fabric. A moment later, it occurred to her she watched *her* breast under assault. She squirmed. Silver-eye picked that moment to squeeze a little too hard. His hand over her mouth stifled her attempt at a scream.

Silver-eye forced her to the side and bent her over a row of trash bins. The harder she struggled, deeper he dug his fingers into her breast. His left hand crushed into the base of her neck, forcing her cheek against the freezing metal refuse bin. Anna growled, shoved, and squirmed. The man had too much strength, too much weight; her palms slipped over the rain-spattered lids rather than pushed her up.

"Leave it out." She pawed at his arm, trying to get his claws out of her chest. "You're gonna tear my tit off."

She hadn't been accosted at a police checkpoint. Anna had no reason at all to surrender to these men, but her withdrawal-wracked body lacked the energy to care. She closed her eyes and went limp, half hoping they would kill her afterward. A hand slid into her pants, icy against her most intimates. It shocked her conscious enough to notice Penny's sobbing in the dark. No longer did the threat of rape loom over only Anna. The person she cared about most in the entire miserable world suffered with her. She tried to get away from the unwanted hand, but his weight crushed her into the refuse bins as hot breath slid over the left side of her face.

"Noice and yummy, the clam ain't got no beard. Moi favorite."

Anna growled as his fingers pressed tighter. Drops of sweat fell on her head; he ground his hips against her ass and panted like a dog. His other hand crushed her neck and made it hard to breathe. She *could* protect herself. She *could* protect Penny, but if she did that, she couldn't let the

Crossmen live to speak of it. How would Spawny react? How would Penny react if she learned what Anna could *really* do? She bit her lip as his fingers sank deeper inside. It didn't matter what they did to her. She had no dignity left to save.

But...

Penny's pleading scream made up her mind. If Anna sat there feeling sorry for herself, her only friend would be forever damaged. It didn't matter if the CSB found her again. It didn't matter what Spawny thought. It didn't matter if her powers horrified Penny and she never wanted to see her again—she had to protect her.

Anna drew a breath and opened her mind to the air around her. She pulled static electricity from the air around her, amplifying it into arcs that swam over her, crackling like spider-legs between the metal trash bin and the wet ground. She gathered the sense of the power, calling the lightning into her body and focusing it into the hands touching her.

Bang!

The unmistakable smell of burnt skin surrounded her.

Silver-eye flew backward and smashed into the wall on the other side of the alley and landed as a twitching unconscious heap atop bagged refuse. Anna pushed herself upright and whirled about, cradling her aching breast in both hands for a moment before she pulled her pants up and fixed her belt closed. She shuddered with shame and anger, rage growing, at the lingering ghost of his hand between her legs.

Anna needed more power to kill.

She reached out with her mind, searching for a source. Twenty meters away, a streetlamp glowed in the blackness. Anna called to the electricity within. A brilliant spark leapt to the puddled ground, snaking in a split second into her boots, climbed her legs, and wrapped around her chest. Electrical energy built up on her skin, hot and tingly. She curled her lip in contempt and raised her right hand, palm facing the man who had groped her. An intense bolt of lightning leapt from our outstretched fingers, searing a black trench over his chest. Foam burst from his mouth. When the brilliant glare faded, his face had become a dark purple mass of swollen flesh.

Two great arcs snapped like whips in the air, connecting the streetlamp to Anna's back, responding to her call for more power.

Penny screamed again. Anna's gaze shot to the sound. Peacock had her bent over a trash bin, dress lifted, frozen in a gawk at her. Penny's desperate struggle had thus far frustrated his progress at doing anything more than ripping her smalls off. The *boom* of the fatal bolt she'd thrown into Silver-eye had startled them frozen.

"Get off her," snarled Anna, her already dark glare accented by little blue sparks crawling over her face.

Peacock tightened his grip on Penny's hair and pulled her upright as a human shield. "Who the fuck are you talking to, bint?"

Tower continued pummeling Spawny, too into his task to notice anything going on.

Anna narrowed her eyes, and let her arms crawl with sparks. "A soon-to-be dead man."

Penny wailed in pain as he torqued her hair back. She scrabbled at her coat, going for the knife she kept in the pocket. While Peacock stared at Anna, she flicked the blade out and plunged it into his thigh. Roaring in pain, he bounced her head off the bin and staggered back. Penny slumped to the alley, both hands cradling her face.

Anna narrowed her eyes. "Oh bugger all. You just pissed me off, fucko."

Anger surged. She drew forth a lingering arc from the streetlamp. It struck her between the shoulder blades, sizzling for several seconds, filling the air with the stink of ozone. She forced the current to wrap over her limbs, basking in the warm rippling surge as she channeled the electricity around her arms. Beyond furious, Anna commanded the dancing lightning down her arms with intent to kill. The bolt went straight for the metal blade embedded in Peacock's leg.

The dead end alley lit bright as day for several seconds from the arc connecting the streetlamp to the Crossman with Anna in the middle. Penny gasped, cowering against the wall.

He went stiff as a plank on his feet and fell face down, smoke peeling from his mouth. Sizzling came from where the knife touched flesh. What once had been eyes oozed out of his skull as white foam.

The Tower stopped using Spawny's gut for Frictionless practice and stared at her. It took him only seconds to decide to haul ass, and he jumped for the fence Penny had failed to climb.

"Where you goin'?" Spawny choked from the ground. "I ain't done wif you yet."

Anna thrust her arms out, firing white-blue arcs from her fingertips into his back. The shock paralyzed him and he fell from the wall, landing landed on his chest in a large puddle. Anna stalked closer, arms out to the sides, fingers splayed. She called a fusillade of long, blue arcs to her from an air handler on the Greek restaurant to her left and mains power lines on the other side of the alley. Crackling lightning swirled around her in a nimbus of energy.

The Tower moaned and rolled over in the puddle, staggering upright. He yanked a truncheon from his belt and growled.

She mimicked the noise, a mouse taunting a lion.

Penny's distant whimpering fanned the fire of her anger. Anna thrust her arms down, ten narrow streamers of lightning leapt to the puddle. Tower's screams almost drowned out the repeating whip-crack electrical discharges. Realizing she only caused pain, Anna surged, projecting a thick, scintillating shaft of electricity from each of her arms. The bolts lapped up his legs from knee to groin before crossing at his chest. The alley walls shimmered in the flickering radiance and the scent of seared meat filled the air. Mechanical noise from the air handler faltered. She grunted from exertion, roaring and crying, pouring all of her shame and resentment into the blast. When she couldn't press any harder, she sagged forward and fell to her knees, the sparks gone.

The alley seemed much darker than before her attack.

Tower slouched on his feet, arms slack at his sides and legs apart. Eyes half-closed, he remained still for a few seconds before falling forward with a wet *splat*.

Heat wrapped her skin, but she found it comforting.

"Jesus fucking H," whispered Spawny, before coughing up blood. He shifted around, holding his gut, aghast at the dead man nearby. With one elbow, he dragged himself closer to the women and scrunched up his face at the breeze. "You're right, luv. You should'a skipped the pickles. Gaw, that stinks."

Anna vomited again.

Penny scrambled to her feet and pushed her dress back to rights.

"Your smalls are showin'." Anna pointed at the cloth around Penny's ankles.

Penny blushed and fixed them in place.

Anna looked up. "You okay? Did he…"

Penny sobbed, shaking her head. "No. You? Are you all right?"

"Just fingers. I've 'ad worse from Old Bill. I'm tired though."

Penny shivered hard. "These aren't constables, they're street trash. No one'll miss 'em. Don't get all wound up."

"Oy, bit on the rough side what I 'eard 'o these blokes," muttered Spawny, before spitting blood to the side.

"Pen..." Tears streamed from Anna's eyes. "I didn't throw up 'cause I killed 'em. It's the zoom. I feel like shit and a half. I..." She covered her face with her hands. "It ain't the first time I had ta do somethin' like this."

"Bugger me," wheezed Spawny.

"Cripes, Anna." Penny crept closer. "You should've told me. That Carroll bastard is bad news. He's put you up to this, has he? You never did tell me what sort of biz you did fer 'im."

Anna hung her head, like a child who'd been caught nicking cookies. Even if her friends were now terrified of her, at least she could live with herself knowing she had spared Penny from rape. She expected them to cringe against the wall to get away from her. It caught her off guard when Penny flew onto her, sobbing, squeezing, and showering her with thanks.

Spawny rolled flat on his back. "Cold, alley's kind of comfortable ta be honest. P'raps I'll replace me bed with wet pavin'. Could get used ta this I fink."

Penny helped him sit up. "Bugger. I can't carry both of you."

Anna wiped bile from her lip with the back of her arm. "I'll be okay. I'm just... It's been a long time since I cut loose like that. Feels like I got hit by a lorry and then par boiled." She glanced at small burns on her clothes. "Not quite the perfect control I used ta have."

Spawny coughed and spat more blood, then glanced up at the scuff of an unseen step. "We best shoot off. Fink we got someone up on the roof watchin'."

Penny hauled Spawny upright and dragged him along. Anna staggered behind them. The thought of what the trio must look like, sober Penny and her two drunken friends, made Anna laugh.

"That's a bit psychotic, innit?" Spawny held his stomach and gurgled.

"We look like a pack of drunks." Anna lost her balance to the shakes and fell to all fours. "Cripes, we look a mess."

A few blocks later, they huddled together in a dim booth at the back end of a small restaurant. Anna went through six cups of coffee before anyone spoke.

"Quaint li'l noshery, this." Anna's attempt at a smile lasted a few seconds.

Penny stared. Anna couldn't read the look: fear, pity, or shame. Perhaps all.

"That's why I started on zoom. Workin' for Carroll got the CSB up my arse. I figured I could use it to keep the involuntary bit under control, but when Tommy got shot... I just..." Patterns reflected by overhead lights shimmered in a hypnotic ballet upon the surface of her coffee.

Penny reached across the table to hold her hand. "It's awright hon, doesn't change a thing. I'm actually happy for ya. All these years, I thought you'd been nonced."

Anna flinched. Despite how he'd been, the suggestion her father might've molested her made her angry. "No. Never. My dad beat the shit out of me. He was terrified of my... abilities. He'd never do anything like that."

"S'right. Not a fing. I seen worse." Spawny stretched back in his seat. "This one time, Ol' Bill hucks a great honkin' dazzle bomb at the lot of us. I'd taken a spill in this wild punch up and landed on me arse. The bloody fing bounces and lands right on my jubblies, but it don' go off. Was a dud. S'were I got me name."

"Flashbang in the cods?" Anna hid her face as the waitress set a plate down. "Aye. Bit o' luck that, no doubt."

The interrupted conversation became polite smiles and nods at the waitress until she walked out of earshot.

"You got me by the short and curlies now," Anna said, and took a bite of her sandwich. "Either one of you could get outta Coventry if you sold me out to the Crown."

"Bugger that." Penny squeezed her arm. "No way in hell. Besides, you ain't got 'em ta getcha by."

Anna blushed.

Spawny perked up, keenly interested in the topic shift. "Aye."

They all laughed.

Plates and cups rattled with a shiver plaguing Anna's body. Withdrawal—like the Four Horsemen—was coming, and it would be a right bitch and a half. She only had to make it long enough to finish the job for Mr. Orange and then she could crawl in a hole and die for a few days. Spawny could've gone running for the cops, he could've been shitless, but he laughed and grinned at her like nothing had changed.

Maybe I will let him fix me to the bed. For my own safety, of course.

"She's roight. Gub'mint don't much like people even known about that sorta thing. They'll bag and tag us all. We give you up, we fuck ourselves." Spawny tapped himself on the chest. "An' no one fucks me, not even me."

Penny stuck her tongue out at him.

He slithered over the table, voice dropped to a whisper. "Havin' none of that, Pix. We're bezzy mates."

17

FOG AND RUST

I n the shadow of a dozen gleaming office towers, Anna huddled under the awning of an autocab station, ignoring the digitized voice asking if she needed a transport for the fortieth time. The rain came in waves so thick the wind made an aurora borealis of water in the sky. Mesmerized by the pattern against the silvered windows of the immense structures, she lost time watching the ephemeral serpents dance.

Electrical humming announced the arrival of a spherical advert bot the size of a soccer ball hovering along as it tried to sell various bits of rain gear. A plastic-coated Chinese paper umbrella perched above it at the end of an articulated metal arm. Glistening amoeba of reflected streetlamp light disappeared as it moved, revealing white stylized dragons. The red umbrella gave the bot the look of a massive cocktail that had gone off wandering. It rotated to face its central lens at her. Deep within, a faint haze of violet brightened. A sweeping pattern of laser-light shone past rain specks on the glass. It searched for a NetMini to see what it could sell her.

She stared, as much as one can lock eyes with a four-inch lens, waiting to see what it would do. Trails of water ran off its parasol, following the spokes. Anna mused to herself how sad the orb must be. She imagined brows over its one great eye, despondent it couldn't find a mini's beaconing signal anywhere on her. If it had lips, it would surely pout.

With a whirr, it drew closer and nodded down to raise the actuators directing its ion thruster. A selection of umbrellas shimmered into view upon a white holographic pane, bathing the area in a soft glow.

Occasional raindrops glinted like fallen stars when they struck the panel of light.

Something about this poor forlorn sphere of metal made her sigh; she almost felt bad, as if it were a young boy forced to hawk wares in a storm. It pivoted a few degrees to the side, simulating a head tilt while switching its display to raincoats.

"Not bad, little thing. You almost seem like you're worried about me." Anna sighed, staring up into the downpour through the clear awning of the autocab port. "Sad that only the robots care about the little things anymore."

The orb drifted to the left and tried to hold its small umbrella over her head, too.

"Bother that, it's so small. You'll short out if you get wet inside."

A sad digital whine added to the sense of sentience she projected onto it, pushing her guilt to critical mass. She plugged her credstick into a tiny socket on the orb, surrendering forty credits on the least expensive umbrella on its list in the hopes of making it feel better.

It continued floating at her side, trying to shield her from the rain that slipped past the narrow awning. Anna squinted at it.

That's odd. Little buggers usually race off after they suck credits outta ya. What's its game? Does it think I'm going to buy something else? It almost seems... concerned. Was its *concern* for her something other than attempting to endear itself into selling more?

A man's voice emerged from the monsoon. "Evenin'. You Pixie?"

She turned, glancing at a nondescript man in a shiny coat. Black on the shoulders, sleeves, and grey in the middle, it covered him from neck to shin. His eyes radiated orange light, as if his eyeballs had been replaced with bulbs. Glowing spots on his shoulders appeared to be responsible for a faint blue dome-shaped field above him where the rain wisped away to steam before it could strike his short, dark hair.

She figured him to be a little older than her, twenties still, but closer to thirty. A black metal case in his right hand gave him the look of a government agent, but he lacked the air of superiority they often wore with it. The orb offered him umbrellas.

Anna raised an eyebrow. "You must be Mr. Orange."

"Indeed."

He gave her an up-and-down glance, picking at Spawny's borrowed denim jacket to appraise the smallness of the woman underneath. Anna tensed, not wanting him to discover she caved in on the way here and had three derms of zoom in her left pocket—just in case. The rainy night made her shivering seem not so out of place. She lost track if it came from the rattles or a genuine chill. The cold sweats covering her face looked like the effect of rain.

For once, she didn't mind that it poured.

"You're a wisp of a thing, lass. Not quite what I was expecting. Are you even fifteen yet?"

Anna tried to remember what it felt like to be confident, and straightened up. "I will admit to being a little rusty, but this isn't the sort of job I'd have taken before. Too basic."

He leaned back, appraising her with a finger tracing his cheek. "If I've learned nothing else, it's not to trust my eyes. Carroll's not the sort to play games. He's gotta have something up his sleeve to send a kid."

"I'm not a bloody kid. I'm short. You got a problem with short?"

Orange chuckled. "No, but shall I take your nervousness as a warning?"

She shivered again, not knowing which of two potential causes to blame. "Feck. Don't mind me, I'm on edge tonight."

The umbrella-bearing bot circled in, aiming its ads at Mr. Orange.

"Bugger off." He swatted at it.

It zoomed off, careening around the corner of a building a block away. Two seconds later, it peeked out like a frightened dog. She frowned at it, finding herself feeling sorry for a thing that had no soul. Another bot, this one long and boxy, glided up. Mr. Orange leaned back and tucked a hand into his coat.

"Keep your hair on, the wee one guilted me into orderin' an umbrella."

He relaxed, but didn't pull his hand out until the flying rectangle spat out a compact, extending umbrella and rocketed off. "Right then. I need to get up to the top of that one." Orange pointed at an office bearing the logo of British Telecom.

Anna examined the wand-like umbrella, searching for what to push or twist to make it open. Her new umbrella exploded in a *pop* of nylon without warning, she jumped.

"A *little* on edge?" asked Orange.

"Aye. A touch." She walked out from under the awning with her new portable rain-shield and brought a merciful end to the terminal's incessant inquiries about a ride. "That's a big 'un. How you fancy that? BT 'as their own police ya know."

"I got it sussed. I had been expecting Carroll to send me a leg-breaker despite being told I needed a nimble sort. Wasn't expecting a girl... That actually works out. How good's your drunken tart?"

She glared under flattened eyebrows, her voice as cold as the wind. "I think I can fake it well enough."

"Good."

He lifted his left arm, case and all, and peeled back his sleeve. Upon the forearm, a small black panel glowed with buttons and a holographic display unit. A few finger taps later, a field of light formed around his face. Pixels and streaks of green orbited into a cyclone of data that coalesced into an altogether different person.

Anna blinked at the sixtyish silver-hair looking back at her. Obviously a hologram, but a damn good one. Unable to resist, she touched his cheek, fascinated at how the image rippled away from her fingertips. He took her arm by the wrist, pulling it away from his face and holding her hand.

"Don't touch it, that'll give it away."

She gasped. The voice had changed; he sounded like the old man he appeared to be.

"Vox unit... What, do you live in a cave or something?" He frowned. "I thought Carroll was sending a pro."

She grumbled. "I am. I'm not a fan of implants..." *and I'm a little rusty.*

"Nothing at all? You're not even armed, what is it exactly you expect to do if we run into problems?"

Anna flashed a wry smile. "I've got it sussed."

"Touché." He regarded her again. "Before I stick my neck out, I need a little more than that."

"Can I trust you?"

He gave her a look. His mere presence on this job proved he worked contrary to the law. The reminder of that made her look at her boots.

"Yeah, sorry. Silly question. I'm... Unregistered."

"Oh." Orange seemed to grow tense. "Right then. I guess that'll do."

Anna took his elbow, not having to work too hard to emulate an intoxicated stagger. She added incoherent babbling about the latest Frictionless match, complaining the ref had made a bad call in favor of Arsenal—by virtue of the claim *any* call in favor of Arsenal was a bad one.

Orange grumbled at having to support so much of her weight. She ignored him as it made the act seem more real. Her legs ached; more effort went into her ability to speak than she allotted to locomotion, and having him there as a leaning-walking post helped.

He dragged her through the lobby of the building across the street, some manner of financial services firm. She babbled on about never having been with a man his age before and hoping he would be able to keep things lively enough for her. Two security officers, a man and a woman at the front desk, looked up and smirked at the unlikely pair. Their glares carried the type of disapproval that could be aimed only at someone they recognized.

At the elevator, he held his hand up to the wall. Tiny mechanized struts extended from his coat sleeve and arranged an electric field over his hand. Orange held it near the palm reader, and waited until the light turned green and the door slid open. No reaction came from the security people. Evidently, they hadn't noticed the mechanical assistance.

"Oh, I can't wait." Anna dropped to her knees, grabbing at his fly in the elevator.

The security officers looked away, the woman blushing.

"What the feck are you doing?" he hissed.

She continued for several more seconds until the door closed and she whispered. "They looked away, didn't they?"

"You can wait until we are upstairs. They've cameras in 'ere." He pulled her by the jacket back to her feet and whispered, "Are you acting like a wreck or are you ripped?"

Wobbling, she made a dizzy face. "Awright, but you better be good for the credits, luv."

Anna collapsed into him again, grabbing on for support and hoping he would think she only *acted* like a strung out whore—not actually *was* one. The clarity that came with the absence of zoom filled her with sufficient shame. She wanted to leave that life behind. For Faye, for Penny, perhaps even for herself, the coming hours would be six shades of hell.

Damn it all, why did I buy more? She could almost feel the chemical beckoning her. *I know I'm gonna cave in. Just gotta do this, go home. Let Pen take the shit and hide it from me. I'll never manage it on my own.*

The chromed panel walls mocked her with how red her eyes had become; she struggled to find the energy it took to keep them halfway open. She squeezed her jacket where the zoom waited; she had three ready to go.

It's right here. This hurt will stop if I want it to...

Daydreams of zooming kept her floating on the elevator ride. Anna debated the seriousness of her desire to quit. Her fear of the CSB battled with the different version of her the art students saw. She wanted to be the girl on the paper, not the girl sitting on the pedestal—and definitely not the girl in the cage. Before she knew it, tears of shame soaked into Mr. Orange's shoulder. Her subconscious squeezed her hand tighter, trying to get to the zoom beyond the barrier of plastic and cloth.

He glanced at her sniffle, lifting an eyebrow at the look on her face. "What the feck is wrong with you? So help me if Carroll has buggered me..."

The elevator door pinged and opened.

Anna wailed, clutching at his lapels. "I'm sorry guv'na, please, I need the money. Okay, fine... I'll let you give it in the bum. Please don't send me away."

A few employees working late looked up. A Nicohaler dangled from the lip of one man, his mouth agape. Somewhere out of sight, something dropped to the floor with a *plop*. Several employees pretended not to notice anything. One woman in a clinging sea foam dress gaped at him in abject shock, shifting in her chair from sympathetic discomfort.

"Don't just sit there gawking like an imbecile. You're quite welcome to join us." Orange held his other arm to the employee.

The woman flushed crimson, aghast at what had been said to her in the workplace. Anna turned, rolling her back into Mr. Orange's chest like an affectionate cat. Her tears turned into giggles.

"Look at 'er gov'na. Bets ya she likes the rug instead."

"Subtle." He muttered into the top of her head.

The woman got up and stormed past them to a different elevator, muttering about going to HR in the morning. Mr. Orange led Anna by the arm past the open area full of desks, a cube farm to the far end of the floor and a row of offices along the outer wall. He ducked in a door bearing the label 'R. Sturgis — VP Operations', and moved with haste to the window. Outside, the BT tower glowed against the indigo night across the street. The other building was shorter than this one, the roof in plain sight from here.

Once the door closed, he pushed her into the wall. "You better have your head on."

Anna swallowed. Everything hurt. Dry throat, sore muscles, and the burned spots from the Crossmen fight throbbed. She gazed into his eyes. Her attempt at a confident face became a pleading one. He spun away, cursing Carroll's name.

"I just need a minute. Look, I'm fine. I... I had a bad night. Pushed myself too far and I'm sore. Took some painkillers."

"Painkillers?" Orange shook his head. "You're a lousy actress."

She frowned shame at the floor.

"That's not what I mean. Okay, fine, you're a lousy liar. If you're wrecked, we need to get out now."

"I'm good." Anna took a few breaths and composed herself.

Orange moved to the window and focused his stare at a four-foot white obelisk streaked with threads of red light. It perched atop a metal box with large wire-guides leading down into the building. Anna had seen enough hardware to recognize it as some kind of network relay transmitter. A powerful one at that. The energy inside it called out to her from here.

"Pretty, isn't it?" Orange patted her on the shoulder. "That's what I'm looking for."

"Yes." She glanced back at him. "But it's over there and we're over here."

"I've got it sussed."

From under his coat, he produced a rifle-like device with a large black box at the rear end. The tip of an e-mag protruded from the bottom of the pistol grip. She followed him to a back exit of the VP's office, down a hidden hallway past the executive washroom, and out onto a patio.

As soon as they went through the door, holographic images formed at the edges, simulating a tropical beach. The effect provided stunning realism, aside from a square of pitch-black night sky directly above them. During the day, the illusion would be perfect.

"End holo."

Orange's utterance dispelled the swaying palm trees. With the light source out of the way, he moved to the railing and sighted the strange rifle at the BT tower. Anna sensed an invisible pulse of energy rush down the length of it like the energized magnets of a rail gun, only the projectile had a fraction of the velocity of such a weapon.

The whirring of unspooling cable broke the still air for a few seconds before it ended with a distant metallic *clank* from the other side. Orange backed up to the wall, holding the butt-end of the thing against the plastisteel panel. With the flick of a switch, it energized and electromagnetically adhered to the structure. A belabored mechanical whine came from it, as the cord tensioned.

Orange took another device from his coat, a small black box with two rubberized grips. One side had a lever like a motorbike brake. After clipping it to the wire, he smiled at her.

"Off ya go then."

"Are you serious?" She suppressed a shiver. The thought of sliding down a wire in her current state added the nausea of fear to the milieu of her misery.

"You are the protection, are you not? This spot is safe. You need to go first in case there's some unpleasantness waiting on the other side."

"I know. I know. That's not what I'm worried about." She plucked at the near-invisible line. "I haven't done wire work in about two years."

"Is it the painkillers?" Orange cocked an eyebrow. "Or the lack of 'em?"

She scowled. *Screw it. I've lost weight since last time, should be easy peasy.*

Anna jumped up and grasped the handles; the wire kept her toes off the ground. Not trusting her life to her grip, she swung her legs up and crossed her boots over it.

Orange grinned. "That button changes direction. It's motored. Squeeze the lever to move."

"Yes, yes… I actually *have* done this before." She sighed. "Not that you'd know it by looking. What're you grinning on about?"

"Trying to understand how someone so small can protect anyone."

"I'm psionic. It doesn't matter how tall I am."

She clutched the metal handles. With an almost imperceptible whirr, the contraption pulled her forward along the wire, out over the street some ninety stories down.

Anna kept her eyes closed and tried not to think about her sore muscles or her difficulty not letting herself degenerate into a shivering wretch. The zoom waited right there in her pocket, but her will to remain alive bound her hands to the grip, preventing her from reaching for it. Venturing a peek, she gurgled at the sight of being only halfway across. The mechanized handle took no effort on her part, but the belabored pace with which it crept down the line made a manual climb almost feel welcome.

A blaring horn tricked her into looking down. An involuntary tremble preceded a full-body convulsion. Her gaze followed a sluice of what remained of her dinner on its way to a soon-to-be unhappy motorist. The stripe of greenish-beige slime fell as a column for several stories before it broke apart into a shower of tiny droplets, which faded into the backdrop of the distant lights of traffic. She coughed, spat, and coughed again before looking up at her hands.

Before the zoom, something like this would have been fun. In her time working for Carroll, she'd done a few high-altitude jobs using the full works: thermal-masking bodysuit with armored panels, goggles, climbing rig. The man had even talked her into carrying pistols in case she'd found herself needing to kill someone without a handy source of power nearby. Carroll's assurances his connections with the government would protect her if things went pear shaped never comforted her much. Carroll wasn't the sort of bloke to be sentimental; as soon as she went from asset to liability, he'd forget ever knowing her. Going over a line in her street clothes felt as reckless as doing it nude. Granted, BT didn't exactly qualify as a high-security installation. The odds of them having thermal cams on the roof were slim to none.

However, in possession of muscles she had to beg to obey and wracked with the pain of a phantom beating, she could only cling for her life and pray for the ride to end before she lost her grip. When something scraped across her ass, she snapped her eyes open, then pulled her body up a second before a perimeter of concertina razor wire would have shredded her new pants. Once she cleared the barrier, she let go and dropped to the roof.

The hand carriage shot back up the line to Mr. Orange. She frowned at the bouncing wire way over her head, wondering how she would get back onto it. Ahead, the presence of electricity in the machinery sang to her. The gloss white shell of a nine-foot tall obelisk brimmed with wire bundles that fed the massive transmitter. Glow from fiber optic piping seeped out the gaps in the panels, creating the red lines that segmented its otherwise featureless sides.

She paced, gathering her jacket against the rain and severe wind she hadn't noticed on the way over, too petrified of falling to care about anything other than her grip. Her new pants were lovely in terms of protecting her from prying eyes, but did little against the cold, especially when the wind held the wet material so tight against her legs it looked like black paint.

Anna wandered around the corner of the relay. A sudden electronic *buzz* made her heart skip a beat. An automated sentry sprang up from a sunken chamber on the roof. About the size of a human head, its spherical body rose on a robotic arm. An extending three-barrel cannon spun to a stop with a sharp *click* before swiveling to aim at her.

Faster than conscious thought, her old instincts drew the power out of the mechanism before it could fire, leaving it slouched and twitching. Her hands trembled as she stared at it. With fading panic came the realization she couldn't stand there concentrating to keep it dead; she had to deal with it in a more permanent way. Anna opened her psionic senses to its form, hunting for the connection to mains power. Filaments of amber light traced over it, brightness and thickness corresponding to the level of amperage in the wire. Upon finding the brilliant glowing branch going up the actuated arm, she pulled electricity from the building into the sentry gun, overloading its circuits.

The turret shuddered, sputtered, and smoked before falling against the concrete roof panels with a *clank* like an out of tune bell, its Myofiber muscles limp. Mr. Orange sauntered around the edge with the cable rifle balanced over his shoulder, glancing at the smoking remnants.

"Not sure how you managed that. P'raps Carroll was right about you."

"Guess it didn't much fancy the rain."

Anna had more than her fair share of practice at lying, but cringed inwardly at the weakness of that one. She rubbed her forehead and leaned against the transmitter array. Carelessness would get her killed or put in a cage and poked by the intelligentsia. Of course, the zoom had also put her in a cage. She debated which kind of poking was worse.

Dark red light glimmered in the corner of her eye from an open access panel. Orange flipped it upward into an awning against the relentless downpour. Glowing bunches of optic cable wound over each other inside in a mystifying tangle of complexity. Groups of fiber as big around as a man's wrist went in every conceivable direction. Individual threads within the clusters shimmered at random, flickering here and there from the millions of conversations, images, sounds, and other traces of the modern age they carried across the GlobeNet.

Each nanosecond flash could be a hundred messages going to a hundred people. Daydreaming about the information made her head hurt. She took the umbrella she had bought from the sad little orb out of her jacket and popped it open, relaxing against an HVAC unit as if she waited at a tram stop.

Orange worked at a feverish pace, picking at the bundles to expose single threads of fiber. He appeared to be searching for a specific one. Anna squatted, peeking over his shoulder.

"How can you tell them apart?"

Orange's, looked up at her and blinked his orange glowing eyes once, the old man illusion gone. "I can see the data in real time."

That made her head hurt even more. She stood again, ignoring him, drifting between watching for danger and trying to tamp withdrawal back down into a can she would open later. Orange spun thread after thread betwixt his fingers, smirking at each for a second or two before discarding it to the side. After what felt like forever, he drew one out from the rest, farther than any other, and grinned. She straightened up, taking her weight off her back.

"That's the one," said Orange.

"Good, my ass is getting numb."

Somewhere in the dark, a hovercar whined its way across a sky of low-hanging charcoal grey clouds. For a moment, she thought it a good thing the weather decided to suck tonight. If she couldn't see the light orbs from the ion engines, whoever drove it couldn't see them.

Orange removed a one-inch black sphere from the case. When he squeezed it, the device split open like a clamshell, and he clamped it around the single fiber before pushing a button on its side. White light appeared in small seams for several seconds before it dimmed to lime green. Once the color changed, he connected the wire lead from the splicer into a cyberspace deck, safe from the rain inside his armored black case.

"Ok, lass. Here's the dangerous part. I'm goin' inside now. I'm gonna be like a corpse out here—"

"Yeah, I know. I'm not a total blonde. I've done this before."

"You're not blonde at all." He hesitated. "I hope white isn't a more extreme version."

He winked. With a flick of a thumb, the M3 wire clicked in behind his right ear and he sagged forward like a Samurai after committing seppuku. His arms fell limp at his sides, his black coat fanned out over the roof behind him. A dead man knelt upon sheets of rain, awash with dark crimson light glinting from each droplet beaded on his shoulders and sleeves.

Anna gazed into the swirling patterns of dancing rain, wondering why the wind fought so hard to keep the water from falling. A sudden flash of cold paralyzed her; the withdrawal had gone from hot that kept her almost comfortable out here into the chills phase. She sank into a squat and clutched at the umbrella handle. Diving into the North Sea in February would have felt warmer than she did at that moment. Each gust of wind rattled her teeth and chased feeling from her fingers and toes.

The gale threatened to tear the umbrella out of her grip. Not wanting to lose something she paid forty whole credits for, she collapsed it and let the rain hit her in the face. At this altitude, the droplets flew at her sideways, rendering the umbrella moot anyway. Within a few minutes, the sensation passed and the hot phase returned. Her clothes soaked to the skin almost became pleasant relief. She daydreamed about a nice warm autoshower tube.

Orange grumbled; his body twitched as if he had let out a one-second chuckle at something not quite humorous enough to warrant a full laugh. Anna glanced at him, wondering what he saw in cyberspace to elicit such a noise. Did something amuse him or did he fight for his life? Anna had worked with hackers before, and they sometimes spoke of their experiences on the other side. They worked in a virtual world as real as this one, only death meant an hour of misery rather than the end of one's life. She would never know what it was like. For her, cyberware remained an impossibility. Never mind how implanted cybernetics tended to deaden psionic abilities... she couldn't keep a NetMini for more than a week without frying it. Electronics *inside* her would be a disastrous idea.

She nibbled on her fingernails, finally taking a good look at the defenseless man Carroll paid her to protect. Not harsh upon the eyes, and not the sort of man who would have shown up at the club to watch her dance. He exuded high class, or at least higher-class than those idiots. She fantasized about having a man sweep her off her feet and save her from her wretched life, carrying her off into the sunset like the knight from the vids she used to watch. She leaned her head back until it hit the metal behind her with a *thud.*

Who am I kidding? They're called fairy tales for a reason.

Orange grunted again; this time, she felt sure the sheen on his forehead came from sweat, not rain. Curious, she peered at his surface thoughts. Flashes of hallway, white and black marble, passed amid a hail of chipped stone flakes flying from errant gunfire. He fought shadowy things that looked like men only alien, tall, and spindly. Anna recoiled and leaned back, letting the mental link drop. The last thing she needed was more fuel for zoom nightmares.

She shivered, clamping her arms tight about herself. Sometimes, zoom changed things on her. The hallucinations could return when the brain starved for a fix. Only, those hallucinations would be dark and threatening. While high, the drug made a user see things depending on their personality. If, for example, an innocent child got a hold of zoom, they'd probably see pixies and faeries and elves, smiling mushrooms, and happy things. Sometimes, Anna saw the faerie forest, but when despair set in, the visions changed. Her fantasy world vanished, in its place, demons and ghouls, goblins and devil faces. Everybody's Friend told her zoom brought out the user's inner personality. Every so often, a pixie would return, chased by an ogre with her father's face.

The bad trips.

She startled and looked up at a sharp pneumatic hiss. Rain threaded off her nose into a rivulet. Cold embraced her in every sense of the word. The *thudding* of heavy boots on the roof echoed from the other side of the giant electronics cabinet. Orange remained in the pose of a post-seppuku samurai. She stood and peered around the metal housing toward the approaching footsteps. At the edge of the roof, a little red umbrella peeked up for an instant and dipped out of sight.

Deep and foreboding, a man's voice echoed over the rain.

"Gotta be over 'ere."

"Yep. Got two on thermal."

Shit.

Anna forced her twitching muscles to still themselves. With a gulp, she balled her hands into fists and waited. Two men came around the corner. Glistening grey armor covered their entire bodies, a blue BT logo emblazoned upon the corner of their chest. Each had a rifle aimed forward in a one handed grip like huge pistols. One frowned at Orange, the other looked at Anna and his gaze softened.

Not constables, private security employed by BT. If they didn't simply shoot and dump them in the Thames, the company would likely stuff her and Orange in a holding facility somewhere in the building with no trial, detained at the whim of some executive. Illegal yes, but Old Bill couldn't care about things Old Bill didn't know.

"Looks like we got a snoop what brought his strung-out kid along," said the guard on the left.

Their size scared her witless for an instant, until she sensed the augmentation in them. Either probably had the strength to toss a car on its side one-handed. In an instant, mouse became cat. She stepped away from Orange, stepping toward them.

"You two best be on your way then, this doesn't concern you. No 'arm to BT, just borrowin' a backbone connect."

They exchanged a disbelieving glance. The one on the left chuckled while the other spoke.

"Who the hell do you think you are? Get on the ground, now."

"Really, I don't want to hurt you. Piss off then, and forget you saw us."

Grimacing from a muscle cramp in her left thigh, she tilted her head. His laugh stalled as something by the edge of the roof caught his attention. She glanced back but nothing appeared unusual.

"Look, hon, you're young, you're pretty, and you got no weapons. Don't give us an excuse to break that sweet little face."

Her hands shook. The trembles had her, and they wouldn't stop for some time yet. Adrenaline soaked into her dried-up brain. She'd slipped into a cold spot again, and her body wanted only to shiver. The headache created a barrier between her and her power. The security men moved closer. One raised his weapon at her. Anna tried to focus despite the feeling of a skull packed with cotton balls. She glanced at Orange, helpless. She felt stupid for even thinking she could do this.

"Not telling you again girl, get on your face."

Come on! Damn drugs...

The man on the right grabbed her by the collar, tightening a bundle of jacket against her neck. She cringed.

Calm down. She brought the sound of Penny begging the Crossmen to let her go into her mind. The memory of how it felt to surge with power crept in behind it. Anna raised her arms as if to surrender. Her body shuddered, but she let herself go.

With a *crack* like a gunshot, a narrow spark leapt from the tip of the obelisk and struck her in the back. The guard holding her jumped away, howling and shaking his hand. The beautiful amber filigree of subdermal wiring traced over their bodies, outlining all their implants. She reached for the transmitter array, clawing through the air at the two men. She grasped the power, pulling it out of the machinery and willing it into the world. A web of lightning arced from the corners of the metal box, scoring burns across their armor and knocking them flat to the ground. They skidded back several meters into the wall of the elevator enclosure.

She tugged her coat back into place and made a 'come here' motion at their weapons. The power cell for their rifles' firing circuits dissipated in a tiny crawling shimmer of blue along the wet roof. Their guns went dark, the absence of glowing LEDs revealing their uselessness. Anna glanced at Orange, wishing he would hurry up and be done with whatever he did in the GlobeNet. He still knelt in silent meditation, a techno-Buddhist lost in a world imagined by machines.

Anna swayed against the vibrating chamber of fiberoptics. Her touch sent little arcs creeping in two directions along the frame, while a one-handed grip kept her from falling. Her hands shook, her legs twitched, and the roof wavered back and forth in her vision. Bile leaked past her lips, trailing to join the water she stood in. Hot and cold came one after the other, so fast they blended into an entirely new level of awfulness.

A moan emanated from one of the security men as he sat up. With an exasperated grunt, Anna latched her mind onto the power lines in the elevator and created a blooming orb of lightning six meters around that swelled out from the wall behind them. Both men convulsed for several seconds before she released the power. The guards fell flat, moaning, steam rising from their armor. She didn't have anywhere near the level of anger she'd experienced in the alley with Penny in danger. In the midst of withdrawal, her body could only handle so much power. Anna swooned to her knees, sparks dancing out from where her hands touched wet metal. Pain like a dagger in her skull set her heaving. She would have thrown up again if not for having an empty stomach.

"What the hell...?"

Orange had returned.

Anna looked up, twitching from a mess of sparks lapping at her body. He stared with both eyebrows lifted; his eyes brightened to almost yellow. The man's monk-like calm gave way long enough for a 'please don't kill me' smile.

"Well fuck me, you really are a psio. Nasty one too. Carroll wasn't dicking around this time."

"I'm rather cack-handing it at the moment. Little rusty."

He slammed the panel closed like a mechanic having finished his work. She forced herself up and zombie-walked over to him, no longer having the energy or desire to hide how bad a state she was in.

Orange caught her fall and pulled her into a platonic embrace. "Easy Pixie, guess that took a lot out of you."

He doesn't know I'm a drugged out wreck. "Yeah..."

"No worries lass. I'm good with secrets."

"Thanks."

Associating with people who operated outside the law provided some comfort. He would be disinclined to approach the government to report an unregistered because they would ask him questions he didn't want to answer. Anna did her best to walk as he pulled her along to the edge of the roof. The sound of the rain upon the tiny lake they stood in gave way to the spectral keening of razor wire being cut and peeled. Doing it one handed slowed him down. The moaning security men stirred. Anna glanced over at them.

"Sorry I'm spent so fast. Not quite the protection you asked for." She trembled. "I've 'ad a rough patch, an' I'm tryin' ta find me legs."

"No harm, girl. I needed protection when I was online, not so much now."

Time blinked out of existence for her until she something tightened around her wrists, binding them together.

Plastic zip ties.

"Ow, what the hell are you doing? I thought…"

"Trust me… You're in no condition to hold on to anything but the floor."

He turned his back on her, pulling her arms over his head like a living cape. Scrapes of plastic armor on metal signaled the security men dragging themselves upright. Orange stepped off the roof. Anna clung as tight as she could, which wasn't all that tight, and breathed into the thick bundle of wool at the base of his neck.

Every bit of wind in her chest burst out as their fall slammed into a sudden deceleration. Gasping for air, she ignored the pain in her arms and looked up at a one by three foot rectangle connected to Orange's shoulders by hair-thin cables, ashen grey against the near black of the sky. The edges rimmed with yellow light from the glow of micro ion emitters. While the collapsible foil lacked the lift necessary to keep them in flight, the thrusters provided enough power to increase the effect of the tiny airfoil to that of a large parachute.

Her head to the side, Anna recoiled from the sweeping line of a laser sight—the security men searching for them in the dark. Orange chased the updrafts between buildings on Long Acre, heading southwest to a gentle landing in the middle of Leicester Gardens. The parafoil split in half, each piece folding into itself twice more before vanishing into compartments in the upper portion of cybernetic shoulders.

"You're just full of surprises, Mr. Orange."

The binding came apart with the flick of a small knife; she slid down his back and hit the grass like a sack of wheat. Sprawled in the wet, she propped herself up, bracing her fingers in the cold green behind her. A silly smile happened despite her body refusing to stop twitching.

"You're in rougher shape than I thought, girl." He shook his head, clucking his tongue. "On the rattle, eh? Well… Good luck to you. Can't imagine what your lot goes through."

She would have shrugged, but didn't want to fall over backward.

Orange crouched, pulling her upright. "Look here, Pixie, is it? There's a man over at Oxford... Doctor Mardling if I recall properly. I've seen some stuff in the net about him. He helps people like you, and he doesn't much like the government. Rather hates their treatment of psionics."

"M-Mardling?" she asked, before losing control to a seizure.

Orange's voice swirled into the oblivion of her unconsciousness, muttering something about not wanting to leave her out there. He sighed as she collapsed in the grass, unable to stand on her own. Arms tightened around her, followed by a sense of being lifted.

She didn't care at all about being helpless in his arms. Anything he did to her would be better than how she felt.

A MOMENT OF WEAKNESS

Blurry pea green haze filled the entirety of Anna's vision, indistinct in distance or composition. Weightless, she drifted in time detached from the world. Dull aches teased at her muscles and every breath sliding in and out rushed like a gale in her skull. A faint breeze tickled and plucked at individual hairs.

Her reality sharpened to the drab confines of a motel room that explored every imaginable shade of vomit green. Anna moaned, waiting for the fire in her lungs to stop. Eventually, she raised her left hand to her forehead and rubbed it, forcing her fingers into her hair in an effort to dislodge the anvil compressing her brain. A line of bruise wrapped around each wrist; the sight dragged the parachute landing back from the depths of her memory.

Something stuck to her arm brushed her nose. *Feck.* Anna froze. Lifting it up from her face, she stared at the zoomer adhered to the tender skin. Rage and despair became screaming and tears. She couldn't remember how it got there, but she also couldn't find most of yesterday in the dark halls of her mind. Furious at herself, she rammed a fist into the bed at her side.

"Damn!" *All that hell for nothing. Right back into the shit.* "Why?"

Anna curled on her side, gazing along a trail of clothes between the bed and the autoshower. She stared at the derm, picking at the edge with her nails. She wanted to pull it off, but something inside her couldn't do it.

Sobbing, she berated herself for buying the zoom. She knew how bad the quitting would be, especially cold turkey, and had chickened out before she chickened out. All those stories of blackouts, crazed fits, had to be true. Her body demanded zoom and took over to get it. Anna wailed and clawed at the derm, scratching red lines in her ashen skin. The little beige square might as well have been an impenetrable manacle chaining her to Coventry.

"No, no, no."

Anna curled up, arm clutched against her forehead, and bawled, cursing herself and her life. Moments later, she opened her eyes. Spawny's jacket, draped over a little chair tucked up to a table near the bed, shimmered into focus. Two more zoomers waited in the pocket. If she put them both on at once and slammed them, good chance her problems would come to a permanent end. Anna pushed herself up, sitting at the edge of the bed in a fog.

Surges of driving rain hammered the window. Anna shivered, staring at her protruding ribs, her thin bony legs and prominent hips. Credits that should have gone to food had bought more chemical chains so she could tie herself to this misery. She didn't want to go back to the club, or be a plaything for the police, or continue to wallow at the edge of a society that didn't want her. Her own father had been ready to kill her. Maybe she should be dead.

Father knows best, right?

She wobbled to her feet and approached the jacket, peering into the gaping darkness of the pocket. Naked in a cheap motel, high, and with red marks on her wrists, the shame of what the sight would imply sent her to her knees. Anna collapsed on her knees and rummaged at the coat until she found the sheet. Thin white plasfilm gleamed in the grey light from the window; the beige bits of rubber beckoned with the offer of bliss or permanent release.

Anna lost track of time, staring at the drugs while pondering her life. She had agreed to go back to the art class later that afternoon. The thought of the two dozen sketches of 'Innocent Anna' there sent warm streaks down her face and balled her hands into fists. She imagined the angelic versions of her moving, turning to look at her and laughing, pointing, mocking the whore with no willpower.

They're all lying to me.

She punched the back of the chair, knocking it into the desk, dropped the sheet of derms, and fell on her side on scratchy, worn green carpet with her face buried in her hands. Something bounced away from her thigh and hit the floor.

A small black plastic ingot sat amid the green haze. It sprouted tiny arms and tried to drag itself to her, grunting. Anna chased the hallucination away and blinked at a device the size of her thumb, flat and rectangular. As thick as a coffee stirrer, it had one button on its otherwise featureless surface. Curious, she picked it up and squeezed. The device projected a holographic light panel. Within, the face of a man hung above a monochromatic green background. He looked in his thirties with shoulder-length brown hair and a precisely sculpted goatee and mustache. His distinguished, almost prominent, nose gave him an air of sophistication. The man lifted his right eyebrow a touch as if to say he'd discovered the secret of enlightenment. He smiled as the image rotated a quarter turn; text filled in to his right.

Anna, apologies for leaving you alone last night but I am bound to certain deadlines by certain individuals that despise tardiness. Don't worry about the room. I've taken care of the fee. This is the man I mentioned regarding your problem. Doctor James Mardling, of Oxford. He might be able to help you with your issue.

Cheers,

Mr. Orange.

Anna blinked. She was high, but the feeling of the holographic man smiling *at her* seemed more real than part of a looping animation or hallucination. She traced her fingers over the image as if petting the hair of a doll.

Can this bloke do a bloody thing for a worthless wretch?

A man's voice out in the hallway said something too far away to understand. Shadows moved in the light leaking underneath the door. She gasped, and tried to cover herself as if being watched while curled up naked on the floor of a seedy hotel room. Anna glared at the door and pleaded with every higher power she could think of the person outside didn't walk in.

The voice from the hall yelled, "Blimey, get away. For the last time, I don't want a bloody umbrella, damn nuisances."

Those bots are relentless. She relaxed.

Anna fussed over the crinkled derm sheet to make sure the doses were intact. Faye and Penny's faces came to mind, heaping on yet more shame for considering checking out. She wrapped her arms around herself, crying, picturing Penny's reaction to learning she had committed suicide. After, her brain forced her to experience a hallucination of walking in to find Faye dead and blue on her bed, her arms covered in derms.

Somehow, the younger girl had come to represent Anna's destroyed childhood. She'd known her for a week, but it felt like she'd stepped in as a temporary mum. Faye still had a chance. She couldn't let the same things happen to her. Her parents hadn't tried to hurt her; they merely failed to listen to her.

She picked at the small black device. The presence in her hand reminded her Mr. Carroll still owed her a great deal of money. Well, chump change to him, but a fortune to her. She stuffed the derm sheet and the holo recording into the jacket and clutched her stomach. With the credits she had earned, her little 'family' would eat well for a few weeks. She used the chair to pull herself standing, holding onto it to stop the spinning room.

The thought of admitting to Penny she had caved and dosed up crushed her. She dreaded the stares of the art students again; she had betrayed the charcoal angels. Could she lie to Penny, try to go cold turkey again and stay the hell home? *No. I'd have to tell her. I... can't do this alone. I'll black out again.*

Glancing at the clock, she stumbled over to the shower tube. Her body refused to let her mind rid itself of zoom. Anna brushed at the derm patch. Anger came out of nowhere. With a snarl, she tore it loose and hurled it into the corner. The pain made her stumble into the wall; a droplet of bright crimson glistened against the white of her arm where the chems had weakened her skin. She couldn't free herself without help. Perhaps she would go see this Mardling fellow.

She wouldn't let the zoom win.

A BOFFIN IN TWEED

Free of withdrawal, Anna seemed at rights when she had met Mr. Carroll at the chippery. He paid her as promised and hinted he might have more work coming up. With all her faculties about her, lies came easy. She left him thinking all was well and she looked forward to another job. He would give her a ring when the time came.

As fate would have it, the art class took place on the other end of the same campus where Mardling worked. Having spent the night in the city proper, she didn't need to cross the police line and went directly to the university on the London Orbital maglev. Petrified of running into more Crossmen as if they would somehow recognize her, she kept her head down, scurried across the platform, and hopped a shuttle to the campus.

Surrounded by people a year or three her junior, she felt uncomfortable even breathing the same air as the Propers. Most of the people around her appeared to be students with promising lives ahead of them, and she was dirty trash.

No! shouted the voice in her thoughts. She might be trash, but she wouldn't be *dirty* trash any more. Her dignity lay in a tatter, but what little of it she found, she would cling to. An evil little smile curled onto her lips as she daydreamed about electrocuting Constable Brown if he tried to take his tax again. The smile faded. In all probability, she would cave in and let him do it. Killing a policeman would bring far too much heat down on her, and probably the rest of Coventry, but it offered a comforting daydream on the ride. Anna narrowed her eyes. Perhaps she could find the right amount of lightning to make it look like a heart attack.

🐿 🌾 🛡 ⚗ 🏺

PALE YELLOW WALLS SURROUNDED THE TINIEST WAITING ROOM SHE HAD ever seen. Old fake leather chairs lined up against three walls, crowding around a little table full of e-magazines like herd animals looking for water. A lilting metal desk in one corner held an overweight middle-aged woman more interested in what lived under her fingernails than anything going on in the world beyond.

Anna stood at the edge of the desk, glancing at thirty years of collected kitsch from various vacations and office supply vendors, as well as award for long-term service.

Didn't know they gave office trophies for nail maintenance.

The file stopped sliding back and forth as the woman looked up with an angry glare. Anna glanced to the right.

"What's that?" asked the woman.

"I didn't say anything."

The old woman squinted at her. Anna's lips hadn't moved, but perhaps her frustration had let something leak on a strand of telepathy. She flicked her gaze back to the turquoise claws, striated with white and blue. Like a master violinist, the receptionist scratched the file back and forth.

"Is Doctor Mardling in?"

"You're touring the campus prior to applying?," asked the woman without looking up. "You look a bit young."

"No. I'm here..." She squeezed the little box again, looking at the text to the right of the apparitional head. "About his Horizons project... I wanted to talk to him about volunteering."

"The Doctor isn't seein' anyone today 'bout that. 'E's quite busy with his class schedule."

Anna's gaze hit the floor with a thud she almost heard. She stood there, silent as furniture, trying not to let her disappointment leak out of her eyes. A few minutes later, the nail file came to a halt again, but the sour woman didn't look up.

"You still 'ere?"

Anna hooked her thumbs in her pants pockets, slouching. A wisp of cool air caressed her waist.

The woman suppressed a snarl and shot her a glare. She opened her mouth to speak, but paused. "'Old on a minute. Wot's that?"

The woman leaned forward, using the nail file to point at the two blue spots where the tattooed pixie's antennae protruded over Anna's belt line.

"A tattoo."

The old woman frowned with a protruding lower lip. "What of?"

Anna pushed her pants down over her hip far enough to show the tattoo without revealing anything too rude.

"Cute." The file resumed sawing at her nails. "That one of them faeries or what have you?"

"Yeah… It's a pixie. It's kind of my nickname."

The fiddle came to an abrupt stop. "'Ave a seat, luv." After twirling the file over her fingers, she poked it into a holographic button. The presence of an open audio channel made the room feel larger. "Doctor Jim. I think that faerie, pixie, whatever you were talking about's 'ere. Shall I send 'er in?"

Something heavy hit the ground in the back room, Anna startled at the impact in the floor. Blinds parted at the behest of two fingers, revealing a pair of brown eyes. A woozy feeling spread over her mind for a few seconds before the blinds snapped closed. Footsteps echoed over the intercom, followed by a loud shuffle of junk on a desk.

"Send her in straight away," said a man, his voice laced with highbrow education.

Following the pointing file, Anna stepped past a self-opening grey door into an office not much larger than the pitiful waiting area. The man on the other side of the desk spiraled about the space in an attempt to collect the contents of a dropped box. Pants the color of over-creamed coffee matched the tweed blazer draped over the back of a steel chair painted hospital green. His hair looked more disheveled than the portrait let on, as if he had been up all night. Two walls held large clear boards aglow with squiggles of blue and green writing, sketches of brains, and more math than she had ever seen in her life.

At the *whoosh* of the closing door, he whirled to face her, smiling over an armload of datapads. His shirt hung open two buttons and he wore the anticipatory grin of someone going *to* a job interview rather than giving one.

He extended a hand, leaning to the side to retain his bundle. "Hello there. I'm Doctor Mardling."

She returned a pleasant handshake and sat in a battered brown excuse for a chair on wheels. He tromped to the side of the room, dropping the mass of electronics into a box all at once. The order with which he kept them seemed to fit his general disheveled state. Anna stifled a giggle, having expected some sort of pompous ass from the look on the face of his hologram.

"I'm Anna."

He fell into his seat, sending the belabored squeak of decades-old rusty springs into the air. Mardling put his feet up on the desk, reconsidered, lowered them, and rubbed his chin. His delighted expression made her think he'd found the one nugget of gold in an entire mine. Pulsing strangeness swam around in her head. She couldn't tell if it came from zoom or lack of sleep.

"Are you all right, guv'na? You seem a bit edgy."

"It's a pleasure you meet you, Anna." He at last settled upon leaning back in the chair with feet down and hands tapping the desk. "Blinds… Lights…"

The window blinds rotated closed and the lights dimmed almost all the way off, leaving the room dark except for the blue-green glow of the drawing boards.

Anna crossed her arms in her lap and slouched. "So what's this all about then?"

"It's about basic human rights. You are here because of the Horizons project, correct? About a certain sort of individual the Crown isn't too fond of?"

One finger picked idly at his cheek. His lips twitched as if he wanted to grin, but was too nervous. She swallowed hard. Saying the wrong thing to the wrong person could create a whirlwind of shit in short order.

"I suppose. You're not with them?"

"Certainly not." Insecurity faded to perfect confidence. "You seem a bit of a mess, luv."

Shame reddened her cheeks. Doctor Mardling's expression changed in reaction to the images of self-degradation in her thoughts. Anna fidgeted, unable to look at him anymore, afraid he would see a dirty drugged-out whore and not the charcoal-sketched seraph she longed to be.

"I…" Her hand covered the red mark on her left arm, kneading at it. "I'm…"

The cumbersome metal beast of a chair creaked as he sprang to his feet. He ducked around the desk, sat on the corner, and took her cheek in his hand.

"My dear, you are greater than you could ever have imagined. You need to stop abusing yourself."

Eyes blurred with tears, she turned away as he touched the red spot on her wrist. The drug had a few hours of effect left in it, not enough for a high, but enough to keep away the need for more. The sense of his fingers on the tender spot embarrassed her worse than if he had ripped her clothes off.

He knows I'm a piece of shit.

"You are not a piece of shit, Anna." His hand cupped her chin, forcing her to look at him. "Those grotty bastards do not possess even the slightest inkling of what you are. No, girl, you are capable of great and wondrous things. Your dignity is in there... somewhere." He patted her atop the head. "I would love to help you find it."

She gave him an incredulous look. "Sorry, guv'na, but..."

Dr. Mardling smiled. His voice entered her mind. *All things are not as they appear to be.*

"You..." Anna swallowed, unable to breathe at the realization she'd met another psionic. Of course, she knew others existed, but she'd never met one before who wasn't either running, on the leash, or dead. Overwhelmed, she flung herself onto him, clinging to his shirt. "You're psionic?"

He gathered her hands from his shoulders and eased her into her seat "It would do well to keep it down, my dear." He rushed to the window and looked out. "The fools think I'm some boffin in tweed."

Anna giggled.

"Let me have a look at you then." Dr. Mardling leaned on the near side of his desk, staring dizziness into her mind. Over the next few minutes, rushes of hot, cold, floating, and shivering with abject terror cycled. He stopped when her trembling broke eye contact. "Easy, luv."

"What did you do?" She clamped her arms over her chest in an effort to stop shaking.

"Electrokinesis is a very rare gift. Not many can exert control over electricity. I see a little Telepathy as well, but I suspect you do not avail yourself of it much."

"No, sir. I've been too scared of the CSB. Haven't done much of anything for a while."

"Hmm." Mardling rubbed his goatee, eyes hardening. "Those blighters are a bit of a nuisance, are they not? Granted, they are much tougher when they are detaining children. The dimwits can scarcely contend with ordinary psionics. They have no idea about us."

"Ordinary psionics?" Anna blinked. "That's a bit of a contradiction, innit?"

"I will explain more as we go." He grabbed his coat and rushed to the door. "Come on then. Let us get you scrubbed up."

Anna forced herself standing, too ashamed to make eye contact. "Yes, sir."

DETOX

S hame sent her to a small campus market for cosmetics to hide the red square on her forearm. Doctor Mardling was kind enough to wait while she sat for the art class. She forced herself to remain still, perched on a pedestal naked in as close to the same pose as she had used the preceding session. Dr. Mardling hovered at the door, chatting with Professor Gresham for the most part. Every so often, he'd send a reassuring telepathic whisper into her head.

Her old friend the stuffed owl sat above the door, though she'd found a new sight to focus on: tiny wrinkles formed around Mardling's eyes as he smiled at the art instructor, the two men joking as if old classmates. He seemed unassuming, unthreatening, one of the kindest men she had ever laid eyes on.

Mardling laughed at something Gresham said, loud enough to turn the heads of several nearby students. Anna couldn't help herself but grin at his hands-in-pockets posture and whimsical affect. The sense of having someone there to 'hold her hand' made the arduous two hours tolerable.

While the students shuffled off to use the bathroom and peruse snacks on a twenty-minute break, she hid behind the changing partition in the back, bundled in the white sheet. It would be a waste of effort to dress, but she couldn't bring herself to sit out in the open. Dr. Mardling knocked on the barricade after a few minutes of quiet isolation.

"Brought you some coffee, Anna." His hand came around the edge with a cup.

She took it in both hands to her chest, siphoning the warmth past the thin sheet. "Thank you, Doctor."

She had about two sips left when the sound of students returning filled the room.

"We are ready for you, hon," whispered Gresham.

Anna cringed, embarrassment mixed with the first physical signs of her need for more zoom: dull threads of pain up and down her bones. *This is art, right? High class.* She held her head up and strode back to her perch.

THE PERIOD OVER, SHE DRESSED BEHIND THE PARTITION AND SAT FOR A MINUTE hugging her clothing to her skin. When the din of departing students faded to nothing, she skulked out into the room. The spot on her arm burned a sense of unworthiness into her as she moved among the easels, refusing to look at them. Mardling's hand caught her arm, and she startled up to see his smile.

"You should see how they came out."

Anna pulled at him, trying to leave, but he held her firm.

"You need to see them."

He walked her around from one to the next, making sure she studied them all. Twenty-four versions of her, innocent and pure, stared off at the undrawn owl, in contemplation of some mysterious question. How many hundreds of men had seen her naked at the club, yet none of them saw this.

"Perception is in the mind of the observer." He squeezed her shoulder.

She glanced up into his eager-schoolboy face, still perplexed at why he had been so excited about meeting her.

"You *are* a beautiful woman," he whispered. "The only person here who sees you as a tramp is you."

She shuddered, thumb rubbing against the sore spot. "I don't want to be trash anymore. I've tried to quit, but I keep running back to it."

"Shrugging off that leash takes a lot of work. Fortunately, you have keenly piqued my interest and I shall help you." He glanced at his NetMini for the time. "Come along then, we can get to the nitty-gritty of the research after a quick stopover at the clinic."

"Clinic?"

"Yes, you see… When you introduce substances like that into your body, certain physiological changes take place in the brain to cope with it. Over time, these changes create dependency, which triggers both the craving for the substance as well as the withdrawal symptoms that come on when the chemical is absent. The good lads at the clinic use nanobots to make minor adjustments in regions of the brain… the subthalamic nucleus, dorsal striatum, and sometimes the medial prefrontal cortex. Most especially the nucleus accumbens septi… that is where the incredibly addictive drugs do the most damage."

Anna stared at him without saying a word for a full fifteen seconds, and blinked. "Well, you certainly sound like a doctor."

"Geneticist mostly; however, as of late, I have chiefly studied the brain." He helped her turn a corner and guided her down some steps to the outside.

She forced a plaintive smile. "Umm, right… about that… I'm not so sure I want some tosser rooting around my noggin."

"Rubbish. It is all done with nanobots. You will not feel pain."

DRAB GREY, THE WAITING SECTION OF THE CLINIC EMBODIED THE SAME SORT of lifeless pervading Anna's being. Ten hours after waking up in a motel room, the lack of zoom had changed her head into a mass of iron slag wrapped in cotton. Her brain screamed at her for making it suffer painful withdrawal, then the tease of a dose, and now nothing. She imagined tiny little brains sitting in a nest, mouths agape and chirping like chicks waiting for worms. The thought was so patently ridiculous she burst out laughing in a silent room. When the humor left her, she leaned her head back against the hard metal wall.

Next time I hit I'm gonna see those things.

Doctor Mardling glanced at her from the counter a few meters away, lifting an eyebrow at the sudden outburst. His eyebrows jammed together, a face she thought he would have made at the sight of tiny cheeping brains. With a shake of his head, he returned his attention to the clerk.

"Zoom. Yes, the narcotic," said Mardling, his voice dripping with sarcasm. "Surely, you *have* heard of it working here? Synthetic psychedelic with opioid enhancements… you do have a programme for something like that, do you not?"

"Is she your wife?" asked the clerk in a bored monotone.

"No."

"Daughter?"

"Hardly. Do I look that old?"

"Yeah, you do. Sister?"

"Oh for Pete's sake, are you going to play silly buggers all day or get on with it? She is my student." He flashed an ID from the college.

"Beggin' your pardon mate, but regs won't let us process her on your register unless she's a blood relative or spouse."

"Do it on hers then, I shall cover the cost." Mardling waved her over.

"Give 'er a swipe." The clerk pushed a small box across the counter.

"I don't have a 'mini." Anna offered a hesitant smile at the Doctor. "It's a long story."

The clerk grumbled; the irritation of having to do something more than gather dust showed quite evident on his face.

Doctor Mardling waved his hand about while speaking to the ceiling. "Oh, sorry about distracting you from slummocking about. They do pay you to do more than warm a chair, do they not?"

The pudgy man in white scowled, his anger focusing almost all on her. "Name."

"Anna Morgan."

"PID?"

"Don't 'ave one."

He sighed, shutting his eyes to search for calm. The protracted 'Ohmmmm' from Mardling made his face redden.

"National or private?"

She fumbled around in her purse and showed her public assistance card.

"Oh, bother that." He smirked at it. "She's on the dole. Gotta put 'er on a list and wait for the approval to come down. UHS, mate. Might 'ave her in the door in six months if she's lucky. That is, of course, assuming she's got a job lined up and a place to stay. If she's a Cov, they're going to deny it."

"Your faculties at cognitive processing have rotten to uselessness," said Dr. Mardling. "Did you not hear me say I am going to pay for her car?"

The clerk reached for his handheld, ready to dismiss them both. "Can't 'elp it mate. Regs. Counts as income. She's on the dole, so it's gotta go through the works."

Anna pouted, sliding her badge of disgrace back into the purse. The man seemed pleased he finally had a reason to ignore them.

"Look here, you insufferable twat." Dr. James Mardling stared into the attendant's soul. "You are going to put her in the programme right this instant."

Undulations rippled the clerk's paunchy cheeks. Already pasty, they whitened to a shade as pure as Anna's hair. Sweat exuded from his face as if in time lapse, forming into visible droplets at the tip of his rat's nose.

Doctor Mardling leaned close over the counter, his words falling to a half whisper. "Right. This. Instant."

Anna didn't know how to feel. No one had ever stood up for her before; she had never felt protected at all. Even her own father barely tolerated her sharing the roof with him. Shaking, the clerk waffled his hands at the holographic displays, pushing bits of light around. After several taps, he nodded and spoke in a voice so hollow it sounded like an android.

"It's done guv'na. Ten minutes, tops."

Smiling, James took her elbow and led her back to the waiting bench. "It's all a matter of knowing how to ask nicely."

Anna stared up at him, trying to sort out what had happened from how she felt about it. Seeing proof of his psionic abilities chased the last of her doubts out into the street.

Within six minutes, an older woman in a white coat emerged from the back. Silver hair streaked with black hung to her belt in a single ponytail and she wore a perturbed face as if she'd been distracted from something fun.

"Hello. I'm Doctor Heath. I'm afraid there's been a bit of a misunderstanding. The schedule was empty for today and there's no UHS file for your... um—"

"Student." Mardling stood, offering a pleasant smile that faded away into a flat line before the 't' finished peeling from his tongue. He whispered, "Sorry for making you wait."

Emotion fled from the older woman's face, replaced by placid calm. "Sorry for making you wait."

Doctor Mardling gestured at the door, still whispering, "Right this way and we'll get her set to rights."

The woman mirrored his smile, waving her arm in the same manner. "Right this way then. We'll get her set to rights."

The clerk glanced up with disbelief at Dr. Heath's sudden change in demeanor. He raised his eyebrows at Mardling, as if to apologize for misunderstanding his influence. Anna stared at the floor as they followed the MD into the back. A hallway later, she entered a small procedure room with a tiny desk, chair, and a large transparent cylinder perched between two metal platforms, one on the floor and one built into the ceiling. Various lights ringed both. The one on the ground had vents and slats while all manner of tubes dangled from the upper one.

"All right, miss. You can leave your clothes on the chair there. Step into the tube whenever you're ready and we'll begin."

"Must I?"

"Afraid so dear. Medical nanobots will destroy anything that isn't biological matter or metal."

"I'll be right outside." Mardling smiled at Anna, then tugged the medic around to stare at her. "You will do all you can to remove her addiction. When you are finished, you will not think one whit about her."

Doctor Heath blinked off the zombie-like stare a few seconds after James moved away to the hall. Anna disrobed and stepped up onto the lower platform, gasping at the freezing steel. The silver-haired woman pulled a facemask down from above and held it up to her face.

"Since we aren't working on your lungs today, we'll use the green stuff." Doctor Heath attempted to sound reassuring. "This gel is not breathable. It's much less frightening when you don't need to inhale liquid. Think of it like taking a nice warm bath, only standing up. Try to relax. You'll need this mask. Don't try to take in the gel. You'll be under for about forty-five minutes. Do you have any questions?"

Anna grasped the apparatus with trembling fingers, finding it odd to be eye level with the tall woman for a few seconds before her dazed brain remembered the raised platform.

"Will it 'urt? Will I feel anything?"

"Nothing but warm liquid, hon. All the work's going on in your brain, and its small things... you have nothing to worry about. You'll feel weightless. Relax; sleep if you care to."

"Why don't the nanobots eat this?" Anna tapped the breather.

Doctor Heath gave her a patronizing smile. "Well, sweetie... It's made from a specific type of plastic that the little robots ignore. They're so small they don't have a lot of room for program instructions on what not to dismantle. The medical processes are more important than a laundry list of 'do not destroy.' Plus, trauma wounds often have fragments of clothing embedded in them. We need the nanobots to clean that out."

"Oh."

She flicked her thumbnail over the black plastic breathing tube. She had tried to break the chains of zoom on her own and it didn't work. Being stuck in a tank didn't thrill her, but winding up dead in an alley wasn't any better. With a nod, she set the notch in the hose behind her teeth and pulled the straps around her head. Doctor Heath checked them, pulling them a little tighter than Anna cared for.

A clear plastic cylinder rose from the pedestal, rotating to seal against the roof. Soon, viscous green fluid burbled up out of the floor. The pleasant warmth of it slid up and over her body, filling the tube. As the fluid level passed her breasts, her weight left her feet and she hung amid the slime, neither floating nor sinking, eventually adjusting to the sense of breathing with a hose. Faint tingling filled her ears and nose. She wondered if it came from millions of tiny robots crawling inside her.

Through a lime-hued lens, she gazed upon the shadow of Doctor Mardling's hair in the window. He stood with his back to the room, right there if she needed him. She wondered what effect this chance meeting would have on the rest of her life.

A sound like a distant balloon losing air swept over her skull; faint, it cried out at the bare edge of noticing. *Little blighters are loud.* Doctor Heath worked a few feet away, sideways to the tank, fingers dancing around holographic images of Anna's head. She found it disconcerting to look at her own brain, even a digital representation thereof.

She averted her gaze and focused on the shadow in the doorway. The little thing in the back of her mind was ripe for a tantrum. Free of its zoom cage, it would lash out if her emotions became too strong in any direction. With machines inside her brain, she did *not* want electrical mayhem tearing the room apart.

A wave of nausea came over her; she scratched at the glass and clutched at her face. Doctor Heath's grandmotherly voice echoed in the substance.

"Hon, if you need to vomit, there's a squeezy on the side of the mask. Pinch it and you can pull it loose for a moment."

She did so without thinking, pressing the button and blowing chunder into the green. When the convulsions ceased, she fumbled the mask back into her mouth and tried not to think about the flavor. The cloud of hours-old food expanded in front of her, disintegrating over the course of several seconds until nothing remained. Millions of tiny robots attacked the contamination like piranha too small to see.

Threads of numbness ran down her arms and legs, followed by a feeling of bugs crawling on her. Hot chased cold around her body and she fell sick again. The room twisted and spun into a sense of vertigo as if she fell. She curled into a ball, waiting for all the strange feelings to go away.

An eternity later, the chaos subsided. She looked up at the sound of metal tapping on plastic.

Doctor Heath knocked at the tube with a light pen. "Put your feet down, miss."

Once she straightened out, the older woman swiped at the holographic terminal and the fluid drained. The tube filled with a thick sucking sound, her weight settled into her legs, and she braced a hand against the tank wall to steady herself. The doctor approached, holding a white towel, and hit a button to open the barrier. As soon as the sinking tube became low enough to step over, Anna tried to leave the chamber, but her foot shot out from under her. Doctor Heath, evidently used to dealing with clumsy slime-coated patients, caught her in the towel and held on until she found her balance. After a wipe-down, Anna dressed, then sat on the exam table and endured routine poking and prodding.

James walked up to stand beside her while Dr. Heath held a sensor with a bright light to her eye. "How did it go?"

"I've 'ad worse. Am I cured?"

Doctor Heath cleared her throat. "Well, Miss Morgan, the long term use of the synthetic hallucinogenic opiate known as 'zoom' causes a strong addiction reaction in most. I can tell by the condition of your brain tissue you've been using it for quite some time. If I were a betting sort, I'd wager you had developed somewhat of a tolerance and could suppress the hallucinations during all but the initial onset."

She nodded and stared down, no longer able to look the doctor in the eye.

"Well, with such a deep addiction, there is only so much we can do on a physical level. You'll need to stay well away from that junk for the psychological cravings to go away. You will suffer some physical symptoms over the next few days, but it'll be about a tenth of what would have happened without this procedure."

Mardling nodded at the doctor. "Nothing to fret about there. I've got a spare bed at my flat."

She got up, pulling her little jacket on. "Doctor Mardling, I couldn't impose… Besides I don't want my friends to be worried."

"I can send them a message for you. Anna. You need your rest. One moment then, luv. I shall follow you in a moment."

She walked into the hall, glancing over her shoulder long enough to see him locked upon Doctor Heath's vacant stare. The woman offered a mute nod and whispered, too soft for her to pick up from the hall. James turned with a smile, leaving the doctor standing there with an expression as though she didn't remember her own name.

"Is she all right?"

"Yes, yes… Perfectly peachy. In a few minutes, she will be right as rain." Taking her arm, he fell in step alongside her, muttering. "And will not remember ever having seen you."

The doors of his gold Mercedes opened as they approached. Anna fell into a passenger seat that shifted to fit her size, weight, and posture. She glanced at him, sighing in her mind, unsure how to process someone other than Penny being concerned for her. Beyond simple concern, a Proper *standing up* for her left her speechless.

"Shall we go to my flat then?" He flashed a placid smile.

Anna stared at her lap, picking at the thigh pocket. "Perhaps in a few days… I don't want to leave Twee alone there."

He looked at her for a long moment, an instant of exasperation flashed over his face before a placid smile overtook it. "You see yourself in that one, don't you? You want to protect her, spare her the same life."

"Well it's a bit less complicated for her. She's not got the curse."

"Psionics are not a curse, my dear Anna. If I am able to do anything for you, I shall hope I can convince you of that." He pulled out of the lot, dodging a flash of plastisteel and red that shot past the windscreen. "Damn bloody advert bots are everywhere."

"Indeed." Anna rubbed her face; sobriety felt alien. "Doctor, I want to make sure she gets home before she winds up stuck in Coventry. She's had a rough bit. I, umm… Maybe that nonce next door needs to have a fatal accident?"

Oh blimey! I didn't just say that…

"A little indelicate I think." He picked at the control sticks. "That could attract undue attention to people with your special skill set. I would rather you didn't. See after the girl then if it makes you happy."

The automatic drive had no programmed destinations for The Ruin; he took manual control and navigated the streets of London toward the police barricade. Soon, the black smear of Coventry Tower loomed high in the endless grey sky, a spire of dread amid the rolling gloom.

As the car came to a halt at the checkpoint, Dr. Mardling fiddled with his NetMini.

"Right, mate. What's your business here?" asked a constable.

Dr. Mardling regarded the man with a disdainful smirk. "I'm doing research for the university. Nothing out of the ordinary 'ere."

"Right, mistah. Nothing out of the ordinary. Carry on." The constable nodded and waved him by.

Mardling looked ahead, resting his hand upon Anna's folded in her lap. "I am worried about you. This place holds so much temptation. I want to help you defeat this addiction. You need a stable and safe environment."

She squeezed his hand. "I know, Doctor. But so does Faye. Let me sort 'er out, and I'll take ya up on that offer."

FRIENDS

Penny portioned breakfast out over four plates, her hands trembling. Anna edged up on her seat, ready to jump up and offer help if her friend appeared to need it. Faye sat with folded arms and the imperious pout of a child dragged out of sleep early on a day with no school, her blue hair draped over her face. Spawny slouched forward in his chair, both hands in his pockets. The shirtless skeleton stared with intensity at the incoming meal, a length of drool working its way into his dense scrub of chest hair.

"Buck up, Twee," said Spawny.

"Don't call me that." Faye leaned back as Penny put food in front of everyone. "My name is Faye."

Spawny winked. "You'll always be cute li'l Twee round 'ere."

The girl narrowed her eyes at him and jabbed her fork in a sausage. Spawny grunted and shifted in his seat.

How's Penny holding up? Is there anything I can do?

Anna's voice startled his half-awake brain; Spawny almost fell out of the chair in a fit of flailing. His sudden reaction drew a startled yelp from Penny and a disinterested sidelong glance from Faye. After a breath, Penny sat.

Spawny fell upon the food straight away, scarfing it down like he had thirty seconds to finish or he'd lose it all. "Damn, Pen, nang brekky."

Penny abandoned her half-hearted attempt at nibbling eggs. "Don't thank me. Thank Anna. She paid for it."

"'Mazing you found a place wot'll send bots to us 'ere." He inhaled half a sausage in one bite, the ecstasy of food preempting whatever else he wanted to say.

With a smirk at the faces he made, Anna cut hers into bite-sized bits. "Any place will send delivery bots anywhere, if you pay for the risk fee."

"The Boys use bots for target practice sometimes," muttered Penny.

"What'd you nick?" blurted Faye, still not having touched a bite.

"Sod-all. I 'ad some work." Anna sensed the look on the girl's face. "No, not that kind of work, some corporate fuckery, strictly legit. Kinda stuff I used ta do before… Okay, maybe not 'legit,' but it wasn't on me back."

Penny looked up. "Kinnel, Anna. You're not in with Carroll again, are you?"

Anna looked down at her potatoes. "Aye. The money's good. Was just a bodyguard bit. Nuffin' manky."

Faye appeared more interested in pushing bits of OmPlus around her plate than eating it.

Penny leaned toward her. "G'won eat. That's as close to real eggs as you can get without ownin' a chicken."

"Oi, Luv, there any more?" Spawny smiled like a great hairy four-year-old begging for seconds. "What's wrong with 'er then?"

"Leave her be," said Anna. "She's thirteen, away from home, scared witless…"

Faye blushed. With both Anna and Penny patting her on the shoulders, she forced herself to eat a little. Penny got up and tossed the two remaining sausages from the pack into the pot with the rest of the eggs.

The girl's glance shifted to Penny without her head moving. "What're you so shivery about?"

Penny almost dropped the pan at the question. "Don't bother about me, eat your brekky."

Anna answered in a flat tone. "We were attacked in an alley."

The pan of OmPlus crashed into the table, the impact came close to spilling the bowl of gravy mushrooms.

"You needn't worry the child with that," said Penny, shivering into her seat.

Anna looked at a clean streak down the center of the grimy window. "Pen… She's thirteen. It's not all faeries and unicorns anymore."

"I know..." Penny stared at her food. "She's got somewhere to go home to. No need to traumatize her."

Anna shifted in her seat, her face on fire with blush. "I'm sorry, Penny. I... shouldn't have waited so long. I... It's my fault." She looked up, watery eyes locked on watery eyes. *I should've killed those bastards before they laid a hand on you. I'm so, so sorry.*

Penny burst into tears. "Anna... Don't blame yourself."

"She's right," said Spawny. "If'n she stays out 'ere, it'll be 'er soon enough bent over a rubbish can wif someone grabbin' quim."

Faye froze, staring at her plate. After a brief silence, she stormed out of the kitchen.

"You had to say *that,* didn't you?" Anna scowled. "You'll make a brilliant dad someday."

Penny propped her face on her hands, hiding behind her untamed hair. "I don't blame you, Pix. You had to hide your... umm... Yeah."

"Pen?" asked Anna.

She parted her thick, black hair like a stage curtain, sniffling. "Yeah?"

"You gonna be okay?"

"As okay as I can be, what with Spawny almost getting' killed, 'aving a Crossman tear my smalls off, and watching you kill three men."

A distant door slammed.

"Kinda terrifying, actually," said Spawny, his emotionless face snapping into a smile. "In a good way. Must'a been a bad night for 'em blokes. Crossmen' ain't usually so handsy wif' the birds."

"You've been there for me every step for ten years... I couldn't just stand there and let them—" Anna sniffled.

Spawny extricated himself from the kitchen as Penny walked around the table to comfort her friend. Anna held on, and they cried on each other's shoulders for a good ten minutes. Neither paid much attention to the muted cheering of a stadium of Frictionless fans in the living room.

Once Penny calmed down and went to sit with Spawny, Anna got up, gathered Faye's unfinished food, and tiptoed across the hall to her apartment.

She found Faye hiding between the bed and the wall in a full on cry. Anna set the food on the nightstand and sat on the bed with her back facing, quiet until it became apparent the girl wouldn't speak first.

"Don't mind him, kiddo. He doesn't know what happened to you." Anna lowered her voice. "Was me what got bent over the rubbish bin that night. Living out here makes you wanna give up. I was going to just lie there and let him." She remained quiet for a moment. "I couldn't let 'em do it to Penny."

"He's an ass." Faye muttered.

"I'm not gonna lie to you. He was tryin' to scare ya into wantin' to go home to your folks. We all think you deserve a real life."

"They don't want me. They think I'm a liar."

"Twee..."

The girl punched the nightstand. "Don't call me that."

"Look, Faye. They might be idiots but they—"

"They don't believe me." The girl lunged to her feet and kicked the side of the bed. "Mr. Bell did that to me... what Spawny said. Handful of... He touched me and they think I made it all up for attention."

"Want me to kill 'im then?"

Faye stayed quiet for a full minute until a little whisper slid past her teeth. "What? Did you just ask me if I wanted you to kill him?"

Anna sat still as stone, save for the small bundle of lint she rolled betwixt her thumb and forefinger. Back and forth it went; she watched, unblinking, as little fibers split apart from the rolling mass. The girl walked in front of her, red-eyed.

"Yes. Do you want Bell dead for what he did to you? Would you go home if he was gone?"

Faye sank onto the bed, sitting next to her. "You're not bloody serious?"

"I don't care what 'appens to me. My life is already down the pan." Her thumb traced over the faint red footprint from the last dose of zoom. "I don't want you with me in the same gutter, you still have a future. Besides, I'll probably get away with it." *I'm good at making accidents.*

"No." Faye shook her with both hands. "I'd rather be here with you than home and 'ave you rottin' in some jail. Bell's a piece of shit, but it's not worth what'll 'appen to you for it."

Anna at last made eye contact, her eyes every bit as puffy as Faye's. The lump in her throat grew. "You need to go back to your folks. I want to help. You have parents that still love you, even if they are obtuse about it. My dad wanted to kill me. I had no choice but to run away. I don't want you to make a mistake that'll ruin your whole life."

Faye cringed at the guilt and shame in her eyes. "Did they?"

"The Crossmen got handsy. Old Bill showed up before it got to that point. Bastards almost arrested *us* for public indecency."

"What? Arrested *you*? You were almost raped!" Faye gasped.

Hands clasped, Anna looked down. "We're Covs, Faye. We don't matter. If you stay out here, it's only a question of when. What Bell did to you is horrible, inexcusable, and I'll kill him for it—but worse waits for you here. Go home."

Faye sniffled. "I don't want to look at him. He lives right next door."

She pulled the girl into a hug, patting her on the back. "Don't worry about 'im, luv."

The girl sobbed on her, letting out a burden of shame and guilt. Anna did her best to comfort her, sitting in silence for some time after the tears stopped.

"You need to finish your brekky. I worked hard for the credits, almost got shot for it. Eat."

"What? Shot?"

Anna handed her the plate. "I never went to university. I either gotta wag my tits or work for interesting people doing interesting things. You really need to get—"

"Pixie?" Penny yelled from her apartment. "Get in here now. You have to see this."

They scurried across the hall, finding Penny pointing at the vid. A bored Spawny bemoaned the interruption of his Frictionless match.

"Play it again from the start." Penny playfully swatted at the back of his head.

He flailed. "Oi, knock it off, woman. Calm the feck down."

She grinned and went to swat him again. He caught her wrist and pulled her over the couch into his lap.

A tiny holographic panel appeared by Spawny's hand as he swiped a finger across the progress bar. Scrolling text identified it as the hourly news update.

"The Metropolitan Police today released these images taken from a triple murder in downtown London. Three members of the 'Crossmen' street gang were found shot dead in an alley behind Zaimi's Restaurant."

The feed zoomed in, showing the three men that had attacked them lying where they had fallen, but with additional ventilation. All of the bodies had been shot, once each in the approximate center of the forehead. The conspicuous electrical scoring on the one man's chest was gone.

"The execution-style shooting is just one in the latest series of violent incidents involving inner-city gangs. Chief Inspector Edmond Green had this to say…"

The image shifted to that of a middle-aged man in uniform with half-grey brown hair. Thick and tall cheeks wagged as he spoke out from under a curtain of diaphanous white eyebrows.

"At the moment, we are attributing this to a retributory attack conducted by either the East End Boys or Clan Brannagh. As you know, the Crossmen have a reputation for vigilantism and attacking other gangs who they believe get away with breaking the law. The violence in this case appears to be related to territorial disputes among rival organized groups and we do not feel it represents a significant threat to the law-abiding public."

The reporter, a wan fellow in his later forties, came back to the view seated behind a desk. "There you have Chief Inspector Edmond Green with the Met—"

The holographic panel flickered and imploded to a tiny point, leaving silence and darkness in the corner where it had been a second ago. Spawny looked at the two women, his finger still stuck through the intangible power button.

Penny shivered and held on to Spawny. Anna reached over and held her hand, trying to calm her nerves. Faye, not wanting to be alone, sat on the arm of the couch.

"What the devil was that?" Penny looked back and forth between them. "Those men weren't shot… Anna…" She stopped herself, glancing sideways at Faye.

Spawny ran a hand up and down her back. "Not the first time you've seen news changed for easier digestion?"

Anna stared at the window, having thought she had seen something moving. "What 'appened in that alley was some gangbangers killed some other gangbangers. That's all the Propers can 'andle, and that's all Old Bill will allow them to know." She squinted at Spawny. "Who's winning?"

"Arsenal," said Spawny, sounding defeated.

"Shite." Anna scowled. "Bloody figures."

"It's that damn Pryce bastard. Luckiest feckin' striker I've ever seen." Spawny threw the remote at the far end of the sofa. "He made a shot from the halfway point, bounced it offa Cummin's bloody noggin."

Anna scowled. "Horseshit."

"Bloody hell right, horseshit." Spawny spat to the side.

Penny whimpered.

Spawny set about muttering reassurances to Penny about how no Crossmen walked away from the scuffle, and none of them would be coming after her. Anna found herself amid a three-way hug, still seething about Man-U behind in score *again*. The way they'd been playing lately—not to mention that magic bastard Pryce—she figured they'd lose.

"Geez, you guys should have a threesome and get it over with." Faye grumbled.

"Capital idea, lass! G'won back to Pixie's flat so we can get on with it."

Anna smirked at him. "Honestly... I'd rather you knocked that bit off. It'd be like havin' a shag with me brother."

Spawny made a pained grimace halfway between a cringe and a smile. "Never thought of it that way."

"Anna, you know he's only sayin' that. He's not serious." Penny, head in his lap, looked up at him. "You're not serious, right?"

"'Course not." Spawny huffed.

Anna moved to the edge of their bed, the only other seat in their 'living room.' Faye followed, sitting close. Everyone stayed quiet for a few minutes until Spawny flicked the sound on and the blare of a goal horn rang out. Penny's sniffling twisted at Anna's gut.

"I'm thinkin' of gettin' a regular job," said Anna. "I don't want to dance anymore."

"Are you blushing?" Penny shifted upright, leaning on Spawny.

"Probably." The charcoal figures flashed across her mind in series, her voice lilted between a whisper and speech. "I don't want to feel like that anymore. I..."

Penny tilted her head. "What'll you do then?"

Anna shrugged. "Heard Sainsbury's is lookin' for cashiers or stock people. Minwag, but it's got a spot of dignity to it."

"That's the umm, hydroponic joint, innit? The one wit' tha real 'spensive shite." Spawny embraced Penny from behind. "'Ow bout we just cuddle tonight then?"

With a grin, she squirmed around and kissed him before looking back to Anna. "The green apron will suit you I think. Better to be seen in public with that than your last work uniform."

"I rather preferred the former." Spawny offered a bawdy wink.

Red-faced, Anna pulled Faye to her feet and went toward the door. "We'll leave you two alone then. Looks like you want some privacy."

Faye glanced at the Frictionless players swarming over the holo-panel before giving Anna a suspicious look.

$$\text{\small ⚓ ☙ 🏛 ◔ ♆}$$

CASCADING WAVES OF WATER THRUMMED INTO THE PLASTIC TUBE, ALL BUT drowning out the screaming in her head. Anna curled at the base of the shower, shoeless but otherwise dressed, soaked as a wharf rat and lost to uncontrollable shaking. Lights at the top made her feel like a creature on display in some old and forgotten exhibit. The rest of the apartment lay quiet and dark. Dr. Heath said the symptoms would still come, but they'd be a tenth of what would have been otherwise. Still, she'd spent the better part of the last day in and out of bed using Faye as a living teddy bear for support while careening along a roller coaster ride that went from feeling like she had a mild flu to wanting to die to escape the agony.

Fuck me. This is a tenth of it?

She laced her fingers in her hair, massaging the ache to different parts of her scalp while daydreaming about the taste of a fresh dose of zoom. It often manifested as a slight metallic presence in the back of her throat. Her tongue flicked at the roof of her mouth, hoping for some trace of relief from the uncontrolled spasms. Her friend's laughter ripped at her brain, painfully loud despite having several walls between them.

At least Penny is coping.

Thunder rolled over her body as if lightning hit the ground between her feet. She curled into a ball, head between her knees. It happened again, a feeling as if the entire shower tube came under assault from heavy artillery. The third time, she looked up at Faye on the other side of the glass thudding her shoe into the wall.

"I thought me dad was cheap… Never saw no one tryin' ta scrub up and do laundry at the same time. Mind leavin' me the loo for a min, need a gypsy."

Anna nodded and clawed at the walls in an attempt to stand and reach the control panel. A swipe at the flashing colors set the dry mode into full tilt and she whirled about once in the powerful cyclone before falling into a heap. When tube opened, she spilled out onto the floor on her back, semi-damp.

Faye shook her head. "Oi, you're a complete hames."

The girl pulled her from the autoshower, dragging her by the armpits for the door. She gave up trying to get her out into the bedroom and propped her back against the wall. Anna slid to the side, fetal upon the ground and shaking. She closed her eyes and tried to exert control over her muscles, but couldn't tell if the shakes remained or if she only imagined them. Black mortar and white tiles blurred into a spiral of grey.

The sound of a flushing toilet peeled her eyes open. The black of

Faye's shoes wavered inches from her face amid a blinding field of white. The girl had turned the lights on, flooding the bathroom with pain. Moaning, Anna tried to crawl away from the glow, but bumped her head into the wall. The sensation of impact ran down her body, bounced off the soles of her feet, and came back up into a blooming migraine. Faye once again pulled her up into a sitting position and set her shoulders to the wall. The girl took a seat beside her, threw an arm around her, and held on.

Time slipped in and out. Anna became aware of a blanket, and clung to her roommate of circumstance to keep from sliding to the ground.

"You've been in there for hours, think you've washed out." Faye padded at her forehead with the towel, catching the drips the fell out of her hair. "'Ow long are you gonna be this bad?"

Anna coughed to clear her throat, triggering a bout that ended in a half-vomit. When she could again breathe, she spat the bile and sighed.

"I dunno, luv. Never got this far along in a try to quit before." She took Faye's head in both hands. "Promise me you'll never do this shit."

"Why the hell do you care?"

"Look at me." Anna clung to the child tight, so she could feel every tremble. "Do you want to end up like this? Do you want to be dead in an alley somewhere before your twenty-fifth?"

The girl looked away, frowning. Amid the upsurge of pain in Anna's mind, she picked out the occasional bit of Faye's surface thoughts. It hurt to flex the psionic muscle, like jabbing a finger on a bruise. Her parents had threatened to take her to a psychiatrist for 'making up lies' and 'acting out.' They didn't believe her about the neighbor. Her father thought she had gotten into occultism, her fondness for The Dead Ballerinas music being the start. Running away had been a desperate ill-conceived idea as frightening as staying in arm's reach of Mr. Bell. Faye was terrified he'd do it again, and next time, she wouldn't be able to get away before all he did was grab her through her pants.

She erected the tough-girl attitude as a defense. Faye was shitless.

Anna grasped fistfuls of her shirt and shook her. "I'll not let you cock up your life like I did. I'll set it right."

She pulled Anna's fingers out of her clothing and held her hands a distance away.

"I'm fine."

"You're as fine as I am." Anna's semi-psychotic laugh echoed out into the bedroom. "Which ain't very fine... I'ma deal with that problem of yours and you can go home where it's safe. You can grow up as a Proper, not throw yourself into this shit." She tried to stand, but shoved clumsily at the wall. "I'm gonna show that nonce what it's like to be touched in a bad place."

"No." Faye yelled, slapping her. "Stop it! You're scaring me. Don't kill anyone." The girl stared at her, flushed and furious for several seconds before she burst into tears. "I don't want you to go to jail for me. Don't leave me here alone."

Anna blinked. Intense pain rode upon a shock wave that started at her cheek and slithered in slow motion down her body. The impact had stalled the shakes as well as her thought process. She stared aghast at the blue-haired person in front of her. It took a full minute to realize the girl had slapped her, then clamped on in a tight hug, sobbing out of control into her shoulder, begging her not to do anything stupid and make the police take her. The more upset Faye became, the angrier Anna felt.

If she did anything else before Coventry killed her, she would help this kid. The bathroom lights faltered and buzzed at her hatred of Deacon Bell.

DANCING IN THE RAIN

Smears of light and color flashed by. Storefronts, streetlamps, and advert bots all came together in a disorienting spiral that followed whichever direction Anna's head swayed. She remembered plucking Faye's home address from her surface thoughts while putting her to bed, promising to speak to her parents and not do anything stupid. Nine Clifton Hill shouldn't have been difficult to find, though it took most of her effort to remain on two feet.

No memory of her navigating the police barricade remained. As far as she could recall, she had gone right from her flat to the middle of London. Blaring horns chased her across streets and armies of faceless blobs avoided her undead gait. She felt a few hands on her searching pockets, though she had forgotten her jacket and the credstick in it back at Coventry. She had nothing to steal, so she ignored them.

She gazed into the sheen of a streetlight reflecting from the pavement, mesmerized by the ten-foot long smear of radiance shimmering in the light rain. She had become so painfully sober she felt high; every muscle took too long to react and reacted too much when it did. Block after block drifted in a dissociative smear of time. More bots floated up to her, offering various things they guessed she needed: hangover cures, stimpaks, antipaks, vitamins, jackets, and her friend with the umbrellas popped in to check on her as well.

She tried to hug it, remembering the little orb that acted so concerned for her. Evading her lunge, it slid off down an alley leaving her to embrace a puddle. The jolt of the icy water on her chest sent her upright with such speed her head felt like it stuck to the ground for a moment before snapping into place. The frigidity stunned her lucid and she noticed she had strayed way off course.

During the reprieve from delirium, Anna oriented herself and jogged in the direction she had meant to go. A few alleys over, she caught a whiff of chemicals in the air—a cruel hint of Flowerbasket. Her body followed the source of the fragrance despite the mental screams of protest. Five young men had propped themselves up against the crumbling brickwork of an old tenement. She tumbled over a stack of refuse cans and hit the ground on all fours.

Anna remembered surrendering her last zoomers to Dr. Mardling. His reassuring face appeared, telling her she would no longer need them. The fragrance of chems came on as a smoky whip, shattering his face into fragments of falling flesh-colored glass.

Don't. Don't. Don't. Go away. Get up and walk away. Get your worthless arse out of here, Anna!

"You guys got any zoom?" asked a voice that sounded like hers.

She crawled toward them, trying to smile. Cold water washed over her hands from puddles, the rain fell like needles through her thin half shirt.

A hand on her shoulder pulled her up until she sat on her heels. Her hard, wet boot soles jabbed into her rear end, sheer nylon offering no protection.

"Look at this skank, Donner… She's wild for it."

The men melted into little more than a sea of blurred colors and the fragrance of stale synthetic beer. A hand drifted past her face holding a crinkled white sheet of plastic. Only one tiny object in the entire world appeared in clear focus: a small one-inch square derm.

Zoom.

No, you dumb whore. Get up. Run!

She reached for it, but they pulled it away. She chased, swatting and grasping at empty air. Before she realized, she stumbled toward them, not remembering standing up.

"What'll you give us for it, bitch?"

You left the money at home anyway. I don't need money to kill that piece of shit. Anna rubbed her forehead. *No. I'm talking to parents, not killing nonces.*

She patted her bare abdomen, hunting for absent jacket pockets. The man laughed, knowing the look on her face. Her eyes tracked the bouncing derm around in a circle, still the only thing in focus.

"'Ow bout a show then, bint? Dance and you can have it."

Fuck. Don't do it. No... You should have stayed with James.

Her body twisted into a drunken imitation of her club routine. She slipped in a flooded pothole and hit the ground hard, but scrambled back up and continued. Laughter echoed around from all sides. Darkness, a flash of light on bricks, darkness, blurry men surrounding her; she went in circles until the dance ended atop a rubbish bin.

"Get yer kit off, give us a real show."

Don't you dare you stupid worthless whore!

Her hands moved without consent. In her head, she screamed as if someone else stripped her against her will. The wet half-shirt slid off, her breasts bounced free. The derm flashed right in front of her eyes, so close she could have snagged it if she had had any reflexes left. Whistles and clapping came from everywhere.

She continued to dance, chasing the bouncing patch like a cat after a toy. Cold water hit her feet as she stumbled out of her boots, and then her pants vanished. She didn't know, or care, if her disobedient hands did it or one of the men. Anna pranced naked in the rain, dancing like an inebriated moth in pursuit of a candle that taunted her ever out of reach, a candle that would consume and burn. It—oblivion—beckoned, and she chased it with a big grin on her face.

The droplets fell on her, the voice in her head sobbed, begging her not to do it.

Around and around she spun, the derm came and went. The light on the bricks flashed white in the dark.

"Please... I need it so bad..."

No. You don't. Stop! The angels are crying. A dozen easels bearing white squares formed in her mind. Shadowy outlines of herself animated, covering their faces, weeping.

The hand flicked, the beautiful deadly sheet of plasfilm spun like a shuriken, flying in a left-curving arc into a pile of trash. Anna scrambled after it and dove headfirst into the pile, clawing with desperate fury at the refuse.

The men laughed.

Finding it at last, she held it up with a triumphant grin and picked at the backing. The derm slipped away from the plasfilm with surprising ease and fell to the alley—but she caught it.

Don't you dare.

She smashed the thing against her arm, squeezing down on it and biting her lip with anticipation. The rain fell stronger, cascading in waves over her back, the hard paving chewed on her knees and shins; the laughter grew louder.

Nothing happened.

Whimpering, she peeled the derm back and found the pad dry and dessciated. They had teased her with a used one. Her humiliation had been for nothing. Shame hit her with the force of a lead blanket. She curled into a ball and tried to cover herself with her hands.

Stupid girl. You deserve this. Don't even try and say it's not your fault.

The squeaking of wet rubber on pavement drew her attention. She whirled to stare at the handful of young men in red and white sprinting off, having stolen her clothes. One man held up the bundle of clothes, taunting. The rest hurled insults and mocking laughter while taking image caps of her with their NetMinis. She crawled into the pile of trash for cover, shivering when the rain found her anyway. The patter of droplets upon the plastic bags overpowered the distant sound of traffic as well as the voice crying in the back of her head.

A lamp on the wall exploded, plunging the area into midnight and showering her with fragments of hot glass and sparks. She stared at the mouth of the alley, watching the occasional car slip past. Trapped by her embarrassment for the better part of half an hour, she bit her knuckle at the memory of her march of shame.

Abject humiliation had murdered the mental urge for zoom. Whatever force had taken control of her had run off with the thugs. The walk to Plonk's flat a few days ago hadn't been a big deal. She needed zoom, he had it, and she didn't care at all what people thought of the naked harlot stumbling down the street with glowing blue wings.

I don't want to be a harlot anymore.

Another car passed the end of the alley. The rain strengthened and the wind grew colder. Staying out in this would be bad for her health, but it took another ten minutes for her to drum up the nerve to stand. She covered herself with her hands at first, but when she reached the sidewalk, she reconsidered. If she acted ashamed, people might laugh and make fun of the situation. Those cyberfreaks with cat ears, tails, and claws often walked around naked and got cheers for it. If she acted nonchalant, she could feel in control. If she seemed desirable rather than embarrassed, it wouldn't feel so bad.

That lasted ten steps.

No sooner did she realize people stared than her hands flew in a desperate search for modesty. Eyes down, she tiptoed forward at a demure pace. A few people called out asking if she needed help. If she stopped, the police would get involved and start asking questions both fear and shame would prevent her from answering. Chasing drugs or planning to murder a nonce, neither one made for great conversation with Old Bil. In her delicate mind-state, she might even blurt about being psionic.

When she ignored offers of help, the mood of the people changed. A woman her age nude in public not frantic, not crying, and not making eye contact had to be on drugs. She had to be someone from Coventry. The first voice that called her a whore caused her to cringe from the disgrace of it. The monster in her head killed a streetlamp. Nothing reined in her emotion, and the little thing leapt into the world frothing at the mouth. Anna kept her head down, gathering her arms tighter around her body as she put one foot in front of the other, faster and faster to get away from the horrible words.

"Such a tramp," a disgusted older man yelled.

If it bothers you so much, why are you looking?

Anna shrank a little more and a nearby vendomat blew up in a shower of sparks.

A shrill female voice cried out. "Pervert."

An air handler two stories above detonated with an electrical zapping sound. Clanging fragments of metal fell to the street, sending some of the Propers scrambling.

A block later, a man shouted. "Put something on, you bloody tart."

I would if I had anything you tosser!

A great arc of lightning flew from a nearby streetlamp into the puddle below it, followed in seconds by the bulb going off in a report that echoed for blocks.

"She just wants attention, so shameful."

No, I don't. Stop watching me!

All the power in a passing car arced from the in-wheel motors to the wet road, with a deep *boom*, leaving it dead in the street and a dozen people diving to the ground. She came to a halt, looking up with the startled realization she could force some of them not to see her. Her clothing could take the form of telepathic invisibility. The gathering of mental energy, and the accompanying grin, dispersed at the feeling of a hand on her arm.

"Do you need hel—?"

A man stood right behind her, about to offer his coat when he made contact. The instant his fingers touched, an intense electrical jolt threw him into the air and sent his body bouncing off the thick resin window of a bakery full of stale pastries. The clatter of his hitting the window drew the crowd's attention.

Anna backed away, staring at the victim of her accidental discharge. He moaned, still alive, at the edge of consciousness.

"I'm sorry."

Terrified of the police inquiring about an unexplainable assault, she ran off, slipping and skidding in the driving rain on the smooth metal sidewalk. Sliding into walls and bouncing off vendomats, she slowed to a normal stride two blocks over and three down. Under the cover of a dark section of street, she came to a halt and tried to catch her breath. Motionless, she folded her arms across her chest and sank into a squat. Anna stared at a trail of water that ran off her nose, falling between her knees to rejoin the ankle-deep river in which she perched on the balls of her feet.

Freezing water sluiced toward the storm drain, the gurgle of its descent into the oblivion of the sewer louder than the air rushing past her teeth. The wind threw the downpour in her face with each gust, her body wracked with shivers of exhaustion and cold. Anna considered letting gravity take her to the ground, lying there and giving up. Rapid breaths slowed to a calm intake and release of air. A moment later, the sense of a crowd having formed nudged her back to her feet.

What the devil are so many bloody people doing outside at this hour?

The rain left the footpath slippery. She wanted to run, but fatigue and fried muscles added to the numbing cold, leaving her balance unsteady. Anna forced her legs into a deliberate trudge, gaze downcast and hands in place as best she could to retain as much dignity as one of Coventry's residents could possess.

Derisive stares came from all sides whenever she walked away from offers of assistance. People here would call the police for finding a woman traipsing about in the all-together, not like the lousy sections of town where the Neko cyber junkies went starkers as a matter of routine. Generally, Old Bill didn't care too much about it in *those* parts of town.

She moved up to a trot to avoid as many stares as she could, her hands in a constant battle to shield herself from prying eyes. Bursts of dazzling orange flecks leapt from streetlamp after streetlamp, her thinly veiled humiliation reaching out into the world. All around her erupted a fanfare of blue arcs and sputtering electronics. Anna trailed a cavalcade of fireworks, dead lights, and car alarms for two more blocks until she spotted the welcome blue-green glow of a Britain's Autocab station.

Under the beautiful dryness of the teal awning, she spent every ounce of willpower she had left to steel her nerves and ignore the small crowd collected around to watch her Lady Godiva performance. The aqua colored podium created an unending train of car icons that scrolled in a holographic cartoon city from left to right. Their grilles and headlights formed smiling faces intended to be appealing, but even they laughed at her miserable state. She reached out with a quaking hand, exposing her rain-soaked breasts to the chill of the wind long enough to tap the request button.

For several minutes, none of the crowd said anything; some took vids of her while others feigned shock. She thought of saying she had lost a dare, but her voice hid in a deep dark pit beneath her self-respect. She positioned herself against the rear wall of the autocab booth, rattling against the cold plastic, and tried to cover as much of her body as she could.

A middle-aged woman, one of the Propers, glared at her. "What's the city comin' to, the 'ores prancin' about like this. No morals left."

Anna's face burned red. Before she realized anger took over, she found herself facing the crowd and screaming. "You're no bleedin' better for staring at me, ya old cow. 'Ave a little damn respect and look the other way. I'm tryin to get the hell inside you demic old witch! I was bloody mugged."

A gasp swept over the crowd. One by one, their NetMinis and other personal electronics burst in flashes of disintegrating plastic and blue crawling sparks. One man howled as some implanted headware overheated, spinning around in a useless attempt to evade a burning piece of metal in his skull that he couldn't get away from.

Anna sank into a squat, her back sliding over the green and blue plastic. "Go on then, piss off. Stop staring at me." The shout petered out to a timid whisper. "Please…" She touched her face to her knees and sniffled.

At a loss to explain why all of their handhelds failed at the same time, and perhaps feeling a tiny bit of compassion, some of the crowd meandered off. Anna cupped her hands over her mouth, exhaling into them in an attempt to force some small bit of warmth back into her fingers.

One man reached up to remove his coat at the same instant a tiny green driverless Cooper rounded the corner and came to a halt, a burst of cold fog wafting from the e-motors in its wheels. The headlights and curved grill had been designed to form a cute smile, and the hubcaps bore yellow happy faces, which stopped upside down.

The side door opened upward and she leapt in before pulling it closed, then scooted over the coarse cloth bench until she leaned against the far wall, curling into a fetal position. Deafening raindrops drummed on the roof, but they no longer nipped at her exposed skin. Another bench faced to the rear, the same cheap fabric-over-hard-plastic without even an attempt at cushioning. Still, it beat wet pavement. Even inside the heated car, she kept shaking. The cold had soaked to her bones.

"Hello, welcome to Britain's Autocab!" chirped an electronic male voice. "Where may I take you on this fine evening?"

She tried to ignore the threads of ice crawling down her back, speaking with chattering teeth. "N-need to f-fare on the reverse. D-doctor James Mardling, please... of Oxford."

Huddled in a ball in the back seat of an autocab, she shied away from the faces looming at her outside the foggy windows, everyone straining to get a peek at the naked wretch in the car. Reality melted away; she found herself stuck inside a capsule in an alien world of scowling, mocking faces. Nothing existed outside her little spaceship but scorn and derision. Her humiliation edged toward the realm of rage but she held it fast, lest the autocab suffer the consequence. This thing had to remain intact. It would carry her out of her nightmare.

A bleary voice murmured from the console. "Who is this? Do you have any idea what bloody time it is?"

Doctor Mardling's face appeared in hologram a few inches in front of the control terminal. A hand floated into the image, wiping sleep from eyes that widened when he saw her.

"Great Caesar's ghost! Anna, what the devil's happened to you? Please tell me you've not been—"

"No, no... I just got... Someone pinched my clobber is all." She blushed and looked to the side at the seat. "I need 'elp. Please."

"The hell would anyone steal your dirty rags?" A voice that emanated only from his side of the terminal drew a scowl. "Yes, yes. Bloody hell, I'll accept the fare."

"Thank you for using Britain's Autocab!"

The cheery singsong jingle faded away and the car lurched forward. Anna lay sideways on the seat, fetal and shaking, trying not to give in to the emotional load wanting to come out of her eyes. Doctor Mardling cared. He wanted to help her from the moment he had seen her.

Staring down at her soaked and trembling body, it hit her that maybe... just maybe... she might be in need of some assistance.

23

DELIVERY

Jostled about in the back of the tiny car, Anna hid low to the seat in an effort not to give other motorists a show. Amid the alternating pattern of teal and orange squares woven into the light grey fabric, she searched for what she would say to him. The heat had kicked into high, fogging the windows over to an opaque pattern of drifting lights and traffic. Blobs of whitish-yellow and red light shot by on both sides.

She curled upon the seat, shivering, staring at the emergency steering controls: tiny nubs in the front dash, a toy version of the control sticks for normal cars. The law required them in case of a system failure, but in practicality, the minuscule things would be impossible to use.

The autocab whipped around a corner. A sudden downhill lifted her weight off the seat, sending her sliding ass-first into the far wall when the car pulled a hard right. Seconds later, it jammed to a halt, throwing her to the floor.

"Thank you for using Britain's autocab. Your travel fare is 143 credits, paid collect. Have a wonderful morning."

The single gull wing door lifted skyward, leaking pure white fluorescent light into the cabin. Anna curled into a ball again and stared at the blinding patch of outside. The dark silhouette of a man moved closer. Dr. Mardling faded into view and reached toward her, holding out a blanket.

Anna blushed as she sat up, so ashamed of herself she had to cling to the handles to keep from shaking into a spill. She emerged from the tiny, sheltering car into the cold post-midnight air of a subterranean parking deck. Air as frigid as the concrete under her foot surrounded her, but at least the underground parking area blocked the rain.

He wrapped her with a warm embrace of fabric that tickled at her thighs an inch above the knee. The amazing feeling of no longer being exposed sapped the strength from her legs. He caught her off guard by scooping her up like a babe.

"Welcome to your new life, Anna."

She leaned her head on his shoulder as he carried her to a nearby metal door. The autocab had been kind enough to drop her off adjacent to the elevator, and in short order, they ascended to the forty-second floor. A few people returning home at this hour from various functions and late nights at the office all paused to ask if everything was all right. James made something up about her being robbed down to, and including, her clothes. It felt strange to have people act concerned; none of them knew where she came from.

Hallways, white walls, and green carpet glided by. She stared at the scallop-shell flanges of frosted glass throwing light up to the ceiling in cones every few feet. By all rights, anyone would call this a middle-class residence tower, but to her, it felt like a palace. Any second now, someone would scream at her for daring to set foot in such a place.

His apartment was darker than she expected it to be. Deep browns and burgundy dominated most of the décor. A leaping gazelle hologram galloped across the far wall between the two exterior windows, casting a radiant blue and green light. A maroon cloth couch faced an unpowered vid-bar, its silver shell glimmering with the motions of the illusory animal.

She floated over the threshold in his arms, gliding past the couch, an arch to a kitchenette, and down a tiny hallway with three doors. The first, on the right, led to a quaint room with a single Comforgel bed near a small table. The second, on the left, looked to be his bathroom. She assumed the far door led to the master bedroom, but he stopped at the bath.

James gestured to the shower. "I'll imagine you'd like to get the smell of whatever refuse you'd been frolicking in off of you."

"More appealed to the warm of it." Anna tried—and failed—to stop shivering.

A pained expression crossed his face. "Yes, you should. Your lips are turning blue. I'll fetch you a nightshirt."

Anna nodded and hurried into the autoshower. Soon, a spray of warm water thawed her bones.

James knocked moments later. "Shall I leave it by the door or bring it inside."

"You can bring it in." She put her back to the door, not too embarrassed, as he'd already seen the whole of her.

He entered and left with speed borne of tact. Anna peered over her shoulder, eyeing a large black button-down shirt draped over the sink. After running a double dry cycle, she stepped out of the tube and pulled the shirt on. It hung so big on her it counted as a short dress. Satisfied at being covered, she padded out into the hall. The scent of Earl Grey drifted in from the kitchenette, so she crept toward it.

Doctor Mardling slumped at the table, clearly in protest of being awake at that moment. He offered a bleary smile and indicated two cups of tea arranged on either side of a tray of small pastries. She took a seat and clasped her hands around the cup. It smelled a bit off from what she'd had before. He chuckled at the look she made.

"Hydroponic… I take it you have not had the genuine article?"

Regardless of how hard she stared at the surface of the tea, she couldn't see her mother in it. "I have, but it's been a very long time."

Clattering rose from her hands. The shaking returned, she let go of the cup and blushed.

"It's all right, Anna. That is normal. Your brain still wants that drek in your veins. It will pass."

She nabbed one of the pastries, dipped it, and ate it almost whole. Another one died a dry death in two bites. After a sip of tea, she stared at her lap, enamored by the black and gold tiger stripe pattern in the buttons while listening to the crumpets' faint screams emanating from her belly.

"I lost my bearings downtown, tried to get some more."

Stretching across the table, he put a hand over her wrist. "That couldn't have been easy to admit, Anna. Thank you for trusting me enough to do so. You will make it. The way you are acting tells me you are not proud of yourself."

"I've not been proud of m'self for quite a span."

A grin crept across his lips, matching a glimmer in his eyes. "You should be. I will help you find the life you deserve. It is my duty."

Eyes down, she took a long sip of tea and savored the core of heat it created inside her. "Thank you for paying the autocab... I was—"

He squeezed her hand. "I know. You have accepted at last that you cannot do this alone. You have taken the first step. Your body no longer craves the drug at a physiological level. We need only convince your mind of the truth of it."

A comforting smile drew a tenuous companion from her lips. She thought about her mortifying walk. "All those people talked to me like I was some kind of piece of rubbish."

Anger flashed over his face, gone as fast as it had shown itself. "No, Anna. You are about as far removed from rubbish as is possible to get. You are perfect, more than they could ever hope to know."

Anna's blush outlasted the remainder of the Earl Grey. After seeing her attack the tea pastries, he made her something a little more substantial to eat. Some manner of instant meal with fish. Far from glorious, but it handy and quick. Once she had eaten, he led her by the hand to the spare bedroom. She sat on the edge, looking up at him. Memories of the cold trek across the city kept her shivering. Anna thought back to her emergence from the autocab, naked into the world from a womb of metal and plastic, she had gone straight into his arms.

Dr. Mardling had been there for her.

His amused smile made her blush. This man wanted to look after her. He hadn't cast a single lustful stare her way, nor did he yell or hit. At thirty-five, he was older by about twelve years, but the difference in age wrapped him with a safe feeling.

Unsure of what came over her, she leapt to her tiptoes and kissed him on the lips. His eyebrows shot up, remaining there until after she stopped and sank back onto her heels.

"Anna... You know you do not have to trade yourself any more. I am here because I want to be, not because I expect anything in return. You are special, more special than you understand. I will be here for you... no strings."

She blinked and sat on the Comforgel pad. The weight of her body activated it, sending a ripple of orange-red glow spreading over the otherwise dark violet block. She reclined and slipped under the blanket, her mind swimming in an attempt to figure out why she had done that.

"It's not that, doctor. I wanted to."

On her side, she peered out from a curtain of fast-approaching sleep at the man in the doorway. After exchanging weary smiles, he swiped his hand at the wall panel and the room went dark. Amid the soft glow of the gel mattress, she lay still, watching him back out of the room.

The door and her eyes closed at the same moment. Not having to worry about who or what might interrupt her sleep, she drifted off.

24

WAKEUP CALL

Anna sat on the Comforgel pad, listening to the clatter of cookware echo down the hall while staring at a modest stack of boxes that had appeared on the little table by the bed during the night. The topmost item as welcome as it was mocking, a clear plastic packet of black lace undies.

Someone had stolen her last pair from the club while she danced. The idea of anyone doing that repulsed her, wearing someone else's knickers. She never had the money to spare to replace them. Not that they were expensive, but the zoom monster ate every credit. Besides, what did she need them for anyway? They would have been in a locker or on the floor more than on her.

Her hands shook at the thought of chems.

He had done a fair job of guessing her size. Then again, he'd gotten a full view last night. She slipped out of the shirt and put them on. While appraising how they looked, she caught sight of a mottle of healing red marks on the insides of both forearms, the remnants of derms. It seemed irrational to want to hide them from him. He knew full well what she had done to herself, but she grabbed at the remaining boxes, eager to cover herself before he could see the badges of shame.

He bought her a new pair of pants similar to what she had lost. Long, baggy, black, and bedecked with an excessive amount of pockets. Cloth, rather than nylon, these were much warmer and didn't make the same strange noise when she moved. Another box held a plain white shirt; long enough to be tucked into her belt. Yet another had black socks and a pair of boots that looked less military and a touch more feminine. Despite the one-inch heel, the rubber soles would be good for working with Mr. Carroll. The final box offered a long black coat made of synthetic wool.

After putting on everything but the coat and boots, she followed the clattering and found him nudging two fried eggs off a pan and onto a plate with some sausages. He smiled and motioned for her to sit. Once she had settled in and they both had a mouthful or two, he cleared his tongue with a swig of coffee and gave her a pleased look.

"You scrub up quite well."

"Thank you for the clothes, doctor."

He waved dismissively, a glimmer of light dancing off his fork. "I could not leave you running about in the buff. Think nothing of it. I hope everything is to your liking." He smiled. "Oh, and please call me James."

A touch of pink crept into her alabaster face. "I don't *like* the zoom you know."

He ate a bit of sausage, nodding until he could talk again. "I imagine not. You seem quite keen on keeping that other little nipper away from it."

Anna looked up, pausing in mid bite. She couldn't recall if she discussed Faye with him at length. "Yeah. Sometimes it runs away with itself. Like this thing in the back of my 'ead. The chemicals kept it in a cage so it couldn't hurt anyone or shit on me to Old Bill."

"What exactly does the little imp in your head do?"

She ate a few more bites, trying to avoid answering. He rubbed his chin, as if reacting to the images of her father's fist in her mind.

"Sometimes 'lectric things bugger themselves when I lose control. If I get scared, or embarrassed, or cheesed off… things tend to explode. It's why I don't have a NetMini. Got tired of replacing them."

James made a series of fascinated expressions at her retelling of how tech went haywire whenever her emotional state reached a peak in any direction. Nodding along with her stories of various catastrophic events, he smiled wider and wider as she kept on about working for Mr. Carroll until she had had a close call with strange government men.

"Those chuffers," James grumbled. "They are officially known as the CSB, Clandestine Services Bureau. They splintered off from MI6 some years ago amid William's intense paranoia about psionic individuals."

Anna shivered, rubbing at the side of her neck.

Anger reddened his face. "Yes... The registered are given electronic leashes."

"Bombs, James."

He shot her a hard look.

The contents of her plate became quite interesting. "Sorry."

He set down his utensils, reached across the table, and took her hand. "No, no, Anna. I am not angry with you. It is the whole establishment treating us like we are beasts."

"We?" she whispered, looking up. "You've got a nice flat, nice job..."

"Yes. We are very much alike. Although our areas of specialty differ, we are both of the Awakened."

She nibbled on sausage, speaking between bites. "Wot's that mean?"

He glanced to the window and smiled, waving a hand around has he orated. "Psionics have been known to mankind for quite a few generations... ever since that Sievert girl in the Colony in 2204. Then you had the Moore twins in Hertfordshire six years later, and that poor Myshkin child who barely escaped Moscow in 2243."

Anna gasped. "Is it true they shot her?"

James nodded. "Indeed, but she survived. She told the world about the horrible state of affairs for psionics in the ACC. More often than not, they are killed on sight." He let out a grim sigh. "Sometimes entire families are culled even if only one person displays any psionic abilities."

Anna found it difficult to continue eating while he rambled on about stories of the Allied Corporate Council murdering psionics in front of their own families, too terrified of what they might be capable of to give them a chance to speak. Some, especially young children, vanished in the night without a trace. Many thought they forced them into secret military projects, but others suspected sadistic experiments searching for way to 'cure' psionics out of the human race—or somehow weaponize them.

"Can't say it's much better 'ere." Anna stabbed a bit of egg. "The Crown will stick a bomb in your 'ead and make you dance like a trained dog."

"Exactly, my dear, but to get back to my point..." He spread jam on a piece of toast. "There is something more than simple psionics emerging from the genetic destiny of mankind. The Awakened are a leap forward. We are psionics, yes, but we are much more powerful than the rest. I fear if they discover this, they will become a tad more aggressive."

"You think? So what makes you believe I'm one of these? I've seen about psionics what can make electricity do what they want it to do. I'm not that unique, not special. If anything, I'm poor at it since I can't control it."

"Oh, but you are." He mashed a fist into the table, making the flatware jump. "Electrokinesis has been documented, but so far in all reported cases, the individuals could only redirect existing electricity along a conductor. In order to use it as a weapon, they needed to make direct contact or touch something metal that also touched someone." Scenes of her one-sided battle with the Crossmen came to the forefront of her mind all of a sudden. "Tell me, Anna. Have you ever made lightning arc through the air without a wirepath? Have you ever controlled the flow of electricity inside a device without touching it? Have you manipulated enough amperage to kill a man instantly?"

Anna looked at her lap, fidgeting. "Aye on the lot."

"How difficult was it for you to do? There have only been two other recorded cases of spontaneous generation over the past century and both from old men who had spent their entire lives practicing it... In the Colony of course, and the best they could manage amounted to a nasty stunner. No one has yet been documented who could do what you did."

"Colony? Which planet?"

He scoffed. "No, not *a* colony, *the* Colony. The US... or whatever it is they call themselves now that they annexed Canada too."

"UCF?"

He waved dismissively. "They're a bit more lenient on psionics across the pond. I have half a mind to go there so I can continue my work in peace."

She pushed her empty plate closer to the center of the table. "What..."

A small flat robot slid from a space on the wall and came floating by, collecting the plate, cleaning it, and depositing it back in the cabinet. Anna remained silent until it had once again blended into the white tiles above the sink. "...work?"

"I have been researching the brains of psionic individuals, scanned data mostly, tissue when I can get a hold of it. From a structural and genetic point of view, I am searching for the trigger that causes someone to be Awakened. I think I found at least the start of where to look deeper."

He finished his coffee in one long sip, put it back on the saucer, and sighed. "But it has so far proven to be unrepeatable."

"I don't want a bomb in my head. I don't want to be tied to zoom either. It's gonna kill me. I don't want to feel so—"

"You are not cheap." He stepped around the table and stooped at her side. "You are Awakened, Anna. Your abilities are far beyond what an 'ordinary' psionic is capable of. That is why you fry things when you get emotional. My research has led me to conclude that children born Awakened have a habit of possessing strange traits that can make their nature difficult to conceal."

"How many of us are there?"

"Well." He stood up straight, rubbing his chin. "There is of course, you. I know of one other, a woman, in Britain. I'm of a mind there is one in Japan and one somewhere in the Colony—but all I have to go on are some old files lifted from a genetic research project. Alas, it contained a relative dearth of useful information. Merely some prattle about an attempt to clone and militarize a pyrokinetic."

Anna stared at her hand. "That's fire, right?"

"Indeed."

She felt drawn to this man, this guardian, this protector who shared the same fear—that the government would find them. Anna stood and embraced him, letting him hold her in silence for several minutes before another wave of zoom-trembles sent a spark lapping at the counter from his food reassembler.

"You are not out of the proverbial woods yet with that chemical. You will need support. I would very much like you to stay here, with me, where you can be safe."

Anna nodded once before looking away and to the side.

"What's the matter?"

"I can't leave Penny to wallow in that awful place... or Twee, umm, Faye."

"I'm sure they'll"—another wave of blurriness washed over her mind —"benefit from having you as a friend."

"James... I want to be with you. I've never felt so safe." She squeezed her arms around him. "I have to do something for them first."

Whirring accompanied the small bot as it tended to his abandoned plate and gathered the utensils for cleaning. James glanced at the wall, a faint hint of frown at the corner of his lip.

She stifled another tremble. "Are you angry?"

His face relaxed, his warm breath fell over the top of her head. "No, Anna... I am worried. I do not want you to do anything reckless."

25

OBSERVATION

Nine Clifton Hill sat amid a strip of residences that had been rebuilt a few centuries ago in the months following the Corporate War. Constructed in an archaic style, the buildings all held ten accommodations stacked vertically, each the size of a one-story house. Advertised as 'full-floor flats,' they housed the not-quite-wealthy.

The induced trees sprouting beside the footpath twisted their way up past decorative iron grillwork. Leaves fluttered in the incessant wind. Rain still came, but it had fallen off to a weak drizzle that her new coat shrugged off. Bundled in it, Anna felt like a different person from the one who existed only a night ago. No one so much as gave her a second glance; she looked like she belonged. Her no-longer-bare midriff gave her warmth, and the presence of underclothes embraced her with long lost dignity.

She had become a Proper overnight.

For many blocks in all directions, patches of pale orange light flickered in the gloom of the approaching storm. A dozen-dozen pictures of Faye in hologram, mounted to any vertical surface someone could find. Little devices the size of a thumbnail presented a black-haired porcelain doll to the world, smiling in a pose for a class portrait. *She looks so different with her hair blue.*

Faye Taylor, 13, missing daughter. Last seen two weeks ago.

AF851.185CC.9185F.FFBDD. Reward if found. ₡100,000.

She blinked at the string of numbers, likely her father's PID. It amounted to advertising one's name, address, phone number, resume, and bank account number. An invitation to every cyberspace criminal in the world to come sniff you out.

The man must be nuts to post his PID in the open like that. Daft or desperate.

Anna stood by one such hologram, staring into the virtual eyes flickering with windblown debris. The ghostly face looked as innocent on the outside as Faye did on the inside, devoid of blue hair and attitude.

A tiny grey car squeaked down the street and came to a halt at the adjacent building. A middle-aged lumpy man stepped out in a brown sweater and grey slacks. He squinted into the wind, his eyes receding into a face pasty and puffy. Anna recognized him from Faye's nightmares: Mr. Bell, the man who had stuck his hand where it didn't belong.

Anna thought back to the Crossman in the alley and shifted her stance at the remembered touch, the sensation of the coarse hand where she didn't want it. Faye at least had the protection of pants in the way. She'd managed to escape him before he got them off her. Latent anger swirled as she stared at the nervous potbellied man leaning in the open door to gather things from the car. He seemed to feel the malice in her stare and looked around like a mouse sensing the eagle before the dive. With each second, his motions picked up speed.

Anna glanced at the warm glow in the windows of number nine Clifton Hill, trying to guess which floor the girl lived on, which floor still held the people Mr. Bell tortured by his continued existence, even if they didn't believe him the reason for their daughter's absence.

She drew her coat tight against a building gust of wind, which knocked one of the man's parcels to the ground. He stooped to retrieve it. She imagined the Crossmen finding Faye, and then felt the man on top of her again, the cold metal refuse bin digging into her hips. Her mind taunted her with what could have happened if she'd been an ordinary woman out on the blag with her mate's no-good boyfriend. Her heart raced with dread. She wouldn't have been able to protect her best friend.

Come off it, Anna. If you were normal, you'd have a loving home and would never have met Penny.

At her spike of sorrow, the lamps on the front of Bell's car blew off in a shower of sparks, sending him scurrying up onto the porch with a high-pitched nasal whine.

How like a pig you squeal.

"Evenin' Deacon," said another man on his way out of the building.

The two struck up a banal conversation, the sort of things middle-aged men in a well-to-do section of London chatted about in passing. The sort of things people with no true worries or no true desire to be friends talked about for the five minutes that fate and courtesy forced them to interact.

Anna glanced at the empty false lawn in Faye's yard that approximated the place the old pink bicycle had been left in hers. Her father had only beaten her, drunk and angry at how many things she broke. Drunk and terrified of the creature he shared a flat with, and rightly so. The beating that made her fear for her life had cost him his. What could she do to a wretch like Mr. Bell if she could kill her father for trying to beat her to death?

Mind made up, her knuckles creaked as she stared at the unsavory man scurrying into his den.

Run you fat bastard of a nonce. Your reckoning's come calling.

She shifted her weight from the lamppost onto her feet, pacing at a stalk toward the gate. The rumble of a vehicle brought her head about to the left. A large black van parked a short distance away on the far side of the street. Something about it spooked her train of thought away from vengeance and she kept going, right past Bell's house.

The van slid out from the space like an orca on the hunt. Anna sped up and took the first corner she could. When the van followed, she considered all manner of possibilities as to who it could be. Some disgruntled corporate from an old job she had done for Carroll, low-level Syndicate thugs looking for a new piece of ass, or most likely, freelancers hired by BT looking to pay her back for the other night on the roof.

Her coat trailed behind her as she ran and leapt a hedge, cutting across a yard to get away from the road. A barking dog joined the chase until another fence jump ended its pursuit with the *thump* of a sixty-pound animal having an abrupt meeting with iron bars. The street in front of the adjoining property looked free of large black vans, or much traffic of any kind given the time, and she resumed a nervous walk.

Without warning, a mass of black leapt from the shadows and blocked the footpath in front of her. The huge man stood two heads taller than her with broad shoulders. His all-black suit even covered his face, save for two opaque round lenses for eyes and a filter module at his mouth. The pistols and other assorted devices on his belt didn't look like the sort of thing common people carried—he was an assassin.

She all but ran into him trying to backpedal away, but he lunged and grabbed her wrist, leaving her struggling like a pickpocket who had been nicked.

"Hello, Miss Morgan. We need to talk."

Terror froze her muscles. She whirled to the right at the scrape of a sliding metal door. Two other men, also covered head to toe in black, crouched within the glowing red interior of the van. Puffs of fog burped from the ends of rifles, and a stabbing pain lanced into her back upon two tiny daggers.

A cold burn spread from the point of impact. Only the man's hold of her arm kept her from collapsing flat on her back. Flexible rubberized material liquefied away from of his bald head, sliding into a gloss black ring around his neck. She recognized him from the police checkpoint—the other man who arrived with the telepath.

The CSB.

26

DIRECTIVE 7

Darkness.

Anna floated in a void of whispers with no sense of temperature, scent, or weight. Random images flashed on the canvas of her thoughts, inane things like cartoon rabbits and car tires. Cartoon farms, planes, people she had never seen before all came one after the next. Whispering voices asked questions without waiting for any answer: what time is it, what's your name, who is that, do you remember your mother, how far a ride is it to the West End from Trafalgar?

Air seeped out of her lungs, the moan of her voice rising over the din in her skull. Her toes made contact with a surface smooth and cold. Icy metal met the backs of her legs. Thin, coarse material itched at her chest and thighs, a smock of sorts. Fabric had been tied around her head over her eyes. A thin rigid band squeezed the top of her head beneath the blindfold, tight to her skin.

Anna attempted to raise a hand to her face, but her arm stopped short after an inch, a hard steel cuff digging into her wrist. Sudden panic triggered a fit of struggling. Metal restraints fixed her by the wrists and ankles to a chair. Softer straps crossed an X over her chest, holding her body against the seatback. Her squirming reawakened tender spots where darts had hit her. Chains rattled as she fought to get loose, shackles biting her skin. She rocked side to side, trying to slip out of the chest straps and lean her head close enough to her hand to pull the cloth from her face, but couldn't reach.

A swirl of fear and anger came on at her realization of being trapped. Threads of pain lanced across her brain, an army of electric hummingbirds pecking at random. The thin, metal headband clamped about her skull seemed to be trying to squeeze through the skin to the underlying bone. Burning intensified with her fear. The little thing in the back of her mind leapt at the walls of a cage, zapped every time it tried to touch the bars.

The more frightened she became, the more it hurt. She threw her weight forward, trying to lift the chair and get to her feet, but it barely moved. The noise of her battle reverberated into the distance, the cavernous nature of the sound suggested she sat alone inside a massive structure.

She writhed in her bindings, freaking out at having no idea where she'd been taken. The cavernous space hung in deathly silence, save for the clatter of restraints whenever she tried to move. Fear circled her like a shark in the void. Her worst nightmare had come to pass; she had been taken by the CSB. Anna thrashed against the cuffs, desperate to reach up and touch the side of her neck for proof she hadn't been cut open and rigged with a kill switch. Handcuffs bit into her wrists and ankles.

Screaming from pain and frustration, she sagged limp, out of breath, and ventured a timid "Hello?"

Her voice reverberated to silence. The straps crossed over her chest prevented her from leaning forward at all. She twisted her head about despite the blindfold. The incessant random whispering hammered her mind.

"Stop it!" she screamed. "Let me out! I'm going nuts!"

Another burst of energy triggered a pounding headache and in impotent squirming. Still trapped, she broke down and sobbed. Every time her fear got the better of her, the metal ring around her head delivered such a jolt of pain she found herself drooling. The whispers and random images continued, reaching a point where they changed her fearful struggle for freedom into a manic and desperate attempt to make it stop.

The scuffing of boots broke past the mental noise. Anna stopped moving, her limbs tensing inward as far as the chains allowed. A sense of bodies surrounded her, and she shivered. Whatever garment they had put on her felt like it covered enough, but being stared at in silence by people she couldn't see was more intolerable than being naked in a cage. Random whispered questions changed into comments about her height, about her tits, about how cute her hair was. Scratchy voices teased her that she found her helplessness exciting, told her she liked it, called her a bad girl in Tommy's voice. It needled her, drawing upon her insecurities and throwing them back at her.

Something pressed against her lip. Anna jumped hard enough to shove the chair back. Again, the object touched her lips. That time, she realized someone offered her water. It smelled normal, so she drank. When the cup retreated, a soft plastic object entered her mouth and forced her jaw open. Contorting in the chair, she tried to get away from it. Hands grabbed her head from behind, holding her still while a swab danced around the inside of her cheek, making her gag.

The mechanism relaxed, and she coughed. "Who the hell are you people? What is this?"

No one answered.

A spot of cold metal touched her right bicep, below the short sleeve of the smock. She made a fist and gasped as an air-hypo fired, again thrashing in her seat.

"Let me out this instant!"

The anger that followed her shout grew into a scream from the incredible pain projected into her head. Her body writhed, shaking with involuntary spasms; four shackles gouged into her skin. When her brain unclenched from the sensation of being cooked, she put together that her 'little friend' appeared to be triggering the device every time it tried to do something.

That's got to be some kind of psionic leash... Damn it hurts.

Attempting to stay calm in her current situation would have been a tall request of a Buddhist monk. A tear ran down her face as she prepared herself to feel the pain repeatedly. James's explanation of the Awakened recited itself in her head. She couldn't mention how her power ran away with itself. It would reveal her as something abnormal. She had to stay quiet—if she could.

Men shuffled about amid the clatter of armor and rifles. Fingers slipped between the black cloth and her temple, and the blindfold flew up and off with a sharp tug. The burly bald man loomed over her, offering a bemused smile while he picked at his black goatee.

She found herself in a prison-yellow smock, handcuffed arm and leg to a rigid metal chair in the approximate center of an old hangar with a floor equal parts grey paint and rusty smear. Thirty feet overhead, rows of ancient lamps dotted the ceiling, none of which appeared functional. Intense beams of light focused on her from a horseshoe of freestanding portables, reducing the dozen or so men behind them to figments of shadow and menace. Anna squinted. They looked like British military, common soldiers.

Some manner of springy cord crossed her chest, the kind of thing she assumed commandos used to rappel down the side of buildings. The entire scene blurred as her head moved, swooning about like the aftermath of a drinking binge. A hovercar passed overhead, the pale blue glow of its ion drives leaking through cracks in the ceiling as it drifted by.

Anna's head sagged forward, and she wound up staring at the redness she had fought into her wrists. Red from the digital code-lock on her restraints painted a smear of light on her arm. Moisture drained from her mouth at the realization she couldn't sense the current inside them. Lightheadedness came on. She twisted her hand over.

"They're quite secure, Miss Morgan. You'll not be going anywhere until we've had a chat."

"I have a headache and I don't even know who you are." She let her skull's weight drag her head back against the chair, then peered up at him. "Thank you for at least letting me stay dressed."

He flashed a two-second smile before all mirth faded. "I am CSB Agent Gordon, and that is a military grade psi-inhibitor. You may be wondering why you cannot read my mind, assuming of course, telepathy is one of your gifts… This little beauty keeps us on the same playing field."

He tapped a finger to the thin strip, sending a reverberating explosion across her mind three times. Anna's hand clanked to a halt an inch above the armrest when she tried to cradle the side of her skull in response to pain.

"It will hurt more if you touch it… security mechanism. Anyway, Miss Morgan, you are probably wondering why we asked you to join us at such an ungodly hour."

"This is asking? I'd hate to see if you made demands."

"Mind your chelp, girl. We know." The large man extended his hand to the right as if indicating something that existed in open air.

Anna lifted her head, about to inquire about the empty space when a hologram shimmered into existence. A six-foot square panel created a hole in reality looking into another time and place. The view peered down from the ceiling into a small room with a round table and chair. A little girl, about twelve, sat at the table with a bored expression. She appeared thin and unremarkable—except for her long, white hair. The child glanced up at the camera with a hostile glower; bruises on her face brought back bad memories.

"I am interested in your opinion, Annabelle." Gordon folded his hands behind his back. "Does this look like a little girl who moments ago watched her father die in a freak kitchen accident?"

The child Anna fidgeted, tapped, and folded her arms. She swung her feet while scowling at the wall. If anything, she looked annoyed at being detained, impatient to be somewhere else. At the sound of footsteps, her demeanor changed. By the time a constable walked in, she sniffled and wiped her eyes, thanking him for whatever hot drink he had brought for her.

"You've had a lot of practice fooling the Met." Agent Gordon chuckled, leaving the image frozen on crocodile tears. "We've been watching you. For a while there, we thought you were on to us."

Warmth spread over her cheeks, the indignity of being caught in a lie. Somewhere behind her, a metal door slid open. Footsteps approached.

The image changed to point of view floating down a hospital-white corridor lined with sheet-covered bodies on gurneys. Silver morgue cabinets showed the reflection of a flying holo-recorder, which stopped near the only uncovered body: her father's. Anna glanced away, whimpering from revulsion and guilt. Someone behind the chair grabbed her head again, forcing her to watch. She twisted, biting her lip, her raw ankles chafing.

The camera zoomed in on a hairy leg where a reddened handprint showed clear on the pallid skin of his outer left thigh. Guilt riled up the monster. The psi inhibitor roasted her brain. Anna foamed at the mouth and struggled, trying to look away.

Agent Gordon leaned over her, a smug grin on his face. "We know what really happened to your father."

Images of the three dead Crossmen appeared all around her, the entire hangar shimmered into a holographic recreation of the alley. The soldiers, Agent Gordon, the metal chair, all of it remained as if they had teleported to the street where she had almost been raped. Anna shifted, looking at each body. The mere sight of Peacock, the man who'd attacked Penny, made her furious. A lightning arc of agony speared her brain.

Anna screamed, in so much pain she felt detached from her body.

"You really ought to stop fighting," said Gordon.

Anna's arms shook, tense against the cuffs, fists clenched near to the point of bleeding palms. "I... Take it off. It hurts."

"How much of a fool do you think I am?" Images appeared in floating panels around the area, showing still-frame grabs of her electrocuting the men. Flickering blue lit the walls.

"You don't understand..."

The artificial reality around her restraint chair rumbled with the arrival of the black van. The side door slid open. Four men stepped out. Three walked around her chair, heading one each to the Crossmen's corpses before putting a bullet in their heads. One familiar man remained by the van, watching: Agent Gordon.

The real man stepped through his holographic doppelganger, halting in front of her with a pleasant smile. "The public can only handle so much truth."

The entire false world disintegrated into a snow of fading pixels, the dark alley replaced with a pristine silver floor and a modern white-walled room. Anna blinked, realizing the old hangar had been a lie. The man from behind strode into view with a silver case. Nestled within black foam, a silver triangle the size of a thumbnail sat at the front end of a small bit of wiring and a capsule the size of an aspirin. She shied away, whimpering.

It didn't matter she had no hope of breaking the chains—she tried anyway.

"No, please don't... it'll kill me."

The big man laughed. "That is kind of the point of them, Anna—but only if you misbehave."

You don't understand... It'll go off on its own.

Sparks crackled around the psi inhibitor as it battled her subconscious tendency to ruin machines at the onset of emotion. The terror in her heart at the thought of having one of those bombs forcibly implanted triggered a neural shock that left her twitching out of control for several minutes.

"That is most unusual," said a voice out of sight to her left.

The men seemed curious about the effect, leaning in closer to look. The one who kept grabbing her from behind waved some manner of handheld device past her.

Agent Gordon palmed her head, lifting it so she looked at him. "Now what did you try to do, naughty little girl?"

The condescension in his voice brought her reason back on wings of anger. "Fuck off and kill me already. Stop torturing me."

He squatted in front of the chair, balancing his elbows on his knees, at eye level with her. "I would very much like to ask a favor of you." He held up a small black box, the size of what an engagement ring would come in. "In return, I'll offer you what's in this box instead of what's in that one." He pointed at the micro-bomb.

"Tell me what it is first."

Standing back to his full height, he pondered her request with a thumb to his chin. The other man closed the case containing the detonator; her gaze darted to the *click* of the latch. Fear of the killer implant built on top of her dread of the pain that followed spikes of emotion. The harder she tried to stay calm, the more she panicked. It spiraled into a building cycle that sent her into a spastic fit of screaming and thrashing. The whispers in her head made it worse. She couldn't contain her fear and she couldn't bear the agony that followed it.

"I can't take this anymore. Please stop. You have no idea what you're doing to me!"

"All you need to do is agree to help us out, and it stops." Agent Gordon patted her on the shoulder.

She sniffled, coughing spit past clenched teeth and trying to regain some small degree of composure. "What do you want?"

"Well, as you know, the CSB operates independently of oversight with wide-sweeping powers in matters involving The Concern. Directive Seven gives us the power to terminate any individual deemed to be a threat to Crown or country." He poked her in the forehead with a gloved finger gun. "I could do you right here and no one would say boo."

Anna swayed as if drunk, looking up at him with an unladylike tendril of drool falling out of her mouth. The thrumming distractions in her mind, images and whispered words, chipped at the threshold of her sanity.

"Why can't you say psionics? Is it easier to murder people when we're just 'The Concern?'"

Agent Gordon flashed a frown of contemplation and nodded. "Yes, basically. I rather think of it as being the poor sot who gets stuck working at the pound, having to put down all those puppies that are unadoptable."

Anna closed her eyes, trying to ignore the whispering. "No puppy is unadoptable."

"Dogs then. I s'pose you're right then, the little ones most often do what they're told. It's the ones that bite we have to put down... the mangy ones that live on the edge of town, hiding in alleys and picking at trash, the sick ones who become a menace to society."

She glared. *That isn't me anymore.* James was going to save her. She shot a longing stare at the door, trying to bend reality by sheer force of will and make him appear. Her howl of agony rang across the cavernous space, leaving her bleeding from the nose and shaking out of control.

"You really ought to stop fighting the inhibitor, Anna. It'll only hurt worse and worse."

Thinking of the earnest look on James's face, she somehow found the resilience not to crack and admit she *couldn't* control it. The CSB didn't know about the Awakened, and James didn't want them to.

"It hurts so much. I can't help it. Make the whispering stop, please."

"Can't, lass. That's what keeps your mind off balance and makes it impossible to use your power. If you try to find enough focus to try, it gives you an unpleasant reminder. Relax; most people last three days of wearing one before all the voices make the cheese fly off their crackers. You've only had it on for three hours."

"What do you want me to do? Will you let me go if I agree to it?"

He circled her wearing a smug grin. "There is an individual who some of us within the CSB would like removed. With a little help from us, your unfortunate pappy's death was swept under the proverbial rug." He spun to a halt with a flourish of his coat. Eye contact. "We want you to solve a problem. Make it look like an accident, just like Daddy."

"I don't like killing. That was self-defense. He would have beaten me to death. Can't you have one of these men do it? I'm not an assassin. That's your lot."

"This is a political problem, so we need plausible deniability. You have a unique talent that will set things up nicely as force majeure, and even provide his widow with a nice settlement from the company that manufactured whatever appliance you use as a power source."

"If I do it, you won't put a bomb in me? What's in the other box?"

Gordon produced the small onyx cube once more, pulling it open like a clamshell to reveal a half-inch black chip nestled in the crease of blue felt. "Information... and yes, the detonators are necessary with individuals who can influence the mind and control people, subtle things poor saps like me have little chance to resist. Your talents are a bit more overt. I suppose you are not much different from a lunatic with a rifle." He held out a hand. "Shake on the deal then?"

Even if she wanted to, the handcuffs wouldn't let her reach where he'd left his hand—on purpose. She glared.

Gordon chuckled, lowering his arm. "I will ensure they make an exception for you and leave you off the books, provided you continue to behave yourself." A plastic smile twisted his lips. "Perhaps you could continue in our employ."

She cringed. "I'm not a lunatic… unless you leave me like this much longer."

"So we have an accord then?" He snapped the small box closed.

"I'll need to think it over… I'm not a killer."

He chuckled. "Those blokes in the alley would beg to differ."

Anna tried to leap out of the chair. "They tried to… For fucks' sake, he had his hand in my twat."

The box containing the bomb dangled before her eyes. "Consider this to be the extenuating circumstance in this case then. It's him or you."

Deflating, she sagged. "Not much of a negotiator are you? Givin' me a choice of one clusterfuck or the other."

The hovercar went past again, going the other way. She looked up, but the pristine, white ceiling no longer had any cracks. Whispers scolded her for murdering her father, teased her for being a freak, and mocked her for being unwanted. Chattering harpies called her a whore, called her dirty, and taunted her because some tiny part of her brain enjoyed the feeling of being tied down. Threads of pain seeped into her head as her emotions careened about with wild abandon. Her impotent effort to get out of the chair fanned the fires of her panic; she knew a wave of torture would follow it and this time, it would be unbearable.

Doctor Mardling's voice drifted out of the tormenting whispers. "You are far greater than they know."

Anna gathered her faculties and braced her mind against the barrage of images and sounds, a self-feeding cycle. The more it zapped her, the more emotional she became, and the shocks grew stronger. Her search for calm equilibrium swayed back and forth like an over-steering drunk driver. Cold metal on her skin provided a constant reminder of vulnerability. Desperation mounted away from her control. Blood gushed from her nose. She strained, her entire body locked in a vibrating rigor as she shrieked with terror. Agent Gordon lifted an amused eyebrow; the men behind him took a step back.

More than anything, she wanted the damnable neuro-electric energy *away* from her.

The thin metal strip around her head erupted in a spectacular arc of violet lightning that leapt to the steel chair and then to the man holding the ominous case. Subconscious desire to be rid of the brain static flung the energy off in a random direction, seeking the closest conductor: one of the CSB men. He fell in place, convulsing on the ground, the energy causing a brief flash of skull to glow purple beneath his face. The restrictive tightness clamped around her brain burst apart into the awesome feeling of mental freedom. Metal fragments rolled down her chest.

The desperate surge of power that leapt from her mind called arcs of lightning from one of the freestanding lamps into two of the soldiers. The men flew off their feet amid crackling flashes, slamming into the ground ten yards away, convulsing and moaning.

Anna panted, out of breath from the exertion, and let her weight hang on the cords across her chest. Magnificent silence in her brain brought a smile to her face; the whispers had stopped. Before she could utter a word, Gordon's head vanished beneath black that flowed out of his collar, up and over it like liquid. He had his pistol an inch from her nose in seconds.

"Please! No!" she wailed, cringing and shivering.

The remaining spotlights flickered.

Distant moaning drifted over a minute of calm, the only sound louder than the rattle of handcuffs.

"I must admit, I've never seen that before. I'll give you two seconds to tell me how the hell you blew that thing out or I'm going to open a Tube tunnel in your brain."

Anna cried, unable to get away from the cold pistol pressed into her cheek.

The chirp of electronic firing circuits echoed from the still-conscious soldiers behind Gordon. Anna squirmed in the chains, not caring about the painful chafing handcuffs. She tried to curl into a ball, to get away from all the guns pointed at her. Her gaze darted past Gordon to the men with rifles trained on her. She jerked at her limbs, unable to move, gripped with fear the likes of which she had not felt since the night of her father's death.

The night she thought she was about to die.

Bang. A loud report broke the quiet, right in front of her. Followed by several more pops, and fizzling.

Anna nearly lost her bladder at the sudden noise. She opened her eyes to mystified cursing. The soldiers no longer aimed at her, they swatted and checked their now-dark rifles. One spoke into a communications link that seemed not to work. A startled gasp came from her right, low. The man who had been holding the detonator implant lay on the floor cradling the side of his face, bloody and laced with superficial shrapnel wounds from the half-exploded box. Bits of foam snowed around him, mixed with the scent of explosive chemicals and burned plastic. The charge meant to be attached to a brain stem had gone off in his hands.

Agent Hughes put a hand over the silver nub behind his ear, eyeing the destroyed box.

Gordon twisted his gun to look at its side, thrusting out a lip as he appraised the dead weapon. He tucked it back into its holster before placing the point of a combat knife under her chin.

She tried to hold her hands up in a defensive gesture; two chains clicked. "Please don't kill me. It was an accident!"

"Sir, the prisoner burned the inhibitor... She's dangerous," said one of the soldiers. "All of our gear is toast. We should fall back."

"I'm inclined to believe her," said Hughes, raising an eyebrow. "You saw what she did in that alley. Even you should accept it as self-defense."

"Get Wiltshire out of here." Gordon poked her in the chin, forcing her to raise her head and look away. She struggled to rise out of her seat in a search for distance. He plucked pieces of the scorched headband out of her lap, appraising each before tossing them one by one to the side. Then, much to Anna's surprise, he tugged her smock down to cover more of her thighs.

Two soldiers dragged the bloody man away.

"Those things ride up when you squirm." Gordon glanced to his left. "What do you think?"

"I can't tell," muttered Hughes. "Her thoughts are walled off. Feels somewhat like a mind block, but not entirely. She isn't supposed to be a strong telepath, but I'm having difficulty getting in. Of course, if she is erecting a block, then she won't be able to do anything else."

"That was a rather fortuitous accident." Gordon smiled, seeming to enjoy the risk of her brain being off a leash. He lowered the knife enough to let her look at him. "I believe you had something to say?"

Anna struggled to rein in her shivering. "Electronics freak out if I get emotional. I'm shitless right now."

"I kind of got that impression from the trembling, crying, and whimpering," said Gordon.

"You kind of have that effect on women." Hughes winked.

Gordon picked his eye with his middle finger.

"It's why my dad beat the hell out of me. I'd get scared or angry and some appliance would bugger itself. The more it cost, the worse I got it. The night he… I thought he was going to kill me."

"Going for the sympathy card now?" Gordon sighed.

Agent Hughes gave her a pitying look. "Gordon…"

"I don't know how I broke that thing you put on my head. It was awful. Maddening."

Hughes put a hand on her head, tracing his thumb over the burn mark. She cringed. "If her electrical abilities are operating at a subconscious level triggered by emotion, the inhibitor was probably creating an escalating feedback loop. The more it punished her, the more her brain fought back. Incredible." With Gordon unable to see Hughes face, he seemed genuine in his concern. "I've never seen anything like this before, but it was… needlessly cruel. I'm not sure what we're dealing with here. She's the first person I've ever seen without total conscious control of her abilities."

"You're going soft on me, Hughes." Gordon chuckled. "Well, Miss Morgan, it seems the Bureau has a lot to learn from you."

"I don't think it's dangerous," said Hughes. "The involuntary outbursts are simply… inconvenient."

"Yes, sir." Anna stared at her bare knees. Her present circumstance terrified her far more than a shithead constable wanting to molest her. "It's why I've not got a NetMini. They kept breaking."

She struggled to get up, fearing the CSB meant to keep her for good. The X across her chest seemed to squeeze even tighter, cutting off her ability to breathe; she focused all her mental energy on staying calm. Gordon held up a placating hand and put his knife back on his belt. Shadows moved behind him from the men around the dying lamps shoving themselves to their feet and staggering away. Hughes held up what remained of the detonator implant, eyes wide.

"There are methods other than crude devices to ensure cooperation," said Gordon with a wry curl to his lip.

"Aye, like 'ow 'bout treatin' us like people?" Anna balled her hands into fists, knees together.

Hughes shifted to hide his face from Gordon.

"We need a problem eliminated in a manner that appears to be accidental. You have three friends who need to stay out of jail."

Anna froze; blood drained from her cheeks. Handcuffs rattled. "You... No."

"I'm not talking about normal prison. I'm referring to a shadowy governmental 'no one ever sees you again' prison. You know, the places the tinfoil hat crowd insist are real, but we deny having?" Gordon patted her upon the cheek. "Consider this assignment a test run. Once it's done, you will work with us if you want them to continue to enjoy the sight of blue sky."

Tears streamed down her face. She sagged.

"Do we have an accord? You know those holding facilities wouldn't be a very nice place for young girls. Twee is it?" Something in his smile said he probably wouldn't do that to her, but Anna didn't fully trust anything about him.

"Don't hurt them. Leave them out of this." She made a fist and yanked at her right arm, scowling at the floor. "I'll do it. Forgive me if I don't shake on it."

"Excellent." Gordon waved to someone behind her.

A hand came over the seatback and pushed her head to the left. Before she could get out much of a yelp, icy metal pressed into the side of her neck with a *hiss*. Cold spread up into her head and down over her chest. Sound blurred, and Gordon's condescending grin warped into a spiral of color. Agent Hughes's face slid into her field of view; his hands cradled her head.

His voice chased her thoughts into darkness.

You will be fine, Anna.

27

RESISTANCE

Gentle rocking lulled Anna into a stupor of comfort. For several minutes after regaining consciousness, she lay on her side like a corpse. Salty air wafted about, creating small whorls of dust over the dull grey-green surface stretched out at the right side of her vision. The soft lapping of water against thin plastisteel provided a rhythmic backdrop to the intermittent cry of gulls and the distant echoing laughter of men. The scent of ocean water lingered in her mouth.

She pulled her arm up, hand sliding over rough cloth then a patch of coarse traction coating, and onto her face. A stripe of pain circled her skull, tender to the touch like a burn from a hair iron. With a groan, she forced herself into a sitting position. The small rowboat in which she sprawled drifted a few yards from a rocky shoreline. She peered over the side into inky black water, a mirror of the night sky, then at a stained concrete pylon leading up to the underside of a pier.

It took her a moment to realize she was dressed in her own clothes again. The yellow prisoner smock felt like a foggy memory. Anna gathered her coat to her chest, struggling to remember how she had gone from stalking a nonce to sitting in a rowboat. Despite bundling herself tight, the air over the water chilled her bones. Her eyes widened with the realization of who had taken her. She probed her neck with her fingers, starting to panic until she could find no trace of an implanted detonator. Anna slumped in relief and tucked her hands into her armpits for warmth. Red marks ringed both wrists. Agent Gordon's voice came back to her, threatening to whisk Penny, Spawny, and Faye off the face of the Earth. She curled up, arms around her knees, and bawled like a child from guilt.

Kill an innocent man or my friends suffer? Anna wiped her eyes. *He's a politician. How innocent can he be?*

Anna leaned against the shallow wall, staring up at the lights of the city. The panic of the past several hours melted away as the little boat bobbed with the gentle motion of a calm sea. Head in her hands, she cradled her skull against her knees and tried to forget the torture caused by the device they had put on her. She eventually noticed a clean black satchel next to her, as out of place as she, and no doubt a gift from Agent Gordon. A twinge of nausea gripped her as she rummaged the contents: a NetMini, a datapad, and a small black case about the size of a large bar of soap.

The datapad, eight by ten inches, caught moonlight in a smear of white across the otherwise onyx surface. Anna tilted it back and forth, using the glare as an impromptu mirror to check her face, relieved at the lack of bruises. Someone had even cleaned up the blood that had gushed from her nose.

She jammed the datapad back into the bag, thinking it far too cold and unstable down here to dawdle. Anger and relief mixed at knowing Gordon could have killed her or put one of those bombs in her, but they had drugged her and set her loose. She shrugged out of her coat and ran her hands all over skin under her clothes, searching for anything out of place. All seemed normal, save for the raw marks caused by the handcuffs.

He must really want that bloke dead if he let me go. She thought of her friends, clueless of the danger she'd gotten them into by merely existing. *Gordon, you bastard.*

The NetMini was obvious in purpose and went into her coat pocket before she moved on to examine the small black case. She spun it around in her fingers until she found a release button. It popped open, revealing six small red cylinders with red crosses on the ends. Believing them some manner of narcotic, she shook with a nervous giggle.

Trembles flung the autoinjectors out of the case, clattering to the floor. The sight of them made her mind crave zoom despite never having dosed it from a pneumatic syringe. Anna clutched her arm to her chest until the shaking ceased, and gathered them back into the case except for one. In another life, she had carried stimpaks while working for Mr.

Carroll. Each injector contained a solution of synthetic adrenaline, neutral base material, and nanobots. The combination could repair minor damage to the body as well as provide a burst of energy.

Anna picked one up. The safety cap went flying at the behest of her thumbnail, and she pulled her sleeve back to expose skin. She pushed the end into her skin and bore down on it. The stimpak emitted a faint *hiss*, its contents forced into her body via pressure. The empty slipped from her fingers to the bottom of the boat with a *clack*. Icy coldness swam up her arm as the nanobot-laced fluid migrated into her veins. Warm tingling circled where the restraints had been. Red marks vanished, and burning pain receded to dull discomfort. Her toes and fingers had become two shades shy of numb. The howl of the wind brought cravings for a warm place to hide. Anna forced herself upright, wobbling on her feet in a shaky boat. Seconds later, she fell on her hands and crawled to the front.

A rusty ladder led up the side of one of the pylons about ten feet ahead. She reached over the bow and pulled at the mooring line, hand over hand, drawing the tiny craft forward. The wet rope further chilled her hands. By the time the boat thunked against the concrete, her teeth chattered. Anna hung the satchel over her shoulder and dragged her achy body up the rungs until she could peek over the edge. The dock stank of industry and pollution, though the air was a touch warmer than below. Without the shield of the sunken waterway, the stiff breeze fluttered her coat and hair. She forced herself over the top and hurried out of the gale into the cover of stacked cargo containers.

Light drew her through a maze of enormous boxes to an alley alongside a warehouse. Conversations and the occasional fit of laughter wandered in from the lit frontage. At the edge of the building, she peeked out of the dark and stopped breathing.

A group of about a dozen men in long black coats emblazoned with silver crosses arranged themselves around a loading dock by an old, dead lorry. Some stood at street level, leaning on the platform, others sat on crates up top, and one rummaged a shipping box in search of an unopened synthbeer.

Quite a few had sunken lines traced over the side of their faces, the telltale mark of implanted neuralware. Here and there, an obvious mechanical eye glowed emerald or amber. A lime green light within the pupils of otherwise normal looking eyes gave another man away as augmented.

Four women sat among them, wearing the same coats, some sporting visible cybernetic augmentation.

Anna retreated into the alley with a spin, back pressed to the wall. The sight of Crossmen sent her sliding down the wet metal until her chest met her knees. Despite the fog of the miserable state she had been in that night, it came back as though it had happened only minutes before. She held her trembling hands out, staring at them. Guilt came on at the question of what her life would have been like if her father didn't beat her for breaking expensive things. How could he have known the more he yelled, the more it happened? Those Crossmen wanted to pay Spawny back for stealing. They would have attacked her regardless of what she could do—without her power, she would have been helpless.

James' words came back to her, calling her magnificent and superior. Her abilities protected Penny, protected herself. She had no reason to fear street punks.

Anna gathered her wits and stood, thinking she might try walking out into the street and away like nothing was amiss. Her present location offered two choices: go swimming in freezing water, or wander past them in plain sight. She glanced up at a broken window two stories overhead, but had no way to climb up to it. A long exhale came with the thought that maybe they'd leave her alone if she didn't look at them. While they'd recovered at the noshery, Spawny, baffled by the attack, said the Crossmen had a reputation for vigilantism. Some had been known to steal augmentations, and they routinely got into turf warfare with other gangs. By far their reputation came from inter-gang violence, with very little mention of attacking women. That struck her as odd, but then again, every group had its rotten apples. Who could say how they'd react to her alone.

More likely they'll be after me like hounds on a fox.

Venturing a peek, she squinted at their number. Thirteen. Too many to influence with her telepathic invisibility, which could deal with a handful at most. All things considered, it would be far better to slip away into the night. She took a deep breath, shivering at the memory of fingers sliding between her legs. Her fists clenched. *No. I don't need to be invisible. I'll blast the first sodding bastard to come near me out of his boots.*

Anna held her breath and edged into the street, as far away from the gang as she could get against the right side wall. She walked as if carrying liquid nitroglycerin in a Dixie cup, hoping not to attract their attention by fast movement.

James's choice of boot earned him a future kiss; the padded soles made no sound.

Anxiety manifested as sweat, the taste of salt upon her lip. She felt like a mouse sneaking past snakes.

"Hey bitch!" yelled a man.

Somewhere behind her, a NetMini detonated.

"Fetch me a beer," yelled the first man.

"Gah, the feck?" shouted a different man.

"Sod off," replied a woman. "Fetch this."

Voices laughed.

In the second or four it took her to rein in her startlement, two more small devices erupted with sparks. *They're not talking to me.* She resumed breathing.

"Hey," said a man, so close it almost stopped her heart.

Anna whirled, finding muscular Crossman two steps behind her. She splayed the fingers of her right hand, ready to strike.

"Nasty part of town, this. You shouldn't be alone, kid."

She couldn't move or breathe. Her gaze dropped to her chest for an instant before snapping back up to the man's face. The baggy coat hid her breasts, her height made her look young. Heck, Faye stood near eye level with her. *Run with it. Maybe they won't want to jump a kid.*

"I-I'll be okay." She forced a smile that lasted only a second. "Thanks."

"Some nasty business goes on 'ere at night. Where's your folks?"

Fingers relaxed, hands stuffed in pockets. "Waitin' on me. I should go."

She started away, but he clasped her shoulder. Anna froze.

"You sure? Things out here would eat you alive."

Anna made eye contact and opened herself to his surface thoughts. He thought her fourteen or so, a runaway and attributed the terror in her face to fear of a pimp—not being arm's length from a Crossman. She couldn't believe it. *He wants me to go home. This is a Crossman?*

"S-sorry. I… Friend of mine got attacked by some of your mates."

The man folded his arms. "Oh, what'd they do to pick a fight?"

"She…" Anna looked at her boots; fear became anger. "They almost raped her."

"Bollocks. That's not how we operate."

His anger made her take a step back. His surface thoughts were… *true.* The concept of a Crossman committing rape offended him as much as it horrified her. She turned to the side, confused, nauseous. The stink in the air didn't help settle her stomach.

Impostors?

"Did three Crossmen die a few nights ago?"

"Aye," he said, nodding. "What're you gettin' on about? You know somethin' bout it?"

"Yeah... I was there."

He pushed her against the wall, holding her firm, but not hard enough to hurt. "What's your game, luv? What are you tryin' to do here?"

She stared into his eyes. His anger waned at the sight of her tears; his thoughts said his confusion equaled hers. Anna explained the events of the alley, leaving out how she killed them, and pinning the deaths on unknown men in black coats to fit the 'official' story. Her retelling left her sounding like some street kid Penny had taken under her wing.

"Bollocks." He rubbed his mouth, pacing back and forth. "We're not like that, girl. *Cross*-men. We're the good guys. We do what Old Bill won't. We wouldn't do that, especially not to a schoolgirl." He pointed at her, finger an inch from her nose. "Somethin' aint right."

"Innit." Anna bit her lip, thinking about the trickle of blood on the side of the one man's head. "I-I gotta go."

"Gatherers lurkin' that way," he said. "I'd rather not leave you alone."

"It's awright. I'm little and I know how ta hide. They'll come after you. I ain't got no parts installed, they won't bother me. Look, mate. I'm not a kid. I'm twenty-three... I'll be okay."

The Crossman scowled at the street, obvious in his discomfort with letting her wander off alone. "I don't like it but, if it's what you want. Somethin' 'appens, holler. We'll be there."

Anna gave him one long, confused stare before she walked off. Rows of darkened streetlamps lined both sides of the road, shot out years ago and never replaced. Shadows crept along the ground from the moon, drawn by bodies that lay against old buildings. The wharf district played home to the type of augmented crazies too far gone even for Coventry.

It looked empty, but any one of the dark spots ahead could be hiding an attack. Here, she ran little risk of being violated in the traditional sense. Gatherers wanted body parts. If she had no cyberware to steal, they might take organs instead. Rumors abounded. Some claimed they occasionally ate their victims.

That which terrified most people reassured her. The more cyberware someone had, the more vulnerable they became to her. Confidence gave her the walk of a soldier. She made it two blocks before the high-frequency whirr of a vibro-blade powered up behind her.

A group of a half dozen creatures that could no longer truly be called men shambled out of the darkness between two abandoned warehouses. Many stooped to one side under the weight of crude, bulky replacement arms that looked like parts stolen from industrial loaders. Hoses, wires, whirring bits, and glowing eyes leered at her. What patches of living skin remained visible under the spaghetti of tubes glinted dirty and pale. Grins bared yellowing teeth. Their posture told her they looked forward to the chase as much as the kill.

Anna frowned at the lead man raising a bladed arm. Amber threads of light swam over him where electricity surged within wiring both beneath and outside his skin. The power cell in his arm glowed like a miniature star. Smiling, she clawed at the air and drew her clenching fist away from him as if pulling at unseen fabric.

Blue lightning flashed out of his body, lapping at the ground and crawling up his face. With a flick of her wrist, she drew the power into herself. He whirled about and fell to the ground. The impact sent crawling sparks searching the wet pavement in random directions.

Anna took a step at them. "Who's next?"

The Gatherers hesitated; the street hung in quiet stillness disrupted by whirring cyberware and questioning murmurs. Glancing from her to their wounded man, they neither attacked nor retreated. When the injured one gasped and pushed his chest up from the ground, James' whispered in her head.

"You are better than these wretches."

A snarl escaped her. She reached at him with both hands. A flower of lightning burst from his back, spinning skyward in a rapid series of blue flashes. Horrendous screaming preceded blood flying from his mouth. His eyes exploded into rivulets of boiling foam and he collapsed to the ground, twitching, dead.

She held her arms apart, palms to the rear and fingers splayed. Sparks cracked between her hands and the wet road. Sympathetic azure flashes, manifestations of ionized air, nipped and popped randomly on the Gatherers' bodies. Anna hardened her glare, hoping she looked meaner than she felt.

"One down. Who's got the next dance?" *Run off, you bastards. Don't make me kill you all.*

The others scattered like roaches from the light. She dusted at her coat, her fingers sending little sparks over the wool. She didn't worry about being obvious. Even if The Gatherers had the inclination to sell out a psionic to the government, Old Bill would shoot them before they had a chance to speak.

Several blocks east of The Ruin, she caught a whiff of food on the air. An all-night noshery nestled in a wedge-shaped building overlooking a three-way intersection. She sent a longing look at it, her initial sadness at thinking of the credstick she had left back at Coventry faded when she recalled the black bag. Anna fished out the NetMini and powered it up. After a few taps into the system settings menu, her old PID displayed, as did her contacts, last vidmails, and a missed call from Mister Carroll. Anna squinted at it.

How the devil long have they been watching me?

She navigated to the financial management section of the GlobeNet, discovering she had a balance of two thousand five hundred credits. The deposit occurred less than an hour ago from an unlabeled source. Hardly a fortune, but plenty enough for a meal.

With the eagerness of a schoolgirl running to recess, she darted toward the glowing windows at the angled corner.

COERCION

Ten minutes after taking a seat in a booth at Bennie's, the warmth of the place eased the numbness in her toes. She cradled an oversized cup of orange herbal tea in both hands, savoring the warmth leeching into her fingers. Small and cozy, the little restaurant held only three people at this hour: Anna, the waiter, and the man in back working the food machines.

"Whod ya do ta yer 'ead?" inquired the waiter as he set a sandwich in front of her.

She touched her cheek. "What?"

He traced a line over his forehead. "Dat's a dodgy sorta burn ya got there."

"Oh that…" The lights flickered. "Jiancorp senshelmet. Damn thing cooked itself."

"Ahh. S'wot you get usin' dat cheap shit. You need anythin' just 'oller."

She rummaged her pocket for another stimpak and stuck herself in the arm with it. Seconds after the initial chill faded, tingling surrounded her head as well as the handcuff marks. Rubbing her ankle through her boot, she scowled at the food. Sudden remembrance of the devil's bargain she agreed to dulled her appetite with worry for her friends long enough that she pulled out the datapad and turned it on.

A middle-aged man smiled up at her from the holographic display while she nibbled. Subsequent pages of data sent her into a choking fit that made the waiter run over to check on her. Careless in appearance, she made a deliberate motion to flip the pad upside down by the time he arrived. Once sure she wouldn't choke to death, he walked away. She slid the datapad off the table and held it in her lap, out of sight.

Gordon wanted her to assassinate Lord Connor Thompson, a moderate among the Lords Temporal. He'd sent her to arrange a lethal accident for a Member of Parliament. The datapad held maps, schedules, access codes, and lists of names of everyone expected to have contact with him on a daily basis. Every bit of information an assassin could ask for sat at her fingertips, enough to plot infiltration from any number of angles.

Anna switched it off, stashing it as fast as possible into the bag. If anyone caught her looking at such a thing, the authorities would be after her even if she chickened out. The Gatherer in the alley was a wretch of a creature, a hazard to anyone normal. She felt only a little guilt about killing him, less than the Crossmen who had attacked her and Penny. In light of what she'd recently learned of them, a new wave of unease settled in. The idea of murder for money, even if it would keep her two friends and an innocent child out of secret detention, seemed impossible to consider. While she *had* killed in the employ of Mr. Carroll, she had not done assassinations. Those fatalities had happened in self-defense.

I kill him or they hurt the only people I love. No way out. I could just off myself.

On an intellectual level, she knew she should eat, but didn't feel hungry. Forcing herself to pay attention to the food, she let her stare wander over empty seats and tables to the forlorn waiter half-asleep by a reefer counter full of desserts. Beeps and explosions from whatever game the cook played in the back echoed over the din of a small holo-vid player hanging from the ceiling by a terminal bedecked with small lottery adverts. Reruns of the day's news dwelled at length on the results of a Frictionless match. Man-U had nothing to do with it, so Anna ignored it.

At quarter to three in the morning, Bennie's had the same sort of somber atmosphere one would expect at a wake. The few people who showed up didn't really want to be there, didn't care to speak to anyone, and focused on finishing their meal as fast as possible. Hours from now, the place would be alive with impatient businessmen, tourists, and a twenty-minute wait for a seat, but now, it held only wretched loneliness.

No sooner did she think of Twee than the words 'Faye Taylor' come from the video screen above the counter. Devon Meath, a reporter on the

BBC news, stood in front of Nine Clifton Hill above the scrolling text 'Molester Deacon Confesses.'

"... as far as we know has not been located," said Devon. "Ordinarily, the BBC does not report the names of victims of sexual crimes; however, Miss Taylor is missing and presumed at high risk. The Met is asking anyone who may have seen the girl to contact them."

Anna leapt from her seat, jogging to the counter by the image. "Oi mate, turn that up."

The man reached up over his head and swiped a finger at a holographic green bar, dragging it to the right.

"I'm here outside the home where, in a startling turn of events, Mr. Nigel Bell, respected deacon in the C of E has recently made an announcement confessing to the fact he engaged in inappropriate contact with a neighbor girl, a mere thirteen years of age."

Devon Meath adjusted a small mic bud on his lapel and glanced over his shoulder at the puffy-faced man on the porch flanked by police. A crowd of citizens gathered on the sidewalk, behind a line of more police. The image, no doubt a bot-mounted camera, swerved left away from the reporter, closing in on the beady-eyed Mr. Bell in his powder-blue pullover.

"I could no longer bear the guilt of what I had done to the Taylor family. I lured their daughter into my flat under the pretense of minding my dogs while I ran errands. Once alone with her, I held her down and proceeded—"

The audio cut out, replaced with Devon Meath's voice speaking over images of a shocked crowd. "Suspect Bell is giving a graphic description of his crimes, which we have elected not to transmit out of respect for the victim and her family.

Audio returned with Bell in mid-sentence. "...holo-recorded the entire event for my later use. I have turned that recording over to the Metropolitan Police force, having rendered a full confession."

The crowd gasped; the video swept over them to capture their reactions. Anna blinked at the face of a man at the rear of the crowd: Doctor Mardling, tweed coat bundled about in a wind that tossed his hair. He met her gaze and smiled at the camera as if somehow *really* looking at her.

Constables escorted Mr. Bell down the steps. Two officers held back a furious man, no doubt Faye's father. The crowd turned, their silent shock morphed into derision as they hurled insults as well as objects.

Amid the pelting, the constables stuffed him into a marked car and drove off.

The camera returned to Devon Meath, flanked by a sobbing man and a woman who looked as though she had been crying continuously for hours.

"I'm here with the missing girl's parents. Missus Taylor, if your daughter is watching, what would you say to her?"

Anna looked away, unable to suffer the mother's sniveling apology for not believing her daughter, begging her to come home. Her father, too upset to talk, wept, squeezing his wife's shoulder.

She had to get back to Coventry and take Faye home, whether the girl wanted to go or not. With the last half-sandwich jammed in her mouth, Anna mumbled at the waiter to prepare her check, and swiped the NetMini past the reader. The gesture, so foreign, stunned her.

After swallowing, she glanced at the door then back to the man. "Where's the nearest autocab terminal?"

He tilted his head. "Are you all right, miss?"

"Fine… why?"

"Yer 'oldin' a 'mini, why d'ya need a street term?"

Anna stared at the small slab of technology in her hand, feeling acute in her stupidity. She had gone so many years without one that the convenience of it had slipped her mind.

"Been up too long… forgettin' meself."

She swiped at the screen, summoning an autocab to her location. By the time the little car arrived, she'd finished eating. Now realizing she had the ability to—she called Penny.

The third time she got voicemail, she had to concentrate not to destroy anything. Neurotic Penny couldn't ignore a ringtone; the woman would get the sweats if she left a text message unanswered for more than ten seconds. Anna rattled about the inside of the cab, fidgeting and worrying until it stopped at the edge of The Ruin, refusing to go in.

She ran into the muck, finding it much easier to jump over the fragments of old paving without the haze of zoom, and raced for the lone tower block that jutted up from the destruction. Had anything dared surprise her at that moment, it would have been bad for both parties. Worry removed her hesitation about hiding her power; nothing would keep her away from her friends. Ol' Jack lay on his back in the ground floor lobby, smoke peeling out of his mouth. Two small, metal cylinders as big as shotgun shells stuck to his chest.

Stunners?

Anna grabbed them, gritting her teeth as she shrugged off the crippling electrical shock and redirected the power into the wall. The cannon-like sound of the discharge shook dust off the ceiling. Ol' Jack drew in a breath as his ability to move returned. A long, low moan leaked from his lips as he sat up.

"Christ on a crutch, Anna... what the feck. How did you touch—"

"Are you all right?"

He coughed. "Someone got me BVR, no idea what..."

"BVR?" Anna helped him prop up against the wall.

"Beyond visual range... sorry. Sniper or something."

"Shit." She looked torn between him and the stairs.

When he waved her on and gave a thumbs-up, she ran up a dozen stories. Gasping for air, she froze stock still at the sight of Penny's door half open. She found her apartment empty; no sign of Faye, only a small white bear perched at the foot of the bed with zip ties on its paws.

"No," she yelled, turning and sprinting past two doors into Penny's flat.

Spawny's hairy ass greeted her as she rounded out of the little access hallway past the bathroom. He lay bent over the couch, beaten bloody and secured hand and foot by plastic zip ties. Penny was on the far side of the couch, naked and hogtied, but didn't appear hurt. Anna skidded to a halt on her knees by her friend, holding her fingers a half-inch apart on either side of the plastic. A brief spark melted the bindings. After freeing her, she hauled the ragdoll of a woman into a hug, patting and shaking her until she moaned.

"Anna?"

She helped her friend stand, guiding her to the bed and wrapping her in a sheet. "What the bloody 'ell 'appened?"

Penny swooned in a chemical fog, her arm flopping at the sheet in an attempt to grab it. "We were shaggin' when we heard Twee scream bloody murder. He got up to go check on her and these men kicked his ass in the door. They came for me when I tried to run. They nicked Twee, didn't much look like the filth."

She brushed green crystalline residue off Penny's shoulder. A thousand tiny wounds from minuscule needles created a rash-like patch tacky with blood. "No... They weren't. Are you all right? They shot you with a tranquilizer needler."

"Little shaken, but all they did was put us out of their way." Penny squinted. "The devil is a whatever the hell you just said?"

"Solid block of chemical tranq, shaved into shards and shot out of a gun. Best tool for abductions."

"I'm not gonna ask how you know that." Penny squeezed, sniffling into Anna's shoulder.

Anna held her until Spawny moaned. She melted the binders from him and hit him in the back with a stimpak. His bruising lessened, the blood dripping from his nose stopped. He groaned while crawling down onto the rug into a fetal position. A liberal dose of obscenities fell from his mouth.

"Bastards." Anna threw a blanket over him and squinted at the wall.

"I didn't do a fing!" blurted Spawny.

Penny gathered the sheet tight to herself and roamed about, plucking her clothes off the rug. "Why would they arrest her? She 'asn't left the place since she arrived."

Spawny dragged himself onto the bed. "Cops smelled sweet meat. She's probably getting the ol' pig on a spit right now."

Penny threw his underwear at him. "How can you say that?"

Anna's voice came cold and soft. "No. She isn't. Cops don't 'ave 'er. CSB does. Besides, the cops don't come in here lookin' for it."

"Wha?" Spawny lifted an eyebrow. "That's a pile of cack, she's not... umm..."

"Like me? No." Anna shook her head. "It's got nothin' to do with 'er."

After pulling her smalls and dress back on, Penny abandoned the sheet and put an arm around Anna. "Are you all right, Anna? You seem... different. Don't think I ever seen ya this, umm..."

"Confident." Spawny moaned. "Ye look like a cat what's eyein' a mouse."

Penny sank into the couch at Spawny's side, shaking. The sight of the woman who had protected her for ten years reduced to a shivering, terrified wretch sent sparks dancing up and down Anna's arms.

"Oh, someone's 'bout to 'ave a bad day." Spawny blinked.

"I'm sorry." Anna looked down. "This is all my fault. I won't let them hurt you again."

Anna stormed for the door.

"Anna! Wait!" Penny yelled, breaking into sobs. "What's going on?"

It took every ounce of Anna's willpower not to turn around. "I have some things I have to do to keep the people I love from being hurt. Don't worry about me. Protect yourselves. I gotta go."

SECOND OPINION

Anna clung to the NetMini, standing at the edge of The Ruin while waiting for the autocab. She had forgotten how much of a lifeline the little devices were. A group of constables by the pod building eyed her with suspicion. Constable Brown stood among them and seemed about ready to have a heart attack. She glared at him.

What are you thinking about, you pig?

Her heart fluttered as she touched his surface thoughts. He knew. The CSB had been here. They told the officers to leave her alone. They told Brown they'd 'black bag' him if he touched her again. They showed him how close he'd come to death. He had seen the alley video; he knew what she could have done to him if she wasn't high. In that moment of eye contact, he froze like a deer staring down a hunter's rifle, wondering if she would kill him. Brown tugged at the collar of his shirt, looking like he couldn't breathe. Her chilling glare sent him scurrying inside like the filth he was. The Sergeant came outside, no doubt to see what had spooked Brown. He tilted his head at her, and approached.

Anna looked off toward London proper, waiting for the squishing footsteps to stop. "Good day, sergeant."

"Indeed, girl. You look like a different person. Off the poison?"

"Couple days now. I'm trying, sir. 'Tis a bastard of an albatross." Her anger ebbed. "I'm not sure what they told you, but I'm not dangerous. All I want is to be left alone and live like anyone else. I've no interest in trouble with the law."

"That's good to hear." He glanced at an approaching pair of lights. "Sorry about Brown. Damn union got involved. I couldn't ship him off. Looks like you've a lot on your mind."

The autocab pulled up and opened its door.

"It's the CSB, sir. I probably shouldn't say more. People could get hurt."

"Aye. Take care of yourself." He started to walk back to the pod, but stopped to smile back. "Oh, and eat something."

Anna almost returned the smile, then settled into the car. She recited Doctor Mardling's address and closed her eyes. The engines whined as it got underway, and the gentle sway of the ride lulled her into a nap.

♫ ⚘ 🏛 ◌ ♋

A HAND ON HER SHOULDER JOSTLED HER AWAKE. SHE LOOKED UP INTO blinding bright light. From behind the glare came a woman's voice.

"You all right, miss?"

She had fallen asleep; the autocab had parked in the subterranean parking deck of James' building. When she didn't get out, it summoned the police. The fatigue of such a brief sleep kept her emotion neutral as she dragged herself to her feet.

"Sorry 'bout that, I've 'ad a long day."

The female constable waved something in her face. "Breathe please."

Anna exhaled on it, making it chirp.

"All right then, you're not intoxicated. Do you need assistance?"

"Been awake almost twenty hours, constable… Just comin' 'ome."

"Which one's yours?"

She gave James' door number. "It's not my flat. I live with my boyfriend."

Electronic noises came from another constable a few yards away as he looked her up in the system. He gave a nonchalant nod to his partner, who relaxed. Her file evidently remained clean.

Minutes later, she wobbled up to the door and hit the buzzer. The greyish-white panel slid to the side, revealing a bare chested and weary James Mardling in long flannel pajamas. His delirious frown became a smile at who had stolen him from sleep at five in the morning.

"James! I need help!" She all but tackled him in the door. "They've taken Faye. They're going to kidnap Penny and Spawny as well if I don't do what they ask."

He rubbed his eyes. "Calm yourself, Anna. The girl should be able to go home now."

"You made him confess?"

"Of course." He chuckled. "Men like that do not simply develop a conscience and give themselves up." James's grin fell flat. "I had half a mind to make him embellish what he'd done to her, but his collection of holo-disks couldn't hold a candle to my imagination."

Anna fumed. "You should've let me kill him."

He patted her shoulder. "The girl whacked him over the head with a porcelain cat to get away. Gave him a slight bump, less than he deserved; however, I suspect he will get far worse in jail. You need some sleep."

"James, there's no time." She pulled on him. "They took Faye!"

"You... need... sleep."

His words echoed around her mind in a repeating circle. The next thing Anna knew, she lay on the couch under a blanket, boots and socks off. The overcast gloom from the windows offered little clue as to the hour. Fog hung between her ears. She sat up and stretched, momentarily confused by the red lines around her ankles. Her finger traced the mark, and soreness brought everything back in flashes. Anna bounded to her feet and sprinted toward shifting blue-orange light in the rear hallway.

James sat at a desk of gleaming silver and glass, manipulating images of blobs, atoms, and bits of brain. Holograms floated, twisting and growing in response to his fingers brushing the light. Almost everything hovering there went way over her head.

She swooned into the doorframe and wiped her eyes. "What time is it?"

He swiveled around to face her, smiling at the sight of her. "A touch past noon."

"Oh, shit. Faye..."

James rushed from his seat, catching her as she started to collapse from dizziness, and guided her to a small green bench at the back of his office and took a seat next to her, holding her hands together.

"You were utterly exhausted. Take a breath and tell me what happened."

"I went back to Coventry Tower to get Faye. I saw a news bit about that nonce confessing and wanted to bring her home, but the CSB took her."

"What?" James let go of her and leapt up, pacing. "Why would they do that? It makes no sense for them to pay attention to a small girl. She is neither a political matter nor psionic."

Anna recounted her brief abduction. The retelling of it sounded lifeless in her woozy state. Nonetheless, the more she talked, the redder James' cheeks became. By the time she got to the point where she'd come to on the boat, his eyes contained a terrifying level of anger. He seemed to take notice of her fear and forced a disingenuous smile. She leaned into him, clinging.

"They want me to kill this man. They said if I did it, they'd leave me off the register. If I don't they'll take Faye, and Penny, and Spawny and shut them away somewhere forever."

He pondered, at last shaking his head. "No, I doubt they will harm your little friend. We should step up my plan to relocate."

"James... I can't just leave her to them. Gordon told me they could do whatever they wanted. They will kill her if I don't do what they ask, I know it... and I can't let Penny wallow in Coventry." Her head returned to his shoulder. "You've saved me from that awful place... I want to go with you, but I can't be happy if she's still stuck there."

Doctor Mardling glanced at the wall. "Lord Thompson is a moderate. He is pushing an agenda of more lenient treatment of psionics. Rumor is that his son has the gift, but no one has proved or disproved it. He represents a true possibility for change, Anna. If he were to die, it could spell disaster for every psionic in the UK."

"I don't want to kill him, but what choice do I have? I'm not sure leaving Britain is a good idea... it's all I've ever known."

"As much as it pains me to leave"—he dropped volume to a conspiratorial whisper—"it is my home too, after all"—he raised his voice —"it would be less risky for us all."

"How do you figure that?" Anna gripped the carpet with her toes, feeling lost.

"In the Colonies, the government does not possess the insufferable paranoia of King William. They have psionic constables as well. It would be far easier to get on there and not arouse undue suspicion. Would you not find it pleasant to exist without the need to hide your nature?"

"Colony? You mean the UCF?" Anna tilted her head.

"Is that what they call themselves now?" James rolled his eyes. "Certainly the little girl is better off in custody than on the street. She is not psionic, so they have no reason to harm her. You should ignore

Thompson and take this opportunity to come with me where they cannot reach you. It is sad, but sometimes the world is a sad place."

"I suppose..." Anna wandered back to the sofa and fell on it. "I can't toddle off to the far side of the pond and leave them in that grotty shithole. She's always been there for me, I..."

James studied the ceiling for a moment.

"Besides, you've eliminated the reason Faye couldn't return home. I don't want to leave her to those bastards. There's got to be something we can do!"

"Agent Gordon, is it?" He ran a hand over her hair. "Perhaps there is at that..."

James scurried around his work area, knocking stacked datapads from his desk in a feverish search for a blank holodisk. He popped it into a writer and waved Anna to join him.

"Pull up that chair."

She padded over, sitting as close as she could, cross-legged on the chair. James rested one hand on the optical writer and cradled the other around her head. The warmth on the back of her neck made her shiver.

"Doctor Mardling—"

"James," he said, smiling.

She glanced down, matching his smile and blushing. "James, what are you doing?"

"I think you should pay Thompson a visit. Now think about your meeting with that tosser, Gordon."

His words filtered into her mind. Lightheadedness crept over her. James' eyes seemed to glow as the room around him blurred. Once more, she found herself restrained in the chair, screaming at the silent echoes around her. The scene played in her memory as if on fast forward, slowing down only when Gordon spoke of his plan for her. When the remembering ceased, her consciousness returned to James's study. She broke down in sobs, trying to rub the soreness out of her wrists.

James rushed over and held her tight. "Anna... I am here, Anna. Everything will be just fine."

TEMPORAL SHIFT

Lord Connor Thompson's estate sat northwest of the city center, far enough removed that the land allowed a copious front lawn with a reflecting pool. Anna glanced at a massive marble statue of a man on a horse, hanging inexplicably above the water. When it shimmered into a frolicking marble nymph, she knew it to be a hologram; multi-ton statues didn't often float in midair. Her nerves had gotten the better of her despite her concealment atop the brick wall. She lay flat on her stomach in the shade of a trio of huge evergreen shrubs inside the corner. The wide and tall perimeter barricade hid her from patrols going past on the ground, so long as she stay prone and motionless. The swaying branches blocked direct view from the house.

For an hour, she remained still, observing the pattern of patrol teams circling the grounds while cold seeped from the bricks into her clothes. The rain had taken a holiday for the past two days, leaving the wall and the grounds as dry as they were likely to ever be. According to the datapad, the perimeter was rimmed with sensors, which would trigger alarms if they lost power. If she got any closer, her body heat would give her away.

A private security company operated here, each group consisted of two men and an artificial dog. She had little doubt the hound bot used night vision and perhaps thermal; the men would be easy enough to get past, but her pseudo-invisibility didn't work on things that had no brain.

She slid to the ground outside, convinced crossing the yard would be foolish. The wall offered only two entrances, a big gate out front and a smaller one at the back. The rear offered the best chance of entry, monitored only by a single live guard. After sneaking around the side, she crouched in the shadow of a disused stable and checked the time on her NetMini. If the information Gordon provided was accurate, a cleaning crew should arrive in minutes. Lord Thompson, an ardent backer of the Labour Party, insisted on providing jobs to people rather than machines. Instrumental in the ban on non-sentient dolls, he made a public show of hiring real people for every function in his estate.

A day and a half of research had taught her the schedules of everyone involved with the property. It brought her back to her time working for Carroll. As odd as it was to plot the infiltration of a governmental residence, it made her feel alive again. She advanced as close as she could, lurking in the shadowy alcove of a building across the street, waiting. Right on time, a white van whirred into place and pulled into a tiny parking lot by the rear gate. Anna squinted at a post-mounted camera pointed at the area, sensing the electricity inside and forcing it away. Three men and three women in white jumpsuits got out. One man, the oldest of the lot, moved to the security booth and chatted with the guard. The others gathered supplies from the rear and side doors. A short Indian woman remained at back end after unloading two wearable vacuums.

The lights on the camera winked out, attracting the attention of the guard. Anna sprinted across the street during the distraction. She ran up behind the straggler, grasping her at the neck and covering her mouth.

"Sorry, miss. Need to borrow your coat."

A modest shock knocked the woman senseless. Anna shoved her into the van and climbed in on top of her, pulling the doors closed. While the guard punched his monitor station, Anna relieved the woman of her white jumpsuit and cap, then put them on. She smirked at the dark-skinned face on the ID clipped to her breast pocket.

"Oh, this'll be interesting."

The woman moaned as she came to. At the sight of Anna, she cowered. "Please, I have two kids…"

"Shh." Anna covered the woman's mouth. "I've no interest in harming you."

"Sod it all," yelled a voice from outside. "Stupid new cameras—oh, wait… there we go. Must've been a power cut."

Anna spun to glare at the wall of the van: racks of cleaning supplies and maintenance parts. She hogtied the cleaning worker with some spare power cords, earning a harsh glare as she taped over her mouth.

"Really sorry about this, but a little girl's life depends on it."

Anna slipped out the back doors and adjusted her hat before picking up both vacuums. The other cleaners entered the checkpoint in single file, swiping their ID cards at the terminal before a guard waved them in. She trotted over to the end of the line, tugging down on the visor. When she got to the machine, she locked eyes with the incredulous security man. Making his brain see a different person was much easier than forcing it not to acknowledge anyone at all.

She thrust her telepathy into his head. Anna's pale face and snow-white hair turned dark in his perception, and she forced him not to notice the faint whimpers and banging in the van.

That's right, Nate. I'm Sajala. See me as who you expect me to be.

The face of Sajala Kaur appeared in hologram to his right as she swiped the card past the sensor. Nate broke out in a cold sweat, shivering. He knew something wasn't right, but his mind caved, unable to deal with the oddity.

"Are you all right, Nate? You look a bit peaky."

"F-fine… 'ave a good shift."

The gate opened and she hurried to rejoin the other cleaning staff. None looked back as they walked in single-file for the servant's entrance. Anna kept her head down, using the visor to hide from cameras. Once inside the building, she ducked away from them into the first doorway she found—a storage closet.

"Sajala, why don't you head—" the elder cleaning man stopped. "Sajala?"

Anna flattened into the wall, avoiding the curious man peering out the window. As soon as he moved away, she tossed the hat and slipped out of the jumpsuit, bundling them together and stuffing them behind a pile of boxes. Once the hallway sounded empty, she eased the door to the side and peered out. Sudden motion came from her right. Anna flinched a split second before a pistol cracked her across the head.

The impact knocked her stumbling back into the closet on her ass. One of the estate security people, a tall dark-skinned man in a black suit complete with sunglasses and earbud, pounced on her before the room stopped spinning. He rolled her face down and put the gun to her head.

"Don't try anything, luv. Hands behind."

Anna gathered herself, focusing on a disabling shock. Before she could deliver it, another strike to the back of her head bounced her cheek off the floor. Her senses returned as the electric whirr of metal binders locked her wrists at her back. Less-than-gentle hands roamed her body, though the contact was brief and professional.

Fuck.

"No weapons."

"Roger," crackled a voice from his ear.

Double fuck.

"On your feet, lass." He hauled her up by a fistful of coat. "I don't suppose you'd care to make this easier on both of us and just tell me what the feck you're doing here?"

Anna put on her most innocent smile. "Sorry, sir. Was a dare from me mates. Please don't tell my parents."

He frowned.

She narrowed her eyes, gazing at his crotch. "Hey… It's a 'armless prank. How bout I give you a gobble and you let me go home? Even?"

His face reddened. "What sort of man do you think I am?"

She loosed an exasperated sigh. "A fine, upstanding officer of the law, apparently."

He shoved her by one shoulder toward the door.

"Sorry."

The man looked down at her. "You're a bit past sorry, lass."

"No, I mean… Sorry." She gathered a charge at the closest bit of exposed skin to him: her nose.

The spark hit him in the face, knocking him flat. Her eyes watered, the jolt hit her like a punch. Anna shook it off and reined in her fear. She tensed her arms, pulling the binders tight to her skin. Sparks lapped at the metal as her brain felt its way around the current paths within the device. A shape formed as a trace of amber light in her consciousness. She disregarded the complex tangle of circuitry and focused on the contact points of the actuator motor. With a little voltage forced into the right place, they whirred open.

It took all her strength to drag the security man close enough to one of the installed shelves and cuff him to it. She grabbed the binders, pumping them full of too much current until smoke peeled from them, ensuring he would be stuck there until someone brought cutters. She swiped his earbud and threw it across the room.

They'll have called Old Bill by now. I don't have much time.

She ran out, following as best she could recall the map she had been staring at all morning. The hallway led to the kitchen, dark and empty at this hour. At the far end, she fed the head butler's code into the wall panel and gained access to the main part of the dwelling. She hurried down a well-lit stretch of lacquered wood floor flanked by miniature marble lions, and slipped behind a dark burgundy tapestry at the clamor of approaching boots.

Two security men tromped by in silence, trailed by snippets of radio conversation going along in their surface thoughts, coordinating with someone watching cameras trying to find her. She concentrated on them, refusing to allow them to see her. When they disappeared around the distant corner, she left her hiding place and crept further down until the floor turned from decorated wood to thick carpet. The décor provided an even more ostentatious display of wealth than his hiring of live servants instead of cleaning bots.

An armored elevator waited right where the map said it would, and the codes Gordon provided worked like a charm. Somehow, he had gotten a hold of a special sequence that also disabled the cameras. No doubt Thompson used that feature for clandestine meetings.

On the third level, a less festive hallway of muted brown wood and royal blue carpet went from the elevator to his private chamber. She sprinted past a library, atrium, and several unlabeled rooms, halting outside the office. After a few seconds of listening to muted voices inside, she rolled up her sleeves and burst in.

Anna kicked the door closed behind her and raised her hands. A security man on either side grabbed her forearms as the startled Lord Connor Thomson gaped from behind a mammoth black marble desk. She closed her eyes, concentrating on where her bare arms made contact with the security men's hands. With an electric *buzz*, two slabs of unconscious meat fell to the ground, one on either side of her.

Lord Thompson raised his hands. "W-w-w—"

When she walked toward him, a feat she thought impossible occurred —his face grew whiter.

Clutching at his chest, he gasped. "Please…"

She shifted her hips and sat on the edge of the desk, crossing her legs and smiling at him. "Relax, old bloke. I'm not here to hurt you. I came to warn you."

He sagged down in the high-backed chair, struggling to breathe. "W-who are you?"

"That's not important." She peeled open a pants pocket even with her right knee; the sharp rip of the Velcro closure made him jump. Anna dropped a holodisk in front of him. It wobbled like a top, four chromatic plastic discs on a central spindle. "That is."

Lord Thompson stared at his reflection upon the silver surface, hand hovering an inch away as if it would burn him to touch it. He swallowed hard and picked the holodisk up in two fingers. "What's this about?"

"The CSB is trying to have you killed. They want to slip their leash... what little of one there is. As far as they're concerned, I've been sent here to kill you and make it look like an accident."

"That's preposterous!" He broke out in a sweat. "What proof do you have?"

She gestured at the disk. "Oh, don't give me that look. If I were here to kill you, I'd not be talking. I'm not an assassin."

He poked at his desk. A six-inch square of the top rose upward without a sound, exposing a recessed chamber with a receptacle for the holodisk. He set it in and the compartment sank closed. A few seconds later, one file appeared on his screen. Lord Thompson poked his finger at the holographic screen, opening it. Blurry video, crisscrossed with faint blue lines, replayed her memory of Agent Gordon's chat. The point of view was hers, the image smeared away to fractal patterns every time the inhibitor smashed her brain into pulp. Anna looked away, not much caring to re-watch it for a third time.

When it stopped, Lord Thompson looked at her. "This file... This is quite damning, was this you?"

Her expression gave it away. She couldn't explain how James had taken her memories and put them on a holodisk; some ability he had with machines combined with Telepathy.

"There's no K-N on this video, how do I know it's real?"

She looked at him. "My thoughts don't have a Karsson-Neimand checksum, milord. It's a direct transfer from my brain to disk."

Staring into old grey eyes, she forced tidbits of the experience into his mind.

He tensed, grasping his forehead from a phantom inhibitor burn. "You're a psionic? You don't have a tag."

"I'll die before I let them put a bomb inside my head. We're not damned animals. Would you put one in your son?" At the mention of it, his surface thoughts betrayed the truth of the boy's ability. "I thought not." She paused a few seconds in search of calm. "A friend of mine believes you are on our side, trying to make things better for us here. Agent Gordon wants me to kill you so he can go on some kind of heretic-burning rampage. I'm sure he'd savor the irony of a psionic killing the MP trying to help psionics."

Swallowing hard, Lord Thompson edged away from the desk. "I see…"

"Do you really think I'm going to harm you? It's what he wants. It would start open season on every psionic in Great Britain. I've come to warn you and ask for your help. You have to stop them from hunting us like wild animals. We're people just like you."

"If… If this is true then—"

A blaring electronic ring all but knocked Lord Thompson out of his chair and stopped Anna's heart for a beat. The VidPhone flashed with an incoming call. Paralyzed from the shock, the old man seemed capable only of staring at it. Anna leaned over and hit the answer key.

The black holo-screen that scrolled open offered no video feed. After a second of silence, an eerie female voice flooded the room from speakers mounted in the ceiling.

"Hello Anna… Milord Thompson. You should consider getting down rather soon, preferably away from any place you can be seen from the outside."

Anna glanced from the source of the voice to Thompson and then to the window. Amid a black window in a building across the street, a glint of moonlight flashed.

"Sniper!" Anna screamed, diving over the desk.

She tackled him to the rug, cringing as shattering glass rained down. The *crack* of a suppressed gunshot chased the sharp *ping* of a slug bouncing off the marble desk. Anna scrambled onto her knees and dragged him to the right behind a patch of solid wall between two floor-to-ceiling windows. Panting, she sat with her back to the stone and stared at him.

"That's a bit odd, milord."

"You don't say?"

Anna smirked. "Seems you're more terrified of me than you are of 'aving a sniper taking pot shots at you."

"I've been shot at before… I know how bullets work, but I've never been alone with an unregistered psionic."

"Other than your son?"

He cringed.

She patted him on the thigh. "I'm easier to talk to than a bullet."

Two shots tore neat holes in the brickwork between their heads, spraying them with dust.

He pulled her to the ground. "Nonetheless, I think that fellow outside is attempting to interrupt our chat."

FIT UP

Lord Thompson crawled away from the wall, moving on his own as much as she pulled him "Bugger it all, where the hell is the security team?"

"Sorry about them, milord." Anna pulled her sleeves down.

The men lying on the rug moaned as if in reply.

Another shot nipped the back of his coat, leaving a tear in a suit worth more credits than Anna had ever seen in one place. She pounced and held him as low to the ground as possible until the plaster stopped flying. The last two shots felt aimed for her. Shouting came from outside as security teams converged toward the front gate.

"Guess they're pissed at me for not offing you."

He flashed a grim look. "If they kill us both, they can make up any story they damn well care to."

"Bastards." Anna froze for a moment. "They were gonna say a psionic killed you and kill me anyway. Even if I'd done what they asked, they'd have done the dirty on me."

"I do so enjoy politics," he said, holding up a finger.

The silence made her think the sniper had decided to reposition or flee. She hauled Lord Thompson to his feet and made to run with him. One of the security men recovered and lunged at her. He stiff-armed her across the chest, knocking her back over the marble desk. Unable to breathe, she slid with a landslide of office supplies and small gold statues, hitting the ground on her front. He seized her from behind in a bear hug, crushing the rest of the air out of her lungs.

"Get 'er!" he shouted to the other man.

The other bodyguard flipped a collapsible truncheon out to length and took aim at the side of her head.

Lord Thompson barreled forward, putting his hands on the massive arms around her chest. "Stop it, she's not the threat."

The security man's anger continued to flow from his great biceps into her ribs. Hot breath fell over her head from behind. She squirmed but couldn't move.

"Dammit Ben, let her down this instant."

The goliath released his grip and she stumbled forward, sprawled over the desk, breathless and fighting to avoid passing out. Between getting pounded in the chest and squeezed, the room spun. Realizing she lay draped with her ass in the air, in perfect view of the sniper, Anna let her weight take her to the floor, kneeling, leaning against the cold marble.

She wheezed, gesturing at the wrecked terminal. "Holodisk—"

The other man had already ushered Thompson out of the room, and the remaining man glared at her as if he wanted to finish the job. His surface thoughts focused on anger at being made the fool by such a tiny woman. After a momentary stalemate, he shoved her out of the way and almost tore the desk open in his effort to retrieve the disk. He smashed his fist into the desk several times until finding the right spot to open the reader. With the disk in his pocket, he grabbed her by the shirt and hauled her to her feet.

"Look… Ben, is it? We're on the same team right now. Please don't make me kill you. You're huge and I'm little. My only chance is to toast your bollocks off and I'd really rather not."

He squinted.

"Ben…" That same eerie voice emanated from the speakers. "Would you be a dear and turn ninety degrees to the right?"

For no particular reason, he complied. As soon as he stopped moving, a bullet came in the broken window and lodged in his cybernetic left arm with a sparking *clank*, rather than his heart.

"Thank you Ben." The vid call hung up.

He ran out the door, dragging Anna despite her pounding on his natural arm. Once in the hallway, he set her on her feet where a number of other, much smaller, security personnel gathered around Lord Thompson.

Before she could get a word out, he pushed her into the wall and gathered her arms behind her back. Anna sighed as someone patted her down.

"No weapons sir," said a voice from somewhere above her head.

Lord Thompson moved closer, waving off the man securing her with handcuffs. "That won't be necessary, Clive. She could've killed me easily if she'd wanted to. What's going on?"

"Everything is on that disc. The CSB wanted a psionic to kill you to stir up paranoia." She waited while the guard removed the restraints. "They're terrified at the thought you might regard us as actual people."

"Sir, we've got reports of hostiles outside. It's not safe here," said another man, grabbing at Thompson's shoulder.

Anna adjusted her shirt back into place. "Seems your security can take it from here, milord. It would be healthier for everyone concerned if I was nowhere near you. Am I free to go?"

"I never did get your name, miss..."

She had little time to debate the thought. The CSB already knew who she was. Having an ally in Parliament couldn't hurt. "Anna Morgan, milord."

Lord Thompson nodded at her with a grateful smile, then gave a nod of assent to her departure.

Having little need for stealth, she ran for the main stairwell and followed it around a graceful sweeping arc to the ground floor. Tall bay windows offered a view of the utter chaos reigning outside. Security forces swarmed the grounds in search of the sniper, trading shots with unseen assailants. Anna headed for the main entrance, but crashed to an abrupt halt with a fleshy *thud* against unmoving doors. A quick psionic tug drew the power out of the magnetic locks and she shoved one side open. When she released her control of the electrical system, the magnet pulled it closed with such a *bang* some of the men whipped about thinking a shot had been fired behind them.

Two bullets bounced off the porch near her boots, sending her into a panicky sprint toward a row of security vehicles collected in the roundabout by the door. A van, two cars, and three motorbikes sat unmanned in the glare of floodlights. Anna leapt onto one of the e-bikes, which started to roll forward from the force of her impact.

Another shot nicked the left side mirror as she accelerated across the grounds and steered for the half-closed gate. When the tires hit street, she fishtailed to line up with the road, then gunned it. High-pitched whining came from both wheels as electric motors spun the treaded loops that served as tires. As it picked up speed, the frame extended. The bike grew longer and lower. She leaned forward, trying to remember how to ride; the last time she touched one of these had been before she touched zoom.

"Like riding a bike, right?" she muttered.

At a flash of light in the remaining mirror, she peered back and up. A small military VTOL craft, large enough to carry two people, swerved around a tall building and bore down on her. Black stealth coating ate the light, making the parts not windows or weapons seem like a void. It resembled a baby fighter craft, short and stubby with a fat central body. Red lights winked from both tips of the 'V' shaped tail, and the downward canted wings bristled with rocket pods.

A man leaned out the open side door, raising a rifle.

Sweet mother...

Anna wrenched the bike into a hard left around a corner a second before a cannon on the craft's nose cut loose. Glass shattered behind her. The VTOL lumbered after, skidding into a turn, almost clipping buildings. She let out an uneasy wail when her balance faltered on another skidding turn. Bullets skipped off the road behind her. After another near-crash into the side of a high-rise, he pilot climbed out of the canyon of office towers.

She accelerated on a straightaway, believing she had lost the plane. A near miss sprayed her in the face with fragments of paving. Too scared to speed up, she hit the brakes. Another shot gouged the road in front of her. The VTOL vanished behind a glittering tower ahead on the left. Anna leaned into a right turn and twisted the handgrip. A sudden burst of speed drilled her into the seat and came close to throwing her into a row of shrubberies along a central island in the road.

The VTOL zipped into view up ahead, the whine of ion thrusters roaring. Two small, unguided rockets leapt from the wings. Screaming, she pinned the accelerator and flattened her body to the motorbike trying to keep it from flipping over in a wheelie. A wave of heat and light fell on her from two successive explosions *way* too close to her back tire. In the mirror, the wreckage of a parked car spun, flaming, into the street.

They've lost their bloody minds.

Buildings and streetlamps tore past in a blur of color and shrapnel. Turn after turn, the damnable thing managed to follow. Not brave enough to push the bike faster than she had done already, she searched with wild eyes for anything she could do in order to get away. A couple of blocks ahead, an old red sign beckoned her to an ancient stairway boarded up longer than she had been alive.

The Tube.

Anna drove the bike through splintering planking as the VTOL swung around into view between two buildings. She leaned on the throttle and bounced down stairs into the old abandoned Tube system. The pavement behind her erupted into a fireball with a deafening concussive *whump* and the reek of burning chemicals.

Debris blew past her, laced with flames driven by the downblast from the VTOL lurching to a midair halt above the subway entrance. Anna focused on the small patch of headlight offering a glimpse into the darkness of another world.

The Tube scared the hell out of her—but the VTOL couldn't follow.

TUNNEL FLIGHT

Unseen drips broke the silent dark with intermittent chirps. At a standstill, the electric bike made little noise other than a below-audible hum that made Anna sense an otherworldly presence nearby. She twisted the handlebars, panning the headlights over cobwebs, decay, and the dust covering everything on the old train platform. With the advent of autocabs and the maglev trams, the old Tube system had been left to the use of those desperate enough to venture down there.

Rumors abounded regarding what lurked below the city. Some believed ordinary poor people, much like those in Coventry, eked out a living in a sort of neo-primitive society separate from the world above. Others claimed various military research projects involving gene manipulation had been exiled down there, but most regarded those stories as beyond credible. Tales of cyber gangs, organ thieves, mad bot-makers, and everything else one could imagine had circulated at one time or another. What had once been a mover of London's people had become a mover of London's imagination.

She slumped forward, resting her forehead on her arms across the handlebars. In a place the VTOL couldn't follow, she hoped for a moment of peace. If its crew jumped out and tried to chase her on foot, she felt confident that random turns she had made over the past few spans of tunnel would've left them as lost as she'd gotten herself. Or maybe all the stories and legends would keep them out.

Anna jumped at a *crunch* of splintering wood and whirled to the rear with a gasp. A vibrating light source slid along the curved wall of the track tunnel. To the right, the clatter of multiple people moving broke the silence. She pivoted the handlebars toward the noise, the sudden glare stunning half a dozen men. Clad in greyish brown rags, they wore a mixture of old cloth, leather, and scavenged bits of metal. Like feral beings, they reacted to light with growls, shielding their eyes with their arms. Knives, swords, and crowbars gleamed.

"S'pose you chaps are the welcoming committee…"

With the *boom* of a gunshot, white tiles exploded away from a column inches above her head. A headlight hovered at the point where the track tunnel opened. Another bike idled there, a large figure upon it.

Agent Gordon's voice echoed over the stillness. "I thought we had an arrangement."

A baritone laugh preceded another shot and more tile dust. *Yeah, you wanted to arrange me right into the fecking ground, bastard.* She twisted the accelerator and the bike surged forward, pulling a small wheelie as she leapt down to the tracks. Gordon's headlights came around the curve behind her, gaining. A camera flash of azure lit the tunnel as he fired again. A ricochet pinged above her. Her console flickered, threatening to burn out from her surge of fear.

Old light mounts flooded the shaft behind her with showers of orange sparks. Her panic tugged at forgotten power lines. Up ahead, the tube split at a fork; she jumped the tracks and went left, hoping Gordon would flub the maneuver and wipe out. Alas, he kept right on her.

Barricades came at her one after the other, appearing in her headlights seconds before she had to react to avoid them. Whoever lived here had fortified this tunnel against attack. The pounding of her heart in her ears overpowered the whine of the e-motors at the thought she headed right into the den of a gang. Sweaty hands loosened her grip. She gritted her teeth and growled, trying to stay more angry than terrified.

Gordon's headlights vanished for an instant behind a heavy cloud of brown fog and smashing noises. He had taken a barricade head-on.

Weaving around the debris slowed her to a pace not much faster than she could have run, though it had an equal effect on him.

"There's no point to running, Morgan," he yelled. "I'll find you anywhere in Britain you go."

Soon as Faye's at home, I won't be in Britain.

After a dozen improvised walls, the barricades stopped. On clear track, she got up to about sixty-five. Gordon's bike rushed up behind her. A glint of a handgun flashed in her rearview mirror. She yanked the bike left, dodging two quick shots, which sparked off the walls. He kept firing at an almost casual pace. She imagined him aiming, squeezing off a shot and savoring the sound it made before shooting again. The taste of dust and mold made her cough. She let go with one hand in an attempt to pull her shirt over her face. A wobble in the steering ended made her slam both hands onto the grips to keep control.

Gordon yelled as he fired, whatever he said lost to the thunderous echo of his sidearm in the confines of the Tube. Anna ventured a peek back for only a second, screaming when she looked forward again—a hanging cloth came out of nowhere like a glowing wraith in the dark. She drove into it, unable to react in time. It tore loose from the ceiling and wrapped over her, sending her into a fit of frantic screaming and flailing. Terror hit a crescendo that caused her power to leap out of control. Both bikes flashed with azure clouds of staccato lightning and went dark.

Sudden deceleration threw her forward over the handlebars, tumbling head over ass in the air twice before she crashed into the curved tube wall on her back upside down. Pain from impact didn't register until after she slid to the ground. Somewhere in the dark, Gordon's bike crashed.

Anna leapt upright, desperate to get away from him.

Her head throbbed; the total lack of light made her feel dizzier. Gordon moaned… somewhere. She grasped at the wall, hurting all over. By some miracle of luck, she hadn't broken any bones. *If I make any kind of light, he's going to shoot me.* Before she could take a step, the headlight of her e-bike came back on, projecting a cone in the heavy, swirling dust. A second later, Gordon's bike lit up a dozen meters behind.

Anna sprint-limped for her ride, but tripped over the bracing struts between tracks and fell flat on her chest. Gordon fired over her; the timing of the miss was too perfect. *He's bloody toying with me.* She closed her eyes and projected a bright arc into the rail. The sudden flash made him yell.

He growled.

Having no interest in waiting around to see how long he would stay blind, she hauled her motorbike upright and threw a leg over. Her entire body tensed from pain as she twisted the handgrip. The rear tire shot a spray of gravel and dirt.

Gordon fired out of the dark; the shot burned a slice of pain over her left thigh from a graze. She curled her body tight to the bike, trying to find the courage to drive faster in such an environment. Artificial light glowed from further down the tunnel, indicating the presence of another station.

Seconds later, the tunnel expanded to a platform. She steered for a stack of wood, hitting it like a jump ramp that catapulted the bike up out of the recessed tracks. It came down hard, swerving on dusty red tiles. Anna scrambled to maintain control and not dump it. The bike slammed into an old trash bin, tearing it loose from a column and sending it bouncing, vomiting old cups and cartons. Gordon followed her maneuver, destroying the impromptu ramp in a spray of planks and splinters. He weaved into a gap between support columns and accelerated, coming up along her right on the other side of a blur of passing white archways. Driving close to the openings between pillars created a thrumming sound as frightening as the bullets.

He grinned as if he hadn't had this much fun in years.

Anna's gaze darted back and forth from him to forward. Bad timing and a lucky column foiled his next attempt to shoot her. The end of the platform came on fast, and he rode farther away from the tracks.

Gordon sighted over the weapon again, lifting both eyebrows when she hit the brakes without warning and swerved away. Anna's bike sailed off the edge, falling hard on the track surface with an impact that numbed her tailbone. Behind her, Gordon's pursuit came to a sudden halt with squealing tires and the crunch of wooden crates. Her landing didn't go quite as well as she hoped, and she wound up airborne off the bike before she knew she was in trouble.

Fortunately, she had slowed enough to where she stopped skidding with mild bruises and a scuffed hand. Added to the pain of her last crash, she came close to giving up and lying there waiting for death. She didn't want to think about how many injections it would take to get rid of all the diseases she had probably picked up skinning her hand open here.

Hot tears streaked out of the corners of her eyes as she thought of Faye still missing. Growling past clenched teeth, she forced herself up and limped past the beam of dusty light from her bike's headlamp. Gordon's irritated snarl echoed in the tube, followed by the clatter of a pile of debris shifting.

Not dead.

For a moment, she debated finishing him off, but fear urged her toward fleeing. She threw a leg over the bike right as his headlight jumped from the platform to the tracks. Anna zoomed onward before he recovered enough from his landing to fire. His next shot went high. Wide-eyed with terror, she risked accelerating to seventy and begged thin air to keep her path free of anything capable of causing a fatal crash.

Grey tunnel streaked past. She dodged the occasional hanging cloth or pile of debris, this section far less fortified by the natives. Another platform passed on the right, but she made no move to go for it. A series of still-working lamps blew out in sequence as she drove by, drawing a frustrated howl from Gordon. She stared teary-eyed into the ghostly glow of her headlights while careening around a rightward curve that took her deeper underground.

Headlights behind her crept closer. Accelerating well past her comfort speed, she screamed and clung to the vibrating metal until every muscle ached. The tunnel leveled off and she bounced over a light uphill grade in time with a gentle curve to the left. Two circles of wobbling light provided only about thirty yards of warning for death on the ground. Keeping up the focus necessary not to smash into anything had taxed her brain to the point of surrender.

A shot blew off her remaining rear view mirror; a second holed the windscreen and left a burn mark on her right shoulder. Another hit the back end of her bike with a jolt she felt in her clamped thighs. Fear pushed her hand around the grip, tipping the speed up even more.

Once the tunnel showed a hint of straightaway, she risked a peek to the rear. Headlights in the darkness bounced about like a murderous will-o-wisp. Dingy walls covered in grime flashed with another blue muzzle flash.

I'm done with this. This is some kind of sick game to him. He's not even seriously trying to hit me.

She pried her trembling right hand off the grip and held it toward him, opening her mind to her bike's power core.

The tunnel crackled with the brilliance of day for a split second as a great arc leapt from her hand into Gordon's bike, sending sparks bursting from several points. Her bike faltered and died, continuing to coast.

In the aftermath of the lightning, absolute darkness enveloped the tunnel. Scraping metal and sparks preceded a wail of surprise from Gordon. That scream drowned amid the screeching of his motorbike going down and skidding in the dirt. The *whump-whump-whump* of an armored body tumbling over the old tracks preceded a loud crash—then silence.

A few seconds later, her ride came back online.

Unable to see what happened and unwilling to turn the bike to check, she slowed enough to release her white-knuckle grip and kept going until she found another station platform. She drove up a maintenance ramp and emerged amid a small tent city, startling several dozen people who had made a village out of the place. Women snatched children off their feet, stuffing the filthy urchins into tents and reaching for swords and pistols.

Anna waved at them. "Hi. Don't mind me. I'm lost; I don't want trouble."

She maneuvered past the settlement away from a group of men who closed around with knives and pipes. They might have been simply curious, but she didn't want to run the risk of getting jumped down here in the dark. Her tires squealed around the hallway at the far end of the station, leaving the boarding platform behind as she rode across an approach mall. More tents dotted the area, but she didn't stop or even look at anything.

Anna skidded to a halt at the bottom of a massive non-working escalator to the street. Dust particles glowed in thin streams of light leaking in past the barrier at the top. She tried not to think about how much more pain she would be in if she wiped out trying to drive up metal stairs. Her legs ached, her thigh and back burned from bullet grazes, and her hand stung where she had skinned it. Metal piping clattered along the ground behind her, the locals approached. The tone of their grumbling didn't sound welcoming.

After walking the bike back a few paces for a 'running' start, she eased on the throttle. The motorbike took the stairs with less trouble than she thought, though she still emitted an uneasy whine out her nose the entire way. At the top, she accelerated at the wooden barricade and crashed through, sending pedestrians diving for cover from the explosion of flying debris.

She let off the throttle and slumped over the handlebars. Once the bike rolled to a stop, Anna slipped off and tumbled to the ground on her back. An automatic kickstand kept it from falling on top of her. She lay still for a few breaths, staring up at the stars and savoring the feeling of not being underground. Faces appeared in her view as the bystanders approached to check on her.

A man in a black suit stooped over her, glanced for a moment at the hole she put in the barrier, and extended a hand.

"Are you hurt, miss?"

She let him help her up. "Yes, thanks. Damn dodgy GPS gave me a bit of a wrong turn."

THE PIXIE

The elevator let her out on the thirty-ninth. Anna glanced out a contiguous ribbon of windows at a pleasant view of Finsbury Park to the east. From all the light at the north end, she assumed a Frictionless match was underway. Plodding down a hallway lined with heavy blue carpet, she staggered past bits of silver sculpture composed of numerous free-floating pieces held aloft in magnetic fields. Orbs, triangles, and other constructs no one had invented names for spiraled about in some artist's attempt to associate moods with shapes.

Apparently, six spheres of ascending size spiraling in a graceful curve equated to serenity, while two pairs of counter-orbiting cubes somehow meant lust. Her head hurt too much to contemplate esoteric philosophy as she fell against the door to apartment 3915. Carroll had been oddly forthcoming with the address. That 'you owe me a major favor' smile had her shivering the entire ride here.

As if the impact of her body didn't make enough noise, she pounded her fist on the door twice.

A few minutes later, it slid open with a pneumatic squeak, leaving her falling forward into the arms of a muscular man with thick black hair. Much of his shoulder and neck area had been replaced with dark metallic cyberware, which gave way to a texture like living tissue halfway down his biceps. He looked quite different without the coat, but familiarity glowed within his orange eyes. The sight of her made him blink.

"Did you take a nosedive off a moving car?"

"Motorbike actually… Twice, in fact. I'm shocked the NetMini is still alive. Bloody thing only survived because I've kept it off, I bet. I didn't want 'em using it to track me. Orange, I need your help to find someone… I don't know who else to trust."

He carried her inside, past a sunken living room three steps down from ground level in a pool of grey rug with a couch, table, and holovid player. A kitchenette covered with imitation black marble tiles went by on the right. She floated down a hall to a bedroom where he set her on something soft and warm. He spent several minutes wiping grit out of the abrasions on her chin and forehead, a spritz of Aeroderm here and there erased the damage from her skin under a cold, tingling foam.

After, he flopped into an oversized chair surrounded by a wall of technology: three rows of holo-panels on top of each other, each with four screens. "So, shall I assume you were pursued the old-fashioned way?"

Anna ogled the display screens, as well as the rack of components and three individual net decks on the desk behind him. White squares, one inch thick, emblazoned with spirals of concentric lines stood off from the wall on silver pegs of various heights. The three-dimensional effect made the room feel expensive. She moaned, hurting everywhere.

"How the hell do you afford this place?"

"I have many benefactors, only some of whom are aware of that fact. So, please, tell me why you're here? Did Carroll give you something you couldn't handle?"

"No. It's the CSB."

He had her halfway to the door before her begging made him stop. She hung suspended by one hand holding a fistful of shirt and one in her belt.

"Please, Mr. Orange. A little girl needs your help."

"Yeah, sure. You're not that small."

"Not me, Faye. She's only thirteen."

He bowed his head and grumbled. "Do I look like a missing kid's charity? Damn CSB. How can you be certain you weren't followed?"

"I told you the other night, I've done this before. Besides, they are trying to shoot me, not stalk me. If they'd spotted me, bullets would be in the air already."

He walked her toward the door.

"Wait!" She clung to him. "Please… There isn't much time! I can't go to Carroll again. The CSB is probably watching him, and if they bribe him well enough I'm done. I don't know anyone else good enough to find her. They wanted me to assassinate a Member of Parliament. I couldn't do it. They're going to kill her to hurt me; I just know it."

Orange held her for a full minute in the doorway, gazing at the ceiling. "For all I know, you've led the authorities to my damn flat."

"I will admit to being rusty." She pulled herself up until they almost touched foreheads. "But, I know I wasn't followed. I lost them underground and I didn't take an autocab here... I nicked a scooter. There's no trace. Please, Orange. I'll do anything you want."

"Anything?" He raised an eyebrow.

"Well, maybe not take it in the bum."

He slouched, staring at her with uncomfortable pity that made her feel like a Cov again.

"Don't look at me like that. I was tryin' to make light." She looked away. "Sorry if it wasn't funny. I'm not in a great mood. If it's what you really want... Faye—"

"No, Pixie." He sighed. "Not every man in the world is looking to use you."

She cried, keeping her face away so he couldn't see. Orange shifted and carried her back across his flat and set her on the foot end of a king-sized Comforgel pad. He glanced between her and the terminals, opening his mouth as if to say something, but changed his mind.

Anna gathered her composure. "Does this mean you'll help?"

"Aye. However, I *will* call in that favor you offered eventually. It'll more than likely involve getting shot at."

"Awright." She stretched, cringing from sore muscles.

After feeding him all the information she had about Faye, Agent Gordon, and the timeline of when they took her from Coventry, she let gravity take her backward onto the bed and waited. Soft, warm padding made her bones throb. Scenes of flying into white faux-brick walls replayed in her mind.

The elaborate chair whispered a soft breath as it reclined. Mr. Orange plugged into one of the decks and laced his fingers together over his abdomen. Anna stared upside down at a large sheet of paper covered with Japanese writing on the wall over the headboard. Traces of the Far East adorned the room. A little pagoda carved from red jade sat by an incense platter carved in the image of a Samurai. Paper lanterns hung across the rim of the bedroom window and a small door led to what seemed like a Shinto shrine.

"You fancy Japan?"

Orange chuckled. "There's a lot of high-paying work there. The country is fragmented, corporate warfare is part of their culture, and they have some of the best network security in the world. I enjoy the challenge."

She remained still, eyes closed but awake, until the pain in her shoulder and thigh became too much. After kicking off her boots, she sat up and undid her belt. With a grimace, she peeled her pants away from the wound and slid them down to her knees. Once she had plucked all the stray threads and splinters from the graze, she flicked the safety cap from a stimpak and pressed it into her leg. Inside of a minute, her milky skin looked as pristine as if it had never been touched. The synthetic adrenaline caused a wave of pain in her overtaxed muscles.

"Nice tattoo."

She jumped at the sound of his voice, blushing, feeling a spike of gratitude toward Doctor Mardling for giving her underwear.

"Would you mind?" She pointed at her shoulder with her second to last stim, and held it out to him.

The wire auto-ejected from the socket behind his ear and reeled itself back into the deck before he got up. She rolled over, tensing without conscious thought as his weight settled into the Comforgel next to her and the presence of a man loomed over her back.

"That's a nasty scrape."

"Ahhh," she yelled, biting the covers as he picked debris out of her back. Gasping, she turned her head away to the left and let herself go limp. "I'm lucky Gordo is a shitty shot."

"Who's Gordo?"

Another scream slipped past clenched teeth wen Orange plucked a nugget of rock from her shoulder. She relaxed, whining, once the pain spike passed. "CSB agent."

"I've never met a CSB agent who was a poor shot."

"Maybe it's 'cause we were doing sixty-five in the Tube on e-bikes. You think—"

She tensed at the touch of the cold metal injector, moaning as her shoulder filled with the cool fluid. Anna gnawed on the bedclothes when the relaxing chill turned to itching. Orange's warm hand brushed over intact skin, sending a shiver down her back.

"Wound's closed." Mr. Orange patted her on the uninjured shoulder. "You definitely got an angel watchin' out for you. From what I've seen, those CSB blokes are all former MI6. Most have SAS training. Damn miracle you survived."

She rolled over, staring up at him. "P'raps he bricked it riding a motorbike through the Tube."

He gave her a shrug. "Or he wasn't really trying to kill you."

"What the devil for?"

Orange raised both eyebrows. "You said he wanted you to take out a MoP. Maybe they'll do it anyway and leave you alive to stand trial for it."

I gotta get the feck out of London. Oh, James. She shook with emotion, fear, love, and anger. It subsided seconds later with the singular focus of not abandoning her friends.

"Thanks for this, Orange. Mind if I use your shower?"

"Go right ahead, I've still got some digging to do."

"You're not done yet? Why'd you log out?"

"The pixie caught my eye."

Anna blushed at the small cartoon head grinning over the waistband of her panties.

She squinted. "Well it *is* in a bit of a spot, innit? I'm kinda sorry I got it."

He looked at her for a moment and frowned. "Go get cleaned up. I'll send your kit off for laundry."

"Okay…" She ducked into the bathroom and hid behind the door while she stripped.

After leaving her clothes outside the room, she availed herself of the autoshower. When she finished, she padded over to the door and cracked it open. Orange lay out cold on the chair, lost in cyberspace, seemingly meditating. Anna clung to the edge of the door, watching him breathe for a few minutes. She hadn't noticed the four katanas mounted vertically upon the wall behind the monitors before.

Seeing no sign of her clothes, she edged the door open a little more until it hit the plastic-wrapped packet he had left on the ground—full of clothing. She grabbed it, closed the door, and broke the seal, filling the room with the scent of fabric softener and the subtle hint of some manner of chemical. He had used one of the good places; the rips and bullet grazes had been stitched almost to the point where no sign of damage remained.

Anna put on everything except her boots, wanting to leave them off for comfort while Orange worked. A glance at the window on her way to the bed changed her mind, fearful the CSB might show up at any minute.

He remained motionless for several minutes. Anna got up and paced, then helped herself to the reassembler in the kitchen and made a single serving of coffee. Twenty minutes later, she fidgeted with an empty cup. Seconds before the desire for more overcame her laziness to go and get it, he sat up and swiveled around. His expression didn't fill her with much hope.

"She's still alive? Please tell me she's still alive…"

"Yeah." He pulled the wire out and leaned forward, resting his elbows on his thighs. "She's being held at a high security facility outside the city. The kind of place they use to hold nutter auggies. What exactly did this brat do?"

"Something bad…" Anna stared at the ground. "She met me. The bastards are using her as leverage."

A tray slid out of one of the black boxes on the rack. He plucked a holodisk from it and tossed it to her. "Well, I got all the information I could on the place, but by the time you get there, the codes I could get will have changed."

"Can I convince you to be a digital guardian angel while I go in?"

His lips parted in a mischievous smirk. "Will you owe me a second favor if I do?"

"Of course. So what's the big deal about the tattoo?"

He exhaled, crossing his hands behind his head and sat back. "Well, that's probably something I shouldn't have mentioned."

Anna squinted. "What do you mean? You've seen it before?"

Orange yanked a large handgun from under the desk; he hesitated, not quite aiming it at her. "And this is why they round you lot up. Look, I trade in secrets that people kill for. Stay the hell out of my head."

Anna scampered away over the bed, hands in front as if they would stop a bullet. "Sorry! I only hear surface thoughts… I can't deep dive."

His finger left the trigger; the lights on the side went dark. He stared at her for a minute, something between anger and pity in his eyes. His expression filled her imagination with a debate about how easy it would be to clean blood from his bed.

She cringed. "I'm sorry, Orange. I'm desperate. Really, I didn't look deep. All I heard was what you were thinking about right at that moment. I swear I won't peek again. It's a habit… Only thing that's kept me alive sometimes."

"You wanna know? Okay, fine." He tossed the gun on the desk with a clatter. "Maybe someday you'll understand why people keep secrets."

Orange shoved at his desk, rotating to face his rig. He swiped at a virtual display panel. One of the numerous holo-screens went from flat grey to showing a black box inside a blue frame. His finger poised over a holographic button. Conscience seemed to get the better of him, and he waited.

"Are you absolutely sure you want to see this, Pixie?"

She walked over and put a hand on the back of the chair. Her voice carried a hint of dread. "Yeah."

His finger pierced the tiny square of light. A video feed filled the frame. A ceiling-mounted camera looked down into a messy bedroom, aimed at a queen sized Comforgel pad. She squinted at it, sensing something familiar about the horrendous shambles. Shadows moved across the sheets, dark azure light from an opening door spreading over dark brown walls. A pudgy balding man waddled forward, dragging an unconscious nude girl with holographic filament wings. As soon as Anna saw them, she clung to the chair to keep from falling to her knees.

Blake, from Bristol City, was carrying the woman she used to be. He paused a step inside the door and gave her a light throttling, screaming about her costing them money all day long and shouting about her lying there like a turd. Anna had no memory of it at all.

"This is what happens to whores who can't handle their junk," Blake shouted.

He threw her face-first onto the bed, the electronic wings fluttering along with her brief flight. Her body landed limp as a corpse, stopping with a dull *splat* upon the gelatinous mattress.

Blake looked up at the camera, tinkered with the angle to get more of the bed in frame, and whispered to the lens.

"And this is how you make up for the money you lost. Greetings my loyal followers! Tonight we have Pixie for your viewing pleasure. No, the useless bint ain't dead, she's strung out to hell and back like usual."

With that, he stripped and climbed on top of her. Anna stared in horror, unable to turn away from the rape of her unconscious body. Orange looked to the side, one hand up to his temple to block his peripheral vision of the screen. The color in his face gave away that he'd seen it already.

Blake rolled her onto her back to give the camera a front view, then pulled her legs apart, giving the camera a perfect view of the grinning tattoo. After a minute's pause for the viewer's benefit, he resumed his attack. Blake didn't even stop when his motion began to knock vomit out of her throat with each thrust.

Anna turned away, shaking. "That's enough… I don't want to see any more. Where did you get that?"

"He sells the videos on the net, but it's on the side. Not official from the club. I find them here and there in forgotten network nodes when I go hunting for data with trade value. Think I found that one in the archives of some investment firm in the city."

Shame and rage got into a scrap. Orange's monitors all flickered at the same time. Anna forced herself to think about Twee. If she let her emotion out right here, all of this expensive stuff would fry, and he'd never help her.

Her voice blurred from the urge to sob. "Can you delete it? I mean… all of it?"

A pained expression crossed his face. "I can try to slap together a hunter construct to track down and wipe the file wherever it finds it, but it won't be able to touch offline storage and it could take years to get every copy."

She bit her lip. "Please start it. I gotta go. I'll call you when I get out to the site."

WRATH

T he sky rumbled with the thunder of unseen lightning. Anna looked up into the reflection of the rage boiling beneath her sorrow. Rain approached. It would soon be no weather to drive a motorbike in. She stashed the scooter in an alley behind Orange's flat, covering it with enough junk to keep it safe at least for a few days in case she needed it again. Cold whistling gusts sent ripples over her white orb of hair. She stood motionless, a lone piling in the river of people. Intermittent voices, pleasant greetings as well as pick-up lines, churned into an endless din of shuffling feet and traffic.

A great burst of wind and water vapor swept down the street as a maglev tram whisked overhead. The row of silent metal cars flowed around a sweeping curve, ascending a long ivory thread into the tenth story of a building. Anna observed the world happen as though the city existed without her in it, a detached spectator looking from afar.

She lowered her gaze, catching sight of an orb bot with a red umbrella peeking out from behind a massive beige and brown vendomat. It cringed behind the thousand-pound purveyor of synthetic Black & Tan. She continued to watch the spot until the autocab arrived.

As the car pulled away, the red umbrella appeared over the top of the vendomat, rising until the single lens eye came into view. Once the car got underway, the orb emerged and skimmed along the sidewalk above the crowd.

Her whisper fogged the window. "Damn bloody thing's after me…"

For several blocks, the orb pursued. High enough not to hit or even be noticed by most pedestrians, it followed wherever the cab went.

Someone's hacked it. "Autocab, please stop here for a moment."

"Abort current trip?"

"No. I need some air."

"Trip pause feature is an additional two credits. Do you accept?"

"Fine, whatever."

The autocab came to rest along the edge of a circus in the shadow of an old statue. Other cars continued past as the AI in the taxi announced she had five minutes before it would assess another fee. The red umbrella zipped around the corner a few seconds later. She tracked it drifting, waiting and watching until it passed near a streetlamp.

She lifted her palms upward and focused on the lamp. A jolt of power leapt into the sky from the exploding fixture, wrapping over the orb and continuing into the clouds. The concussion of the detonating lamp sent pedestrians diving for cover. Surrounded by flickering lightning, the small bot emitted a high-pitched squeal of distress. The umbrella caught fire and the flying bot wobbled out of control. People on the ground held cases and coats over their heads to shield themselves from falling droplets of molten plastisteel.

The digital scream grew louder and the orb rocketed forward into a spiraling, flaming corkscrew before smashing into the road. Several cars ran over it, breaking it into progressively smaller and more numerous fragments. Anna glared at the smoldering junk in the street, watching the chaos no one connected back to her. She wondered if the little thing that had showed concern for her had always been *them* watching her, or if the twinge of guilt she felt at 'killing' the little guy was deserved. She pictured a remote operator grabbing their head and screaming.

"Whoever you are, I hope that hurt."

Early in the afternoon, the main room of Bristol City held a lie of tranquility. It contained only Lawrence the bartender and shafts of dusty sunlight piercing cracks in the black-painted windows. An aroma of musk and alcohol had seeped into every fiber of the place. Taking one breath in here tasted like sticking her face in a woman's nethers. The soft metal song of hanging cages creaking back and forth filled in the silence.

Lawrence wagged his head at her. "Oi, we ain't open yet. Come back after two."

Anna traced her fingertips across the round tables, ignoring him.

He came around the edge of the bar. "Hey, you deaf? I said we're not open yet."

They met at the edge of a silver stage with three dancing poles. He towered over her, not yet ready to lay a hand on the small woman in the black coat.

"Sod off, Larry. I got business with Blake."

"Pixie? Zat you?" He gasped, eyes roaming. "Crikey! You look so different... Oi wait a minnit, didn't Sanjay give you the sack?"

Two lights exploded in the rafters. She knew he meant fired, but Blake's naked paunch wobbling back and forth filled her mind.

Lawrence jumped away from the fall of glass and sparks. "Bloody 'ell."

"Like I said, I got some business with Blake."

He stared at the smoking electronics, raising his arm at her. "Look, Pix. You know as well as I do I can't let you walk in back. 'Specially after you've been fired. Company policy and all, ex-employees might be up to no good."

"Oh, I'm definitely up to no good." She flicked her eyes toward him. "Did you 'appen to know of Blake's video library?"

"Video library?"

Anna relaxed when Lawrence's surface thoughts gave away his true ignorance of what Blake did to his girls. "He's got a holo-recorder rig in his bedroom. He..."

Lawrence slackened his aggressive posture at the sight of a tear on her face. He looked away, shaking his head. "I'll beat that fucker to death myself." He punched the bar.

Anna put a hand on his shoulder. "No, Larry. It's not your fault. I was smacked out. Too far gone to scream. I didn't even know it happened until..."

"If Old Bill asks, I never saw ya." He touched her arm as she moved to walk away. "You sure you'll be okay?"

"Aye. Safe as houses."

The coldness in her voice made him take a step back. He returned to the bar, muttering, calling himself an idiot for not noticing what his boss had been doing.

Double flap doors to the rear part of Bristol City opened without a noise at the urging of her hand. The air stank of desperation and sex, the grey carpet soaked in both. Crunching over flaked plaster, she stalked the corridor.

Those doorways reminded her of being dragged by a fistful of hair. A dislodged tile in the drop ceiling made her remember where she had stumbled and been *encouraged* along by his police baton. The water cooler she had fallen into still lay on the floor in the corner; no one had bothered to clean it up.

The women's dressing room was open and empty. Blake had removed the door long before she had started there. The shower tubes, benches, and lockers sat idle; none of the girls would even be awake at this hour. Anna swallowed the nausea climbing the back of her throat, searching for the one thread of dignity Doctor Mardling had extended for her to grasp.

A shriek came from behind Blake's door. The gold plate bearing his name brought back the feeling of him using her face to open it. She clasped the knob, trying to sort out if the female screams behind it sounded like participant or victim. A mild tweak of Electrokinesis worked the latch, and she brushed the door out of her way.

One of the new girls cried out in rhythmic squeaks with Blake's motion. He held her by a black cord binding her wrists behind her back as well as a handful of candy-red hair. The girl's surface thoughts didn't contain the panic of an unwilling participant, though she wanted it to end sooner rather than later.

Anna glanced at the amber threads spreading across the walls, wherever power ran in wires. She found six cameras, their cables all running back to one device concealed in the nightstand.

She flung her arms to the sides and the walls came alive with sparks creeping like great crackling azure spiders. Wires flamed out of the fake wood panels, holo-cams burst into showers of orange flecks and debris, and the nightstand jumped back against the wall with a deep *boom* before black smoke belched from disjointed doors.

Blake let out a startled cry before shouting, "What the bloody hell?"

In the aftermath, the only light came from a single beam of sun sneaking past a gap in heavy crimson curtains. The woman screamed, shying away from creeping blue lightning while struggling at her bound wrists.

Anna remained in the doorway, her voice cold and lifeless. "Still looking for that raise, Bree?"

Blake shimmied backward off the bed, turning on her with an angry glower. "What the fuck are you doing here, bitch? Your strung-out ass ain't wanted. You got exactly three seconds to get out of my face before—"

She didn't move, or even look at him. "Before what, pig? You rape me again?"

Bree nodded her hair off her face. "Pixie? I thought they sacked you."

"Get out of here, Bree. You don't want to watch this."

Blake pointed at the redhead. "Sit still, whore. We ain't done yet."

The *boom* of an explosion shook the ceiling. One of the air-handlers out on the roof suffered for his words.

Bree squirmed, staring at the stained drop ceiling above the bed. "This is gone pear shaped, Mister Blake. I wanna leave. Somethin' ain't right. Cut me loose."

He glared at her past the hazy smoke. The taste of scorched electronics settled on Anna's tongue. She met his converging eyebrows without blinking.

"I saw the holovid, shitsack. I know what you did to me."

"Holovid?" Bree grimaced as she fought harder at the rope. Arousal became mortification; she tried to cover herself with her leg. "You're recording us?"

Anna glanced at the charcoal lines on the walls, her gaze settled on a scorched hole where one of the cameras had been. "He *was*. Not anymore."

The nineteen-year-old turned her back on him. "Mister Blake, please untie me."

He palmed her head and shoved her face-first into the pillows. "I said we ain't finished yet. Sit your ass still. I gotta deal with this hag first."

Blake snatched his police truncheon from the bureau. Bree tried to run when he leaned away, but he hauled her back onto the bed and brandished the weapon at her. The young woman scooted into the corner, back against the wall, and lapsed into bawling. He whirled on Anna. When he raised the club over his head, lightning pooled at her shoulders, spiraled around her outstretched arm, and nailed him in the gut. He flew off his feet and landed on the bed, twitching and gurgling. Trapped under his girth, Bree screamed.

Anna stooped and picked up the baton. Glancing between the smoke wisping off the end and the undulating mass of flesh, she shook her head and threw it to the side.

"Compensating much?"

"Pixie, please don't hurt me." Bree thrashed trying to get out from under him. "Please, he said I had to do this or they'd sack me." She broke into uncontrollable sobs.

No wonder Blake had it in for me. I told him to go fuck himself.

"Bree?"

"Yes?" she sniffled.

Anna patted her on the head, trying to push her anger aside enough to sound soothing instead of cold. "As soon as he's off you, run and don't look back. I'd appreciate it if you kept what's happened here our little secret."

The younger woman nodded. Blake shook his head in a search for coherence. When he saw Anna, he roared and rolled to his feet. She had little difficulty avoiding him. His clumsy lunge crashed into the desk, causing a reverberating *thud* of sheet metal. He grabbed and pawed at stacks upon stacks of holodisks in small clear cases, which fell to the ground with him, a waterfall of porn.

Bree scrambled to her feet, running off into the club after bouncing off the doorjamb, not bothering to ask Anna to untie her. Blake recovered, climbing the desk to get back up. Memory fobs and empty holo-disk cases adhered to his gut. He faced her, heaving great breaths, staring as the stuff clinging to him peeled away and fell one at a time.

"You cost us—"

Another bolt of lightning launched the fat man against the wall; he bounced off the desk again, bending it, and rolled to a halt on the rug with smoke peeling from his head.

"I'm not going to allow you to even attempt to justify what you did. I don't blame you for my landing in this shithole—that was my fault. I do blame you for other things, Blake. Other things that've made me decide to introduce you to the person I was before."

Anna examined her fingernails.

Groaning, Blake clutched at the hair on his chest, his hands twitching. Tiny sparks rippled along his face, arcing across the thread of drool between his lips. She jolted him again, sending a scream bubbling up past thick fluid in his throat. He tried to say something, but managed only a weak whimpering gasp.

"I'd considered torturing you until you begged for your life, but I'm a bit pressed for time. I'd ask if you had any final words, but pigs don't talk."

Lightning wrapped around her legs, threaded across her chest, and shot down both arms into Blake's mountainous belly. She leaned into the effort, ignoring the draining sense of fatigue enveloping her. Opening the floodgates, Anna sent her rage out into the world, the electricity her wrath made physical. He clawed at the rug for only a second before his body flopped about in uncontrolled spasms. Self-generated power didn't have the strength to kill, especially not a man his size.

Blake moaned.

She beckoned to the flow in the wall wiring, drawing a great arc to burst out from the paneling. It crackled over her twice in a great, blinding tendril. Anna pulled the electricity across her skin, guiding it down her arms and into the wretch on the floor with a long, sizzling discharge. Foam sprayed from his mouth, his eyes exploded, and the scent of burnt meat filled the air. A charred hole yawned from his chest at the point the spark connected.

When the flickering blue ended, Anna slumped against the doorway, winded from the exertion. One droplet of sweat fell off the tip of her nose. Blake's mouth hung open, smoke pouring into the air. Dark bloody fluid leaked from the corners of his eyes over the sides of his head, pooling on the carpet.

"Well, Blake... was it good for you?"

35

SPARE THE INNOCENT

The countryside flashed by in waves of green and brown. On an old-fashioned paved road, among the sparse traffic of the hour, she had taken the bike up to a hundred and ten without even thinking about it. She weaved around a handful of autocabs ferrying commuters out of the city as well as the occasional lorry packed with hydroponics and armed guards. Few people in London owned personal cars anymore. Anyone with a NetMini could call a ride within minutes, even out in the middle of nowhere.

Anna dwelled on the image of fire licking at small circular mirrors, consuming the mound of holodisks. She had ignited the carpeting, destroying the recorded shame of countless damaged women. She didn't much care if Lawrence could put it out before the whole club went up in flames. Even if he did, it would look like the overburdened electrical system had finally called it quits.

Every so often, she glanced at the display between the handlebars, watching her location update on the NavMap. The spot Mr. Orange had located drew ever closer. Fifteen minutes after turning off the main road, the silhouette of a giant farm complex slipped out from behind a hill against the reddening sky.

The sun sent shimmering waves over the countryside on its retreat into the horizon. She had so seldom been away from the decaying old city, the grass, trees, and fields glimmered like an alien landscape. When the magic wore off, she dismounted and leaned the bike against a tree.

The farm complex no longer served as such; rows of hundred-meter-long hydroponic tanks, stacked six high, sat idle. The robotic arms that used to tend them hadn't moved in at least a decade. Orange's data said the CSB had appropriated this facility eight years ago, using it as a prison for criminals with too much augmentation for standard jail. The only lucky break was that they seemed to staff it with regular army and only a handful even knew it as a CSB installation.

Anna sat on the hillside. Arms folded over her knees, she sulked. The House of Lords deemed forcible removal of cyberware unethical from individuals not officially declared insane or incompetent regardless of their crime. The government cared so much about the rights of killers, but allowed bombs in the heads of innocent psionics. Hardliners even advocated rounding them, and their families, up and shipping them off world.

No wonder her father hated her; she could have gotten him killed. Anna shivered, trying to stop seeing his face the moment she'd electrocuted him. He had thought her power a mere annoyance. "I'm sorry, Dad. I couldn't stop myself."

Her pity train screeched to a halt with the memory of Doctor Mardling's voice. She imagined him chiding her for going down such a path, telling her a father should have shielded and protected his child from the government. No real father would have thrown her to the wolves, or punished her for her greatness.

She smiled despite tears, trying to forget the awful video. Thoughts of James pushed themselves over her mind, filling her with a sense of contentment. Her father's horrified face morphed into James', smiling and surrounded by a faint golden aura. The horror melted away from her heart as she became distant from that memory, from the kitchen full of smoke and the smell of scorched flesh. His smile broadened. She felt like a real person.

Shame crashed on her with Blake grunting. She fell to the ground as if his cheese-scented mass crushed her to the Comforgel pad. Anna mused about asking James to take that memory away from her. Her jaw tightened.

I don't want him to see me like that.

Anna fought out from under the emotional burden, one hand clamped around her wrist. Zoom would make the awful memory of that video go away. Seeing it from the outside would make it easy to think it was someone else, someone other than her. The Pixie was not her anymore. It could all be a nightmare.

No. She spat. *I'll not be any good to Faye or Penny if I get high again. I'm almost free. Hitting that shit again will throw me right back into the gutter.* That meant dealing with pain, not running from it any more. She covered her face in her hands, concentrating on her breathing until she calmed. Anna focused on how terrified Faye must be. *Everything wrong with my life can wait.*

She took a tiny electronic bud from her pocket and snugged it into her ear, wincing at the insect-like sensation of the cold metal moving, adjusting its shape to fit without gaps. An electronic tingle spread over the side of her head with Mr. Orange's voice as loud as if he stood inches away. It required no microphone, picking up the vibrations in her skull.

"Signal's good, Pixie."

"Call me Anna."

"Nathan."

"Hello, Nathan. I'm waiting for the sun to go down."

His voice carried a smile. "Understood, Anna."

While waiting for darkness, she observed a dozen men in grey uniforms and black-visored caps patrolling the outer perimeter. Most on foot, but one drove a six-wheeled rover bearing a mounted cannon. Aside from the men in military garb, the complex maintained an innocuous appearance that would cause anyone passing on the road to disregard it as yet another abandoned farm.

By the time the sun slipped behind the western horizon, she had gotten a fair sense of their pattern. Her jog down the hill slowed at a sense of energy in the air.

"I'm sensing a field at the outskirt."

"One moment..." He sounded different; grim and deep, with a Japanese accent.

"What happened to your voice?"

He laughed. "I'm in the net now. It's my avatar modulation. Does it bother you?"

"No, it caught me off guard."

"It's a trigger field for explosive restraints. I bet the auggies have bombs around their necks or put inside them."

Anna advanced, chilled silent by the thought of something like that on Faye. Fifteen meters later, he told her to wait.

"Okay, that's got it. I've nixed the thermal sweep on this sector and replaced most of their security monitoring with a four-second loop of empty space. Go in three...two...now."

She darted ahead, bounding over the grass down a long slope before she reached a metal fence.

Electrified, cute.

Anna leapt onto it without hesitation; her power guided the current across her skin harmlessly. By the time she leapt to the ground inside, the charge had made her feel as though she'd drank an entire pot of coffee.

After a short dash over open ground beyond the fence, she slipped among old hydroponic tanks. This close, their massiveness made her feel like a mouse. The stack stood a touch past forty feet tall, each individual row about seven. White metal glistened in the starlight, framing murky transparent plastic coated with ten years of neglect. Most large food producers used orbital farms these days, making gravity and real estate nonissues. Due to economy of scale, land-based farms had almost died out except for the third world.

She jogged to the end of the row, leaning up against a tank while waiting for the patrol. Due to their spacing, her best bet would be to walk right past one. When the guards came around the corner of a red corrugated building, she latched onto their mental presence and forced their brains to ignore her.

Striding out into the open, she bee-lined for the nearest door. Two soldiers passed within an arm's length, not even batting an eyelash. Anna ignored Orange's frantic shouting until she arrived at a grey door.

"Relax, I got a few more tricks."

"I... I don't even wanna know how the hell you just did that." His rapid exhale flooded her ear. "One sec, I'll get the door."

She squatted low, keeping her body in shadow while examining the code panel. The next pair of guards would come around the corner in about fifty seconds. Based on her count, these two would have a live dog. She had never tried telepathic invisibility on an animal before, and had no idea how to make it not smell her.

Come on, Orange.

A pleasant beep and a dull green light signaled the acceptance of the forged code from cyberspace. She ducked inside, closing it two seconds before the next patrol walked into view. The room looked like an old storage barn converted into a garage for military rovers.

Nathan's voice in her head made her jump. "Cameras are off, go now."

Anna ran into the dark toward a small light on the wall and another code panel. It beeped green a half-second before she reached it. The door opened, allowing her into a sparkling metal hallway. The harsh change from dark garage to bright passage left her blinking and seeing nothing but whiteness.

"Left," he whispered.

She dashed to the side, rubber soles squeaking across the gloss black floor.

"Duck behind the bulkhead, now."

She squeezed herself into the wall in an effort to become part of it. The sound of voices went by in an offshoot corridor.

"Clear. Take the next right turn and go for the elevator."

Two silver doors opened in the otherwise featureless grey wall, taking her into a large octagonal chamber with silver grating around a polished black center.

"Sublevel three."

She flicked a finger at the controls and the room rumbled. The elevator, basically a huge slab of plastisteel, sank into the floor. Reinforced struts braced each angled part, gaps in the walls created a gear track in the wall, the nubs bigger than human heads.

Bloody elevator could lift a tank...

"This is a right bit of overkill for a little kid. What the hell did I walk into?"

Orange snickered. "Cyborg prison, remember? This is the only facility the CSB has complete oversight on. Anywhere else they tried to stash her, some other agency would have noticed. I'm surprised they slipped a little girl in here without anyone saying a word. I bet your friend Gordon is operating a small cadre within the CSB that isn't exactly playing by the whole rulebook."

"Probably not even one page."

The great elevator crept downward. What it had in carrying capacity, it sorely lacked in speed. Anna came close to screaming out of impatience. When the doors opened, she edged into another corridor of silver, black, and white. A single row of lamps along the ceiling painted glare spots down the hall in both directions. Two guards walking away glanced at her, yelling and going for rifles. Anna raked her hands downward, calling lightning from the overhead lights. Rapid-fire flashes connected thin threads of electricity to their skulls with a series of *cracks*. The woman passed out without a sound, the man managed a weak gurgling howl before he fell. Lacking the time or the strength to drag them anywhere, she secured them in a handcuff hug before frying every bit of electronics on them. Communications, rifle firing circuit, and binders sizzled and smoked.

"Way to impose a time limit, girl. Next patrol will find them in a hair under four minutes."

"I could've let them shoot me instead."

Orange sighed. "Don't argue with me. Run."

Every ten feet, an armored door stood emblazoned with a four-digit number.

"Crikey, Nathan. These doors would stop an airstrike."

"Right turn. Go to the end and wait."

She fought the urge to sprint, moving as fast as she could without making too much noise. Heavy scrapes and moans came from some of the cells, making her jump. Something smashed into a cell door on the other side; a grungy face appeared in the tiny strip of armored window. A man with a half-metal face howled at her and licked the glass. More whooping and screeching made the place feel like an asylum more than a prison.

Anna's heart resumed beating. "This is what they call sane enough to keep cybernetics?"

"What's that? Signal fell away there."

"I'm okay, at the end of the hall."

"To your left is a monitoring station with two guards. You'll need to get past it and go straight; do not turn right at the node. I'd suggest not frying the systems counter. That will set off alarms and might make it impossible to get the doors open."

Peeking around the edge, she attached her thoughts to two minds and commanded them not to see her. A slow but deliberate walk took her across an octagonal room with an arrangement of consoles at the center. A man and a woman in grey military dress monitored security cameras, sometimes looking in at cells from which a particular amount of noise emanated. They spent most of their time watching hallways.

"What the fuck is that?"

The man's voice almost stopped Anna's heart.

"What?" asked the woman.

"There's a thermal anomaly floating down the hall…" He looked right at Anna. "I see a heat signature right there. A little woman, but there's nothing."

The female guard jumped up, reaching. Anna leaned out of the way, avoiding the woman's fingers by inches.

"Doesn't feel warm. Must be that dodgy sensor again. You fill out the IT request this time. I did it last night."

Anna held her breath and edged out of the chamber. She finally gasped for air forty meters down the subsequent hall.

"You have to show me how to do that." Orange's chuckle reverberated in her skull. "Would come in so handy."

"You missed a thermal."

"Sorry. I made it go away."

"It's a lot harder than it looks. I can't run while concentrating. Which one is it?"

"Another ten meters, hook left here. There ya go, fourth door."

Anna stopped at the indicated point and stood on her toes to peer in a strip of six-inch thick transparent resin forming a window. Faye trembled in a ball on the bunk at the far end of the room, wearing an oversized yellow prison jumpsuit. Bare toes poked out from under the loose pant legs of a garment made for someone much taller. She hid her face against her knees, blue hair spilled down over her shins. Multiple vomit puddles littered the floor.

"Sons of bitches. Orange, open this fucker." Anna smacked the door.

Clanging metal played background to his voice. "One second... one second..."

"What's the racket?"

"A swordfight."

"A what?" She blinked. "Did you just say a bloody swordfight?"

"Yep. Security construct found me. Doesn't much like me being in here. Just a moment."

"You're playing a bloody video game while I'm up to my tits in a military prison?"

"It's..." He grunted, the sound of clashing blades clear in the background. "Not a game. Defense software."

After a quick left-right glance, Anna stretched upward once more. Faye stared at the window, clutching at the bedding with a terrified expression. Red ringed her eyes. As soon as she recognized Anna's face, she shouted. The immense door reduced her words to a weak murmur. Seconds later, muted banging and screaming echoed inside the cell. She managed to shout "help!" loud enough to be clear.

Anna clawed at the metal, the wait agonizing. After an intolerable seventeen seconds, the door rumbled with a heavy *clank* and rolled to the side. When the gap became wide enough, Faye squeezed through and wrapped her arms around Anna, trying to speak, breathe, and cry at the same time. She smelled like vomit and cheap food, and couldn't get a word out between sobs and coughing. Anna held her, patting her back. Finding the girl's neck devoid of anything that could go boom, she relaxed.

"We haven't time... We have to go."

Faye sniffled. "W-what d-did I do? They w-won't tell me."

Anna squeezed the air out of her. "I'm so sorry they took you... It's my fault. They wanted to use you to make me kill someone."

"I want my parents!" Faye bawled.

She propped the girl up, holding tight. "Be quiet. I'm going to bring you home, Faye." Anna wiped tears from red cheeks. "I need you to be strong for me, okay? You can fall to pieces once we're out of here. We have to run."

Faye's fear turned to petulant anger. "I can't. I'm—"

Anna took her hand and pulled the girl behind her down the hallway. Three steps later, Faye stumbled and fell, hitting the ground with the squeak of skin on plastisteel. She got a hand over her mouth to mute the whimper of a banged knee, but when she tried to gather her legs underneath, metal clattering made it obvious she had chains on her ankles.

Aghast, Anna helped her up, pulling at the oversized jumpsuit to expose the glimmering silver links of handcuffs. Faye cringed, a cloak of shame on her shoulders growing. Anna stooped and pulled the leggings further, revealing a high security electronic restraint. She cast a disbelieving glance upward, pondering for a second. A healing bruise on Faye's lip triggered understanding.

"How many of these chavs did you hoof in the plums?"

The girl fidgeted her thumbs at the pockets, staring down. "Four."

"Good for you. At least they're electronic. I can get them off but it might pinch a bit."

Anna put her hand on the shackle above the code-entry pad and mentally mapped the threads of current within, looking for the contacts to operate the drive motor. The circuitry of these was more complex than the ones from Lord Thompson's staff, but the hasp motor felt the same.

Faye yowled and leapt back, almost tripping over the short chain. "Ouch."

"Shock or too tight now?"

"Shock… What the fuck did you—"

Covering her mouth with her other hand, Anna shook her head. "Quiet, sorry, and you're too little for that word."

The lack of a smartass remark for being scolded on language worried Anna.

Faye grabbed onto Anna's shoulders, crying and trying to break the chain with kicks. "I wanna go home, I wanna go home!"

"Hold still!" Anna looked back and forth to make sure no one was coming, and focused again. A second gap in the circuit path proved more fruitful; when she zapped it, the motor revved and threw the hasp open. Faye jumped and flailed, trying to get her other foot away from Anna's hand when two false zaps made her hair stand up. The girl fell, scooting backward to get away from the painful shocks, but Anna held on to the loose end of the binders and pulled her close.

She concentrated, ignoring the tugging and whining. The third try worked and Faye yanked her foot free, then gathered herself against the wall, shivering and sobbing. Anna held up the restraint and made sure the girl saw them fry. Faye went to cling again, but Anna grabbed her about the wrist and took off at a run. The girl scrambled to stay upright, slipping and sliding on the floppy pant legs. Anna stopped at the corner, peering at the security station. Faye grabbed on from behind, crying into her back, trembling.

"Nathan, still with me?"

"Who's Nathan?" Faye whispered, on tiptoe to peer over Anna's shoulder.

"Yeppo, I'm still here," said a voice in her ear.

She patted Faye's hand. "The trick I used to get past the sentries on the way in won't work with a passenger. Got any suggestions?"

"Depends. Lethal or non?"

Anna furrowed her brow, thinking of what they did to Faye; but these two were only grunts doing their job. "Non-lethal if you can. She doesn't need to see anything more."

"Who's Nat—"

Anna put a hand over Faye's mouth and pointed at the earbud.

"Ten seconds," said Nathan.

Whirring made them both look up at a circular aperture opening in the roof. An orb bot sank into the room and pivoted toward them. Faye emitted a pathetic squeak. Anna shoved her against the wall, raising a hand.

Orange's voice vibrated her skull. "Hang on, I'm the ball bot."

"Little warning next time, I almost cooked it and Twee nearly bricked." *Didn't yell at me for calling her Twee. Oh, no.*

Anna rubbed the girl's back. "You'll be safe. I promise. I'm sorry it took me so long to find you."

The hovering robot zipped around the corner and went off down the hallway. Several seconds later, the sizzle of electrical arcing and gurgling followed. At the *thump* of bodies hitting the floor, Anna set off running with Faye in tow. Having shocked the sentries into unconsciousness, the orb spun about the octagonal room in a playful orbit.

Faye looked down at the twitching bodies. "Are they dead?"

"No, hon."

Nathan cleared his throat in her ear. "You got a bit of a problem, luv."

Anna made tight fists. "Feck, what now?"

"I think her suit has a chip in it somewhere. They've noticed one of the prisoners out of their cell. You got men on the move."

Anna grabbed the lapel of the yellow prison jumpsuit; amber light glinted from of a network of hair-thin metal threads.

"The whole bloody thing is an antenna…"

Faye stared up at her with terror in her eyes.

"You've got anything on under that?"

"The bastards stole my Dead Ballerinas shirt." Faye went scarlet. "I just got me smalls. They wouldn't even let me keep a bra. Said I'd hurt myself with it. What kind of bollocks is that?"

"Shit. I'm not dragging her around here in only her knickers." She grasped Faye's shoulders. "They're gonna catch us if I don't get rid of that transmitter. I don't know how much power it'll take. It might not be pleasant. I don't want to hurt you."

Faye shook her head. "No way I'm taking it off. I ain't running around starkers. No way. Do it. I trust you."

"It might hurt."

"Do it!" Faye rasped, trying to yell at a whisper. "They're coming."

Anna took two handfuls of the fabric, channeling electrical power at the smallest amount she could perceive. Faye's hair shifted, rising to stand on end as the energy increased. She went stiff as a board and convulsed. Two sparks rode down her legs a second before a loud *pop* preceded smoke rising from the back of her neck where the suit caught fire. The stink of burning silicon and molten plastic stung her eyes.

"That's got it," said Orange. "Signal dropped."

Frantic, Anna swatted at the flames while Faye collapsed into her whining, "Owowowowow."

Anna hugged her. "Sorry."

Faye fought back tears as she pointed. "Anna! Look ou—"

She whirled around as a soldier leapt from an opening door and pounced on Anna before she could react. Arm across her chest, leg sweeping hers, he swung her over and drove her chest into the floor. Stunned by the impact, she thrashed impotently. He grabbed a handful of hair and pounded her face into the floor twice before pinning her with a knee to the back and gathering her arms behind her back.

A sudden fleshy *thwap* preceded a squeal; the strength holding Anna's arm down faded. Faye lunged at him, shoving her off Anna. He rolled against the wall, red-faced, cradling his groin. Anna shoved herself up into a squat.

"Five." Faye folded her arms across her chest, backpedaling with a slight limp that favored her right foot, and shivering.

The soldier went for a stunner, glaring death at Faye, who backed into the wall, whimpering.

Anna hurled herself on him before he could go after the girl. He jammed the taser into her neck and squeezed. Blue sparks danced, crawling up and over Anna's face like a gentle caressing hand. She drew the power into herself, feeding from it.

Faye screamed, sobbing "No!" over and over, venturing a hesitant reach. She recoiled from crackling buzz.

Anna thrust her arm up, palming the man's face. All the energy of the device, plus as much as her anger could draw from thin air, burned a handprint into his cheek. He fell in a heap, hot saliva bubbling between her fingers.

Faye swallowed hard, glancing at the twitching body, then at the hallway where they'd left two guards unconscious. "Is *he* dead?"

"No, hon." Anna wiped her hand on his back, dragged herself to her feet, and took Faye's hand again.

Boots echoed as a handful of soldiers approached from the right. Another opening in the ceiling released a stationary sentry gun, which pivoted in the direction of the security detail, firing a few shots before they came around.

Orange's voice flooded Anna's head. "I got this... I'll keep 'em pinned down while you get on the lift."

She ran for the elevator, which opened at their approach. Between tear-blurred eyes and floppy leggings, Faye stumbled after her as best she could. Anna dragged her past the doors, diving to the side as two bullets bounced off the wall. Gunfire sent Faye into a shrieking ball on the floor, her screams echoing in the confined metal space even after the elevator closed.

Her face twisted with emotion, she squeezed Anna's coat. "What now? We're in an elevator. There's gonna be a million guys waiting for us when it opens."

Anna pulled her upright and held on. "I will get you out of here."

Nathan chuckled. "I got it sorted, turrets here and there keeping them occupied. I created a phony tracking signal, so it looks like you're on the other side of the facility. I'm also flooding their security cameras with awful movies."

"Awful movies?" She made a confused face.

"Let's just say you probably wouldn't let that kid watch these."

"What the bloody hell are you doing that for?"

The sounds of the turret gunfire grew faint as the elevator climbed.

"Increases the distraction effect. Some of the blokes might be more inclined to linger to watch it. They'd ignore something goofy."

Faye's teeth chattered in time with her shivers. Anna wanted to take her mind off the situation at hand.

"That weasel of a neighbor of yours confessed. The filth took him away."

"He what?" She looked up with blue lips. "Really?"

"A friend had a nice long chat with him and convinced him that what he did to you was wrong. He felt so bad, he confessed in front of the news with the Met watching. There's nothing stopping you from going home."

"Are Penny and the idiot okay?" Faye sniffled.

"Yeah, little bruised, but okay."

Faye wiped her face. "Okay. I wanna go home."

Anna smiled. "Were your parents always such weepy saps? Ugh, the way your dad blubbed, he couldn't even speak."

Faye's attempt to laugh while crying produced a strange noise.

A roar of distant gunfire, shouting, and alarms burst in when the elevator opened. Anna rushed to the right. Faye followed, scrambling on too-long floppy pant legs that became tractionless socks. Sounds of war nipped at her heels, hounding them back the way she came, to the garage.

Hopping in one of the transport vans was tempting, but she didn't know how to drive anything with military-style controls. Besides, the huge, slow, and obvious vehicle would make it simple for the CSB to locate them. Anna led Faye into the blue-indigo darkness, ignoring the hulking machines. She hoped a nationally broadcast return home would keep the girl safe from the CSB.

Anna slid against the wall next to the final door, with a hand on the girl's shoulder. "Faye, once we go out this door, we have to run for about two hundred yards. I have a bike. Whatever happens to me, you keep running."

"No." Faye cried again, gathering up the jumpsuit leggings. "I don't want you to die."

"If they kill me, they have no reason to hurt you anymore."

Sniveling, she clamped on and shook her head. "Not gonna leave you."

Anna nudged the door open far enough to peek. Orange must have killed the lights; outside, the air was so dark it felt solid.

"Perfect timing, Orange," whispered Anna.

She shoved the door open and slipped out.

Orange emitted a confused noise. "Eh? What?"

The door clanked closed behind her and beeped.

"With the outer lights," whispered Anna.

"What outer lights?" He asked, worried. "Bugger all! Something's happening to the connection."

Anna's heart stopped.

Brilliant light bathed the area, projected from four armored vans, revealing a row of a dozen soldiers, rifles aimed. Faye's arms encircled her from behind, squeezing tighter.

"Shite." Anna held her hands up.

36

MONSTER

Twelve men stared at her. Twelve little red dots swarmed like bees at the center of her black coat. Eight rectangles of white light glared, searchlights mounted in pairs upon four armored vans. A cold breeze blew across the silence.

Anna squinted at them. She had endured the shame of being despised by her own father. She had been a faceless Cov kicked around by Old Bill. She'd let Plonk use her to score a fix, caring only for an easy way to flee her grey reality. She had abandoned her dignity, prancing naked in front of horny men while Blake treated her like a veritable slave. The thought of his doughy body sliding all over her filled her with such humiliation she no longer cared what happened to her. Out of all that, her deepest regret was the innocent little girl clinging to her suffering because of what she was.

"Twee?" Anna muttered, scarcely audible. "I need you to let go of me and take a big step backward."

Faye squirmed around front, putting herself between rifles and her friend.

"No," she whined, the pathetic sound eerily loud.

"Twee? Do you want to go home?"

"Stop calling me that! Fuckers won't shoot if I'm on top of you."

"Do you trust me?"

"Yes."

Anna lowered her gaze to the ground, raising her hands higher and farther apart. "Then please do what I ask."

Faye sobbed. The arms around her slackened, and Anna opened her mind. Tiny sparks leapt from one rifle to the next; ammo counters went dark, firing-circuits dead. None of them seemed to notice, all too on edge about the *monster* in front of them.

Faye. Get behind me this instant and keep your eyes shut!

The child jumped at the telepathic shout and dove against the wall behind Anna.

Glowing amber threads swarmed over the vehicles in Anna's mind, connecting into a brilliant shimmering mass deep inside—the fusion generator core. A soldier lifted one boot as if to walk toward her surrender. He shook, pointing the useless rifle at her face.

Faye's crying grew louder. "Please don't hurt her!"

The troops shivered with fear in their eyes. Surface thoughts told her they had seen the video of the Crossmen.

The soldier's boot thundered to the pavement. Faye curled tighter against the building, knees to her face, a sniffle seemed as loud as a gunshot.

Anna spread her fingers, beckoning to the power within the armored trucks. The eight searchlights wavered and grew a touch brighter. Eleven pairs of eyes twitched at the change in the light. A few squeezed useless triggers at the flash. Anna's mind pulled; the man took another step. Faye sniffled again. James' face filled Anna's mind, smiling at her. Rage at what these people did to an innocent girl narrowed her eyes.

I am Awakened.

She called upon the monster.

Eight jagged streams of lightning flew from explosions of melting glass as the spotlights died, bouncing in great serpentine streams across the ground and up Anna's legs. Men screamed. Rifles twitched and fell abandoned. The soldiers reached for sidearms, but too slow. The electricity flooded into her body with a surge of adrenaline. Roaring with anger, she flung her arms forward, projecting one scintillating arc around the horseshoe of men.

None of them lived long enough to scream.

Blood and body fluids boiled in seconds. Eyeballs burst, skin ignited, and several of the men split open. Random arc spiders crawled among the carnage, fizzling off into the ground when she released the unrestrained energy of the vehicles' power sources.

Several seconds of dark silence passed before the troop transports recovered from the severe drain and their headlights flickered back on. Far dimmer than the dead mast lights, they outlined a mangled pile of bodies dotted with patches of ember. The scent of cooked meat and melted plastic hung in the air. Faye huddled against the wall, face buried in her arms.

"Anna?" whispered Faye.

"Aye?"

"Are they dead?"

"Good chance of that." Anna kept silent for a moment. "Don't look over there. I'm sorry. They were going to shoot us both. And, what they did to you cheesed me off a bit."

"A bit?" whispered Faye.

Anna stooped over her. The girl shivered out of control, terrified to lift her face away from her knees. She put a hand on Faye's back and braced for the painful transition of going from friend to terrifying monster. The child had been spared the sight of it, but who knew what kind of scars hearing the screams would leave.

"Do you think I'm a monster?"

Faye swiped at her hands and held on, keeping her eyes closed as she burrowed into Anna's hug, sniveling. "I think that was fucking brilliant."

"Come on then." Anna pulled the girl standing. "And mind the swearing."

Faye blurted a laugh. "I don't mind the swearing."

"Cheeky…" Anna poked her.

The girl managed a feeble laugh. Anna kept an arm over her, shifting to put her body between Faye and the carnage as they ran for the distant fence, leaving the alarms blaring behind them.

An hour later, Anna pulled over within eyesight of London, guiding the motorbike to a halt in a small copse of trees. She stumbled away and collapsed on all fours, dry heaving. Faye ran up and rubbed her back.

"Are you sick?"

"I… didn't want to kill them."

Faye squinted into the night breeze. "They were going to kill us."

Anna took out the NetMini and stared at it. If she turned it on, they would find her. "Nathan?"

Silence.

"Did Bell really confess?" Faye sat next to her, tugging at the yellow fabric to shield her feet from the cold.

"Yes. He even turned over a recording he took. No way to worm out of it. The cops found recordings in there... dozens of other victims."

"He recorded me!?" Faye lurched to the side, her turn to dry heave. Anna held her until the coughing subsided. Faye's surface thoughts raced from panic to shame to anger before she burst into tears.

"I want to die."

"No." Anna shook her. "No, you don't. I know exactly how you feel... Same thing happened to me." She shared a toned-down story of what Blake had done to her. "Bell's vid was for personal use. Only the police saw it. He'll get what's coming. Don't let that bastard beat you. Don't give in to shame."

"Like you did?"

Anna pulled her tight, patting her on the back. "Yes... Like I did. Don't be an idiot like me."

"Anna?" Orange's voice crackled over the earbud.

"Nathan!"

"What the hell happened? They cut me off; I didn't see you get away."

A wry smile spread over her lips. "I think the soldiers were a bit shocked as well."

"That's not at all funny," he muttered.

"Can you scrub a NetMini? They're going to be watching for this one. I need to buy Faye some new clobber. Can't take her into London in a bright yellow prison thing. Old Bill will be all over her."

"I'm not changing out here in the woods!" Faye's yelp dropped to a whisper toward the end.

"Forget the NetMini. You'd have to turn it on for me to get it, and they'll see that. I'll send something out to you based on our comm signal. Sit tight."

"Oh, Nathan? Can you do me one additional tiny favor?"

LONDON STREETS STREAKED BY, TINTED IN VARIOUS DEGREES OF GREY WITH the occasional smear of neon. Faye clung to her from behind. Anna didn't push the e-bike up too much past sixty miles an hour with a young passenger, and neither of them wearing a helmet. She sank into a fog, oblivious to all but the feeling of shame that crept in behind her receding adrenaline. Wherever the street became dark, an image of the Pixie and Mr. Blake appeared. The thought of it sickened for the rest of the ride.

She parked at the end of the street, glancing at a crowd of news bots hovering in front of Faye's building. The parents stood on the porch, squinting into the lights. Constables and other people in white uniforms walked in and out of Bell's building next door. Too far away to hear, Faye's father looked and moved as if befuddled at all the media activity.

Faye shivered. "Anna?"

"Yeah?"

"Am I safe?"

Anna got off the bike and took her hand before walking toward the chaos. "See all those news bots? The whole of the country's about to see you come home. Those tossers wouldn't dare go after London's little darling. They'll leave *you* alone." She let slip a tear or four. "*You're* not a monster."

Faye stopped and gave her a flat look. "I'm not afraid of you. I don't think you're a monster. I won't tell anyone how you saved me, only that you cared enough to find me."

Self-pity had already formed quite a large lump in the back of her throat, and Faye's words made it swell. Anna prodded her up to the gate, coaxed along by fingertips in her back.

"Mister Taylor, is it true your daughter was secreted away by the government?" yelled a reporter.

A dark haired woman tried to squeeze closer to the porch, flanked by flying orb camera bots. "Mister Taylor, our sources tell us she was taken as part of some manner of governmental conspiracy against the House of Lords? Do you have anything to say?"

He flailed, waving at them to go away. "I have no idea what the devil you're going on about. My girl ran away because I was too stupid to believe her."

Faye pulled at her hand. "Come in and see my mum and pa..."

Anna couldn't talk. The squeak of the gate made one reporter turn and point, lights bathed them, then a mass of bots whirled around. When Anna saw the overjoyed expression on Faye's dad, she had to stare at the ground to mask her jealousy. Her father never once looked happy to see her. The man shoved reporters out of the way, barging a path to his child.

Fay ran to him, and he scooped her off the ground into a spiraling hug. Anna's dad would never have lifted a finger. He would have been happy she'd vanished.

Anna felt smaller and smaller as the man sobbed all over Faye.

More like an outsider—more like a monster.

Faye's mother's joyous wailing pierced the din, raking down Anna's back, pushing her away at the same time it warmed her heart. Following the lost daughter, the ocean of bright light moved back to the building, leaving Anna in the dark.

A hornet's nest of bots, reporters, and two frantic parents roiled on the porch. Anna stood still as a statue amid a flock of pigeons while a number of constables ran past her and joined the fray. Present and absent at the same time, she felt like a bystander to reality. Faye's overwhelming happiness shooed her envy off to the side.

A constable's voice swam out from the blur of stalled time, bringing her into the present once more. "Lord Thompson sends 'is regards."

She swallowed hard and waited for the hand on her arm. "It got a little pear shaped."

"Gordon's gone rogue. He's been officially disavowed. Agent Hughes went with him."

Anna looked over at a middle-aged man in a constable's uniform; he seemed too athletic for it. "You're Bureau aren't you?"

He refused to make eye contact, hands folded behind his back he smirked. The hard lines on his face gave her the answer.

"I don't care anymore. You can do what you want to me. Can we not make a scene in front of her?"

Glancing at the buildings off to the left, he muttered a bit above a whisper. "Lord Thompson wants to return your favor. We'll be watching, but as long as you behave yourself, there won't be trouble."

She reached up, teasing her fingers at the soft skin behind her ear. The thought of a bomb inside her brought chills. "I don't know Agent Hughes. I imagine those two will be after me."

The 'constable' nodded, and squinted down the street to the left. "That is our conclusion as well. Of course, you'll understand that we cannot offer direct assistance."

"Hughes was that telepath."

"Correct." He made it a point to look past her.

The streetlamp above them flickered. "They're not simply going to make his brain go *pop?*"

"Gordon's removed his code from the system. We can't arm the bomb. That, and Thompson's floored a motion to reevaluate that program."

Her arms fell slack. "Oh. 'Reevaluate'."

His jaw tightened. "Some of the soldiers you killed had families."

"They were going to shoot Faye, too."

At last, he looked right at her. "I respect Lord Thompson's request, but if it were up to me, you're too dangerous to be off a leash."

"Am I any worse than a nutter with a rifle? I can't muck up people's brains." She scowled. "If you beat even the sweetest dog enough, it bites everyone who goes near it. I'm what you people made me."

"The Taylor girl will not be bothered. Watch your step, Miss Morgan." He moved forward into the crowd, once more acting a mere constable.

She took three paces into the night before Faye shouted her name, struggling to break away from her parents' arms to come after her. Anna paused, summoning a flimsy smile.

Enjoy your home, Faye. It's much too dangerous for me to be here right now. I'll vid you as soon as it's safe.

Color drained from the girl's face at the telepathic voice. Her surface thoughts floated past a moment of confusion and fear before she realized what had happened. She didn't want Anna to disappear; she wanted her friend to remain in her life. A few drops of rain fell, spattering into the pavement and chasing the crowd inside. The windows glowed from inside, a swarm of news bots lighting the dwelling like a giant jack-o-lantern.

You need your parents now, Faye.

Faye shouted, "Please come in, just for a bit. My mum and dad want to thank you proper."

Anna knew if she looked at the tear-streaked face, she couldn't say no. She couldn't bear to be inside a real *home*. Every breath of air in that place would be a stifling reminder of how her life was a pale shadow of what it could have been.

"Anna! Please!" yelled Faye.

She looked. Game over. Reporters and orb bots parted as Anna trudged across the front yard to the porch. Voices surrounded her with questions: who are you? Are you the person who found the girl? Where had she been? Will you accept the reward? What happened? The parents didn't seem to know what to make of her at first, until Faye wriggled loose enough to reach out.

"Okay fine." She took the girl's hand. "But I can't stay all night."

A STRANGER AT HOME

Electric streetlight comets blurred by overhead in an endless procession. For hours, Anna rode around the streets of London in an aimless search for somewhere to dump off her guilt. As she feared it would, the 'P' word came out in conversation with Faye's parents. Their initial horror clashed with the gratitude of bringing their daughter back to them and turned the usual screaming panic into wide-eyed staring. Not until after Faye's repeated insistence that Anna had protected her, did they stop acting as though they had an escaped wild tiger in the room with them.

At least Faye was safe at home, in bed, with two loving parents to watch over her.

Two loving parents Anna would never have.

The sky rumbled, spitting, but the full downpour hesitated. Killing Blake had not provided the sense of vengeance she had hoped it would. Lightning-lit flashes of his death appeared in the darkness of alleys she drove past. Sometimes, a glimpse of the video formed in her mind, a still image of his sweaty paunch on top of her unconscious body. Murdering her rapist had not undone his crime. All at once, she felt cheap and worthless again. Even if she rampaged over every corrupt constable, every street punk that pawed her, and every man who ever laid a hand on her in Bristol City, the vacuous hollow in her heart would never be filled.

Her father's final expression—the instant his rage became confused fear—came to mind and punched her square in the stomach. She skidded to a halt and covered her face with her hands, shaking. In that moment, she wanted more than anything to take it back, even if it meant she would die that night on the kitchen floor. *Why did I have to panic? Why couldn't I have just curled up in a ball like I always did and wait for him to work it out?* Her eyes burned with tears as jealousy toward Faye gave way to anger at herself.

After a few minutes of sniffling and wiping at her face, the feeling of being alone overpowered her gloom. She couldn't bring her father back. She couldn't jump ten years into the past and grow up normal. However, she could seek the comfort of the family she *did* have: Penny.

By the time she drove out of the checkpoint around The Ruin, her tear-blurred vision made it hard to navigate. The motorbike kicked streams of ink-black mud into the air behind her whenever it struggled to gain traction or she splashed into a puddle. Each time the tire found a patch of broken wet pavement, the bike lurched forward. Anna held on, driving toward the monument to her shame. The e-bikes tires squished to a stop a few feet outside the main entrance to Coventry Tower.

Ol' Jack un-leaned from his post by the door as she dismounted, giving her an unusually wary squint. The kind of stare he often reserved for the East End Boys who came to start trouble. The kickstand sank into the ground, so she leaned the bike against a standing fragment of wall. When she turned back to the building, she found her nose all but touching his chest.

The way he looked down at her got the hair on the back of her neck standing and her heart moving faster. "Ground's a bit squidgy today. Kickstand isn't working."

"You think it's a good idea to be here, Pix? Word is trouble's got your name."

"Jack?" She looked up. "How many times have you saved me from the wankshafts 'round 'ere? I'm only coming home."

He shifted, leaning back as if preparing for a fight. "You're a Proper now, lass. You don't belong 'ere. Too much badness got your scent."

Stunned, she stared at him with tears warming her cheeks. Penny was with her in the alley; she'd been her big sister for ten years. Only Penny could help her cope with the pain caused by that awful video. Only her friend, and a dozen cycles of an autoshower, might scratch some of the grime away.

"Turn it 'round an' don't come back. Don't want anyone gettin' hurt 'cause of what you are."

"What's come over you?" She gasped. "It's me, Pixie... I'm not gonna hurt anyone here."

His expression didn't soften as he motioned at the bike. Veins rose in his forehead and he broke out in a sweat. "We don't know what you're capable of. You're a danger to us all."

Anna glanced up at the thirteenth floor. "Jack. I've known you for years. You're a good man. I thought you knew me, but I guess I was wrong. If you know what I am, then you know what I can do. You've got so much aug in you I could turn you off like a switch. Get out of my way, please. I'm going to see Penny."

He stood firm. "She doesn't want you here either."

The Ruin echoed with a report like a cannon blast. Ol' Jack landed a few feet away, smoke peeling from his coat. He struggled to sit up, like a turtle on its back, making the oddest wheezing moan. Erratic electrical threads shivered across his skin and into his neuralware. The shock left him temporarily paralyzed, but not seriously injured.

Fists clenched, she fought hard to keep her voice sounding confident. "I don't believe that. If she really wants me gone, I'll sod off, but I am going to see her. I owe you for saving my arse many times. Please don't make this unpleasant."

"Hannah?" Jack reached upward. "What's happened, Hannah?"

The unfamiliar name made her look at his thoughts. A woman, a little younger than herself, blonde... so familiar. Anna's eyes widened as though she looked at a sister. She jumped on Ol' Jack and grabbed him by the flaps of his coat, shaking him as much as her scrawny arms could move a half-metal man.

"Jack, sod it. Who is Hannah?"

"Promised... Mother." He wheezed and passed out.

She grunted, struggling to drag him into the lobby where she propped him against the wall. *Was that my mother? Did he know? Why was he so focused on making me want to go away? Oh, no. Something must've happened upstairs and he doesn't want me to see it.*

She sprinted away from him, scrambling past a dozen regulars huddled around a trio of burn barrels. They looked at her like a Proper had stumbled into the wrong part of town; if any recognized her, they hid it well.

Twelve flights of stairs went by in a blur of grey and sadness. Two men saw her in the hallway outside of Penny's apartment and ran the other way. Penny's laughter came out from the wall, followed by the usual snickering Spawny made after he'd said something crass. Anna calmed, feeling even more confused by Ol' Jack's behavior. She'd been expecting a horror show.

Her place looked the same as when she'd left it, with the exception of a pair of fist-sized orb bots floating in the main room. Both swiveled to face her as she walked in, and exploded in a flickering nimbus of lightning the instant she wanted them destroyed. She stomped through the glimmering cloud of debris to the bed, plucking the little white bear from where Faye's abductors had posed it. The pink kunzite earrings waited in their box on the nightstand, their nocturnal resting place.

"Twee..." Anna clutched the bear. The girl's absence hung in the air, tangible.

She's better off. Stop feeling like you had your kid taken away.

Any semblance of 'home' this place may have had seemed absent. She glanced about at the walls, thinking it little more than a hollow shell that no one in their right mind would want to live in. Every flaw, every crack, every draft, stood out. Had she not noticed the ruin while high? Black mold crept down bare concrete. Wires hung in tangles from holes gouged in the drop ceiling. Rats moved beyond sight above and in the walls. The scratch of fluttering plastic tarps came from what had once been a kitchen. Even the roaches stopped coming here; she never had food. Her apartment reeked of dampness tinged with a hint of sour fruit. A few days absent made the stench bad enough to taste.

I don't even want to know what the bed smells like.

Still holding the bear, she drifted out onto the balcony where she had spent many an hour with her legs dangling through the bars, looking out at a city that didn't want her. She stood, staring over the smashed remnants of buildings between here and a glittering coalescence of light, London proper. Numbness set in as she thumbed her NetMini to the GlobeNet presence of Bluebot, a shipping service. She leaned on the railing, mesmerized by distant moving lights whizzing in the air between the tall buildings, neon gnats on rotting fruit. Thousands of small robots swarmed London. The place she had lived in for so long had changed. It felt like the bombed out shithole it was.

One of the gnats came like a shooting star out of the glowing mass; tracing the location of her NetMini. A hoverbot the size of a large dog glided up to the balcony, drifting toward the pocket where she had stashed it. Reading a match, it chirped and played the Bluebot jingle as it opened a side hatch.

She pulled the zip ties off the bear and placed it and the earring box inside. It took her a moment to find a voice before she pushed the lid closed. "Faye Taylor, Nine Clifton Hill, number three, please."

The bot emanated a series of beeps and pivoted to face her. "Destination found. Sixteen credits have been charged to your account. Thank you for using Bluebot."

It rocketed off to rejoin the swarm on the horizon. Anna tracked the flying light until she lost it among the scintillating mass. Faye's things flying away may as well have been the girl leaving her life for good. *She'll be better off without me knowing her.* She glanced down at the single kunzite earring she kept. A tear splattered over it into her palm.

Bugger. She's not my kid. I shouldn't be this upset.

Anna trudged across the apartment she had once called home, out to the hallway, and across to Penny's door. She paused, feeling enough like an outsider she wondered if she should knock. She raised her hand for an instant, but dropped it and walked in. Thick air brushed warm over her face, still loaded with the fragrance of an hours-old meal. Penny rummaged among stacked crates, on all fours amid a pile of clothes.

Spawny reclined on the bed, a hairy flesh-toned break in the black of the cheap sheets covering him from the hips down. Narcotic vapor trailed upward from his mouth and nose. Somewhere between the scent of sausage and potato, a whiff of Flowerbasket teased at Anna's nose.

She took a step toward her friend. "Penny?"

The woman whirled as if an intruder had broken in. Recognition calmed her a little, but she trembled. "Hi Anna." Penny's face twitched, warped with a look of conflict.

"Not you too..." Anna sank onto the end of the couch, face in her hands. "What's wrong with everyone?"

"You're gonna get us killed." Spawny sat up, pointing at the ceiling. He'd likely meant to yell, but it came out sounding bored due to the drug.

"Blake..." Anna sniffled, reaching toward her friend. "Penny, He... He... r—"

Her friend took a step closer, not the fervent embrace Anna needed. "A man came by today, Anna. He wanted to fix me up with a job, a real job in the city. We're getting out of this place."

A faint peal of thunder rolled overhead. Spawny looked up, moving his head as if tracking some great boulder going past. "Oh feck. Here they come. You led them right to us."

"What happened to bezzy mates?" Anna glared. "You said it wasn't a big deal."

He fell flat as his arm slid out from under him. "You's right dangerous. Nuffin personal like. Ain't gonna tell no one nuffin. Jes' don't fancy gettin' nicked."

"It's not that." Penny risked getting close enough to touch her shoulder. "The men after you could kill us for knowing you. We won't say a word, but… It's too dangerous to stay here." She winced as if having a headache, and looked back up at Anna. Fear and concern traded places back and forth.

Blake raped me! I need you… Don't leave me alone now… please.

Anna held Penny's hand tight against her shoulder, unable to speak or even transmit the thought. Penny's eyes vibrated with fear which became love; swooning, she shook her head and blinked as though she'd come out of a waking dream.

Weeping despite joy, Penny fell on Anna with a hug. "I'm getting' out of this place, Anna. I'll be a proper secretary."

Anna held on, shivering. "Penny, I need you… I was…"

Spawny pointed one finger straight up from the bed. "Mind out Pen. Don't touch 'er, she'll zap ya."

A dozen small pieces of electronica around the apartment sputtered into sparklers. Anna sobbed into Penny's side, crying harder when she felt her friend gasping for air.

Penny staggered, leading Anna by the hand into the kitchen—away from Spawny. "What are you trying to say?"

"What's wrong with everyone, Pen? Why does everyone hate me?"

"Well you did kill a dozen men."

She froze as if slapped. "How do you—?"

"A short while after that man came about a job, some other bloke showed up. Said he worked for Carroll. He told us you'd gone off the deep end at some facility."

"Pen, they took Faye!"

"Who?"

"Twee." Anna shook Penny by the shoulders. "They kidnapped her, beat you and Spawny half to death and left you cinched up on the floor?"

"I…" Penny sank into the chair. "What? What's a Twee?"

"Don't be afraid of me." Anna sobbed. "Blake… he…"

"Oh, little Anna. Always crying." Penny hugged her. "I'll look after you, sprog."

Anna lifted her head, her tears stopped cold. That was exactly what Penny said the night they decided to stay together.

"What?" She stood. "You're shaking and covered in sweat. You... You think I'm going to hurt you?"

Penny looked up, eyes struggling to focus. "No. Anna." She shuddered. "Never. Seems like it might be better for everyone if you didn't stay at Coventry."

Startled shouts and explosions echoed from two floors up and two floors down. The little monster raged in her grief. Anna let Penny go, walking backward two steps.

"Penny... I thought you were my... sister." The last word came as a defeated whisper. Anna spun on her heel and flew out into the hallway, blinded by betrayal and sadness.

Penny stared at the slammed door, then at the bed. "What's she on about? I was gonna invite 'er to join us at the new flat in town."

Spawny gave her a look as though she had suggested inviting the Devil to live with them. "Are you nutters?"

"I..." Penny touched her head. "That other man that came looking for Anna... He... I felt so strange when he looked at me."

Anna half ran, half fell down the stairs to the outside. An unfamiliar chime came from her pocket; it took her a few seconds to realize she had an incoming call. Mr. Orange's head appeared in hologram and stared at her unblinking. He seemed pale, robotic.

"Is this a bad time?"

She closed her eyes and looked away, her voice shaky but cold. "What?"

"I found something else you might want to see."

She imagined her naked breasts bouncing in the air, Blake sweaty and grunting. Her body collapsed over the bike, propped up with her elbows on the seat. "Who's screwing me this time?"

"The government, I'd say. Specifically, CSB." Orange's facial expression remained stoic, his voice rote and monotone. "That man you killed wasn't your real father."

Thunder pealed overhead, and down came the rain—full and heavy.

OFF THE WAGON

Trails of water ran along the clear plastic. Little hands poked out of them waving at her. The droplets cheered as they fell into the swirl around the drain. Anna slumped on the floor of the autoshower, having scrubbed herself raw wherever she imagined Blake touched her. She had tried to tell Penny. She had *needed* to tell Penny. She couldn't tell anyone else what Blake did to her. Why, out of all the times she'd been forced to have sex did that bother her so much? Was being unconscious so different from held down by the authority of a constable or the ridiculous notion of it being a 'job?'

Blake left me no choice. He...

Her reflection mocked her, moving while she sat still. Pale breasts blotched pink from furious washing sprouted mouths and wailed at her for hurting them.

Anna's head sagged forward as the machine started again. Pelted with hot water and soap, she reached between her legs and tried to wash the filth out. The bathroom beyond the tube shimmered into a chaos of flashing lights and horny men cheering at her for touching herself. The autoshower, the dancing cage, had trapped her again. She cowered, trying to shield herself from their eyes, looking for a spot to hide in a tube with clear walls.

I have to get out of here!

Her fingernails raked over her breast, drawing blood and breaking her free of the illusion of the club. She screamed at the self-inflicted pain and lapsed into sobs. Blood swirled in the water over her toes, leaping up and forming sanguine garter snakes that hissed before diving into the drain. She stared at her bloody hand as if it belonged to someone else, laughing at the trails of red outlining the zoom patch on her wrist.

Sharp burning pain pulled her away from the hallucinations, leaving her thoughts dull and muted. The hallucinatory trip had come on as hard and vivid as her first time. Doctor Heath was right; her brain didn't know what to do with it anymore. As the rinse started for the fourteenth time, she clutched her knees to her chest and peered with a zombie's eyes at the dead face mocking her from the glass.

Plonk coalesced out of the darkness, his junk dangled over her reflected forehead. "You awright? What was that scream?"

Her skull wobbled upon numbed muscles. She looked at him, naked and shameless outside the shower, and blinked. His manhood perked up, sprouted two little arms, and waved at her. He made impatient gestures toward the door.

"Come on, girl. You've been in there for hours."

Clinging like a lamprey, the suckling zoom patch reminded her of making a deal. Flashes of memory came and went. Losing Faye. Shame at the parents' reaction to what she was. Betrayal from Jack. Betrayal from her only family. Orange's news about the man she thought was her father had been the last straw to shatter everything. All that guilt she had carried for ten years, pointless. So desperate to get away from shame and sadness, she crawled back to Plonk. Her account had been emptied and someone pinched the credstick from her flat. Anna had agreed to shag him for a zoomer. A feeble grasp at the handrail pulled her into a kneeling posture, and she found the door release. She crawled into the cold air over tiles that squished like jellies until her shoulder stopped against his knee. He tapped a pair of furry handcuffs against her head.

"Up for the darbies?"

She murmured something unintelligible, not caring how he used her.

The strength left her arms, sending her into the frigid full-body embrace of the bathroom floor.

When Anna's senses returned to rights, she found herself face down, naked on a warm Comforgel slab. Fire lapped at her left breast, but when she tried to cradle the burning, she realized Plonk had cuffed her arms behind her back and a faux leather-and-chain leash tethered her by the neck to the headboard. Squirming onto her side, she moaned past clenched teeth as the sticky, blood-crusted claw marks on her breast peeled away from the sheet. She cringed, grunting in a brief fight with the restraints. Unable to cradle her wounded bosom, she blew on the damaged skin.

"Plonk? Lemme outta these fuckers." *Ow, son of a bitch.* "I'm rather not in the mood. I'm about to blow chunder all over your bed."

His reply floated down the hall. "One sec luv. Doorbell, prob'ly a client."

Anna squinted at the doorway, curling fetal from pain. "Did we shag yet?"

Footsteps thudded farther away. "Oh, now who's in a hurry miss four-hours-in-the-bloody-tube?" His voice rose to a yell. "No, you passed out straightaway. Awright, awright, keep your bloody knickers on, I'm coming!"

Electronic chirps preceded the hiss of an opening door. Anna rolled onto her back, biting her lower lip as she tried to wriggle her wrists loose. Plonk murmured in the other room, his voice interwoven with that of another man he didn't appear to know. Anna stared into the simmering grey ceiling, swishing her feet about and cursing him for using the cuffs. She liked the escape of feeling vulnerable and protected; at that moment, she hated herself for it. The more she thought about James finding her here, like this, the more she wanted to crawl into a deep, dark place and never come out.

Her eyes shot open at the thought of Agent Gordon.

She went to leap out of bed, but the sex-shop leash jerked her to a halt. She fell flat, gagging from the crushing tightness around her neck. Zoom morphed it into a choking tentacle. Anna rolled off the bed to her feet, the tether forcing her to stay bent forward. Several painful meetings between her legs and furniture knocked the room asunder while she screamed and thrashed at the restraints. The collar tightened in in her zeal to pull away from the bed. Lightheaded, she fell to her knees, choking until she forced herself to slide up and back onto the Comforgel pad.

Panting, she stared wild-eyed at the air, trying to breathe. Zoom painted black phantoms in the window, evil hybrids of the VTOL aircraft that chased her and something from the seventh plane of Hell. Black, segmented tentacles whipped and clattered at the glass. Insectoid hissing rattled her brain. The leash changed shape; the drug made it look like the creature outside had her by the neck. She howled and leapt upright again, pulling at the chain after bracing a foot against the headboard. Zoom's powerful grip on her reality made the hallucination real. Believing the tentacle choked her, her body refused to draw in air.

Anna flung her weight into the collar over and over, pushing with her foot and twisting. She tried to scream, but all the noise she managed came out like a strangled gargle. Desperate fear for her life fueled her muscles. The imitation leather hand-loop at the end of the dog chain broke, sending her flying face first into the nightstand.

Her skull bounced off the cheap furniture on the way to the floor. She hit the ground flat on her back, gagging and gulping great breaths. Incoherent screaming paused long enough to shout, "They're coming! Plonk! Help! Let me outta these!"

Anna rolled around, trying to avoid the serpentine beams of red laser light sweeping the room from the creatures outside. The dangling chain at her neck became an enormous millipede attached by its mandibles to her throat, a creature she couldn't escape. Screaming at the pain of fangs piercing her neck, she fell once more into Plonk's desk, sliding to the ground in a waterfall of drug paraphernalia, condom boxes, and holodisks. She rolled onto her back, scrambling in search of the ability to stand up.

Wild with panic, she ran down the hall to the main room. On the way, she tripped over cartons of old useless electronics, stacked junk, and empty synthbeer cans. Tiny VTOL craft melted through a window as solid as jelly, then morphed into cat-sized wasps. She screamed and took off, the giant wasps chasing her into the front room. A fire exit on the far wall offered the safety of a straight slide to the ground level. The wasps shrank back to little planes, whizzing after her, backing her into the frigid plastisteel door. She struggled to raise her hands high enough behind her to get a grip on the handle. Two fingers touched it when she froze, staring into the hallway at the man there.

Doctor Mardling had found her.

His stunned visage slapped the words right from her mouth and made the creatures disintegrate. The sight of her naked, handcuffed, leashed, bruises all over her legs, beaten bloody about the face, and with trickles of crimson streaked dark against her pale breast discolored his face with rage. He glared at Plonk.

Mardling's voice leaked cold, sinister. "You heard the lady; take them off of her this instant."

Anna let go of the handle. Her wet skin squeaked over the door as she sank to the floor and tried to hide her nakedness with her legs. She wrung her hands about, searching for the derm, wanting to get rid of it before James saw it. Too late. She read his look: anger mixed with pity. He had seen it in her eyes. He had to know how high she was.

"Who the hell do you think you are givin' me orders? It's not what you think, mate. She likes it. Turns 'er right on. We're right about to—"

Plonk rose into the air, rocketed across the room, and hit the wall upside down. Fragments of shelf and plaster dust burst out of the impact point, creating a white cloud in midair. He tried to shout, but something crushed his chest to the point he only gurgled.

"How about I do to your nose what you did to hers?"

Plonk separated from the wall for a second, flipped over so he faced it, and drilled once more into it.

"This is where you learn the discrete difference between an order and a request, you scratter," said Mardling, his voice slow and deliberate. "Code, now."

"They're not municipal… Sex toy," rasped Plonk. "Keys…"

"Well then." James's eyebrows flared, the invisible force crushed the dealer into the wall harder for an instant; more lumps of plaster fell. "Get the bloody key."

With a contemptuous sneer, Mardling turned away and let him fall. Plonk dragged himself along the floor to the bedroom, crimson-faced and gasping for air. Anna cowered at James' approach, unable to look at him or cover herself. James took a knee in front of her, gently unbuckling the leather collar. She wanted to curl up and die as it peeled away from the line of tenderness her panic had crushed into her throat. James must have been looking at her thoughts, since his anger at Plonk faded to concern. He caressed her cheek for a moment, and stood, tracing his fingers away.

He looked a bit shy of toward her, leaving his hand outstretched. "Come on then."

"James!" she yelled, cowering into the wall.

Plonk, still in his robe, had emerged from the back with a combat rifle pointed at them. The report of a shot made Anna scream and close her eyes. When James didn't fall or cry out, she looked. Plonk's aim went high and right. He pulled at the rifle, which seemed to hang frozen in midair as solid as if nailed to a wall. A bead of sweat trickled down the side of James' head, a sign of exertion and perhaps a touch of fear.

Anna snarled, raising her leg to point with her toe at Plonk. The lightning wouldn't listen, wouldn't come out from under the zoom. "Plonk, you tosser!"

"Christ on a rubber crutch," whispered Plonk.

Before he could gather his wits, the rifle flipped over in his grip and caught him across the forehead. Plonk collapsed to the carpet, cradling his head in his arms as the weapon danced around and battered him.

"Okay! Okay!" He flailed. "You win."

The rifle careened into the kitchen, falling into the sink among a rain of shattered tiles. Anna shivered against the wall, trying to scoot away from tiny, fanged gremlins dragging themselves out from under the sofa. The nude figures in Plonk's coffee table twisted about to glare at her, envy radiating from their eyes. One spat a glop of searing green light. From where it landed, the rug caught fire in a thin stream that raced at her. She screamed until James stepped in front of her, dispelling the hallucination.

Plonk crawled into the bedroom.

James helped her up, and she leaned into the soft warmth of tweed, coarse against her chest. He kissed her with gentle care upon the forehead. She rattled the cuffs, yearning to embrace him.

"I'm sorry, James. I... I'm such an idiot. Your buttons are talking to me."

He traced a finger over the scratch marks. "What's this?"

"Bad trip. I needed the pain to snap out of it."

"Look at me."

"I can't." She sniffled. "I almost made it... I thought I was free, but I'm just a piece of shite."

"Anna," he said, in the tone of a chiding father.

She ventured a reluctant glance into the deep chocolate of his eyes, shivering from shame and cold. She wanted to cover herself, to hide this disgrace, to grab him and hold on so he could lift her out of this pit. Images slid to the forefront of her mind as he searched for what sent her over the edge. Bile rose into her throat at everything replaying itself from when she'd set off to fetch Twee to the message from Orange.

James closed his eyes in a pained grimace.

She pressed herself against him in an armless hug when the mental link ended. He removed his coat and wrapped it around her.

He caressed her hair with one hand while leaning past her to call, "Where's that bloody key, you twit?"

Amid the bangs and thuds of heavy objects knocking about, Plonk shouted. "Lost guv'na. She must'a kicked it behind the bed when she lost her goddamned mind. You'd think she'd never been leashed to a bed before."

"Mind your tone, cretin."

Anna shot a fearful glance at the window, straining against the furry cuffs. "James, the CSB is still hunting me. A rogue agent named Gordon, if he gets me like this I'm—"

He guided her to a seat on the couch and took a knee in front of her.

"Do not worry about that twat Gordon. He will regret the day he tangled with me." James brushed a tear away with his thumb. "You were doing so well, Anna, it pains me to see you have run back to the chemicals. I do think the normal recovery process is going to take a bit more time than we have been allotted given recent developments. I cannot let you do this to yourself again."

"I was doing well. I just… It was too much to handle." She looked down. "They all hate me now. Ol' Jack, Spawny… Penny…"

He smiled, lifting her chin. "Wanted you to move in with her at her new flat. She said leave Coventry, not leave her."

"How do you know that?" She squirmed, wishing he would stop staring at her.

James smiled. "It did take me a bit of asking around to find you."

Anna hung her head. The zoom scar on her arm burned with regret.

"Pity, I thought finding out that man you killed was not really your father would have made it easier on you." James growled "What is taking so long, man?"

"I'm looking," yelled Plonk.

"That made it worse, James." She sniveled. "I've had so much guilt for so long. Finding out it was all bullshit…"

"But…" He lifted her chin. "Your own family didn't turn against you. No real father could hate his own child. You might still have family out there, somewhere."

Her mind raced. "I… never thought about it that way."

Something crashed in the back.

James looked up again, yelling, "Will you hurry up?"

"You somehow tossed Plonk into the wall. Can't you break them off me?" Anna shifted and held her arms up.

"I could, but I would rather not break your arms or tear your hands off." He flashed a cheesy grin.

She trembled. "I need to see Penny."

"Alas, that is not a particularly good idea right now. For her sake, you should keep some distance for a while. At least until Gordon and any allies of his are no longer in the equation. Now, there is still the matter of your mental addiction. I will not let you turn to that little patch every time you need help."

"I'm sorry." She squirmed.

"Found it." Plonk shouted from the back with a singsong tone.

He held her face in both hands, forcing her to make eye contact. "Do not be sorry, Anna. Be rid of it. I will help you."

"Okay." She let him stare into her eyes. "Why didn't you do this before?"

He leaned in and kissed her on the top of the head. "Because, Anna. If you overcame it on your own, it is rather unlikely you would go back to it. This…" James gave her a sad look. "This could come undone and leave you craving it hard, beyond rational thought. For the time being, it will have to do. Once we get to the Colony, we can go back to a more natural cure. Although, given the medical detox, dose will not have done much damage."

It didn't matter she was as vulnerable and helpless, both mentally and physically, as she had ever been. With him there, she felt as safe as Faye in her parents' house.

"I trust you, James."

She surrendered to the eyes that pierced her mind. His face shimmered, lit by a faint aura as he held her. Adoration shone in his stare; she offered no resistance to his telepathy.

An angel, sent to carry me out of this dreadful place.

Scrap by painful scrap, her recollections of being high tore away from the canvas of her memory and spiraled into oblivion. Some scenes wound backward as they unraveled, others simply never existed. The zoom disappeared; it couldn't comfort her any longer.

James would protect her.

The sensation of floating ended when he lifted her to her feet. The cold air embraced her when the coat fell off. The change in altitude churned her stomach. She gasped in an effort to hold back the urge to vomit. He steadied her while Plonk unlocked the restraints. Once free, she threw her arms around him.

James stared death at Plonk. "Bugger off. Go teach yourself to fly, or something."

She convulsed in his embrace. The disconnect between what her brain thought and the state of her body brought cold sweat, trembling, and the need to retch.

Doctor Mardling held on with one arm while he collected his coat. "So good of Lauren to remind me to bring these."

Anna held on as he rifled among the pockets. An autoinjector pressed into her back, forcing her up on her toes in response to the spreading chill.

"Ooo, that's cold," she muttered.

While the scratches faded into the milky white of her chest, he pressed a second autoinjector into her leg. This one had a blue shell and didn't feel like ice water under her skin. The sweat stopped, the nausea departed, and the trembles came to an end.

He knew to bring an antipak for zoom; am I that predictable?

Plonk shambled into the hallway, leaving them alone in the apartment. Anna looked down at her nakedness, stark white against the charcoal grey rug. She blushed and flashed a mischievous smile.

"James, we really must stop meeting like this." She leaned up and kissed him.

Aside from the pleased smile that followed, he didn't move. "You are lovely, Anna, but this is neither the time nor the place. As I told you already, you do not need to trade anything for my help."

"But what if I want to?" She traced a thumb over the pristine skin of her wrist. Something about that bit of skin needled at her as having been important. She vaguely recalled using a drug derm, but no matter how long she stared into space, couldn't remember what it felt like to be high. After a plaintive glance, she leaned in close and set her cheek against his chest, staring out the window. "I wanted to dull my mind. It does what it wants when I get excited. I had to hide, they would have found me."

He leaned his head against hers and patted her back. "All of that is behind you now Anna, no more hiding from who you are. No more shame."

She squeezed him.

James stepped back, leaving his hands on her shoulders. "You will need to use the loo once the shot has collected the trash from your system. It is dangerous to let such toxins linger inside. Go have a seat and wait for it.

Get cleaned up and your kit on, and let us be off. We have much to discuss."

"James? Where's Plonk going?"

"How should I know? I would imagine he is on his way to the roof to conduct a practical experiment in applied gravitational attraction."

"Is that really necessary?"

He scoffed. "After the way he treated you?"

"James." She put a hand on her chest. "I did it all to myself. Thank you for showing me that. Please, don't kill him. In some odd way, he's almost like a friend."

Fullness spread into her bladder. She let out an "eep!" and ran for the bathroom. When the most disturbingly uncomfortable event of her life finished, she sat there out of breath, waiting for the fire to cool.

"Flush."

The machine obeyed. She had no desire to open her eyes and see what nanobot-purged zoom looked like. Smelling it was horror enough. Too drained to move, she slumped with her elbows on her knees. *Not my real father.* Scenes of his cruelty flashed in her mind: yelling at first, followed by a tearful apology and hugs. When things continued breaking and she got older, yelling became spanking, then belting, then beating with a closed fist. The apologies faded to fear; he couldn't stand being in the same room with her. Always, though, he had lingering sadness in his eyes.

That was a total stranger? Anna rubbed her hands over her head and through her hair. *Why would he keep me around? Why didn't he ditch me in the street or murder me?* Legs numb from the toilet seat, she stood and stretched. *Was he some CSB agent forced to watch me?*

Anna mused over her past as she cleaned up and dressed. She felt bad for the man, but the guilt seemed distant now, far away as if it had been a bad dream. Each time she reached for it to wallow in self-pity, Faye appeared, smiling at her for saving her life.

Head held high, Anna emerged from the bathroom. Plonk sat on the couch, staring vacant at sportscaster commentary on a Frictionless match about to start.

"Oh, it's Man-U vs. Arsenal. Can we stay a bit? Arsenal's magic bastard Pryce is sidelined with an injury, we're going to smash them."

Anna's run for the couch stalled on James' Arm.

"Catch it on the portable, Anna. We do not have the time."

She flashed an insincere pout, and walked with him to the car. He held the door for her, closing it with a gentle touch once she had gathered her coat.

A musical jingle from her pocket broke the silence, becoming louder when she took it out and swiped at it. The face of Mr. Orange appeared with a trace of a smile.

"Pixie… I have some good news. Got about two dozen hunter-killers scouring the GlobeNet for that vid."

"Umm, all right. Thank you Nathan." Anna cocked an eyebrow as he nodded and hung up, and then looked to her right. "Do you remember me asking him to fetch me a holo?"

Doctor Mardling traced his index finger up and down over his smirk. "It escapes me. Probably nothing of consequence. I believe you may have asked him to destroy the security footage of you killing that Blake fellow."

"Oh." She scowled. "That grotty bastard. He deserved it for leaving me locked in that bloody cage overnight."

"Yes… Indeed he did."

AURORA

Cold didn't quite capture the truth of the floor Anna encountered the next morning in the cramped bedroom of a small house in the woods, South Snowdonia in County Gwynedd. Frigid approached the issue with more accuracy, though frozen came the closest, yet it still failed to completely capture the shock.

Anna's foot numbed in an instant.

"Gah! That's fecking—"

Her next word took the form of a shriek as she leapt back into the bed. She grabbed her toes to make sure none had snapped off and remained stuck to the stone tile. Frantic hands swiped about in a desperate search for something to put on her feet. After, she tried to rub feeling back into her toes through three layers of socks.

The place had no electrical connection to a power grid, only a fubox thrumming on the back porch. A handful of freestanding lamps were, at the moment, all the portable fusion generator had been connected to. The beautiful stone-paved floor was unfit to be trod upon barefoot this early in the morning.

She glared at the floor. *That'd freeze even with shoes.*

Anna shuffled into the main room in an oversized shirt, panties, and boots. She went over to the pile of supplies James ordered and dragged a heater unit to the center of the room near three finger-thick cables entering under the back door. The wires glimmered with amber light, full of electricity. The interior of the vented black mechanism took on a deep orange glow as a bladeless fan circulated warm air.

She knelt in the stream of heat until the numbness left her bare legs. Still shivering, she fetched the food reassembler from the stack of metal boxes. With a grunt, she managed to heft the ponderous machine and wobbled with it for two steps before dropping it on the table, then slumped over it to catch her breath. The old wooden furniture creaked and slid several inches from the force of the device landing on it.

The reassembler, made for camping, operated via internal power with an e-mag like an energy weapon. After some digging around the pile of stuff at the far side of the room, she found the protein fluid tank and twisted it into place in a socket on the left side.

She set an empty plate inside the machine, dialed up some breakfast, and took a seat that made her squeal at the touch of cold wood. Clasping her hands over her mouth, she blew hot hair into her fingers while she waited.

At the center of the reassembler, a cluster of robotic arms the size of chopsticks came to life. Droplets of beige OmniSoy paste exuded from their tips as shimmering blue light formed an orb above the surface. The spider legs whirred about, faster and faster, pecking at the spot where food formed out of thin air.

Anna kept warming her fingers with her breath while the device printed her breakfast, altering the atomic structure of the slime into eggs, ham, mushrooms, and gravy. When it beeped, she opened the door and pulled the plate out, adoring the steamy heat.

Halfway into her meal, a tall woman with snow white skin and blonde hair reaching down to her thighs walked in the back door and glided to the sink, her pink satin robe scandalous in its shortness. The pattern of white flowers spread across it in a diagonal line lent an Oriental feel. Wet and barefoot, the sight of her made Anna feel colder in spite of the heating unit three feet to her right—especially when her footprints became frost.

Anna swallowed a mouthful of eggs and cleared her throat. "Um. Hello?"

The woman turned to look at her with solid black eyes like onyx gems set into the head of a porcelain doll. A bit shy of six feet tall, she had a generous chest and curvy hips that made Anna feel like an adolescent boy by comparison. The strange appearance of this woman startled Anna's chair several inches to the rear.

After a casual wave, the woman laughed. When she answered, her lips didn't move at all, merely a pleasant voice echoing from everywhere at once. "Hello, Anna. I'm Aurora."

Anna squinted. "Stage name? And umm…"

"What?" Aurora cocked her head to the side, thinking. "Oh, no. I'm not a dancer. It's actually Lauren, but I go by Aurora to protect my family. The voice thing? Oh, it's just how my brain works."

Anna couldn't help but stare at the woman's wet feet and the trail of ice-prints leading to the back door. "Aren't you freezing?"

Aurora moved to the sink and washed a piece of fruit she had gotten from a box with Japanese markings. "The floor is warmer than the stream out back. It's quite nice in here."

"It's positively Baltic out there! You went for a skinny in this?"

"It looks less ridiculous than wearing outdoor boots with a man's shirt." She sat at the table, facing her, and bit into an enormous peach.

The girth of the thing stalled Anna's train of thought. "What the devil is that?"

"A peach."

"Obviously, but it's as big as your head."

Aurora spoke between nibbles. "The only hydroponics worth bothering with come out of the NSK. They have these giant artificial islands. So much better than the orbital stuff."

Cupping her hands to her mouth, Anna exhaled to warm up. "Never heard of it."

"Nippon Shōgyō-Kumiai. They control all of the commerce between Japan and the outside world. The country broke up into a bunch of different prefectures… and the companies that own them are always fighting. The NSK plays intermediary so they can continue to trade. If you're going to buy fruit or vegetables and you don't want reassembled, look for NSK."

"You sound like an advert bot." Anna giggled, pushing what remained of her food around the plate. "Well, who are you then?"

Aurora laughed with a haughty air and waved the colossal fruit at her. "Relax, dear. I'm his friend. We work together. I think I'm a bit too odd looking for him to be honest."

"You, umm, do have a unique presence."

"You can stare all you like. I don't mind."

She likes making people uncomfortable.

Eye contact lasted a minute. "You're quite pretty. Thank you for making me feel less pale."

Aurora smiled. "You sleep all day, come out at night, and it's always raining in London. All you need is some sun. I'm stuck like this."

"So what do you—?"

"Do?" Aurora winked. "I'm a clairvoyant, and a spy."

Anna froze, fork halfway between plate and mouth. It hit her where she had heard this voice before. "Lord Thompson's phone?"

"Good memory. Saw the blighter on the roof across the way about ten minutes before he shot at you. Truth be told, I didn't expect the call would go through. You know, I've a habit of telling James where he can find Awakened. You must've had quite the uncertain life, girl. I never saw you coming until a few days ago."

"Yeah…" Anna looked at her plate. "It's been… far from fun. So you see the future?" She lowered the forkful to the plate, uneaten. "Oh and, thanks for saving my life."

"No bother at all." Aurora paused to peck at the massive fruit. "Not all the time, and it's not always so clear. The stronger the significance of an event, the more warning I get. You were a complete unknown to me at the time. It's only because James had asked me to watch you that I saw it. I didn't believe him at first when he said you were one of us, but now I see you are a critical part of his path. Because of you, some innocent children will go where they need to be. You will save lives, Anna. Think you'll ever get over your feelings toward Arsenal?"

"What?" Anna coughed. Once her brain chewed on the question, she scowled. "Certainly not. Pack of wankers. I'll hate 'em and everyone who likes 'em straight to my grave."

"I see." Aurora smiled in an unsettling 'are you so sure' sort of way.

Finally relaxed, she finished off her food and smiled at the bright green-tinted sunlight leaking in the windows. Deep within a grove of trees, the area held a pastoral calm that transcended time. If not for the portable technology, the scene could have been a thousand years ago.

Aurora put a heel on the table and crossed her other leg over it. "It is nice to finally meet you in person."

"Yes… Does the stove work? Firewood? Wouldn't mind some tea."

She waved the peach at the ancient iron stove. "No wood chopped. There's a hot plate in the oven."

Anna stood, heading for the oven, and dragged the portable cooker out. "So, how'd you two meet?"

"Part of his research with the university. Neither one of my parents were gifted. Mum worked off-Earth on a colony for a little while she was carrying me."

Anna sighed at the lack of a faucet. Aurora pointed at bottled water.

"Thanks. What, you're part alien?"

Aurora laughed. "No... No one knows what happened. Space radiation, odd effect of gravity or jump travel." Aurora gnawed on the peach. "For all I know, I could've come out just like this if she pushed a broom in Essex her whole life."

Anna poured three bottles into the kettle. "Are they well?"

"Yes. CSB only arrested me. I think I was sixteen when they hauled me out in handcuffs, in front of the entire street." Anna gave her a sorrowful stare. "They shut me away in some place like where you found your little friend. 'Course... I left straight away. They grabbed me again. I escaped. They started keeping me in a drug-induced sleep."

"That's awful!" Anna switched on the hot plate and set teabags into cups. "I'm so sorry."

"Oh, it's hardly your fault. Mardling was working with the CSB as some kind of consultant. I still don't know how he convinced them he had no ability."

"I think we both know that." Anna winked.

They laughed together.

"Tossers brought me out of the coma, had me lashed hand and foot to a chair, blindfolded, with one of those damn headbands on. They couldn't leave it on too long or I'd go nuts."

Anna fell into her chair, shaking.

"I see you've had the treatment, too.

"James talked me into talking... Somehow smoothed things over with them and he was allowed to 'take me into custody' from then on out. He was supposed to study me and give them a full report on what I was capable of." She took another large bite of peach, licking the wounded fruit. "He never quite got 'round to that bit."

Anna leaned forward, hushed. "Do you always traipse about in such skimp?"

"He's seen your goods more than mine, luv. I tend to leave my togs behind when I cross over, got tired of replacing them."

"Cross over?"

"Have you heard of astral projection?"

Anna shook her head. "No, I've been kind of sheltered."

"Most psionics who can astrally project are able to leave their bodies behind and roam about like a ghost. They can see and hear things, see spirits and whatnot."

Her eyebrow climbed. "Ghosts?"

"You toss lightning out of your hands and you're surprised to hear spirits are real?" Aurora smiled. "Suffice to say, Awakened are quite a bit more powerful. I don't only send my soul into the other world. My whole body goes. Only living bits. I can't bring objects, clothes included."

An eerie feeling accompanied a soft *thump*. Anna looked up to find the empty pink robe settling over the peach on the seat of the chair. She bolted to her feet, and glanced around at the cabin.

Aurora's voice came spectral, echoing, and unearthly. "I'm right behind you, hon."

When Anna whirled about, she stared at empty air. A gossamer presence traced an icy line down the bare skin on the back of her leg. She jumped forward. "Eep!"

Aurora's laughter reverberated across the room, the source moving directly through the table to the other side. As if stepping out of an unseen doorway, Aurora reappeared, solid and nude. The sight of the woman made Anna feel even more un-feminine in her lack of shape. Aurora put her robe back on, retrieved her fruit, and sat.

Anna blinked, mouth open.

"Can't take anything with me. That's how I kept getting away from them. Walls don't stop me." She took another bite of peach. "These are really good, would you like some?"

Sinking into her seat, Anna shook her head. "No, thanks. It almost makes sense why they put bombs in us now."

"Oh they tried that." Aurora narrowed her eyes. "Bloody thing fell out when I crossed. Hurt like a bitch."

It hit Anna funny, sending her into a giggle fit. "You can't have cyberware either? I'm the same… though I'd fry it and kill myself."

"Likely, that. You don't have to worry about it though. James has the CSB right where he wants them. Well, almost. They still exist, so not quite *exactly* where he wants."

"Where did he get off to?"

"He's gearin' up for something big now that he's found you." She glanced up at the middle of the ceiling. "Display on."

Holographic light shimmered into a terminal screen above the table, two by three feet. Aurora flicked at it with a toe, opening a folder and kicking it apart into individual files. Images of people, including small children, scattered about the screen, depicting them taken from screaming families. Some had been beaten unconscious; men, women, and even children carried away battered and bruised.

"Psionics," said Aurora before taking another bite of peach. "He's been sneaking the wee ones out of government *care* for a few years now, and any of the others who want to go. Alas, none of them are like us... They're ordinary psionics."

Anna couldn't believe it; the level of cruelty in the images hit her in the gut like a fist. Some of the parents had been shot trying to stop the arrest of their sons and daughters. Agent Gordon appeared in a handful of the scenes.

"This is all Gordon's doing, isn't it?"

Blonde hair swam about as Aurora shook her head. "No, he's a tool. There's a splinter faction within the CSB that would rather see us all eliminated. A couple of hard-liners want to re-enact the witch-hunts. They've got backing from the C of E. Whole group of them think psionics are a sign of the Devil's power."

Anna closed the files, unable to tolerate at any more. "So what's he doing?"

"Gathering them and shipping them off somewhere. He's told me he wants to create a new society for us. If I had to hazard a guess, he's considering the UCF. Most of Europe is right out. The ACC kills us on sight. Paranoid bastards. No one knows how China feels about psionics, as there hasn't been much information leaked. As far as the Arabs are concerned, they claim they don't have any psionics."

"That's bollocks," chirped Anna. "Psionics are one to two percent of the population, there's no ethnic or geographical preference."

Anna shrugged. "It's propaganda. There's more than one religion that fears us."

"The UCF?" Anna blinked. "It didn't seem as though he cared much for it... called it 'the colony' still."

Lauren almost spit a hunk of peach across the table with her laugh. "He's a condescending bugger sometimes, thinks he's the cat's whiskers."

With closed eyes, Anna hugged herself and thought of his face aglow with the aura. *He is.* She shifted in the chair, no longer able to ignore the nagging presence in her bladder. "So where's the loo?"

"Twenty paces out back."

"Bugger…" Anna stood and shuffled outside, dread hanging on her shoulders as though she walked off to be shot.

AURORA CROSSED HER ANKLES, FEET UP ON THE TABLE, AND SMILED. THE back door creaked closed with a dull *tap*. She pictured Anna galumphing down the stone trail behind the house in those dreadful boots on her way to the outhouse.

"Four… Three… Two…"

Anna let out a piercing scream in the distance.

"Seat's a wee bit chilly, luv."

Aurora ate the last of the peach.

40

ACCEPTANCE

Crunching gravel announced the arrival of Doctor Mardling's gold luxury car. Aurora reclined on the porch, still clad in the skimpy robe, playing with the silk belt as the car slid to a halt a few meters away. The door closed with a *thunk*, and he trudged over as she leaned back on her elbows.

"You are overdressed."

Aurora winked. "We have a guest, and I'm not planning on going anywhere today, unless you need something."

"No. Everything is in order." He glanced back and forth from her to the door. "Why are you outside?"

"Your little Pixie has the heat cranked to the nines, too bloody hot in there."

"Do you associate with the dead or *are* you one?" James shook his head. "You would live in the arctic if you could."

"Sod it, James. I'm not *that* bad. She's got it over thirty eight degrees."

He sent a thoughtful glance at the window. "What do you think of this one?"

"Well, she's rather enamored with you." Aurora stared off into space, silent for some time until a coy grin slinked over her lips. "I think she will make you happy. The chances of her being disloyal are pretty much *zero*."

He chuckled, bowed, and went past her. Heat fell out from the door when it opened. James shot a glance at the portable heater. A dirty fork floated up and poked at the holographic controls. Repeatedly stabbing at the downward arrow, he lowered it to a tolerable twenty degrees before the utensil fell to the plate.

ANNA RECLINED ON THE BED, HAVING ABANDONED HER BOOTS AND SOCKS, lost in a video game on her NetMini.

The *clank* of a fork hitting a plate made Anna look up. She tossed the 'mini to the side and ran out of the back bedroom.

"James." She wrapped her arms around him. "Is something wrong? You look worried."

His expression settled into sublime calm while he endured her clinging. "Anxious is a better term, my dear. Many innocent lives are depending on me right now, yours included."

She glanced out the window, at trees shifting in a soft, whispery wind. "Do you think we'll be safe out here in the country?"

"Reasonably, but it is not a long term solution. Your efforts at liberating your former roommate have created a tenuous climate back in the city. This should afford us the luxury to gather ourselves, and for you to settle your mind. Put the rest of your clothes on. I have a surprise for you."

A few minutes later, with one boot on, she hopped into the front room while donning the other to find James by the door with a large metal case in hand. He went out onto the porch. Anna stepped into her boot, tapped it on the floor twice, and hurried after him. Aurora flashed an impish smile as they went down the steps to the grass.

Behind the cabin, rolling tree-covered hills went as far as she could see in all directions. A hint of a dirt path made its way off to the south, and the air came alive with the sound of birds. She followed him for the better part of twenty minutes into the forest. He commented on the relaxing atmosphere, trying to keep her mind away from everything that had happened in the city. Dense trees foiled the worst attempts of the breeze to frost her bones, and its gentle hiss among the leaves soothed her.

"I missed you this morning when I woke up."

James massaged the back her hand with his thumb. "Sorry, Anna. It came up out of the blue. I was making arrangements for some of the younger victims of the Crown's tyranny to leave the country."

Moved by the thought of broken families, Anna squeezed his arm.

"James, it's so good of you to help those people. It isn't right how they're treated."

He paused in mid stride and faced her. "It was not right how you were treated, Anna. I'll always be here for you."

A spasm twitched in her forearm, two inches south of her wrist. "I know that now."

"I hope to help them even more... One day, I will find a way to unlock their true potential. It may not be Earth, but I will find a home for us."

Their stroll came to a halt at the edge of a modest lake. He nodded toward a decaying wooden pier and the prow of a small rowboat protruding from the water like a shark's fin. Clumps of algae trailed away from it as if the ancient craft had a green beard. She leaned against him to take in the view, smiling at the tranquility.

"Boat ride is not quite an option. Bloody thing sank fifty years ago, however..."

After setting the case down, he unpacked a large tartan cloth, which he flicked out over the grass. Motorized trays lifted up from inside, sliding out into shelves laden with hors d'oeuvres, a bottle of wine, two glasses, and some small sandwiches.

"A picnic? Really?" She giggled.

Grinning, she flopped next to him as the case projected a holographic arrangement of candles in the center of the blanket. A whimsical smile accompanied a lifted eyebrow as he offered her a glass of wine. She overacted high-society, doing a spot-on impression of Princess Daphne for a few minutes before it lost humor.

James muttered about the princess for a short while, amused by the lengths to which the SIS had to go in order to keep the debutante's post-adolescent wild streak out of the tabloids. As they ate, he worked the conversation around to the topic of Annabelle Morgan. She felt safe with him, not caring he pried into her life. She held no part of her past from this man; the more she smiled at him, the more he felt like the protector she had always wanted.

"I feel safe with you, James."

He sipped from his glass, gazing out over the water. "You shouldn't need a protector. Those who have taken advantage of you should have needed protection from you. You are a very capable woman."

She swirled her drink, lost in the twisted reflection of trees upon the merlot. "I never enjoyed hurting people. I always got it. Even as a little girl, they'd all give me hell for having white hair."

"It's beautiful."

"They called me ghosty. Everyone thought I was some kind of monster." *Even my... non-Dad.* Anna took a long sip, thinking about the man for whom she had borne so much guilt over killing. Why had he always seemed so sad after hitting her?

"No Anna... That is your power. Think of it like a fern too great for its pot. You have a great deal of energy, and your head is only so big. You were born Awakened; certain oddities are included with that. Quirks like Lauren's eyes and skin, or the way you burn things out when you get excited."

"Can you make it stop? NetMinis get expensive after a dozen."

He traced his fingertips over the back of her hand. "I was not born with this power. I found a way to unlock it. For me, many hours of telepathic experiments, and a little neurosurgery did the trick. Perhaps it may be possible to make adjustments. I would want to be careful, however. It wouldn't be worth it to lose your gift. A NetMini here or there can be replaced, you are too precious to risk."

A bird glided along a few inches above the surface of the lake, striking unexpectedly at an unseen meal before returning to the trees with a thrashing fish in its talons. Anna glanced down, studying the hand touching hers.

"It's so peaceful, James. I'm almost afraid our being here will ruin it."

He stared at ripples where wind touched the water. "Perhaps. I wanted to offer you the chance to unwind before the storm."

She leaned up and kissed him, a quick smooch on the lips. Jumping back, she smiled at the astonishment in his eyes, and did it again, longer the second time. He gave in, embracing her with a kiss as they rolled onto the ground.

Breath fogged in the air. She ran her hands over his shirt; he seemed hesitant to surrender control of the moment. She kissed over his cheek to his neck. His arm tightened across her back as her warm breath flooded his ear.

"I love you, James."

She surrendered to the hands that worked her clothes away as she continued to kiss him. Cold air washed over the absence of cloth. She reclined, grinning at the sky. He shrugged off his coat and shoes, and threw his necktie to the side with a sly grin. Biting her lower lip, she sat up and helped undo his belt. James leaned forward, lowering himself on top of her. His scent enveloped her; she closed her eyes, reveling in the warmth of his body against her. He kissed her breast before his lips glided up to her neck and he kissed her again. The scratch of his goatee upon her skin sent shudders down her legs, intensified by the rough tartan blanket scratching over her writhing body.

Tiny crackles emanated from the dew-laden grass behind her head.

He stared at her, lost in a dream. "Are you certain this is what you want?"

She pushed, rolling on top of him, staring with adoration down at his face surrounded by a fan of chestnut hair. He slid his hands down her sides, caressing her hips. Anna suppressed a shiver at the puffs of mist their breaths made and the frigid air across her back.

"I am," she said with a breathless rasp.

His grin held a touch of imperiousness when he rolled on top. She squealed, arching her back; paralyzed by the unexpected caress of frosty, wet grass. Their fingers interlaced, palm to palm. He pushed her hands apart to the ground on either side of her head. Her effort to get away from the soaked green only tightened their entwined bodies.

She was his.

Anna gazed at magnificent white clouds floating in an ocean of endless blue. She cried at the sight; until that moment, whenever she had looked up, the sky had always been grey. Electricity crackled somewhere out of sight in response to her heart swelling with joy.

Trembling, she moaned in a voice half shout and half whimper. They moved as one.

A few feet to the right, the holo-projector in the picnic case died a brilliant sparking death—not that either of them noticed.

Giving herself in to bliss, she *made love* for the first time in her life.

AMID A STREWN MASS OF CLOTHES AND PICNIC SUPPLIES, ANNA CUDDLED TO James' side, both of them wrapped in the tartan. She couldn't get rid of her silly grin, staring at the dark spot on his nose and his fluffed up hair.

"I rather fail to see the humor," he said.

He set about fussing with his mane. When it continued to frizz back up despite his best effort to settle it, he squinted at her.

"You are doing that on purpose."

She bit her lip and acted innocent until he shook his head with a faint chuckle. She snuggled against him, and relaxed the mild current so he could set his hair back to rights.

Anna put a hand over her face, rubbing a sore spot. "The nose to nose bit *was* an accident."

He stopped combing with his hands. "I say, having a romp with you is quite an electrifying experience. Perhaps damp grass was a poor choice of scenery."

"Puns, James?" She sat up. "I thought you were an intellectual?"

He stretched past her to retrieve the wine and glasses. "I am, but we are on holiday."

41

WELCOME WORN

A bladder full to the point of pain urged Anna out of sleep. The woozy head of wine passed away into a dull sense of discomfort. Between James and the blankets, she found it quite difficult to summon up the willpower necessary to make the horrible trek outside to the privy. Never mind the waiting torture of sitting on an ice ring.

Country dark was a new experience. For a few seconds after she awoke, she couldn't tell if she'd even opened her eyes. It didn't make any difference. Snuggling into his warmth, she attempted to go back to sleep but the need nagged at the recesses of her mind until she sat up with a growl.

After running all day, the heater had taken the fangs out of the chill inside the cabin. The cold had lost much of its paralytic nature, but still stunned a gasp out of her as the blankets slid away. She stepped on her boot while attempting to get up, and tripped into the wall. Whatever she grabbed for support came away in her hand and she collapsed on all fours.

"Sorry James," she whispered, and put down a canister.

To her surprise, her fall hadn't disturbed him. A short crawl to the left resulted in her head smacking something hard. She cringed and muttered swear words. Once the pain faded enough to allow her to move again, she patted her hands around at the floor in a search for some piece of identifiable clothing. Her full bladder threatened not to wait for her to get outside. In a rush, she created an electrical arc between her fingers for light. In the flickering blue, she grabbed his shirt and stuck her feet bare into her boots. The cold imitation leather against her legs nearly made the walk outside unnecessary.

Anna raised her hand, the spark between her thumb and finger flickering, providing light while she snuck out of the bedroom. She tiptoed past Aurora's door to the rear exit. The night air wrapped her legs with a chill so intense it came on as a blanket of biting needles. She made it two steps along the footpath before her teeth chattered. Impenetrable darkness saturated the forest, except for the shifting blues of lightning-lit trees nearby.

The outhouse door opened with a low drawn out *creak*, leaving her face to face with her nemesis—the frozen toilet seat. Edging into the tiny space, she pulled and latched the door.

"Dammit, Lauren. Why did you keep feeding me tea last night?"

She bit down on her forearm, hiked up the shirt, and sat. Sitting bare-ass on a block of ice would've been warmer. Anna shrieked into her arm, trying her best to muffle herself. Despite the urgency of her need, it took a while to get started. Eventually, relief came, and she sagged forward. The moment of elation ended with a sudden strange feeling. Indistinct amber light wobbled by outside, the sense of it masked by the wall. Anna braced her hands on the cold wood, searching the darkness. When she caught a glimpse of it again, she focused, and her mind created the image of a ten-inch sphere a few inches beyond the wall.

An orb? She froze. *Oh, James! They found us.*

She eased herself upright, holding on to the seat to keep it from making noise. Cold air threaded up between her legs. Between the temperature and the unknown threat outside, she couldn't stop shivering.

Anna peered out a tiny crescent moon hole at blinking red lights floating along in the blackness. They stopped and swiveled to face her. Scant moonlight gleamed on the barrel of a gun extending forward like the proboscis of a rabbit-sized mosquito. She called out to the electricity within the device, forcing a surge to leave the battery and overload the components. The orb glimmered, encased in a lattice of sparks and smoke. It went haywire, flying about in a sped up impression of a moon orbiting nothing, spinning about for several seconds before plowing into the ground and exploding.

A man yelling a distance away intensified her fear. She fumbled for the latch. At last, the door opened, and she sprinted over the frigid grass in the direction of the dim red and green lights on the fubox.

On her way from the outhouse to the cabin, she fell four times, tripping over roots, slick spots of wet grass, and paving stones. She dashed inside, locked the door behind her, and stumbled in the dark, feeling her way to the bedroom. The two front windows flooded with bright artificial light that sent creeping shadows over the room. Stealth became futile; she sprinted.

Anna burst in the door, slamming it open before flinging James' shirt off and throwing it at him. She slipped into her bra, grabbed her shirt, and jumped into her pants, intermittently kicking at the bed while she dressed. He still hadn't moved by the time she had on everything but her coat.

She shook him, speaking in a half whisper. "James, they're here. Wake up."

He moaned; in the passing flash of a searchlight, she made out the shape of his hand rubbing his eyes. "What are you going on about?"

"Orbs... One was about to shoot me in the loo."

Glass shattered in the main room; James sat bolt upright.

Initial fright melted to droll annoyance. "Damn, they are early."

Anna gaped at him. "You were expecting them?"

He shrugged. "Of course. Alas, I thought they would have the decency not to come calling at this awful hour."

His chest glowed in the radiance of a small searchlight. Another orb, inside the cabin above the kitchen table, swiveled to point down the tiny hallway at them through the open door. Anna thrust her arm out, palm facing. With a loud *snap*, an arc formed for a nanosecond between it and her hand. The orb went dark and plummeted straight down, ringing like an out of tune bell when it struck the wooden table. It rolled off the edge, falling to the floor with a louder *clang*. Anna gathered her coat around herself.

"Looks like you have this sorted, my dear." James leaned back as if to return to sleep.

She gasped. "You're going back to bed?"

He paused halfway down to the pillow as true wakefulness came over his eyes. "Damn, there are more than robots out there. Twenty-four men. We have to leave."

A shadow across the window drew Anna close. Outside, a row of intense wavering searchlights lit the forest like daylight, their constant, subtle motion suggested hovering orbs. A multi-legged metal spider the size of a tiny car smashed its forelegs in the window, sending a shower of glass into the room. Shrieking, Anna started to leap back, but a second pair of legs thrust in and grabbed her coat with pincer claws. The two front limbs sprouted eighteen-inch blades, poised to strike at her heart.

It froze, the robotic menace shuddering and straining against an invisible force. James grunted from exertion, battling its Myofiber muscles with telekinetic force. Her eyes widened at the spotlight's gleam along the blades; for a second, she stood without reacting, stunned. At him growling, she shrugged off fear and grabbed the clamps holding her by the scruff.

Blue sparks leapt from her fingers, swimming around and into the metal arachnid. The entire bot convulsed and banged against the stone cabin wall. Panels exploded off its back. Fried to uselessness, the main body fell with a thud that shook the ground. James snarled; in time with his sound of disapproval, the limp legs clattered over the windowsill, out of sight.

As if grabbed by unseen hands, her body jerked to the side seconds before bullets cut the air where she had been standing.

Flying into James's arms, she broke out in a sweat. "No... No... I'm finally happy and they're going to kill us."

"Gather your wits, girl." James squeezed her hand before forcing a patronizing smile. "You may wish to keep clear of windows, though."

Aurora stumbled out the door to the smaller bedroom, satin robe unfastened. She turned toward them, mouth open, as a trio of red lasers streaked across the shimmering dust in the air behind her.

Anna yelled. "Look—"

The ivory-skinned woman evaporated into a cloud of silvery mist in an instant, leaving the robe hanging in midair as if still worn. Three bullet holes ripped open in the center before it fell.

Anna didn't have time to think as another floating orb dashed in the window. She induced an arc between it and an unused cable from the fubox. Orange flakes exploded out of every seam. The flying sphere went dark. The orb hit the floor and rolled across the room with a noise like a bowling ball on stone, fast enough to dent the wall it hit. Anna started for the window again, but James held her back.

"Stay away from the windows. There are snipers. Give Aurora a few minutes."

"What do you mean?" Anna crouched low.

James gathered his clothes. "She has a way with people."

Gunfire cracked and popped in the distant, darkened woods. Anna crawled out to the living room, past the stack of supplies, and over the wire leading to the heating unit. She looked back at James with an expression of frightened bewilderment when the entire cabin shuddered and filled with a deafening roar. Windows rattled, silverware and plates on the table vibrated to the side, and small objects fell from shelves. Beams of light angled in the windows, shifting in response to a brilliant object gliding overhead.

Anna shouted, trying to ask James what was going on, but her voice proved no match for whatever aircraft had settled in above, clearly much larger than the VTOL that had chased her before. The blur of grey and black camouflage snapped her gaze to the windows; from the look of it, six men had hit the roof and rappelled to the ground outside the cabin.

The front door shattered open and went skittering away in several chunks, revealing an immense spider bot as big as an autocab. Its flat white hull blocked the entire opening. Sinister red sensors on the front end had the appearance of eyes. Two hatch plates snapped open on either side of the 'head.' From each rose a cluster of three tiny missiles.

Anna dove away screaming, rolling onto one knee near an unused cable from the fubox. She took a deep breath and grabbed the metal connector. Power from the portable fusion generator coursed into her, covering her body with a web of shifting sparks. Staccato bursts of light flashed, searing the room into her memory as a series of still images.

Six trails of smoke traced a meter into the room in the blink of an eye; the eight-inch missiles hung in midair, throwing fire and exhaust to the rear, but no longer traveling forward. James leaned against the wall, sweating, eyes wide, his hand outstretched in a trembling recreation of a constable halting traffic.

His sneer deepened as the alarm left his face. The fuming projectiles rotated over to point out the door. Anna raised an arm to shield her face from the backblast for a second before they streaked off into the woods. Seconds later, a bloom of tear gas clouds, flashes, and loud concussions broke the darkness, the last one accompanied by a man's startled howl. A soldier appeared in the window, confused eyes staring out from a gas mask.

"Away," said James, twirling his finger.

The soldier jogged off with purpose in his eyes.

Whirring and clicking, the tarant bot shifted about, seeming confused at the misfire. Bladed claws at the tip of its forelegs grasped the frame of the door, crunching into the wood as it squeezed itself in. The other legs folded tight against its hull while it forced its body past the too-small doorway, cracking and pushing stones apart. Another hatch split open along the centerline of its back, sliding down into the body as a rotary cannon came to bear.

Anna drew power from the wire, amplifying it into a two-inch thick streak of lightning that sent the bot into a shaking frenzy of burning wires, twitching actuators, and molten metal. Plumes of smoke filled the air with the smell of scorched silicon. The tarant bot crashed to the ground in a heap, inert legs splayed out in eight directions.

Two soldiers climbed over it and swung their rifles in the door, making entry as another pair came in the back. Another two appeared at the smashed windows; all six of them aimed at Anna, momentarily stunned at dancing flashes of azure crawling around her body.

She pressed her thumb deeper into the socket at the end of the wire and clenched her fists. Before she could react, or the soldiers could fire, James's presence swam over her mind. She turned her head to look toward the sound of his voice; his arms rose to either side, his eyes flickered with a white glow, and his lips moved in a rapid whispering that gnawed at the back of her brain.

The commandos wobbled on their feet, lost in a daze of a telepathic saturation. James had seized each of them, injecting such an amount of different sights, sounds, and feelings they stood there like drug-addled dolts. Anna's mind fogged as well, though not to the same degree. His effect was radiant, not directed at specific minds. Anna assumed being Awakened, her mind mostly resisted it.

Any time you're ready, my dear. Doctor Mardling's voice spoke clear despite the muted chaos, snapping her out of the fascination his telepathic assault caused. *As much as I enjoy entertaining these buffoons, I think they are about due for a bit of a jolt.*

Anna stood, clutching the wire. Lightning sizzled along the heavy rubber insulation, racing to and from the back porch. She let power go in all directions with an angry banshee wail.

Jerking and twisting from a rapid-fire electrical discharge, the solders danced in place. A fusillade of *snaps*, *pops*, and resonant *bangs* flooded the cabin. Smaller sparks sounded like breaking twigs, while the big jolts— the ones that knocked bodies to the ground—sent window-cracking *booms* into the air. Jagged lines of black ash formed on the walls from a stray bolt that attempted to follow one retreating man through the stonemasonry.

"Simply incredible," muttered James.

Anna relaxed and fell to her knees, ready to fall asleep on the floor right there. Beeping alarms from out back warned the fubox carried too much drain. The texture of braided wire scraped against her palm where the insulation had melted away. Searchlight bots closed in on the front, aiming in the windows at her. Not bothering to stand, Anna growled and focused on the hanging orbs, commanding their power to her.

Hair-thin trails snapped in rapid succession. One after the next, the floating machines ignited in place, electricity leapt from their power cores, drawn into her. Bolt after bolt of lightning came to join the cloud of shifting sparks on her body. Other soldiers creeping up below the droids screamed, scattering to evade the hail of orange flecks and falling debris.

A concussive *whump* rocked the cabin as the capacitor in the fubox reached its breaking point. The detonation broke the rest of the cabin's windows and pounded the air in her lungs. She dropped the wire and dragged herself up to the wall adjacent to the front door, hiding behind the dead spider to peek outside.

Confusion swept over the soldiers; they shouted between gunshots. Azure muzzle flashes appeared at random in the trees from troops firing on each other. One man turned, shooting at the soldier next to him before stumbling back as if drunk. Seconds later, fog coalesced around a woman who then froze in place, shuddering and clutching at her head for a brief moment before she raised her weapon at different soldiers. Then, she too swooned with an intoxicated stagger. Some of of the soldiers moved naturally, others like zombies. Two men in the distance aimed at each other in stalemate, neither seeming to know if they faced friend or foe.

James put a hand on her shoulder, nodding in the direction of the back door. "Go now. Be quick about it. Wait for me about a hundred meters out."

Anna let him help her stand. "Aren't you coming?"

He smiled. "Of course." A brief kiss upon the lips made her eyes flutter. "But there is the matter of my destroyed car, and we need a ride. I'll be borrowing one of theirs."

She nodded, backpedaling away from the windows as two more spider bots outside spun in circles, aiming onboard weapons at the disarray.

Anna started toward the back door, but froze when a soldier hustled into the cabin. They stared at each other, both frozen for an instant before she flung lightning into his chest. He sailed off his feet, landing on his back and sliding across the wet grass in a convulsive fit.

Aurora's disembodied voice fell like silk from the air. "Damn it, Anna. That was me. Now I have to find another toy. He's going to be napping for a while."

The dropped rifle shifted on the ground, pivoting to point at James before it leapt into his waiting arms. His casual glance settled on her with a lifted eyebrow.

"What? Do not tell me you are afraid of firearms?"

She looked away. "I'm not a great big fan to be honest. Pointed at me, or getting shot by the cops for havin' one…"

Splinters rained from a trail of bullet holes less than a foot above her head. James fired at the orb bot responsible, but it evaded him with ease and whipped about to shoot again.

He frowned. "Sit still, you little blighter."

The orb wobbled, emitting an electronic squeal as his telekinesis held it in place with its weapon aimed away. Blue light grew bright at the base from the little ion engine overworking itself. A few shots into the stationary sphere reduced it to a shower of metal fragments.

"I could have gotten that…"

He made a shooing gesture at the exit. "Save your energy for the big ones, off you go."

A body hit the cabin outside the rear door, knocking a decorative plate off the wall.

"Anna, don't kill this one," shouted an unfamiliar man.

Clad in grey-on-black camouflage, a dark-skinned soldier ducked into the room. Anna couldn't help but stare at the odd feminine quality to his movement as he took up a firing position at the front wall. He fired a few shots, and laughed.

"I keep forgetting how light the recoil is when I'm wearing a man," he mumbled.

"She's creeping me out, James."

He pointed and raised both eyebrows. Taking the hint, she darted out the door in three strides and ran among the shimmering cones of searchlights from above. The air vibrated with the thrum of ion drives, a grating techno-growl that sent shivers down her spine. Every piece of grass and leaf tingled with electricity from the ionic downblast. Anna absorbed it as best she could, gathering a second wind from the charge.

Two great spots of white light, the main drives of an assault VTOL, drifted over the cabin. This one looked at least three times the size of the one that had chased her along the streets of London. Small vented-thrust ports, one at the nose and each wingtip, hinted at the general orientation of the craft as it rotated to point at where she ran. A rectangle of light appeared in the blackness between the main engines, a weapons bay opening with a mechanical whine. From within the white-walled interior, a dual-barreled particle cannon swiveled to take aim.

Are you fucking serious?

Anna's fingers numbed with cold. Orange glowing light gathered inside the weapon. Fear of imminent death broke past her initial shock and let her focus. A matrix of luminous threads formed over the plane; every power connection, every circuit path, and every wire traced itself out in the vision of her mind. No longer black against the sky, the military aircraft glimmered amber, brightest where power built up in the weapon system.

She seized upon the energy, forcing it away from the particle cannon and into other systems. Drawing as much as she could from its engines, she shoved it to places where the threads were too narrow to hold it. The VTOL wavered in the air and the developing radiance in the gun faded. The cockpit erupted with fire and sparks. The ion drives flickered on and off several times, and the entire upper surface of the plane crackled with roaming lightning. Amid a series of small explosions, fragments and debris rained from the air. The VTOL fell like a brick when its thrusters blew out, smashing trees on its way to the Earth. It hit the ground on its belly, trenching a channel in the soil before it stopped against two oak trees, pushing them into a lean, their roots partially exposed.

Anna collapsed where she stood, too tired to stay upright. Her drop proved fortunate; a wave of splinters and shrapnel passed overhead seconds before the concussion of the crash knocked her into a roll. She came to a halt on her stomach in wet grass. Without the plane, the rear of the cabin faded to the dimness of stars. In the sudden absence of floodlights, she went night blind. Her arms felt like rubber when she tried to push herself upright. She wobbled, staring dumbfounded at the fire spreading over the crashed VTOL and the screaming pilot pounding at the canopy.

"Bloody." *No wonder they want to kill me.* She stared at the plane, sensing the connections to the explosive bolts, and set them off—blowing the canopy into the air and allowing the man to escape.

Shouts and gunfire resonated from the front. Soldiers, bots, and Aurora combined in a disordered mess. Anna crawled to a tree and used it to haul herself to her feet. She held on to keep from falling while gazing about in a futile search for James among numerous muzzle flashes, running soldiers, and searchlights. She whirled at the approach of an electrical source behind her. An amber sphere of energy crept up behind her; the two bright points leading the way connected by a visible spark.

She raised a forearm, protecting her neck. The impact of the orb knocked her down, but she absorbed the shock from a stunner. Her power converted electricity into energy, curing her exhaustion.

"Cute," she grumbled, and grabbed the orb with her free hand.

At her behest, its power cell discharged with a single intense arc. Its ion thruster quit, and she wound up holding all fourteen pounds of inert orb one-handed. She let it fall from her hand in the dirt with a dull *thump.*

Her second wind got her on her feet. A soldier came out of the dark and charged at her. Anna raised her arms to defend against a high feint, leaving her gut exposed. One punch to the stomach put her down on all fours, struggling to breathe. She grabbed his shin. Little sparks crawled over her hand, wavering over the armor like whiskers testing an unfamiliar object.

"Insulated, bitch."

He kicked her in the side, knocking her over. She lunged into a crawl, barking like a stomped goose when he stepped on her back and drilled her face into the mulch. At the chirp of a firing circuit above and behind her, she screamed. Hard metal jabbed into the back of her skull.

Bang.

Anna convulsed, her body lost to primordial terror until a body collapsed beside her. She raked her fingers over wet grass and soil, every muscle tensing at once. After crawling a few feet away, she flipped onto her back, the connection between brain and mouth broken. She could only babble at the sight of Agent Hughes standing over her, black coat fluttering in the wind of a second nearby VTOL. His huge silver handgun leaked smoke, but he didn't point it at her. He'd killed the man about to shoot her.

"Ba... Wha... You..." She stared up at him, shaking.

"Lucky you had a gypsy before this got underway," said Hughes.

She swallowed hard, edging away from the soldier with half a skull left.

"Wha?" Tears streamed down her face. "You..."

Hughes put the weapon under his coat and squatted with his elbows on his knees. "It's a complex mess." He reached behind his ear and peeled the little metal triangle off, holding it up to show it as fake, a metal slug held on by a sticky pad. "What the Crown doesn't know won't hurt them." He winked, and pressed it back.

Anna still couldn't form words. Hughes stood and started to walk away, but paused, glancing back.

"Don't just sit there, Anna. Your ride's almost here."

The glow of spotlights came over the cabin from another VTOL troop transport gliding in low. When she looked back, Hughes had vanished.

She slouched, arms lax at her sides. "Oh bugger…"

Hold on, luv. Do not cook this one. James' voice flooded her mind. *Aurora has the pilot.*

Doctor Mardling stood in the open side door, one hand on the hydraulic strut. He posed as casually as if he directed the military operation himself. The plane's landing struts folded down and the main engines tilted forward to arrest its speed. Its wings grew thick with flaps, a great metal bird ruffling its feathers while coming down in a mud-flinging burst of ions between the outhouse and the little dwelling.

He gathered his tweed against the gale, hanging on as the lower half of the hatch folded forward into a staircase. No sooner had his boot hit the first step than two bullets whistled over Anna's head. She ducked and stared in the direction of the shots. Agent Gordon reached around the corner of the cabin with a pistol, clinging to the wet stonework.

James snarled and grabbed at midair. Gordon's pistol shuddered in his hand; he growled with pain and effort. The gun slipped from his fingers but jerked to a halt four feet away on the wire connecting it to the side of his head. Howling, Agent Gordon grabbed the cord before it tore loose from the socket under his ear. His wail of pain mutated into an angry bellow that rivaled the roar of the idling aircraft.

A telekinetic pull from James snapped the wire and sent the pistol flying a dozen meters forward. Dangling from the metal stair, he reached an arm toward her. "Now, Anna, run!"

She glared at Gordon, holding her arms out. Arcs of lightning spanned the air between them, lifting him off his feet and slamming him into the wall with the meaty *slap* of flesh on stone. He bounced away and fell flat on his chest. Anna spat in his direction and ran for James. She made it three steps before two gunshots in rapid succession preceded blinding pain in her legs, and she went down on her face.

"Damn, bitch," yelled Gordon. "That hurt!"

Both of her shins shattered. She pulled herself an arm's length forward, struggling to look for the source of the attack. Gordon, propped up on one arm, wobbled to get a bead on her with a smaller backup gun. The liquid black of his suit slithered up and enveloped his head.

"Aurora." yelled James.

The VTOL whirled around, bringing the particle cannon to bear on Gordon.

"Aww, now that's just dirty." Agent Gordon's arm fell limp. He scrambled around the corner out of sight.

An invisible force closed around Anna, tight but not painful, and hauled her into the air. She flailed her arms as if swimming, albeit a pointless gesture. The instant she flew close enough, she grabbed onto him. James pulled her into the plane and laid her out on the floor.

"Are my legs off?" She wheezed.

James grumbled. "That was rude of him. Those boots were expensive."

"What?" Anna forced herself to sit up. A finger-sized hole pierced both legs about halfway between knee and ankle. The sight of bloody metal floor *through* her wound caused the world to melt into a blur.

She awoke with James' hand patting her cheek. As soon as she focused on his face, he smiled. "Stop being a drama queen. It was a small caliber. Clean hole. Nothing a stimpak or two cannot handle."

"Ngh." She groaned, staring at her legs, bare from the knee down and smeared red. They still hurt as if she had nails in her bones, but appeared intact. Anna flexed her toes, wincing from the sensation of it, and probed her fingers around the spot she remembered having holes. Painfully tender, but tolerable.

James pulled her upright, helping her across the cabin of the troop transport to one of several seats rigged with cross-chest harnesses, backs against the side walls. A seam down the center of the floor gave her the impression it could open to allow paratroopers to drop. He eased her down and buckled the harness over her.

"You'll be fine, Anna." He toweled the blood off her calves. "The bullet went in and out."

"Ouch." She let her head loll back. "James?"

"Yes?"

"How did Gordon constantly miss me with his smart gun, but put two rounds right through my shins with a holdout using iron sights?"

"You are welcome."

He started to walk down a narrow passageway to the cockpit.

"What? James? Don't be difficult."

Her arm leapt up without warning and slapped into the metal wall.

"Not a great feat of telekinetics to throw off someone's aim, girl." He paused. "I'm sorry I didn't anticipate the pea shooter."

She beamed at him. "You're amazing."

James grasped his lapels and grinned. "I rather fancy the sound of that. Now rest."

An Asian man on the left side of the cockpit held a pistol to the head of a woman at the flight controls. Both wore the same drab green jumpsuits.

James hovered behind them, staring at the pilot.

"I'll need you to give us a lift to Heathrow straight away. Also, be a dear and turn off your communication system and transponder."

The pilot looked up at him; her movements slow, no trace of emotion on her face. "I'll take you to Heathrow. No comms or transponder."

"Good girl." James patted her on the helmet.

Anna grunted as the craft climbed and pivoted. The man lowered the pistol, shuffled around Doctor Mardling into the rear chamber, and trudged down the still open ladder. He leaned forward until gravity's claim on his body became irreversible. White fog exuded from him, the body falling out from the cloud before plummeting out of sight. A man's scream lasted for only a second. The glowing mist flowed back in the door, coalesced, thickened, and turned into Aurora, naked and sprawled on the ground. Blonde hair as long as her thighs whipped about in the wind sucked out the open hatch. "Damn it's hot in here. Ugh, who smeared blood all over the floor?"

James chuckled. "You always were rather good at making entrances, Lauren."

Anna gestured at the opening. "Lauren! What did you do that for?"

"He would have killed you." Aurora offered a blasé smirk.

Yes, but he's was no threat now. If we kill helpless people, it proves them right about us."

Aurora stood, frowned at the smears of crimson on her snow-white ass, and hit a button. Upper and lower halves of the hatch folded together, sealing the doorway and shutting off the torrent of wind. "Are you so convinced they're wrong?"

"Yes!" She stomped, bare foot slapping on steel. Pain like a knife piercing her shin paralyzed her for an instant. "Aaagh!" She cradled her leg, whimpering. Several lights up front flickered in response to her pain.

"Relax, luv. We're only fifteen feet in the air." Aurora stuck her head out *through* the plane's wall, a luminous collar of white vapor ringing the breach. After a moment, she leaned back inside. "Merely knocked the wind out of him. He's fine."

"Aurora. Please don't play these kinds of games with me."

"Indeed," yelled James from the front. "If she loses control of her mood, we may very well crash."

Gravity intensified with a harsh climb, and sudden acceleration shoved Anna to the left in the harness. Aurora flopped in the next seat, as casual as if clothed. Anna looked away.

"Oh, come on. You used to work in a tittie club. You can't tell me you've never seen these before. I know for a fact you used to sit around with other dancers, none of you with a stitch on."

"That's *not* the point. We were, as you so eloquently pointed out, in a 'tittie' club. This is not a tittie club."

"Got a spare kit for me then?" Aurora gave her a sarcastic face. "Thought not."

"You're not going to walk through Heathrow like that, are you?"

"Of course not."

Interior lights changed to red night-flight illumination. The whine of the engines increased in pitch. Aurora's pure white skin glowed in the red, giving her the appearance of a wingless black-eyed succubus. She offered a pleasant smile and secured the harness around herself.

She winked at Anna. "I'll need a favor when we get to the airport, luv." She crossed her legs. "As you said, I can't go traipsing about in public like this. I'll need someone to wear."

Anna gulped. "S-some*one*?"

"Would you prefer we abduct the pilot?"

"N-no."

"Don't worry hon. I'll only be along for the ride. You won't even know I'm inside you."

THE COLONY

Anna reclined upon a lounge chair at the far end of a boxed-in balcony. She glanced down the length of her body, frowning at the black bikini. For two days, she had lain out here in the strange thing called sunlight, and had not succeeded in doing anything more than suffering a nasty burn that required a stimpak to be rid of. She almost missed being a creature of the night. Cool mist settled on her from a miniscule orb bot hovering about spraying coconut-scented lotion on her with an almost inaudible hiss.

Fluffy clouds drifted in a square of blue sky, framed by towers of silver and glass blocking the horizon in all directions other than straight up. The apartment James had secured sat at the corner of the building, affording a view of two streets' worth of hovercars and advert-bots at all hours. Sunlight had shown itself several days in a row, an event in and of itself confounding.

The muted *squeak* of glass doors opening came from behind. She glanced up and to the left, and rolled her eyes at Aurora walking naked onto the patio.

"For heaven's sake, Lauren, you're outside. Put something on."

Aurora settled onto the next lounge chair, sitting on the edge before kicking her feet over in a graceful transition to lying down. "We're seventy stories up. Hovercar traffic is well below." She broke out in a sweat right away.

Anna chuckled. "You'll knock pilots out of the sky from the glare."

"Oh, like you won't?" Aurora winked. "That little strip of cloth isn't doing a damn thing; you might as well let the girls get some sun."

"My 'girls' have gotten enough fresh air for their entire lives already." Anna grumbled, squinting at her paper-white companion. "I'll pass. Compared to you, I'm brown. You want some lotion?" Anna sent the little bot over to her. "Does it bother you being trapped inside all the time?"

Aurora closed her eyes as the tiny sphere covered her in mist.

Her laugh carried a hint of haughtiness. "Oh, I'm not trapped. I wear sunglasses and claim to have a skin condition. It's not as bad as you think. Especially in the city here, people are so busy they don't notice a damn thing."

"It's so hot here." Anna stood and walked to the edge of the patio, leaning her elbows on the railing. "How can they live like this? Metal as far as I can see. At least in London, most of the buildings aren't metal. And there's some grass and trees... and dirt."

The glare on the shimmering city wrapped her with an oppressive heat that drew sweat from every pore. She drifted to the corner of the deck and stared down on crisscrossing lanes of hovercars fifteen stories below. The ground well beyond them had about a tenth of the traffic. Sensing a person, advert bots drifted up toward her, creating an explosion of pink and white holo-panels trying to sell cold drinks, alcoholic beverages, bathing suits, cosmetics, and anything else their programming calculated sunbathing women might want.

"So many hovercars..."

Aurora laughed again. "Yes, well, the UCF doesn't have a paranoid king. Anyone who has the credits can get one, not to mention firearms are unregulated. Almost everyone carries them here."

Anna shivered, then trudged back to her lounge chair. She sat on the edge with her elbows on her knees. "Yeah, but they don't arrest children for being psionic here."

The door hissed open. James emerged in a rush of air conditioning with a drink in one hand and two others floating alongside. The levitating drinks glided to the women.

Aurora fanned herself. "They may not haul them away in manacles, but the government here watches them every bit as much."

Anna shivered at the thought. "They don't put bombs in their 'eads." She squinted at James. "Do they?"

He smiled. "They don't do that anymore, though everyone thinks they do. My friends inside the CSB have been faking it for a while." James raised his glass in toast and took a sip. "It is certainly dreadfully hot. I am surprised to see you outside, Lauren."

"I meant here." Anna picked a fingernail at her glass.

"Oh, no." James chuckled. "They are rather fond of 'civil rights' and so-called 'vulnerable populations' or some such codswallop."

Anna's iced tea vanished faster than she realized. "Why did you pick such a humid place? Really, James, all the way in the south end of East City?"

"Proximity to our goal." He pointed at the skyline. "The Colony's space programme still focuses significant resources in this area. The facility is a relic from the days when craft launching into space could draw giant crowds of spectators."

Ice rattling in her empty glass, Anna stood. "I can't tolerate this dreadful heat anymore."

"Wales was too cold. This place is too hot…" Aurora laughed. "You got a fickle one, James."

"This place *is* too hot," he muttered into his cup.

Having had enough sun, Anna stood and headed inside. Beige interior carpeting squished soft and cool beneath her feet in contrast to the coarse hot concrete on the balcony. She basked in the air conditioning for a few minutes before it grew too cold for a small bikini. Wrapping herself in a dark blue satin robe, she settled into a large sectional couch the color of sand. Soon James joined her there, and she shifted up against him, leaning into the arm he put around her shoulders.

"You smell like a tropical drink." He kissed her.

Anna smiled. "That little robot was spraying me all morning. I suppose it helped. I didn't burn."

Aurora walked past in a black robe with a hem at mid-thigh.

"Are you feeling unwell?" Anna sat up with mocking primness. "That robe is almost decent."

"My attire, or lack thereof, is a product of simple laziness." Aurora kept going on her way to the bedroom. "James, I'm going to scrub up a bit and do a little snooping around the facility."

"This is a nice flat," said Anna. "I thought your money was in a tangle back home."

"The manager of this development is a rather friendly chap. Nice enough to let us try the place for two months without a commitment." He winked. "Of course, he thinks we paid for it."

Anna whistled. "Naughty."

"Well, we won't be staying on the Colony's east coast for long."

"James, it's 2413. I don't think the Crown is going to take it back at this point."

He brushed his hair over his ear. "Perhaps. So, how are you holding up?"

Anna snuggled tighter to his side. "Fine, I suppose. It was a bit dodgy having Lauren sharing my body at Heathrow. T'was like a voice in my head. At least my legs stopped hurting. Why didn't she turn into a ghost and follow us? Did she really want to make me squirm that badly?"

"Yes," called Aurora from down the hall. "One of the few things in life that I find amusing is to put others off balance."

"I mean about you." A soft kiss landed on top of her head. "But, it's rather tiring on her to do that. Having a body is a lot less work."

"And I don't suffer the random attentions of restless spirits... and other things," said Aurora's pervasive telepathic voice.

Anna fussed at his hair and drew in the scent of him. "I don't know how I feel about learning the bastard wasn't really my dad. Who was he? Do I still have a family somewhere? Did I ever? Ol' Jack seemed to know my mother. Where did I come from?"

James kissed the side of her head. "I don't have any of those answers, my dear. Fate brought us together. Somehow, you managed to hide even from Lauren. Do not waste another thought on that wretch of a man. You have to remember you were only defending yourself. You did only what you had to do in order to survive. Knowing he was not your own blood should make it easier to cope with."

"It feels so odd. The way he looked at me after." She brushed her fingertips over the inside of her wrist. "It hit me bad at first, but you know that." Anna looked up. "Oh, I was chattin' with Penny on the vid this morning. She's doing okay, but I miss her. She wanted me to thank you for helping get her that job."

"Think nothing of it. The school will keep paying her until she's dead. She could dance naked and drunk in the halls and they would keep her on staff. You need not worry about her. The woman is set for life."

Anna shot him a look.

"I know you care a great deal about your friend. I made some changes to a few brains on the board of trustees. Nothing harmful." He took a sip of his drink. "They all think she is the bees knees."

She relaxed, settling her head against him. "Are you still sore from the hot tub?"

He drew a breath, grimacing. "The numbness is gone. That little trait of yours is a bit of a nuisance."

"Is there a way I can control it? I'm rather sick of blowing out NetMinis every time a rat scurries over my foot."

"Oh, Anna…" His arm around her shoulders squeezed. "You'll no longer be living among rats. Perhaps there is something, let's have a look."

He leaned close and locked eyes. Lightheaded euphoria came over her, followed by a strange sense of floating away from her body. She fixated on his face, once more adoring the surrender to his presence. He provided the sense of security she had craved for so long. When she had been doing jobs for Mr. Carroll, she had confidence and poise, traits only now starting to return. With James in her life, and the CSB an ocean away, she no longer felt the need to act meek as a survival mechanism.

When her thoughts settled back into the present moment, she noticed a smug smile on his face.

"Did you fix it?"

"Not entirely, although I believe I understand it now. Those who are born Awakened have some modicum of difficulty with their abilities when they are young. Some, like Lauren, experience visually obvious indicators of what they are. Others, like you, have an event or circumstance knock things loose. This is a great deal of power for a little mind to handle."

"What happened?" She pushed at his chest, trying to squeeze the words out of him.

"You may have been a year or two old when you witnessed the CSB assassinate your mother. There is no conscious memory of it left in there, but given your circumstances and what has happened… I believe that to be the case. The event caused a connection between your emotional state and the part of your brain that governs your electrokinesis. While I believe it is physiological in nature, you may be able to overcome it meditation, discipline, that sort of thing."

She sighed. "So I'm to become a Buddhist monk then?"

The unexpected quip made him laugh. "Well, that would certainly be one way to go about it but I think it would be an unnecessary extreme. Besides, they have a dreadful sense of fashion. Perhaps when I unlock the secret, I'll better understand how to adjust such things."

"What did you do with the detainees?"

He grabbed at the air, opening a holo-vid panel up from the silver bar mounted to the wall. Upon the one 120-inch screen, a confusing jumble of program guides scrolled along.

"I sent them ahead with Terrence, who I have entrusted to run things in my absence, to the west coast. Not so different here, is it? Nine hundred channels and still nothing worth watching."

Aurora emerged from the interior hall, dressed in a short white jacket, black leggings, and a blinding cobalt-blue miniskirt. She navigated the periphery of their vision so as not to disturb them. James wagged his fingers to scroll among the stations, eventually stopping on a documentary comparing the physiological effects of off-Earth colony life among six different planets. Anna pulled her feet up on the couch, cuddling up to him and ignoring the braniac drivel spilling from the screen. Aurora's boots echoed from the short entry hallway by the kitchenette and front door.

Anna closed her eyes. "Where's she off to?"

"That is the next part of the plan." He stroked her hair. "The military over here is developing a starship, the largest yet attempted. With it, we can rid ourselves of prejudice and find a new home."

"Are you touched? You're talking about leaving Earth?"

"Indeed."

Anna stared at her feet.

"Aren't you excited?"

"I... Faye was beside herself with tears when I told her I'd left London. Penny and Spawny..."

"The girl has her own family. She will find her way. As for your friends, perhaps we can take them with us. If they want to go."

"What do you need me to do?" Her voice came out, but she felt far away from it.

"Infiltrate the facility of the corporation responsible for its construction, and recover design specifications and access codes. I lack the contacts to find a digital operator in this area within my timeline, plus they likely have what we need on an isolated network, which will require going inside their building anyway. The ship is still several years from completion, however, I need to make sure it will be capable of fulfilling our needs and learn as much about it as possible."

She gave him a look as though he'd asked her to shoot her own dog. "Are you sure?"

James pulled her head to his chest. "Of course. Would I ever deceive you?"

Anna smiled, basking in the sense of safety. She liked the feeling of having him care for her. Penny, as dear as she was, didn't have his kind of strength or confidence. The woman would've done anything for her, but she *was* after all a mere normal. Not even psionic, much less Awakened. it pained Anna to be the cause of stressing her best friend. Deep down, Penny had been every bit as terrified as Anna—she only hid it better. James… Anna squeezed his arm. James didn't fear anything.

He would be her protector now.

RIDDEN

Anna paused against an angled beam of white-painted plastisteel, square and as thick as her body. From where it bolted to the ground, it trailed into an upward spiral before joining the side of the Timmons-Orben corporate headquarters at the fortieth floor. Hundreds more formed a ring around the base of the building, a crisscross of metal in the shape of an inverted hyperbolic cone, as if the corporate tower wore a glass skirt. Transparent panels set into the grid let sunlight in to a spacious round courtyard ringing the structure.

The tower rose past the center of the lattice, a great white needle stabbing at the sky. Hundreds of people flowed to and from the entrance, flowing around several one-quarter scale models of spacecraft, hovercars, and full-scale mockups of ion engines. All the suits and skirt suits made Anna feel underdressed in loose black pants and combat boots she had ordered an hour earlier. She tugged at the sleeves of her loose, grey top and grumbled. Her plain silver mesh belt held one small box at her left hip, a container of imitation white leather the size of a bar of soap. She squeezed it, hoping like hell she wouldn't need the six stimpaks inside.

I don't fit in. All these people are wearing twenty thousand credits of designer crap. I feel like a terrorist.

Lauren's voice laughed in the back of her mind. *Well it's not like we've come for tea and biccies. It won't matter in the courtyard. Like I said, they're all too busy.*

I should have gone with the white thigh-highs, said Anna in her head, then sighed. *The military boots make me stand out. I'm the only woman in sight not wearing dress shoes.*

Anna shuddered at the oddity of *feeling* Aurora roll her eyes.

The bloody things you wanted had two-inch heels. You'd fall on your ass if this goes wonky.

Two security officers walked into the periphery of her vision. Head to toe in black jumpsuits, armor, and headgear, they tromped around the campus with rifles clutched to their chest aimed down to the left. Their approach spurred her into motion before they could get close enough to scan her. Moving as if she belonged there, Anna stepped out from behind the giant metal ribbon and blended into the crowd.

How can you stand it? Lauren's question almost made her jump.

Gathering herself with a breath, Anna shot an annoyed look in a random direction. *Stand what?*

Being this short.

Color came to her cheeks. *I am not that short! You're a bloody amazon.*

I'm only five eleven, hon. You're tiny.

Anna got redder. *Five eleven is a bloody amazon. Knock it off. You'll give me away.*

Okay, okay. I'm not used to seeing the world at tit level.

Anna's left hand reached up and checked the boob on that side.

Little petite, but they've got a good round shape.

She grabbed her left wrist with her right hand, forcing it down to her side. *Stop groping me! Err... Stop making me grope me! You're so unprofessional.*

But, I'm not a professional, dear. That's all you. I'm a freak.

Tuning out Aurora's laughter, Anna focused on navigating. She noted pairs of security men monitoring the crowd here and there. Far too many people flooded the place to mask her presence from everyone, but she only had to avoid notice by the guards. Anna mingled her thoughts with theirs, forcing them to disregard her.

Lauren, can you take over walking? Takes too much focus, slows me to a crawl.

Numbness came over her lower body as her legs vanished from her consciousness. Feeling as though she floated on a cloud, Anna maintained concentration on the patrollers while Aurora kept her at a brisk walk. Into the shadow of the building they went, under the gleaming archway of white plastisteel and glass. She maintained telepathic invisibility aimed at anyone in a security uniform on the way.

Aurora stopped between a pair of nine-foot tall ferns against a gloss black wall.

Care to hit the call button or shall I? Lauren chuckled inside her head.

Anna reached for the elevator control while keeping the security team oblivious. Doors squeaked apart, revealing a mirrored cylinder. Energy filled the air while faint green laser lines traced a grid in the reflective wall. Having no firearms, blades, or cybernetics, Anna didn't worry about the scan.

Since she also lacked an ID, the control panel ignored her. She pressed her fingertips into the console. Flickering amber threads stretched out into darkness as her mind mapped the electricity in the wires around them.

That's bloody keen. So pretty... Lauren's mental voice faded to an awestruck whisper.

Anna glowered at the pattern in the control box, hoping to find a circuit path to bypass the security system. *This is so damn complicated... I should have gone to school for electrical engineering or something.*

Lauren's influence made her head turn to stare at five large amber slabs surrounding the elevator cab. *Bugger the controls. Can you tweak the magnets? Go for the 53rd floor.*

She studied the insane mess of amber wiring and circuits. *I don't think I could figure that out, besides it'll set off an alarm for a malfunction.*

Wait here, said Aurora.

Anna shivered from the chill of spirit fog rolling out of her body. The white mist vanished into the door. A couple minutes passed in agonizing silence. Without warning, the elevator lurched upward. She yelped at the sudden motion, stumbled, and clung to the handrail. Ice cold air crawled up her legs from the floor, and Aurora's presence forced itself into her thoughts again.

Nice fellow at the guard station decided to send us to the correct floor. No, he's not hurt.

Moments later, the elevator stopped, the doors opened, and she stepped out into a blue-carpeted hallway.

Duck into the ladies' loo.

Had Aurora not kept refilling her tea that night, she wouldn't have been awake in the outhouse when the ambush started. Despite wondering what the clairvoyant had in mind, Anna complied without protest. She whistled at gold-plated sinks with reticulated crystal faucets, feeling ever so much more underdressed for being in an executive washroom. Behind her in the mirror, one of the brown-marble patterned stalls contained a pair of legs in dark pants.

Be right back.

Anna clenched her jaw at the momentary sensation of freezing air sliding down her skin. Aurora flowed out of her, leaving her clinging to the sink to avoid falling. Wooziness swam in her head for a few seconds until her body adjusted to being in control of itself once more. A female voice gasped, and the stall opened to reveal a security guard with dark brown skin, wearing Aurora's haughty smile.

The officer walked up to her, head tilted to the side, and nodded. "Yep, you are short."

Anna squinted with folded arms. "What's the point of this? You want to fake arrest me?"

"Hate to disappoint you, luv, but you don't get to wear handcuffs today. One sec."

Anna blushed and turned away, unable to come up with a good comeback. The officer took off her utility belt and laid it on the sink, followed by her armored vest, which she tossed over. Anna caught and looked down at it, bewildered. The security woman placed her helmet on Anna's head, then patted it twice.

"Put that on, don't quibble," said the security woman. Aurora walked the guard to the back end of the bathroom and sat on the floor. "Hurry up, we don't have much time. Knock this one out."

She wriggled into the vest before putting a hand on the guard's shoulder and jolting her unconscious.

"Damn that hurts." Aurora's disembodied voice floated over her from behind. "I figure this one will start making noise in about ten minutes Go out to the end of the hall and turn right. You want the corner office. I'll follow."

"How do you know all this?" Anna started for the door.

"While you've been making kissy-poo with James for the past four days, I've been a ghost in this place. Take the damn gun so you look like a guard."

Anna ducked past the automatic door and jogged to the end of the corridor before turning right. The gun in her hands felt like carrying fear in solid form. One bad fright and she could detonate all the ammunition in the magazine. Electronic triggers worked with small sparks instead of a percussive pin; in her hands, it became a bomb. The chime of another elevator opening coincided with her rounding out of sight. Comm chatter in the stolen helmet reported on the abandoned elevator and an unrecognized white-haired woman who had gone into the bathroom. Hearing them coordinate movement made her step up to a run, and she burst past the door of a fancy office.

A startled executive assistant looked up at her. She zapped him without breaking stride, a single thin spark of lightning between the eyes knocking him senseless. The intense *crack* shook the windows and filled the air with the smell of ozone. Anna continued past an interior door to a large corner office. Floor-to-ceiling windows offered a breathtaking view of a cityscape that could have been a mural. White and silver buildings caught the powder blue glow of the sky, while hovercars and advert bots danced like fake snow in a globe. Behind a monolith of black marble serving as a desk, a middle-aged Hispanic man with grey hair peered over a bank of holo-terminals with stunned indignation.

"Who the hell are you? How dare you barge into my—"

A dozen crackling arcs connected her fingers to his desk, destroying every piece of electronica before he could trigger an alarm. He cringed away from the shower of silver dust exploding into the air, and reached for a handgun under his jacket.

He never quite managed to aim it at Anna. The man wobbled in a drunken sprawl and fell over the desk of annihilated components. After a moment, he straightened up, grinned, and tucked the pistol back under his arm before walking out from behind the desk.

"Come on then, luv."

Anna grinned at the English accent. Several more security officers swarmed past them. She kept her head down, acting like a guard on escort duty. Each guard greeted the older man in turn as they passed, apologizing for the disruption. Aurora didn't speak, offering only nods and grunts. After hurrying past a handful of offices and a conference room, the possessed man swiped his badge at a blank spot of wall. One of the imitation marble tiles opened like a door revealing a concealed elevator. The interior maintained the overall opulence of the facility with gold and black panels and a holographic plant in the back corner.

"How did you know that was there? Can you read minds when you're inside them?"

Lauren's laugh sounded wrong in a man's voice. "No, I went snooping about. Walls don't stop me. My, my. This one's a bit cheesed off."

The borrowed executive poked at the elevator controls, sending them down several floors to a plain grey-carpeted hallway full of cube farms.

Aurora nodded at people as they passed; most everyone seemed afraid of making eye contact with whomever she had taken. At the end of the room, she hooked a left turn into an alcove and walked her victim over to an armored silver door.

A tall black man stood up from behind a nearby security desk, giving the executive a hesitant nod.

"Good morning Mr. Alvarez. Is there something I can help you with, sir?"

"I'm conducting a review of the facility. I'd like to check up on the Angel team."

The guard stared for a long few seconds. Anna sensed doubt in his surface thoughts. He thought something sounded ever so slightly wrong with the voice. Aurora's best lack-of-accent raised suspicion. The senior vice president, military project division, seemed different to him in a way the officer couldn't pick out. He hesitated with his finger inches from the door control, debating pushing the alarm.

"Mr. Alvarez, are you feeling all right?" asked the guard.

Too friendly! Anna shot her thoughts into her friend's mind. *Alvarez is a raging twat!*

Aurora leaned at him with a hostile glare as her smile snapped into a flat smirk. "Is there something wrong with the door or are you just being a simpleton?"

"No, Mr. Alvarez, I'm sorry, must be hot in here today." The guard poked a button.

Two halves of the giant door split apart, sliding open.

The executive spun on his heel, a look of alarm on his face.

Anna, count to two and step left.

She obeyed without thinking. The instant she moved, glass shattered. Fire scraped the outside of her right bicep. A sniper's bullet stalled on the security officer's armor, doubling him over to the ground. Anna's heart resumed working after Aurora all but threw her through the giant doorway. She collapsed against the walls of a hospital-clean hallway and hyperventilated.

Klaxons and red flashing lights erupted everywhere.

Alvarez hauled Anna standing by two fistfuls of armored vest. "Seal the door!"

Lightning crawled up the walls, seeking the threads of circuitry on their way to the motors. The door slammed shut right as a dozen security officers charged into the antechamber outside. Anna and Mr. Alvarez exchanged a lingering stare, the silence broken by their heavy breathing and muted fists pounding at four inches of armor.

"What was that?" Anna leapt up, cradling her nicked arm.

"A shooter." Aurora couldn't help but laugh at Anna's expression. "Buggered if I know. It's outside the plan. I only saw him about ten seconds before he fired."

Not waiting for another question, Aurora headed down the hall, pulling Anna along. Raised floor tiles *clattered* and *thunked* underfoot on the way over a short ramp and into an airlock. Hissing permeated ten feet of overpressure hallway before they reached a door labeled 'Secure Data Room B.' A dozen workers in white coats looked up like prairie dogs from terminals arranged around a central computing core. The amount of power in it called to Anna like a candle tempting a moth to a suicidal dance.

"Freeze!" shouted a deep, male voice.

A huge armored guard rushed at them from the left. Anna cringed away from the flash of a laser sight in her eye.

"About god damned time." The exec barked. "This bitch has had me at gunpoint for twenty minutes."

Anna gasped in shock. Lights and terminals faltered. She held her rifle out to the side, away from her body in case it went off.

"Drop it or I'll aerate your skull!" The guard edged closer.

Techies hit the deck.

Anna let go of the weapon. The super-girly way she tossed it, as if she couldn't wait to be rid of it, seemed to confuse him.

He cleared his throat, sounding a tiny bit less aggressive. "On the ground, arms apart."

She spread herself out on the floor. He ambled over, keeping his pistol trained on her until he took a knee at her side and gathered her arms behind her back. While he fumbled for restraints, Alvarez lunged and yanked the stunner from his belt.

"Sir, I don't think that's nec—"

The huge guard blinked in shock watching Alvarez apply the device to his own thigh, activate it, and face-plant the floor, drooling. Taking advantage of the distraction, Anna shocked the ogre via his grip about her wrist. He groaned and collapsed in place. Trapped beneath three hundred pounds of twitching security guard, Anna growled and clawed at the carpeting, trying to drag herself free. A few techies peeked over cube walls at them. She couldn't pull herself forward, wasn't strong enough to shove him off her, and couldn't breathe under the crushing pressure driving her hipbones into the floor.

After an agonizing few seconds, the guard roared to consciousness, sending techies ducking out of sight. He stood, seized her by the armored vest, and hauled her into the air over his head in preparation to slam her face into the floor. He hesitated, staggering to the left. She fired an arc into his face, which he appeared to disregard aside from changing the direction of his drunken lope to the left.

He stopped, eyes crossed.

"Sorry, Anna," said the man holding her. "This bugger's quite the strong-willed one. You might want to keep a few steps away in case he slips my leash."

The big man set her down.

Anna backed away. "Took you long enough."

SOFT

Wearing the security officer, Aurora rounded the technicians up in the rear of the data room. Anna followed, carrying her stolen rifle only to keep anyone else from using it against them. Aurora-turned-guard shook his head at the way she held it.

His aim point shifted from person to person. "Right, which one of you is the project lead?"

The soft technological thrum of the gargantuan computer almost drowned out the whimpering. Anna skimmed surface thoughts until she found someone thinking about being the project lead. She stepped around the guard and grabbed a Chinese woman by the collar.

"This one's the project lead."

The big man smiled. "Love having you along, dear."

You're not telepathic?

Aurora shook the giant's head. "A bit. Not as much as you. I also can't do it from inside someone."

The Chinese woman shook in her forty-thousand-credit shoes.

"Recognized her face from the personnel records," said Anna. No sense pushing their hostages to the point of pissing themselves. The added terror of psionics on top of the already scary situation could escalate things far out of hand.

"Okay then." The guard dragged the woman to the terminal and tossed her into the chair, almost knocking it over.

"Kinnel! This dogsbody is strong." He blinked. "Sorry. Wasn't tryin' ta hurt ya."

The techies glanced at each other.

Oh, that's real subtle. Anna smirked at him.

Anna removed a blank holodisk from her pocket and placed it in the terminal.

"Log into the system and copy all of the design specification documents for the CSS Angel. Schematics, codes, everything," said Aurora, no longer bothering to hide her accent.

With the barrel of an automatic rifle in the side of her head, the tech obeyed. A three-by-six foot panel of holographic light spread out in front of them, a sequence of file icons filled in across it. Anna kept an eye on the other techs, all huddled in a mass of trembling white coats.

One man pictured his three children, another wondered if he would ever see his wife again. A dark-skinned woman worried what would happen to her cats if she died today. The man next to her couldn't wait to go home to his cyberspace gaming habit; his worst fear was that this raid would cause him to get stuck late at work. Faces of spouses, kids, and pets ran a slideshow in the forefront of their minds. By the time the copy finished, Anna felt sick.

She jumped at a sudden scream. The giant had raised his rifle. Anna grabbed Aurora's arm, doing little stop the tree trunk of a limb from pointing the gun at the Chinese woman's head.

"What the hell are you doing?"

He looked down at her. "We can't leave witnesses."

The employees began to panic until Anna shouted, "No! These people aren't our enemy. We can't kill them."

"If they learn we nicked this data, it will become a big bag of wank."

Anna felt six inches tall, her pull at the arm lifted her off the ground before it altered his aim. "Do you honestly think they won't assume we took everything if they find a room full of bodies? This will give the police a dozen times the motivation to breathe down our necks. We came here to get away from government pressure, not make more. We can't prove them right about us."

He lowered his arm. "Still got a bit of the softie in ya, I see."

The head tech sank to the floor, sobbing and thanking Anna.

"I'm being practical. Killing for the sake of killing won't help us." Anna squeezed past him to the terminal. "There's got to be a way…"

A hint of a smile on the man's face suggested Aurora hadn't intended to follow through on killing anyone here.

Anna ducked out of sight behind a wall of neural memory storage cabinets and called James with her NetMini. In a moment, a small holographic head stared up at her.

"What hell are you calling me for?" He blinked.

"She wants to kill all these technicians. They're not our enemy. We don't need the extra attention from the police."

His lips curled into a patronizing smile, the sort of smile given to a child offering an unwanted gift to a parent. "That's rather precious of you, Anna. Still plagued with a bit of regret I see."

"Think about it, James. If we leave the room bloody, the cops will come after us for the killing and the company will assume we have every bit of data about that starship you're so enamored with. That's what everyone in here is working on, right? If we wipe them out, it's as bad as telling the cops what we took. I don't know what to do."

He pursed his lips. "Yes, I suppose it would be cleaner if they had no recollection of what happened. Very well, transfer the call to a desk terminal and round them up in front."

Anna blinked. "You want them to see your face?"

"Yes, yes. Bring them over."

"What?" Anna peered over the data cabinets at the techs. "What good will that do?"

"Have a little faith, Annabelle."

She approached a desk, waving the NetMini at it as if trying to fling his holographic head off it onto the larger device. James's head streaked off for two feet before it vanished. Seconds later, it reappeared life-sized over the terminal.

Anna pointed her rifle in the general direction of the hostages. "Everyone who doesn't want to be shot come over, look at him."

The crowd stood, wary of the big man. Once they had all gathered around, James closed his eyes, seeming to concentrate for a few seconds. When they opened, Anna gasped. The hologram had surface thoughts, as if he was there in the room.

Technicians stared at James' floating head, their expressions fading to blank when the widening hologram eyes became fields of white digital snow, hollow spots in an otherwise lifelike visage. He looked at them one by one, each individual fainting after a long, pointed stare. When he finally turned his attention to the thin man who wanted to go home to his video games, he smiled.

"You will access the system logs and remove all traces of your supervisor's account logging in today. Do you understand?"

The young man nodded, pivoted on his heel, and plugged a wire from another terminal into a jack behind his left ear.

The static faded back to brown eyes. "My dears, it would be a most excellent idea if you no longer remained in the room when I am done working with these people. We wouldn't want them to see you."

45

AN OLD FRIEND

Alarms flooded every hallway in the building. Anna shuffled against the tide of employees headed for the exits. In their panic, they all mistook her for one of the security team. Her running in the opposite direction only reinforced their belief. She hit the stairwell, following Aurora's suggestion to make her way to the executive parking deck.

Drab grey walls of unpainted concrete passed one after the next over a dozen flights. The air stank of dust and the helmet visor fogged into a blurry obstruction. Comm chatter buzzed with the search for the white-haired woman who had, according to them, tried and failed to kidnap one of the VPs. They also searched for the source of inbound weapons fire from an office building across the street.

At the doorway to the seventy-fourth floor, she collapsed on the stairs to catch her breath. After two gasps, a freezing mass of heavy air settled on her. Clamping her hands over her mouth to stifle the shriek, Anna twitched and let Aurora in. Chilling threads slipped around her brain.

Her teeth chattered. *Little bloody warning, please.*

Sorry, luv. I had to drop the suit somewhere other than the data room to keep the illusion up.

Content to be little more than a presence in the back of Anna's mind, Aurora rode as a passenger. At the end of the stairs, Anna emerged from a door adjacent to a silver elevator and jogged into a lavish corridor of white marble, gold trim, and black carpeting. Two white porcelain angel statues, three feet tall, occupied recessed alcoves in the left wall. Glass comprised much of the other side, beyond which the executive's café teased her with the smell of food and coffee.

You're not seriously considering stopping for a munch are you?

Anna had been, but she kept going. *I should, I'd be eating for two.*

An eerie laugh echoed in her head.

Thirty meters later, the hall descended at a mild grade to a pair of double doors, which opened at the approach of people. Outside, beyond a small cadre of umbrella-bearing orb bots, a handful of high-end hovercars sat arranged in named spaces. Anna went for the nearest one.

Two paces from the car, a severe impact caught her between the shoulder blades, driving her into the fender. Stunned with no air in her lungs, she slumped to the ground, wheezing.

Good thing you've got that armor, eh? asked Aurora.

Whatever had hit her left her in too much pain to reply, even with a thought.

Aurora took over, dragging her under the car.

You all right, Anna?

A sniper just nailed me tits-first into a bloody car. How do you think I feel? She curled on her side trying to breathe. *Thanks for telling me to take the vest. Cripes. Did my spine break?*

The strange sensation of Aurora winking tweaked her mind. *Be glad they got the good ones. Most vests can't stop rifle slugs. No, your spine is perfectly healthy.*

Again in control, Anna rolled out from under the far side and sat up. *You've any idea how to steal one of these?*

Her left arm moved on its own, offering a shrug. *Imagine it's got some manner of biometrics, fingerprint reader most likely. Didn't you nick a few cars when you were little?*

Bloody hell. Anna scowled. *I've never even sat in a hover much less nicked one.*

The shivering chill of Aurora's departure ran down her back, followed by a ghostly voice. "Stay still then, I've an idea."

Anna figured if she could see the man shooting at her, she could force him not to see her. She crept to the end of the car to peek. The taillight exploded from another shot, spraying her visor with sharp fragments of plastic, making her grateful to have the helmet. Without a clue where the sniper was, Anna waited. Nerves got the better of her, and some of the cars nearby sparked.

Flashing lights came over the edge of the roof atop a white and black hovercar bearing Timmons-Orben security markings. It glided to a landing a few meters away, bumper to bumper against the car she used for cover. Rather than point a gun at her, the driver waved her over.

Anna tilted her head after she jumped in. "Aurora?"

He made a hat-tipping gesture. "Good guess. It's easier to steal one that's already moving."

"Yeah sure, if you can fly and possess people willy-nilly I suppose it is."

The guard feigned shock. "What, you mean you can't?"

Aurora slid the car sideways to the side and drove off the edge of the roof deck. Several shots clanked in from the unseen gunman, one of which blew out the rear window. Aurora jammed the left control stick forward, but rather than accelerate, the car tumbled end over end when a detonation hit it like a kick in the trunk. Shouting obscenities, the possessed man lost his British accent for a few minutes, struggling to correct their plummet into a careening dive a few degrees away from actual control. He shot Anna a glance as if he wanted to attack her, but was too petrified to let go of the sticks.

"What the fuck is going on? Why was there some woman in my head?"

"Look out!" shouted Anna.

He swerved past a support beam, howling while wrangling the car into something close to normal flight.

Anna clung to the roof handles, staring out the window at the sloped wall of plastisteel and glass that circled the lower half of the building. The car rocketed around in a downward spiral, swaying left to right, chased by its reflection in the surface below.

The console became a blinking mass of red and orange erupting with lights and warnings. They bumped and scraped over the edge of the thirtieth floor parking deck, the top level of a separate building where the non-executive employees parked. The open parking deck contained thousands of cars in a space large enough to host three concurrent Frictionless games.

Anna's weight crushed into the seat until an impact from below bounced her into the roof. Metal grinding shuddered the frame when the car bottomed out with the tires still retracted. A chaotic eight seconds later, motion ceased. Anna ventured a look. They had come to a halt three inches away from the far edge, having slid between two rows of parked cars without touching a single one. Sunlight gleamed from windows and chrome accents all around them.

Anna blinked at the man next to her. "Fine bit of flying, that."

He glared at her and reached for his sidearm, but his eyes fluttered with Aurora's presence.

Fragments of acrylic showered the interior as a hail of bullets riddled the driver. He slumped dead over the console. Aurora's voice moaned from the back seat, grumbling about how much it hurt to be killed. A plain grey hover-van swooped out in front of them, gliding with the side door open. Three men inside continued to fire assault rifles at the car.

Anna ducked under the glove box, arms crossed over her head to shield from the rain of debris. When the shooting stopped, her fear morphed into anger. She sprang up in the seat and reached out the broken windshield. Dazzling sparks leapt back and forth between her hands before a shaft of searing electricity connected her fingertips to the van with a deafening *cracka-boom*. The riflemen jumped out, their plummet slowed by cables attached to harnesses. All three glided down to the parking deck. The van faltered in midair, but didn't quite go down. Anna growled, drawing power out of the car around her to make the arc thicker.

Ion drives overloaded, detonating the back end of the van into a fireball. It tilted nose down and careened off to the left. Streamers of lightning crawled along the undercarriage, sporadic blue flashes against the black metal. The van lurched over the edge. Silver windows across the street lit red-orange an instant before the deep rumble of a crash at ground level reached the roof.

Amid the fading roar of the explosion, a metallic *clank* rang out from the railing where it had gone over. The three men scattered among the cars to take cover as a fourth came up over the side on a grapple hook. Anna crawled out of the wreck, eyes narrowing into a hateful squint when she saw the long shape of a sniper rifle across the back of the muscular figure pulling himself up onto the parking deck.

One of the men popped over a car and fired at her. She dove to the ground, crawling away from a spray of broken glass. Another plinked at the deck behind her in a series of near misses that sent her scurrying up to a full sprint. She stayed low, using parked cars for cover and heading for the stairwell. The third man slid out from under a car, sweeping her feet. She flew forward, catching herself on her hands, but he pounced on top of her before she could stand again. A fistful of hair jerked her head back and the glint of a combat knife flashed in the corner of her eye. She drove her helmet into his face, buying enough of a distraction to get an arm on his hand and redirect the knife from her throat into her shoulder. It slipped between armor panels and drew blood.

Anna screamed. He rolled over on his back, twisting the knife. She shocked his arm, barely able to concentrate on her power past the agony. It had no effect. He brought his other arm around and hooked his wrist in an attempt to force the blade past the vest into her throat. Anna kicked at him.

Insulated suits. She snarled and bit him on the hand, grinding her teeth into the thin glove. As soon as she tasted blood, she let her fear take over. The electric discharge knocked him epileptic, and hit her like a punch direct to the gums. Boots tromped closer. Disoriented, Anna grabbed at the nearest car, trying to figure out which way gravity pulled. He howled in rage, shaking off the stun and had a pistol in her face while she was still on all fours.

His grin evaporated to an emotionless line. "Hang on, luv. I got him. Kindly don't zap the shite out of me."

The possessed man clicked off a few shots over the roof at someone Anna couldn't see, then whirled a second before another one rounded the row of cars behind them, as if she knew he would be there before he showed up. Aurora opened fire, walking a line of bullets from chest to head. The armored man staggered, a spray of red burst from the back of his skull.

A glint caught Anna's eye from the left. The man with the rifle aimed from the edge of the roof.

"Aura, sniper!" she screamed, and dove for cover.

Aurora swung her arm back over the car, the man's motion jerky and zombie-like due to his fighting for control. She squeezed off a series of shots, having little hope of hitting him with a handgun at such range, but the attempt was enough to make the sniper duck. Anna leaned up, blue muzzle flash over her head, and stared at the man who had shot her in the back.

For several seconds, she concentrated, building up a charge in the metal parts of the long rifle. The sniper broke to the side, seeking refuge behind another car. Several creeping arcs leapt from the ground to the tip of the barrel. Sparks spewed from both ends of the electronic scope as it fried, the man holding it jerked on his feet. The lightning crackled and scored the ground until he managed to toss the weapon to the side, drawing the nimbus of lightning with it. He leapt away from the discharge, rolling out of sight behind a car.

Aurora grabbed Anna's belt, hauling her around like a ragdoll before hurling her over the trunk. She hit the ground on her back, sliding away from the possessed man. Before Anna could ask why, a barrage of automatic rifle fire tore over him, spattering blood on her face. Wheezing, he fell to his knees and over sideways, struggling to crawl.

The last of the three men from the van shouted from behind a vendomat cluster at the center of the parking deck. Clicking noises gave away reloading. "So who paid you off, Paul? I had a feelin' that damn Brit was involved in something fucked up. He was payin' too good to help him off his ex-wife."

Gurgling, the wounded man reached into the air. "Don! No! Something... controlling... me."

"You expect me to believe that?"

Mercenaries? Anna blinked at his surface thoughts.

Don finished him with a single shot to the head. Ignoring the viscous red seep oozing out from the dead man's helmet, Anna forced the last mercenary not to see her. Startled, he rushed forward from his cover, swinging in a leftward arc to aim at where he thought she had gone.

"What Brit?" asked Anna.

He whirled, hearing but not seeing her a few feet behind him. She sidestepped in case he decided to fire at random.

A moment of dead calm passed.

"Annabelle, Annabelle..." sang a familiar man. "Where did you go?"

Agent Gordon.

The mercenary continued to circle, checking behind the next row of cars. He shivered as he walked into a cloud of arctic air. Fog materialized into the outline of Aurora's nude form.

"You should have listened to Paul. Something *was* controlling him."

"Wha—" He screamed, continuing to howl as he scrambled backward, firing into an Aurora-shaped cloud of mist.

She laughed with haughty delight. Her fog-form swam like a mermaid in the air and disappeared into his chest. Curling into a ball, he fell thrashing on the ground and shouted, banging his fist into the concrete until his knuckles bled.

Not seeing Gordon, Anna crouched behind the wheel of a van and yelled, "You've got no backup left, Gordo. They're still in London, or did you get sacked after Thompson survived?"

The crunch of boots drifted from left to right somewhere nearby. "You're simply too dangerous to be allowed to remain alive."

Don's head snapped up, his face red but calm. "My word, this one was stubborn."

Two gunshots came in such rapid succession they sounded like a single shot. Don's head exploded into a sluice of gore, brain chunks, and teeth. Anna stared at the expanding pool of crimson burbling out of the stump of a neck. Aurora's body fell out of a cloud of fog a few yards away, hitting the ground barely conscious.

"Aurora!" screamed Anna.

"Two deaths is too much. Wasn't expecting…" She passed out.

Anna scooted over, jamming a stimpak into her friend's back in hopes that the synthetic adrenaline would help. The pale woman didn't move. She hit her with a second one before the scrape of a boot made her jump to the side and huddle against a vehicle. Anna whined at Aurora.

"Come on, get up," she whispered.

"Two birds with one stone." Gordon laughed. "By the way Anna, I should thank you for sparing me the expense of having to pay those guys. Looks like I'm going to be in the black after all."

46

SHOWDOWN

Anna peered around the back end of the car, balling her hands into fists at Gordon strolling into view with a large pistol in each hand. Threading her mind into his, she moved as fast as she could while concentrating on keeping herself invisible. A field flickered across his brain, some manner of mental screen that made it more difficult to see his thoughts. Anna broke out in a shivery sweat from the exertion, but forced herself in anyway. Gordon staggered, touching his skull as if something burned him. She thought back to the inhibitor. Maybe he had something similar, only designed to keep stuff out rather than locked inside.

His tech isn't calibrated to our level.

Agent Gordon looked to a sudden beeping from his armband display, raising his left arm so he could look over the screen, almost aiming at her with his other hand.

"Well, well. Still playing mind games through a psi screen." He sighed. "This piece of shit is supposed to keep you out of my head. Learn something new every day."

The first time he fired, she had the nerve to trust he would miss. When he corrected, her resolve faltered and she sprinted at him, no longer able to keep up the effort to remain invisible. He flung his left arm out and fired the instant the gun lined up. The slug crushed into Anna's breast, stalled on the armor, but the impact sent her to the ground, wheezing.

"Like pulling the wings off of flies, or pixies as the case may be." Agent Gordon offered a sincere smile before taking three steps to the rear and aiming down at Aurora's head.

Aurora's body dissipated into fog like a bubble popped by the bullet. Anna smiled at the *ping* of the ricochet, cradling her chest and trying to breathe.

"Well that's just rude." Gordon faced back to Anna. "I suppose I'll have to eat the pudding before the meat."

The fog coalesced around Gordon; Aurora appeared solid behind him, screaming and holding her head. Gordon raised an eyebrow.

"Well, I suppose the bloody thing is good for something." He grabbed for her, but she zipped down into the floor. He sighed, shaking his head. "That one's always been a pain in the ass."

Sliding backward, Anna held a hand against her chest where the bullet hit her. Anger got the better of her and she hurled a blast of lightning into the pistol. Gordon flew off his feet, landing on the ground a short distance away, the smoldering handgun skittering away to the side.

He remained still for a few seconds before clasping his elbow and tapping his chin with his right forefinger. "You know, Anna. An insulated combat suit is quite the thing for dealing with people with your particular specialty. That almost tingled."

Anna hesitated; her heart sank. "Why do you have to do this to us? All we want is to live like anyone else."

He made a whimpery noise, mocking her. The condescending smirk she imagined hid behind the black material over his face. She sprang to her feet and sprinted past him to the dropped sidearm. He spun, kicking the back of her right foot out from under her the second it hit the ground. She went down, sliding on her ass and knocking the pistol farther away. He grabbed her ankle when she went to run again, dragging her closer.

Anna flipped over, drilling him across the face with her boot hard enough to get him to let go, and scrambled in a crabwalk away from him.

His laugh sent a chill down her spine. "That legwork might have worked at the strip club, but I'm not impressed."

Telepathic invisibility made him look at the armband once more; when seemed unable to find her, she had a sudden epiphany. *Motion tracker.* She froze. Gordon rotated, searching. She couldn't see exactly where he looked due to the opaque lenses. His display chirped as her hand slid two inches rearward. She held still again, letting him run past her.

With his back turned, Anna stopped concentrating on the telepathic invisibility and opened her mind to the electronics on his arm, calling to the sensor's power cell. It detonated in a bloom of sparks and a spray of molten plastic fragments.

Roaring in pain, Gordon took a knee and clutched his arm. "That's gonna cost you, whore."

Anna jumped on his back and yanked a knife from his belt. As she raised it over her head, he elbowed her in the gut. The strike winded her and knocked her into a backward stagger. Gordon rose to his feet and faced her right as she lunged a second time. He swatted her attack aside with an almost casual deflection, toying with a child. Twice more she came at him, and twice more she met similar results. The third time, he caught her hand, disarmed her, and flipped her to the ground.

Agent Gordon shook his head. "Who the hell taught you how to fight? You're waving that thing like a schoolgirl."

Anna's face reddened as he twisted agony into her shoulder. "No one, you twat. I grew up on the street."

"Oh, that's so tragic." He let go of her and took a step back. "There's no fun in *that*. I could go beat up ten-year-olds all day, but it's not entertaining. Come on, get up. Grab the knife."

Anna staggered to her feet, cradling her arm where he twisted it. "What the devil's wrong with you?"

"I only want this to be fair." The way his head tilted made her imagine the shit-eating grin she hated so much. "Here…"

He pulled another knife from a vest sheath, and held it in a closed fist. "This is your basic hammer grip, good for newbies like you." He shifted his thumb along the spine of the blade. "This is a saber grip. When you learn a little bit more, you can employ it with some footwork." After a brief demonstration of stances and shuffling, he flipped the weapon over, holding it like the first time, only with the blade pointed down. "Now the icepick grip is advanced; once you know what you're doing, you can use it with some of the fancier deception techniques, but you give up some reach for power. However"—he tossed the knife and caught it upright—"you're not even close to that level yet."

Gordon lunged with a teasing attack. Anna evaded it, but walked right into another foot sweep.

He paced around, pinching his temples and shaking his head. "That's sad. Get up. It's gonna take me three weeks to train you up enough so it's fun to kill you."

A crackling azure bolt connected her hand to his crotch for several seconds. He squealed, grabbing himself, and fell to his knees. She leapt at him, flying straight into a ju-jitsu arm takedown that left her kissing the ground with no knife in her hand.

"I was faking. Rubber suit, remember." He tapped his crotch. "Zap away, doesn't do a bloody thing."

Growling, she struggled to crawl away, but he held her fast.

"No appreciation any more. You Covs are all the same." His backup pistol pressed against the side of her head, above her right ear, crushing her skull against the concrete.

The *bang* of a gunshot almost emptied her bladder. Gordon lurched forward, falling on top of her with a loud grunt. She rolled to the side. He jumped into a somersault shooting midway through the roll and continuing to fire on his way upright. A short distance away, a Timmons-Orben security guard stood aghast, red seeping over his white shirt. Three bullets struck within millimeters of each other in the man's heart. Anna sprinted for a dozen car lengths before diving into a slide beneath vehicles.

Gordon snarled, scanning left and right. A small advert bot zoomed in, hovering over the dead man and displaying an offer for medical products. Agent Gordon pointed and burst into laughter, which grew louder when the little machine drifted closer to the guard, and the ads changed to solicit various funerary services.

"I love those things!" Gordon howled and slapped his thigh. "Awesome."

Another security officer emerged from the main entrance, firing as soon as he had a bead on Gordon. From the unsteady gait and expression of confusion, she figured Aurora tried to help. Anna bolted during the distraction in an effort to put as much distance as possible between herself and Gordon while the security man kept him occupied.

A stark white enclosure a hundred yards away offered the respite of a door. She ran hard and skidded to a halt by an entrance stenciled with black letters: 'Roof Access – ID required.' Her hope shattered at finding it locked. She screamed out of sheer frustration.

Bullets hit the wall, chasing her to the right and under the nearest car.

"Planning to fly off the roof, Pixie?" Gordon laughed. "You're running *away* from the door. I suppose you are trying to keep me busy until Doctor Mardling shows up to save his little sex doll. He is coming, is he not? I've got something special for him as well."

As much as Anna wanted James to come save her, being called a sex doll filtered the world red. She sprang up, hurling a twenty-foot long arc of lightning into his chest, which slithered around him to the ground. He didn't bother to act like it did anything. Anna seethed; her anger came in waves mirrored in flickers upon every lamp in the area.

Three cars burst into flames behind her from her rage. Great crackling serpents of electricity burned holes in their hoods and coiled around her. She caressed the sizzling sparks wrapping her body like serpents, then combined them into a blast that flung Gordon off his feet and sent him ass-first into a windshield thirty meters from where he'd been standing. Smoke and the scent of burned rubber filled the air. At the center of his armor, a patch of bare skin showed from a hole melted in his black suit.

"Not so cocky now, Gordo?" she grumbled, tamping out a small fire on her sleeve.

Near exhaustion, she stumbled over to the dropped gun. The effort it took to stoop down and grab it almost made her fall over. She aimed at him. The weapon chirped a ready tone in reaction to her finger on the trigger.

"Drop it!" yelled a man to her right.

Anna froze, shifting her eyes to look toward the voice.

A pair of security guards pointed rifles at her over the hood of another car. Anna rotated her head to stare at them without moving anything else.

"Don't make me shoot you, honey. Drop the fucking gun."

She squinted, an action imperceptible to them from that distance. When she erased herself from their sight, they prairie dogged. To them, she had vanished into thin air. As they spun around searching for where she'd gone, she swung her arm toward them and fired. Three seconds and eight shots later, she stopped concentrating on invisibility. Both locked eyes with her for their last few seconds of life. Anna stared at the readout showing three bullets left. She blinked at the realization she'd killed two men and it didn't make her the least bit tired.

So easy. She no longer even wanted to touch the pistol. *And they're afraid of us? Any idiot with a gun is much more dangerous than me...*

"Hey there," said Gordon, right behind her.

Anna turned, but couldn't duck fast enough to avoid Gordon's boot. His kick caught her in the chest, knocking her flat. The gun sailed off to the side. His fist crossed her face before he grabbed her by the armored vest and hurled her into the door of a car. She sprawled on the ground, motionless, exhaustion from the massive shock and the sudden assault left her head spinning. A grip on the helmet rammed her head into the fender twice, after which she absorbed another punch or six to the ribs. She coughed up blood, and scrabbled at the painted metal in an attempt to stand.

When he reared back for another round of thumping, Anna shoved herself out of the way, leaving him pounding a dent into metal. Her lunge *at* him caught him off guard. She reached for the hole in his armor. Hot skin met her fingers; she called on every ounce of her desire to live, and zapped him twitching. He grabbed her forearm, breaking her contact seconds before he would have passed out. She tried to recoil away, but his grip tightened to the point the bones in her arm creaked, on the verge of splintering.

He drove a downward left hook across her face, drilling her into the pavement. Delirious, she struggled to move as he pulled her helmet off, threw it aside, then lifted her head by a fistful of hair to expose her throat. She flopped a hand at his wrist, a feeble attempt to break his hold before the blade came.

"That is quite enough," said Dr. Mardling.

At the sound of a longed-for voice, she let her eyes close, close to surrendering to unconsciousness in the trust he would protect her.

James had arrived.

The knife twisted itself out of Gordon's hand. Anna struggled to look up at her savior, vision blurred from exhaustion and repeated hits to the head. She felt utterly at peace and safe. Unable to speak, her mind managed a weak telepathic whisper before she fell into unconsciousness.

I love you James…

47

DEALBREAKER

Agent Gordon spun to face James Mardling; his head covering liquefied and flowed into a metal ring on the chest plate, exposing a sweat-covered face and a dark metal headband glittering with numerous pinhead-sized lights. The two men circled in a manner akin to a pair of gunslingers in the Old West. Anna lay unconscious a short distance away. Her hair and strips of torn shirt blew in the gentle breeze sweeping over the parking deck. The distant warble of alarms lent an almost inaudible backdrop to the sound of boots in orbit.

"Killing her was not part of the arrangement, old boy," asked James. "In fact, what the hell are you doing here across the pond?"

Gordon spat, picking at the hole in his armor. "Neither was this. Your bitch almost killed me. How the hell does she generate *this* much power?"

James chuckled with a sinister smile. "Well then, she is apparently stronger than I gave her credit for. That, or whatever you said to her cheesed her off. I thought you SAS blokes had more self-control."

"We had a deal, Mardling. Thompson's gone unhinged. They're calling *me* a rogue agent now. *I'm* the one that's in hiding, not you criminals."

Genuine amusement spread over his face. "Thompson... Lord Connor Thompson, the only psionic-tolerant moderate in the House of Lords. Do you honestly think I would allow a mundane like you to shift the mindset of Great Britain against us even more? You are deluded. What you thought of as a deal was you simply doing as you were told. I should have been rid of you after you pursued her into the Tube on a bloody motorbike. What were you thinking? She could have crashed." Mardling paced, folding his hands behind him, half turning his back on Gordon.

"Your pet pissed me off in Gwynedd, Mardling. That little zap of hers snapped me out of the fog."

"Oh, that is most unfortunate." James sighed. "I had a feeling something was amiss when you shot her. Why did you bother legging her then?"

"So she could watch me kill you first."

James laughed as if he had heard the greatest joke in the world.

A second grey hover van circled in and landed. Gordon grinned as the side door slid open and five more mercenaries leapt onto the deck with rifles at the ready.

Agent Gordon's hand crept behind him. "Psionics are too dangerous; there is no way to properly police them. They could sow chaos and discord, overthrow the government, no one would ever be able to keep secrets. It's only a matter of time before we're all enslaved."

Doctor Mardling's gaze fell upon Anna. His words took on an undertone of anger drizzled with contempt. "Are those men supposed to be some kind of threat? Gordon, I do believe that knife you are secreting into your left hand would look much better in your thigh."

The psi screen went into a flurry of blinking, then smoked and broke into pieces. Gordon's head ran with sweat, his trembling arm extended. His eyes rolled up, as if trying to stare at the broken headband, clueless as to how it could have failed. Gordon sank the blade three inches deep into his own leg. Screaming from terror as well as physical pain, he staggered backward. Mardling glanced in the direction of the mercenaries. He invaded their thoughts all at once and altered their perception of reality. Believing the building crumbled out from under them, the men panicked and flopped to the deck, screaming while locked in a hallucination of plummeting ninety stories to the ground. Within seconds, they all passed out.

Gordon gasped, still staring aghast at the knife in his leg.

James frowned at the blood leaking from Anna's nose and lifted an eyebrow at him. "Give her a twist, mate."

The arm obeyed. Gordon roared and fell to one knee. "You're a bleedin' monster."

"Monsters haul little children away from their families in the middle of the night." James narrowed his eyes, gazing into the breeze. "You are not even a mere psionic, Gordon. You are nothing, and you had the gall to strike one of The Awakened? It is quite lucky for you that we had an arrangement, you know, but you have shown me the folly of charity. You did quite well convincing her it was too dangerous to stay in London, but I didn't give you permission to injure her. Since you have attempted to kill her..." James shifted his gaze to Gordon, eyebrows rising. "I'm afraid, my dear boy, you are simply too dangerous to be allowed to live."

Gordon leapt for his gun, but never hit the ground. He hung in midair, flailing for a moment before ripping the blade out of his leg and hurling it at James' head. The knife stopped two inches short, frozen in space. James turned, waving his hand in a dismissive flick. Gordon sailed into the side of a parked van with an echoing *whump*, jerked across the aisle into the rear window of a car, then hurtled across the parking deck. He careened off a light post before sailing over the edge of the roof.

James released his telekinetic hold on the CSB man.

Black-gloved fingers slapped onto the concrete rim, Gordon's desperate grunt reverberated in the hollow space of the parking level below. James walked to Anna, scarf fluttering over his left shoulder, barely noticing the effort of levitating a knife. The hanging blade glided along until it came to a halt above the black-gloved hand, then rotated point down.

James stared at Anna's limp figure, his words at a precipice between speech and shout. "No savory pleasure to the imperious man above whose head hangeth the spring-loaded combat knife of Damocles."

His frown deepened, and he drove the knife down with enough force to spike the blade into the concrete. Gordon's subsequent scream didn't faze his dour glare, only caused the focus of his telekinesis to shift from the weapon to the hand through which it had been impaled. He shoved Gordon off the ledge, ripping his hand from the blade in a bloody smear. Screaming faded into the distance, then silence.

After a meditative breath, James wrapped his telekinesis around her. Anna rolled onto her back and floated straight up until he cradled her in his arms. He started carrying her to the van, but paused about midway when Aurora emerged out of a cloud of mist rising from the ground. She looked about ready to faint from exhaustion.

James nodded toward the unconscious mercenaries. "Would you mind tending to the rubbish, my dear?"

Aurora padded over to the unconscious men, stooped, and took one of the rifles from their hands. She unloaded the magazine, spraying bullets back and forth over the group. Her skin, the color of new-fallen snow, spattered with crimson until the gun ran dry.

She sashayed to her waiting ride, vanishing into the astral world only long enough to shed the coating of gore.

48

THE FUTURE DAWNS

First Class accommodations on the intercoastal shuttle offered a private room with four large seats, two facing front and two facing rear. James sat at Anna's left near the door while her window seat offered a view of the clouds below. Her body ached, though it showed no outward signs of the beating she had received. Lauren, eyes concealed behind an oversized pair of sunglasses, reclined in the seat facing Anna. She'd her creepy eyes with big sunglasses, but made little effort to hide her skin.

Anna looked away from the swirling whiteness ten thousand feet below, and sent a loving smile at James. When she needed him, he had been there for her. Feeling her stare, he lifted his eyes to meet hers and returned the affectionate glance.

"James... why is the shuttle so high? We're only going to the other coast, not Mars."

He rolled his eyes. "Apparently, the rebels have lost control of most of their land. Some nonsense about cyborgs they sent out there to clean things up turning traitor. Funny bit of karma, that." He chuckled. "The shuttles fly up here to avoid missiles."

"Rebels?" Anna shook her head, laughing. "Now you're beating a dead horse."

"Terrence is doing well in the west. He has already found half a dozen other psionics interested in my philosophy. According to the data you retrieved, we have roughly five years before the ship is completed. That should enable us to set things up quite proper and be ready."

AURORA SHUDDERED IN HER SEAT, SITTING BOLT UPRIGHT FOR AN INSTANT before collapsing again. Anna gave James a worried look. He didn't react to the writhing figure, as though such episodes were a matter of routine. Aurora slipped into a half-awake state, her arms clawed at the air as if to stop from falling.

Overwhelmed with curiosity, Anna peered into the woman's mind. The vision saturated her thoughts, pulling her in and trapping her in Aurora's perspective. They fell through the bottom of the shuttle, sailing out into the sky. Anna screamed in silence, the scene so close to real it triggered primal terror. Aurora recognized a dream vision and took control, riding the air currents and following whatever force pulled her down in a graceful curve.

She moved among the clouds far faster than a normal fall; her trajectory flattened out, skimming over cracked desert ground. Scrub brush and weeds rocketed past, followed by the occasional cactus and scrap vehicle. In the distance, a speck of maroon seemed more distinct than the surroundings, like the one object of color in an otherwise black and white video. Aurora slowed and steered for it. An old wood-walled wagon made from the trailer of an ancient box truck painted burgundy grew out of the speck. Tall white letters dominated one side with the phrase: 'Magic Healer - 10 coins.'

Two living horses grazed to the left of it, detached from the otherwise unpowered vehicle. She swung around to the other side where a line of at least thirty people had formed. Wanderers, bandits, and the unfortunate souls condemned to the Badlands had queued up at a portable metal podium, behind which stood a dark-haired man his early thirties.

He pranced side to side while waving his arm. "Come one, come all, see the great magical healer who can cure you of anything that ails you. Any condition except death can be fixed for ten coins. Anyone who's dead, please fall out of the line."

Aurora's floating point of view glided past the oblivious crowd, heading under where the open side of the wagon formed an awning. Tucked between a small bed wrapped in dingy sheets and a pea-green wooden cabinet sat a small metal cage. A little blonde girl, barely six years of age if that, peered between the bars, her wide, innocent eyes glowing blue. Tears streaked clean lines over grimy cheeks. The child struggled to reach a dying man on the ground by the podium.

She wailed at the salesman, pointing at the man, begging he allow her to help him. He smiled at her, shaking his head to the negative and patted a fat pouch of coins. The man would die because he had no money; the girl seemed more upset over his death than her captivity. Aurora gazed at the scrawny waif clad only in grime. The child made eye contact, as if she could somehow sense her.

Shock at being seen broke Aurora's concentration. The wagon, the crowd, and the desert zoomed into the distance, her point of view sucked up into the sky.

ANNA FOUND HERSELF ON THE FLOOR, WRACKED WITH SHIVERS AND COLD sweats, as dizzy and sore as if she had fallen down stairs.

James helped her into a seat. "Now you know why I wait for her to tell me what she saw. Clairvoyant visions have a rather nasty habit of taking over an eavesdropper's consciousness."

Still asleep, Aurora convulsed and gasped in her seat.

Anna got up on her knees, patting the woman on the cheek. "Hey, wake up. What happened?"

Aurora leaned forward and rubbed the bridge of her nose.

"I just saw… the present, I think." She squinted at the window. "Yes, it didn't feel like past or future."

James raised an eyebrow. "That is quite unusual. You only see the present when something horrible is about to happen, though I dare say I would call that the future."

"What did you see?" Anna returned to her seat.

"No, this was happening right now…" Lauren gazed into space. "Another Awakened, I think. I'm not entirely sure what I was watching."

CLOUDS OF FOUL, STINKING MIST ROLLED OVER THE RAIN-SOAKED GROUND, drifting among a confusing tangle of pipes running in all directions. The smallest as small as Anna's arm, while the largest tube had enough diameter for her to stand inside. An autocab raced off into the distance, as if eager to get away from this area. Anna found it confusing they called them PubTrans here. *Why can't they call them autocabs? Ugh. I'll never get used to that.* She looked over and up at a row of three massive white hyperbolic towers.

She squeezed James' hand. "Is this what I think it is?"

He smiled. "Indeed. Our people have discovered an abandoned power station in a part of town where the police are terrified to go. The place is quite old. They have not used fission in centuries. Fear not, any dangerous material has long since been removed. It makes a perfect metaphor I think. We are more than capable of protecting ourselves from the local rabble."

A young man of about seventeen emerged from a four-story reinforced building, descending a shorts et of metal stairs before trotting over to the approaching trio.

"Doc Mardling is it? It's great to finally meet you in person. I'm Terrence, but everyone calls me Terry."

James glanced upward, transfixed by the eerie lime glow in the windows of the decaying building. He drew in a breath and spread his arms. Anna emitted a little squeak when telekinetic pressure wrapped around her like the hand of an enormous child grabbing a toy doll. James leaned his head back and levitated all four of them in the direction of the roof. Aurora laughed aloud at the face Terrence made. Anna kept her eyes closed until her weight settled onto her feet again. Folding his hands behind his back, James strode to the edge of the wall like an admiral taking command of a new vessel.

The wind picked up, fluttering his hair and scarf. His right eyebrow notched upward. He cast an imperious look of disdain on the city spread out below him.

"Good evening, Terrence. From this point forward, you shall know me as Archon."

fin

ACKNOWLEDGMENTS

Thank you for reading Archon's Queen!

Additional thanks to Jackson Tjota for the cover illustration, Alexandria Thompson for formatting the cover, and 'the group' for being the sounding board for this storyline many years ago in a slightly different incarnation.

ABOUT THE AUTHOR

Originally from South Amboy NJ, Matthew has been creating science fiction and fantasy worlds for most of his reasoning life. Since 1996, he has developed the "Divergent Fates" world, in which *Division Zero, Virtual Immortality, The Awakened Series, The Harmony Paradox, and the Daughter of Mars series* take place. Along with being an editor at Curiosity Quills press, he has worked in IT and technical support.

Matthew is an avid gamer, a recovered WoW addict, Gamemaster for two custom RPG systems, and a fan of anime, British humour, and intellectual science fiction that questions the nature of reality, life, and what happens after it.

He is also fond of cats.

Visit me online at:
    Facebook: https://www.facebook.com/MatthewSCoxAuthor
    Amazon: https://www.amazon.com/author/mscox
    Pinterest: https://www.pinterest.com/matthewcox10420/
    Goodreads: https://www.goodreads.com/author/show/7712730.Matthew_S_Cox
    Email: mcox2112@gmail.com

(Fiction Novels - Adult)

The Roadhouse Chronicles Series

- One More Run
- The Redeemed
- Dead Man's Number

Faded Skies series

- Heir Ascendant
- Ascendant Unrest
- Ascendant Revolution

Temporal Armistice Series

- Nascent Shadow
- The Shadow Collector
- The Gate to Oblivion
- The Queen of Discord

Vampire Innocent series

- A Nighttime of Forever
- A Beginner's Guide to Fangs
- The Artist of Ruin
- The Last Family Road Trip
- The Phantom Oracle
- How Not to Summon Demons
- Ordinary Problems of a College Vampire
- A Vampire's Guide to Surviving Holidays
- An Introduction to Paranormal Diplomacy

Standalones

- Wayfarer: AV494
- Axillon99
- Chiaroscuro: The Mouse and the Candle

- The Spirits of Six Minstrel Run
- Sophie's Light
- The Far Side of Promise anthology
- Operation: Chimera (with Tony Healey)
- The Dysfunctional Conspiracy (with Christopher Veltmann)
- Of Myth and Shadow
- The Girl Who Found the Sun

Winter Solstice series (with J.R. Rain)

- Convergence
- Containment
- Catalyst

Alexis Silver series (with J.R. Rain)

- Silver Light
- Deep Silver
- Silver Quarrel

Samantha Moon Origins series (with J.R. Rain)

- New Moon Rising
- Moon Mourning

Vampire For Hire series (with J.R. Rain)

- Moon Master
- Dead Moon
- Lost Moon

Maddy Wimsey series (with J.R. Rain)

- The Devil's Eye
- The Drifting Gloom
- Dark Mercy

Samantha Moon Case Files series (with J.R. Rain)

- Blood Moon

Immortal Operative series (with J.R. Rain)

- Broken Ice

Four Elements series (with J.R. Rain)

- The Elementalist
- The Black Rose
- The Wakefield Curse

Young Adult Novels

The Eldritch Heart Series

- The Eldritch Heart
- The Cursed Crown

Evergreen Series

- Evergreen
- The World That Remains
- The Lucky Ones
- Nuclear Summer

Standalones

- Caller 107
- The Summer the World Ended
- Nine Candles of Deepest Black
- The Forest Beyond the Earth
- Out of Sight

Middle Grade Novels

The Adventures of Ubergirl series

- My Dad is a Mad Scientist
- Aliens Ate My Homework
- The End of all Halloweens

Tales of Widowswood series

- Emma and the Banderwigh
- Emma and the Silk Thieves
- Emma and the Silverbell Faeries
- Emma and the Elixir of Madness
- Emma and the Weeping Spirit

Standalones

- Citadel: The Concordant Sequence
- The Cursed Codex
- The Menagerie of Jenkins Bailey

www.ingramcontent.com/pod-product-compliance
Lightning Source LLC
Chambersburg PA
CBHW020511260626
47156CB00006B/1972